Dutch Island

A Novel

Curt Weeden

QUADRAFOIL PRESS

Quadrafoil Press
1121 Park West Blvd.
Mount Pleasant, SC 29466

www.dutchislandnovel.com

First Quadrafoil paperback printing: September 2012
Printed in the U.S.A.

This is a work of fiction. Characters, corporations, institutions, and organizations in this novel are the product of the author's imagination or, if real, are used fictitiously without any intent to describe their actual conduct. However, references to real people, institutions, and organizations in the introduction and epilogue are factual.

To my father and mother – a promise kept

To my brother and sister-in-law – *Le meilleur d'entre nous*

– Introduction –

by Bernard J. Fogel, M.D.
Chairman – National Parkinson Foundation
Dean Emeritus – University of Miami Miller School of Medicine

Two of the most memorable characters in *Dutch Island* are Parkinson's patient Rick Weeden and his wife, Betty. As author Curt Weeden writes in his epilogue, the novel's events are fiction but this couple is rooted in reality. Rick is a Rhode Island native who has battled Parkinson's disease (PD) for over thirty years. Rick's wife has been on the front lines throughout that long war. The novel is a tribute to both of them.

Dutch Island is a reminder that Parkinson's patients have a lot of practice in meeting life's hurdles head-on. Granted, the challenges aren't always as dramatic as Rick Weeden's novel-ending, near-death encounter. However, everyday skirmishes have a way of turning frailty into resolve; weakness into grit.

What *Dutch Island* says the most about Parkinson's is just how powerful human relationships can be when dealing with the disease. In the novel and in real life, Rick's connection to Betty is what keeps him moving forward. And it's Betty's devotion and commitment to Rick that solidifies their partnership into a rock-solid marriage.

My own introduction to PD came in the early 1960s, when my father was diagnosed with the disease. Decades ago Parkinson's was a relatively obscure medical condition. Treatment was mostly physical therapy and massages. But even then, it was evident that treatment was likely to be far more effective if a patient was surrounded by concerned and dedicated caregivers.

Through my father, I learned firsthand just how medically important family and friends can be. With incredible determination and strength, my father battled PD until his passing. But he was not in the fight alone. He was given constant support by a network of people who truly cared for him.

Regrettably, not every Parkinson's patient has this kind of strong, engaged circle of family and friends. For those who don't, developing more effective treatment options that will lessen the effects of PD is especially important. Finding and implementing those options is a high priority for a nonprofit organization on the front lines in thewar against PD – the National Parkinson Foundation (NPF).

NPF's mission is to improve the quality of care for PD patients through research, education, and outreach. Our organization works with over forty top-rated medical centers across the globe, looking for ways to prevent and

Bernard J. Fogel, M.D.

more effectively treat PD. At the same time, NPF focuses on improving the clinical care for people with PD through its highly regarded Quality Improvement Initiative.

NPF's goal is to ensure that anyone diagnosed with PD – no matter who they are or where they live – gets the best possible care and treatment. Your donations along with proceeds from the sale of the print edition of *Dutch Island* will help NPF achieve that goal. I know if he were still here, my father would agree with Rick Weeden and the four million PD patients around the world that this is a goal that can't be reached soon enough.

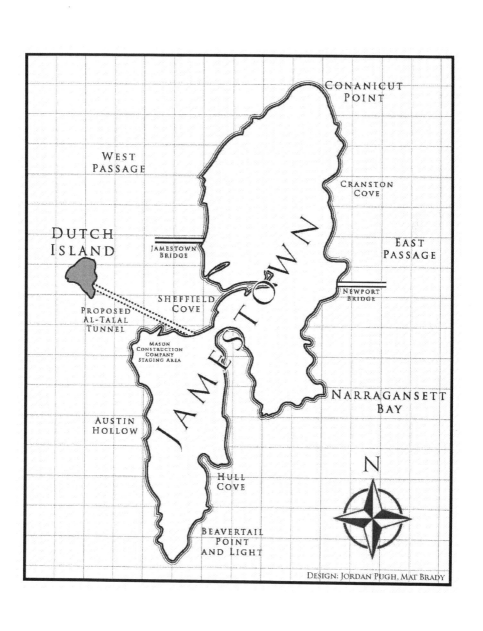

CONANICUT
POINT

WEST
PASSAGE

CRANSTON
COVE

EAST
PASSAGE

DUTCH
ISLAND

JAMESTOWN
BRIDGE

JAMESTOWN

NEWPORT
BRIDGE

SHEFFIELD
COVE

PROPOSED
AL-TALAL
TUNNEL

MASON
CONSTRUCTION
COMPANY
STAGING AREA

NARRAGANSETT
BAY

AUSTIN
HOLLOW

N

HULL
COVE

BEAVERTAIL
POINT
AND LIGHT

DESIGN: JORDAN PUGH, MAT BRADY

Part I

– Chapter 1 –

A three-quarter moon flickered behind a parade of clouds rolling over Narragansett Bay. The front line of a Canadian air mass threatened an end to a spell of unseasonably warm, dry weather that had blanketed southern New England for the first two weeks of September. Earlier in the day, the owner of the Conanicut Tackle Shop had warned a sharp change in temperature was about to turn fishing ugly. So here I was standing shin deep in saltwater at ten o'clock at night, hoping my borrowed surf rod would get lucky before the first fall blast chased away the bluefish and striped bass.

"Got a leash on that dog?"

I half turned and squinted at a man standing on the shell-covered beach behind me. In the dark, he was a tall, slightly slouched silhouette wagging a hand at my fishing partner, a female standard poodle named Olive.

"I asked if you got it on a leash," the man called out again. The usually composed Olive began barking furiously.

"No," I answered and grabbed the dog's collar. Olive's front paws churned up the bay, her long ears flopping wildly. "She's supposed to be friendly." At least that's what Kenneth and Maureen O'Connor had told me before handing over the keys to their six-bedroom waterfront McMansion

"My ass!" the man shouted back in a raspy voice. "I know that dog. Keep it on a line or you're gonna have a problem!"

"Right," I said, struggling to hold the agitated poodle with one hand and the seven-foot fishing rod with the other. "Look, I'm sorry. I'm house-sitting for that place behind you. A couple of weeks while the owners are away. Taking care of the dog is part of the deal."

"Yeah, I know who you are and what you're doing. If you don't want trouble, leash that animal!"

As the dark shadow moved away, Olive's barking subsided and the dog's body relaxed. "Jesus," I whispered. A day and a half into a two-week stay and

I was already on somebody's naughty list. If the water hadn't started boiling a hundred yards to the east, fishing wouldn't have been as important as figuring out how and why a complete stranger knew who I was. But when the bay's washboard surface exploded with menhaden making a run from a hungry school of blues, nothing mattered except the four-inch wooden lure dangling from the tip of my rod. I cocked the shaft and was a half second away from firing when the tall man shouted at me again.

"Too damn soon!"

I spun my head in the man's direction. Now he was nothing more than a slightly bent stick blocking the dull backlight from another large bayside house.

"What?"

"Wait! You cast now and they'll scatter to hell 'n' back. When they're closer, drop the plug in front of the bait fish!"

The man sounded as knowledgeable as he was nasty. So I held back as the desperate menhaden swarmed toward me. I counted the seconds.

One. Two. Three. Four. Five.

When the water began churning thirty feet away, I whipped the rod forward. The birch lure flew into the night and landed inches in front of the surging school. Instantly, the plug was attacked with such ferocity that I was yanked ahead, nearly losing my balance.

Olive shifted her attention from the unfriendly man to what was happening at the end of my line. Her tail motor clicked on and she chirped gleefully as I jammed the butt of the rod against my stomach.

"Set the hook!" the man shouted. *"Set the damn hook!"*

I pulled back hard on the rod and one of the plug's treble hooks took hold. Yards of fifteen-pound monofilament line screamed off my reel. For the next seven minutes, it was an adrenalin-charged battle that left me winded and exhilarated. I maneuvered the fish to my Shimano fishing boots courtesy of Ken O'Connor. Speckled moonlight lit up the greenish-blue dorsal fin as I lifted my catch from the water. "Careful," the tackle shop owner had cautioned me, "bastards can strip a finger to the bone." I used a towel to cradle the blue and worked a pair of needle-nose pliers to free the lure.

"What do you think, Olive?" I asked the poodle. "Eight pounds? Maybe ten?"

Olive whined.

I shot the dog a look of disapproval. "All right, so make it five. Still a helluva fish."

I lowered the traumatized blue back into the bay holding it gently while it gulped water through its gills. Then with one forceful swipe of its tail, the fish darted away.

"Mister!" I called out behind me. "Appreciate the advice!"

The stick figure didn't respond. Olive and I watched as the stranger turned and slowly continued his march along the rock-strewn beach. Before I could trudge to shore, the night swallowed the man.

A third of an acre of well-maintained lawn separated Narragansett Bay from the back porch of the O'Connor's impressive home – enough walking distance for me to mull over whether I should chase after Olive's detractor and clear the air. What I really wanted to do was store the surf rod, wipe down the poodle, and nurse a nightcap. But that option didn't stand a chance once I reflected on what my friend Doug Kool had told me.

"Don't screw up the deal I got for you, Bullet," Doug said – several times in fact.

Dr. Douglas Kool was the undisputed king of fundraisers in New York City. He was hardwired to big money up and down the East Coast, including Ken O'Connor, a fast-food franchising wizard whose deep-fat fryers had made him millions. O'Connor owed Doug a favor who, in turn, owed me a favor. Two weeks free lodging at O'Connor's Rhode Island summer estate while the fast-food mogul and his wife cruised the Côte d'Azur erased all IOUs. There were stipulations, of course. There always were when Doug was involved.

"Make sure nothing happens to the dog," my friend ordered before I left Jersey for the road trip to Jamestown Island. "It's their only child, Bullet. They treat the thing like a kid and if it gets so much as a flea bite, you and I both will be chin deep in dog crap. Understood?"

I understood. I figured pissing off one of the O'Connor's neighbors fell in the "screwing up" category. So, instead of ending the night with pleasant memories of landing the biggest fish I had ever hooked, I parked Olive inside the enormous screened-in porch at the rear of the house, traded my fishing boots for a pair of beat-up sneakers, and hiked after an unpleasant coot ready to explain how little I knew about local leash laws.

The night had cooled quickly over the past hour and a fog was steaming off the warmer water. The moon was now mostly curtained by thickening clouds and navigating the rocky shoreline turned out to be trickier than expected. After slamming my foot into a washed-up lobster pot, I wasn't as keen on setting things right as I had been only a few minutes earlier. Besides, I rationalized, the man had probably made his way back to one of the other sprawling estates lining Beavertail Point, Jamestown's high-end district.

I was set to make a U-turn when I heard a thwack. It brought me to a stop, but I shrugged it off as a dislodged stone or maybe a wave-driven chunk of silverweed that landed on a bed of clamshells.

Thwack.

The second hard thump was followed by a sound I had heard too many times before – a hollow moan that's a sure-fire precursor to death.

Thwack.

And then a splash.

I stumbled toward the commotion, slipping over a wide patch of kelp. Thirty yards away, I caught a hazy view of someone holding a hatchet. Ambient light from a house a half acre back from the shore leaked through the fog. I watched horrified as the ax whipped down, power driving its way into the skull of a man lying with his legs in the water and upper body splayed out on a bed of broken mussel shells.

Thwack.

The hatchet blade cracked bone and this time there was no mistaking the nauseating sound. The assailant yanked hard, but the hatchet was lodged deep in the victim's cranium.

"*What the hell are you doing?*" I screamed. It was pure instinct, no heroism intended. If there had been time to think it through, I probably would have run back to the O'Connor house and hunkered down with Olive. Instead, I barged toward the attacker who jerked the ax free and with a grunt, sprinted into the bay before I got within ten yards of the bloody mess he left on shore.

I stooped down over what was left of the victim's head. The hatchet had cut the neck muscles and the cervical vertebrae nearly decapitating the man. I had enough of a side view of the face to fathom a guess at his age. Probably in his seventies. Gray, thinning hair. Pencil mustache and leathery skin. I couldn't be sure but guessed this probably was my dog-hating fishing instructor.

"Don't you move one goddamned inch! *Not one goddamned inch!*"

A high-intensity beam held steady on my eyes. It was impossible for me see who was holding the powerful flashlight. What I couldn't miss was the barrel of a pump-action shotgun pointed at my forehead. I moved slightly to the right careful not to unnerve whoever was holding the weapon but just enough to peek past the blinding shaft of light.

"Stay put!" the man ordered and cocked the light so as to make me squint again. Still, my maneuver had given me what I wanted – a quick look at a lanky white male wearing wire-rim glasses and a Red Sox cap. He was holding the shotgun with his right hand, the butt of the weapon pressed hard against his hip. The man trapped a long, narrow flashlight under his left armpit and used one hand to punch 911 on a clamshell cell phone.

"I want to report a homicide!" he screeched and followed with a street address. It had to be the man's residence, the house closest to where I was hunched over a dead man. A yellow porch light shimmered in the fog.

4

"Listen –" I started.

"Just shut the hell up!" The trigger finger tensed and I did what I was told.

The man stayed on the phone feeding answers to the dispatcher's questions.

"I'm not sure – head's been crushed – oh, Jesus, Mary – I think it could be – oh, my God – it looks like Harold Mason – no, I told you, I can't be certain – when will they be here? – what's taking so long? – I have the killer –"

Ten minutes later, sirens and blue lights. Two uniformed cops, probably in their late twenties, trotted down a grassy slope, their spotlights igniting the night with cone-shaped arcs. When they reached the shore, there was an awkward moment of silence. Murder didn't happen often on Jamestown Island and the protocol for handling a homicide wasn't something the two young police officers had committed to memory.

"You Roger Standish?" one cop asked the man holding the shotgun. The second cop yanked me to my feet.

"Yeah," Standish answered. After a pair of nickel-plated steel handcuffs snapped onto my wrists, Roger Standish lowered his weapon. I don't own a gun, but thirteen years of street savvy exposed me to just about every firearm ever manufactured. I was looking at a Super Mag Remington, America's shotgun of choice.

"Tell us what happened," the cop said to Standish.

The handheld lights shifted from me and scattered over the crime scene. Now I had a decent view of Roger Standish. The wiry man probably in his late fifties lifted his hat and wiped sweat from his brow with his left forearm. "Damn deer been in my garden," Standish explained. "So I went outside to check."

"Go on."

"Heard something by the water. Went halfway to the shoreline and saw two men fighting." Standish paused and licked his lips. The night was cooling fast but he continued to sweat profusely.

"That's when I seen him," Standish hesitated and gave me a nod before rattling on. "He used a hammer or ax or whatever to beat the hell out of this guy." He gestured to the victim whose lower body rocked back and forth in tempo with the wave action of the bay.

"You had that shotgun with you?"

"No. I had to run back inside." Standish pointed to the misty shadow of his house. "Got my gun and, well, the rest you know about."

The second cop motioned Standish to hand over his weapon. The officer popped out a twelve-gauge shell from the Remington's ejection port and gave the pump-action gun a closer look.

"It's registered," Standish said defensively. "Just finished cleanin' it. For duck huntin' next week." Or for picking off a few backyard deer, I thought.

"Whatever was used to kill the victim," the first cop said, jerking his head at the dead man, "do you know where it is?"

"No. By the time I got my gun and come back, it was over. All I seen was him kneeling by the guy on the ground."

Cop number two pushed me up the grassy incline toward his Ford Interceptor. In the background, I heard the other patrolman chatter into his shoulder mic.

"I know we're supposed to leave the body where it is," the cop said. "But here's the thing. The tide's comin' in."

– Chapter 2 –

Narragansett Bay is Rhode Island's watery crown jewel. At its mouth, the estuary wraps around Conanicut Island, a narrow, twelve-mile long splotch of land hitched to the rest of the world by a pair of bridges – one attached to Newport and the other to North Kingston. Better known by its incorporated name, Jamestown, the island had a long-time reputation for its quiet and largely rural lifestyle. But six thousand residents, an incessant flow of transient motorists, and a growing tourist industry have a way of redefining a community. Throw in a brutal homicide and on this night, Jamestown managed to catch up with the rest of America.

"The man you beat to death – you're telling me you don't know him?"

Lieutenant Michael Ravenel's over-sized hands squeezed the top rung of a straight-backed chair on the opposite side of a laminate table where I had been ordered to sit. Ravenel stood ramrod straight, his broad shoulders pulled back and his chin tucked into a muscular neck. He lacked a New England twang and instead had a different kind of accent rooted in his southern African-American upbringing. It wasn't just Ravenel's skin color that put him in stark contrast to the two white uniformed men who had crammed themselves into the ten-by-ten-foot room. It was his militaristic, no bullshit demeanor that left no doubt who was running the show.

"That's exactly what I'm telling you," I repeated – for the fifth time. "I know *of* him, but I don't *know* him."

I glanced at the eyeball camera mounted high on the wall and the one-way glass window so standard fare for a police interrogation room. "By the way," I added, fully aware every word was being electronically stored, "I didn't kill anyone."

"So, you know *of* the man –" Ravenel said, pulling on what he thought was a loose thread in my last statement.

"If the victim is Harold Mason, of course I know of him. Who doesn't?"

"Just how do you know *of* the man you killed, Mr. Bullock?"

"I didn't kill him. And contrary to what you might have heard, people in Jersey watch TV, listen to AM/FM, and even read a newspaper now and then. Harold Mason has been a headline for the last year and a half."

"Front page headlines," Ravenel agreed. "Which agitated a lot of people – people who would love to read Mason's obituary. So which one of those unhappy folks hired you to make the hit?"

"All right," I sighed. "I can see this is going to be a long night. Before you continue chasing me around the barn, I need to make a call."

"You haven't been charged," Ravenel reminded me. And technically he was right. I had been Mirandized by another detective but I wasn't under arrest – yet. "So why lawyer up?"

"No lawyer. I want to call the O'Connor's next-door neighbor. I need somebody to check on a dog."

Ravenel looked genuinely puzzled. "It's one thirty in the morning, you're a person of interest in a murder investigation that's going to make headlines in every goddamned paper in the world. And you're worried about your *dog?*"

"Not my dog. It's the O'Connor's poodle. And yeah, I'm worried." As well I should be. *You don't want to cross Ken O'Connor,* Doug Kool had advised me before I left New Brunswick, New Jersey, to head north to Rhode Island. *Something happens to Olive and you're a dead man,* he had warned. So yes, I had a right to be worried.

"Go ahead," Ravenel consented and handed me a cell phone. I read his face and knew he wasn't buying my dog story. "If you're looking for privacy, it's not going to happen. I want to hear every word."

Manage a homeless shelter in central New Jersey and you learn how to run legal interference for every kind of lowlife, dimwit, and hard luck Joe who ends up on the street. I knew all about the rights of the accused. When Lieutenant Ravenel began edging over the interrogation line, I could have pushed back. But I didn't feel the need. Not yet.

I pulled Maureen O'Connor's list of emergency numbers from my wallet. The name at the top: Dr. Alyana Genesee, the O'Connor's neighbor who conveniently happened to be a veterinarian. I called the number and the phone rang five times before I got an incoherent answer.

"Dr. Genesee? I'm sorry to wake you this time of night," I opened. "My name is Rick Bullock. I'm taking care of the O'Connor house while they're in Europe."

"What? Is there something wrong?" The woman snapped out of her twilight zone and prepared for the worst.

"Nothing serious. It's about Olive."

"Oh, my God, is she –" Dr. Genesee was now on full alert.

"No, no," I cut in. "She's fine, fine." I hoped. "It's just that I've been – detained. Can't get back to the O'Connor house for a while and Olive's in the screened-in porch, which isn't locked."

"The porch," the woman's whispered words were easily translated into what she was thinking: *You're an irresponsible idiot. This is why you're yanking me out of bed in the middle of the night?*

"Look, I know it's late. But you know the O'Connors. If their dog got loose or something else happened –"

"It's after one a.m., Mr. Bullock. What else could happen?"

How about an ax-wielding maniac cutting off Olive's head? "Is there any way you could check on her? Maybe let her in the house and lock up. The O'Connors said you have a key."

"All right," the woman sighed. "I'll bring her to my place for the rest of the night."

"I really appreciate your help. Oh, and one other thing."

"What is it?"

"Don't go outside until the police show up."

"*What?*" The woman's sleepy voice turned sharp. "What's going on?"

"Look for a uniformed officer at your front door. Should be there in a few minutes."

I didn't wait for a reaction. I clicked off the cell and handed it to Ravenel. "She's going to need an escort," I told the lieutenant who didn't look pleased having been manipulated into making a manpower decision. What choice did he have?

"Get it done," the lieutenant squawked to one of the two uniforms standing to his rear. The cop nodded and trotted away.

"Let's back up," said Ravenel, his tone slightly less arrogant. My phone call apparently earned me a dab of respect. He tugged the chair away from the table and sat, his eyes level with mine. The fingers of his right hand drummed on a manila folder. "We know a lot about you, Mr. Bullock. You have an – how should I phrase it? – an *interesting* history."

Ravenel pulled a single sheet of paper from the inch-thick folder. "Richard Bullock. Age forty-four. Employer: Gateway Men's Shelter, New Brunswick, New Jersey. Widower. No children." The lieutenant paused and ran his finger down a typewritten page. "No arrests. No warrants outstanding. However –"

The detective let a few seconds pass and then continued. "Seems you can't go to the can without running into trouble." He flipped the sheet over and scrolled to several lines marked with a yellow highlighter. "Continental

Airlines terminal bombing at Orlando International Airport: subject probable target. Gunfight at New Brunswick Hyatt Hotel: subject present but not charged. Known relations with organized crime figures in New Jersey and Florida. And then there's the big one that I should have remembered in the first place –"

Ravenel went silent again and let the anticipation build.

"Ellis Island: one homicide and the related accidental death of investment banker, Arthur Silverstein," Ravenel let the words slide out slowly. "Subject implicated but not charged."

The cop behind Ravenel released a low whistle. *Now* he remembered. The photo of me kneeling over one of America's richest men burned to a crisp at a United Way dinner on Ellis Island. Plenty of witnesses had made it clear I wasn't responsible. Yet there was a lingering speculation that I was somehow connected to the incident. *Subject implicated but not charged.*

"Now let me tell you something about me," said Ravenel. "I'm an assistant commander in the Rhode Island State Police Detective Division. For the most part, I work homicides. That means I don't spend much time in Jamestown because murder, manslaughter, and the like aren't common in places like this. But when shit does happen, my division gets involved. Which is why I got a call ten minutes into Letterman and had to make an hour's drive to spend the night with you. Can't say I'm thrilled, Mr. Bullock."

"Likewise," I countered. "Not the best way to start a two-week vacation."

Ravenel leaned back. "Odd coincidence, isn't it? A man who's in tight with the biggest mob boss in Jersey shows up one day and the very next night, Jamestown has its first homicide since no one can remember when."

The file suddenly looked a mile high. "You talking about Manny Maglio?"

"None other. The titty bar king."

"I'm not in tight," I corrected Ravenel's wrong impression. "I met the man once which was more than enough."

"Uh-huh. And you did a dance with his niece for how long? Seems to me you're *definitely* in the family."

It was an easy conclusion to reach. For a lot of convoluted reasons all wound around my pal Douglas Kool, I did spend time with Maglio's niece, an ex-stripper with the stage name Twyla Tharp. I didn't bother telling Ravenel that it was totally platonic because I was certain Twyla's photo was stuck somewhere in the manila folder. One look at the woman's size D boobs, frosted blonde hair, and bedroom eyes would stomp out whatever I had to say about my relationship with Maglio's promiscuous relative. Maybe the file also filled in the rest of the story – that last year, Twyla converted to Judaism, married a lawyer named Yigal Rosenblatt, and was now a happy housewife living in Orlando.

"Look," I said, "I'm about as connected to the mob as you are." The lone uniformed cop who was still in the room grimaced and tilted his eyes to the discolored floor tiles. For a split second, I wondered why my words had hit a nerve. Then I remembered where I was. Rhode Island. A state where people still remembered the underworld's notorious Patriarca syndicate and the way it took care of Cosa Nostra business during the fifties and sixties. A state where the mayor of its capital city was sentenced to five years for racketeering conspiracy. A place where organized criminal gambling, kickback payments, embezzlement, and bookmaking were as everyday as chowder and clam cakes. Unlike the cop in the background, Ravenel appeared unruffled by my mob inference. I took that to mean either he was clean or maybe a mobster extraordinaire.

"Let's get back to Harold Mason," Ravenel changed course. "I want you to understand something, Mr. Bullock. What we've got here is no ordinary homicide. Within the next twenty-four hours, the FBI and a dozen other government agencies will be on top of this case like crabs on a whore. Do yourself a favor and tell me what happened before life gets very unpleasant for you."

As if life hadn't already turned unpleasant. I was the prime suspect in the assassination of a man branded by B'Nai B'rith as "a billion-dollar American turncoat who sold his country and soul to an Arab terrorist." And it wasn't just Jews who were unhappy with Harold Mason. Talking head conservatives had jammed the airways with conspiracy theories after news leaked that the Mason Development Company, one of New England's biggest builders, had put a prime piece of real estate in the hands of a Lebanese oil baron who had no love for the United States.

"Run a men's shelter and you get to learn about the law," I said, pointing my words at the one-way mirror that I knew was a window to a gaggle of spectators in a darkened adjacent room.

"So?" Ravenel asked.

"So, I know you'd be booking me for homicide if you thought I was guilty."

"We can hold you for seventy-two hours before finishing the paperwork for a murder one charge."

"I don't think that's what you're going to do," I said. "You've waded through my file. Probably made a few calls. Your detective DNA is telling you this is a situation where a nearsighted witness who doesn't seem all that bright shows up after the fact and points a finger at the wrong guy."

Ravenel pushed his chair away from the table and folded his arms. "Whether we toss you into a holding cell tonight or let you go home to play fetch with your dog, I can tell you for sure what's going to happen. By tomorrow morning, the press is going to tie your name to this case. Nothing we can do about that."

I pictured the look of horror on Doug Kool's face as he picked up the *New York Times* and the O'Connors gagging on their morning espresso after reading page one of the *International Herald Tribune*. For the first time since being hauled into Jamestown's compact police station, my armpits turned moist.

"This is one of those times when you're going to be considered guilty until proven innocent," Ravenel promised. "Which will make you a hero to a lot of people. But it's going to really piss off some others."

"Such as?"

"Mohammad al-Talal, for one." The name was as familiar as Harold Mason's. The Arab multibillionaire had used Mason to buy himself a toehold on America's Atlantic side. Supposedly it was a done deal, but maybe not. I wondered if tonight's homicide could possibly throw a wrench into the works.

"Any others?" I asked. Always best to know thine enemy – or enemies.

"Just a few million Muslim extremists. Oh, and put old man Mason's sons on that short list."

"Sons?"

"Two of 'em. Both sons of bitches in different ways."

Terrific.

"Where do we go from here?" I asked, checking my watch.

Ravenel mulled over his options before delivering his decision. "We're done for tonight. No charges. But get this straight: you're not out of this. I don't want you off this island and if you try to leave, you'll be a guest in one of our windowless backrooms. Understood?"

I gave the lieutenant a nod and left the room. Ravenel followed me outside the station house front door.

"Listen, what I said about certain people being less than pleased with you –" Ravenel tapped out a cigarette from a pack of Camels. "I wasn't exaggerating."

"Mason's sons?" I asked.

"One of them is known for his temper and the other for running over anyone who gets in his way. Both of them have the money and motive to put you in a bad place."

"Why this heartfelt concern all of a sudden?" I asked.

"You've been around. You know how it works. What went on inside was for the record." Ravenel's cigarette smoke disappeared into the fog.

"So, you think I'm innocent."

"Not necessarily," Ravenel answered. "But you have three things going for you. First, the man who claims he saw you kill Mason is a mental midget."

"Roger Standish?"

"He's a known nutcase," Ravenel said. "Second, apparently you have friends in high places."

The lieutenant didn't elaborate but didn't need to. I was house-sitting for one of Jamestown's wealthiest residents. The cop knew when to tread with caution.

"And third, we found a couple of footprints next to Mason's body," Ravenel added.

"Footprints?"

"We were able to cast them before the tide came in. Look like split-toe neoprene boots."

"The kind you wear with a wet suit."

Ravenel walked toward his car. He wasn't more than fifty feet from me but his dark face was lost to the night. "Still keeping you in my crosshairs, Mr. Bullock," he called out. "So don't wander too far. And watch your ass."

– Chapter 3 –

Alyana Genesee's two acres butted up to the O'Connor's three with a long row of manicured hedges separating the properties. A vine-covered arbor framed a small gate that made for an easy passage between the estates. Cobblestones ran out from either side of the gate telling a tale of two neighbors who had no problem getting along.

I walked to the front of the sprawling two-story house pausing twice to take in the sweeping view of Mackerel Cove and, in the distance, Newport's pricey shoreline. It was ten a.m. and, as predicted, the cold front had pushed the dense fog offshore and left behind a morning that was brisk and clear. A few minutes earlier, I had called Alyana Genesee with a mea culpa for ruining a decent night's sleep and an offer to stop by to pick up Olive. She gave me the okay, but there was a tentativeness running through her words that hinted she may have seen one of the morning TV news programs. The late Harold Mason was all over the networks and so was the one person of interest linked to the millionaire's murder, a mob-connected men's shelter director named Richard Bullock.

When I reached the brick steps running up to the home's impressive front entrance, the door opened and Olive charged out of the house. The poodle's tail whirled and the dog made a few excited turns before washing my hands with her tongue.

"She's got a reputation, you know," said the woman. She stood, arms folded, in the doorway.

"Really?" I knelt and stroked Olive's long ears. "What kind of reputation?"

"She reads people. Sniffs out the bad from the good and turns on her affection meter to let you know where you rate. At least that's what Maureen O'Connor says."

Alyana Genesee took a few strides across the brick porch and sat on the top step. She wasn't at all what I expected. Slim, shoulder-length black hair, great figure. Judging a woman's age was never my strong suit but best guess put the woman in her late thirties.

"Affection meter?"

"Growling and barking – not good," Alyana explained. "Licking and incessant tail wagging – very good."

"I'm honored," I said as Olive slathered my cheek.

"You should be. Olive doesn't usually rate ax murderers so highly."

"Been watching a little TV this morning, have we?"

"And answering an endless number of phone calls from Jamestown's concerned citizens – not to mention my mother who wants me to move before lunch."

I had to smile. "Got some 'splainin' to do, I guess."

"Guess so," Alyana replied. "Although Dr. Kool did a lot of the work for you."

"Doug Kool?" I blinked.

"Maureen O'Connor gave me his phone number," she said. "That's after she called a couple of hours ago in the middle of a panic attack. Did you know BBC broadcasts in Monte Carlo?"

"So you phoned Kool in New York?"

"I did. Dr. Kool gave me quite an earful."

"Yeah, I'm sure he did. By the way, he's not really a doctor. He bought himself an honorary degree." Doug Kool had a paper-thin veneer that was transparent to anyone who took the time to look hard. But the richer the connections Douglas happened to have, the less his background came under scrutiny.

"Doesn't seem to matter to the O'Connors. They consider him a good friend. And he vouches for you. Says you wouldn't kill a cockroach if it was – how did he put it? – crawling up your nose. Or did he say snout?"

"Had to be snout," I said "He has a way with words."

"Dr. Kool said he's been trying to reach you," Alyana informed me.

"I turned off my cell after partying all night in that funky little place Jamestown calls its clink."

"Well when you decide to reconnect with the world, you might want to thank your friend. He called Maureen O'Connor to tell her it wasn't necessary to fly back to the States. Promised her Olive will be fine. Apparently you're still a canine companion at least until you start doing hard time."

Olive trotted up the five brick stairs and nuzzled Alyana. A quick turn and the poodle was back at my side.

"I'm going to let Olive override what I consider good judgment, Mr. Bullock," the woman said and stood at the same time. "Why don't you come inside and have a cup of coffee."

It would be my fifth of the morning. With zero sleep for the past twenty-seven hours, I was running on caffeine and wasn't about to turn down another infusion. I followed Alyana through the door and into a cavernous great room floodlit by a mid-morning sun that streamed through a wall of floor-to-ceiling windows.

"Quite a view," I small talked my way to the kitchen that was a showcase of granite, glass and expensive appliances. "Quite a house."

Alyana poured brewed coffee into a pair of identical mugs branded with the ASPCA logo. "It's all yours if you want to buy it."

"For sale?"

"Yup."

I ached to ask the price but instead let loose with an even more tactless question. "How come?"

"Excuse me?" Alyana's face told me I had crossed into territory closed to people who knew each other less than five minutes.

"None of my business, I know," I tried to mollify the impertinence. "But this –" I made a half-circle gesture with my right hand. "This would be hard to beat."

No exaggeration. It wasn't only the IMAX-sized view of Narragansett Bay or the manicured yard that sloped to the rocky shoreline; it was the dramatic design of the house itself and its eclectic mix of furniture and art.

Alyana let a few seconds slip by. When her face and shoulders relaxed, I took it as a sign that my cheekiness wasn't going to get me tossed out the mahogany-and-stained glass front door. "Yes, it will be hard to beat," she admitted. "But I'm not racing to live bigger and grander. Quite the contrary actually."

"Well, in that case, let me show you a two-bedroom condo in Central Jersey," I said. "Might be what you're looking for – if you can get a mortgage."

She laughed. An easy, gentle sound that went well with her dark eyes. Her smile shook me out of my weariness long enough to give the O'Connor's next-door neighbor a closer look. Alyana wore an off-white cotton oxford shirt tucked into a pair of light-blue denim jeans. The style was casual but right out of Neiman Marcus or Saks Fifth Avenue. Her jewelry was gold, simple, and a perfect accent to her slightly dark complexion. Most noticeable of all – at least to me: no wedding ring.

"Appreciate the offer," she said. "The plan is to shrink the living space and stop paying the college tuition for my landscaper's kids. But I don't hear New Jersey calling."

"Too bad. You'd bring a whole new look to my neighborhood's mean streets."

"Thanks – I think." The smile reappeared and the sun-drenched kitchen seemed even brighter. "I know a little about the Garden State. My husband was born and raised there."

It was the kind of dejection that hits hard. I cursed myself for being such an ass to think a beautiful, rich woman living in a six-thousand-square-foot waterfront estate would be single.

"Really?" I managed to mumble over my coffee cup.

"Near the Delaware Water Gap. His family has deep roots there. So deep, in fact, that they wanted Jeff buried in his hometown."

I connected the dots. "Jeff – Geoffrey Genesee?"

"When he died a couple of years ago, it turned out to be an issue," Alyana reflected. "Jeff loved where he grew up but he loved Jamestown more. And he wasn't into the burying scene. So his ashes were scattered over the bay, which didn't sit well with the Genesee side of the family. Still doesn't."

Geoffrey Genesee was the computer wunderkind whose love affair with fast boats cost him his life. Like most people, I remembered the story. A month after Genesee convinced Intel to buy a majority stake in his business for a number north of one hundred million, he ran his forty-six-foot cigarette racer into a rogue wave. Traveling at close to one hundred miles an hour, the consequences were grim. Genesee was catapulted out of his powerboat and hit the water with such force that his neck and back were shattered. He was still alive when a Coast Guard patrol boat fished him out of the Atlantic, but died a few hours later.

"I'm sorry for your loss," I said. "I didn't realize you were –"

"It's okay," Alyana broke in. "In fact, it's refreshing to meet someone who doesn't know me as Jeff Genesee's widow. I loved my husband – very much, in fact. It's taken a while, but I'm moving on. Time to regain my own identity."

Except she hadn't moved on. Not really. There was a transparency to the nonchalant coating she tried putting on her words. Alyana couldn't hide the emptiness and pain that cut through what she was saying. Not from me, at least. Because it was the same emptiness and pain I still felt thirteen years after a gliomas tumor invaded my wife's brain and slowly, methodically, mercilessly killed her.

"Selling this place – it's all part of the process?" I asked.

"It is," Alyana confirmed. "Now tell me about you. Aside from being an assassin, that is."

"Very funny," I said. "Not a lot to tell. Penn State grad. Worked in a Manhattan ad agency until my wife died. Cancer. Did a professional U-turn and took a temporary job at a New Jersey homeless shelter. Thirteen years later, I'm still there. Go figure."

Thankfully, Alyana didn't pick at the scab that still hadn't healed since I buried my wife. It was a scab Doug Kool relentlessly jabbed by telling me to get a life. To crawl out of my homeless shelter hiding place and rejoin the real world. But when death leaves such a deep wound, the misery of others helps dull your own anguish. That I could possibly find any kind of solace in a men's homeless shelter is something Doug could never grasp. But I had a feeling Alyana Genesee would completely understand.

"Some reason why you skipped over the part of your life where you made every network newscast in the country?"

"Fifteen minutes of fame I'd just as soon forget."

"I wasn't sure at first that you were *the* Rick Bullock," said Alyana. "But your friend Dr. Kool said I should get your autograph. The man who found a missing book of the Bible. And not just any book – the book that spelled out God's definition of when the soul enters the body."

"The Book of Nathan," I acknowledged. "I think you know the end of the story."

"Doesn't everyone? A billionaire investment banker goes up in flames along with a Biblical book that could have been the Waterloo in the abortion battle."

"That's it in a nutshell," I said.

Alyana turned to the O'Connor poodle. "Strange, isn't it, Olive? A billionaire dies a horrible death and who's the last man he sees? Mr. Bullock. Now another multimillionaire gets killed. And who's on the scene?"

Olive replied with a soft yelp.

"You're the Grim Reaper for men with a lot of money," Alyana continued.

"To be crystal clear, I just happen to be around when they depart. I don't kill 'em."

Alyana stooped and stroked the bushy black crown on the poodle's head. "For reasons we don't quite understand, Olive and I believe you, Mr. Bullock."

"Thank you," I said. "I hope I can count on both of you as character witnesses when I go on trial. Although I'm not sure a jury will buy anything coming from a dog named after Popeye's girlfriend."

The poodle cranked her nose high and barked twice.

"Popeye had nothing to do with it," Alyana explained. "Maureen O'Connor was working on her third martini when she met a dog breeder in Boston."

"So she likes olives in her martinis. From what I remember reading, she also likes her husbands well heeled."

"Ken is her third try. I hope this one lasts because Maureen's a very nice lady."

"With a very nice dog."

"More like a fantastic dog." Alyana stood and refilled her mug and mine. Then the light banter turned serious. "Last night, you stepped into a very deep pile of trouble, Mr. Bullock."

"Since you and a dog have found me innocent of first-degree homicide, how about calling me Rick."

"All right," she agreed. "You're Rick and I'm Alyana."

Rick and Alyana. The two names coupled into a mellow sound that stopped me for a moment. For the first time in thirteen years, I felt a hairline crack in the despondency hanging over me like a shroud.

"So, Alyana, what do you know about Harold Mason?"

Another smile. "Not a nice man. Even before he hooked up with Mohammad al-Talal, there was a long line of people who wished he and his two sons would fall off a cliff. Harold got a minus ten on Olive's affection meter."

Now I understood the poodle's frenzy last night. "An old man takes a hike along a shoreline littered with slippery rocks on a dark night. Doesn't even have a flashlight. Make any sense to you?"

"Not to me," Alyana said. "But Harold was different. Obstacle courses were his thing, whether personal or professional. He had this weird obsession where he waited for low tide and then walked the shore from his house to a few lots past Roger Standish's place. Then he'd do an about-face and head home. Didn't matter if it was light or dark, winter or summer. If the weather was decent, Harold did his thing once everyday."

"Whoever killed him knew his routine," I speculated. "Waited in the water until he showed up and took care of business."

"Everyone in Jamestown knew Harold's routine. The local paper even did a piece on unusual exercise regimes for seniors and ran a photo of Mason working his way along the bay front. The story made it sound like he had an obsessive-compulsive disorder. The old man went ballistic over that story."

I drained what was left of my coffee. "Why stage an attack on Mason in front of the Standish house?"

Alyana shrugged. "Most of the waterfront homes have owners and families who don't follow predictable patterns. Me, for instance. As a veterinarian, I'm in and out at all hours. But Roger Standish lives with his ninety-year-old mother. It's almost always lights-out in that house by nine o'clock. Low tide was at ten last night. Roger was supposed to be asleep, but apparently stayed up late hoping to ambush a couple of our local deer."

The audio from a television in another room of the Genesee house filtered into the kitchen. I couldn't make out all the words but recognized the voice. It was Lieutenant Michael Ravenel.

"Give me your best shot," I said. "Who killed Harold Mason?"

"How much time do you have?" Alyana answered. "There are a lot of contenders. The America First crowd is right up there. More than a few Jews would be on the list. Maybe even the Narragansetts. Plus a boatload of people who have been foreclosed or cheated on by the Mason Development Company."

"The Narragansetts?"

"The tribe that lived on Jamestown centuries ago."

"What's the Indians' beef with Mason and sons?"

Aryana's expression lost its pleasantness. My question sparked a flash of irritation – or maybe it was pure anger – in the woman's eyes.

"Their beef, as you put it, is how Mason's company has dumped on Native Americans, especially those of us whose ancestors lived and died on Conanicut Island."

My faux pas took over the kitchen. Another careful look at Alyana Genesee and her heritage was obvious in her attractiveness. High cheek bones, the dark bronze tone of her skin, slightly oval eyes, and her thick, lustrous hair.

"It was a stupid way of phrasing the question," I tried repairing the damage. "I'm like too many Caucasians who don't know enough about Native American life, especially here in this part of the country."

"Who don't know and don't care," Alyana shot back.

"But I'm quick to learn what I don't know. Once I get educated, caring takes over real fast."

Alyana relaxed her shoulders and the fiery look in her eyes cooled. "My mother is a full-blooded Pequot, another New England tribe. My father was half English, half Narragansett. When he was alive, he would tell anyone who would listen how Conanicut Island – Jamestown – is a sacred Indian burial ground and should be treated as such."

"Words land developers don't love to hear," I interjected.

"Especially the Masons. They tore up a lot of graves over the years. But when Harold Mason broke ground for the al-Talal project, it literally killed my dad."

"More desecration?"

Alyana nodded. "Long before Mason started digging, the largest Indian cemetery in the northeast was discovered on this island. My father knew there was an even bigger burial site on land Mason owned. Eight acres of prime Jamestown property that Mason sold to Mohammad al-Talal."

"Eight acres your father wanted protected," I presumed.

"He had hoped Harold Mason would have deeded the parcel to the town or state. Wishful thinking. Two days after a pair of bulldozers showed up to clear the land, they hit the mother lode. Shoveled Indian bone into dump trucks like common trash. My father was already a very sick man when all this happened so I can't say Mason is directly responsible for his death. What I do know is he stomped out my dad's will to live."

I expected another rush of anger to sweep over Alyana. Instead, a sad reflection softened her eyes.

"Could someone connected to the Narragansett tribe have killed Mason?" I asked.

"It's a possibility," said Alyana.

"Any candidates?"

"No, but there's one man who would know if any tribal member might be hotheaded enough to attack Mason."

"Who?"

She said, "Lloyd Noka."

I couldn't disguise my puzzlement. "Lloyd Noka is an Indian?"

"Most of our families adopted Anglo names long ago. To the Narragansetts, Lloyd is Fifth Feather but that's not how he's known on the island."

"I'd like to talk to him."

"He wouldn't be forthcoming with you," Alyana noted. "But he might open up to me."

"What about a tandem?" I suggested. "Let's talk to him together. He might like hearing my first-hand account of how someone turned Mason's head into shark bait."

Alyana weighed the offer for a few seconds. "All right, I'll call him and try to set up a time to meet. He lives on the other end of the island – Conanicut Point."

"The sooner the better," I urged. "I'm only one link away from a Rhode Island chain gang, so if something could be worked out for today or tonight –"

"I'll do my best. I'm staffing our office from noon until six today. Maybe after dinner. Since you don't seem to know where the ON button is to your cell phone, how do I reach you?"

"How about I call you later this afternoon?" I proposed.

"Okay," she agreed and handed me a business card.

Alyana Genesee, D.V.M.
Conanicut Veterinary Associates
North Main Road, Jamestown, RI

We walked to the front foyer, Olive leading the way. When we reached the door, Alyana held out her hand. I braced for the imagery that always swept over me after even the most casual contact with a woman. The ghostly picture of Sloan-Kettering, the hospital ward where my wife lay motionless, the touch of her fingers as death pulled her away. But on this late morning, I felt something remarkably different. Just the warmth of Alyana Genesee and a haunting that never happened.

I made an awkward exit, practically tripping down the porch stairs. Olive pointed her long nose at me and barked, her tail wagging knowingly. Still bewildered by what just happened, I stumbled behind the poodle as she led me toward the O'Connor estate.

– Chapter 4 –

"You're not answering your damn phone!"

Lieutenant Michael Ravenel's wide body filled the O'Connor doorway blocking the bright noontime sunlight. Olive sat at my side studying the black man but didn't render a verdict. Her Olive-o-meter tail was in a locked position. The dog couldn't quite figure out Ravenel and neither could I.

"Cell phobia," I explained.

"I've been trying to reach you all goddamned morning."

I muttered an apology and motioned the lieutenant inside.

"Another thing," Ravenel continued his rant. "Didn't I tell you to watch your ass?"

"Exactly what you said."

"Then why's the driveway gate open?"

"Broken," I said. "Keypad-entry system is shot. The O'Connors have someone coming to fix the thing later this week."

"Later this week you could be nose down in Narragansett Bay like the old man you probably snuffed last night. Now let's go. We're taking a ride."

"What? Where?"

"To see your lawyer."

"You need sleep," I said. "I told you last night I don't need a lawyer."

"Yeah, well that's not what your lawyer says."

I balked, but Ravenel tugged my arm like an aggravated man who meant business. "I can't go without the dog."

"What?"

"If the dog stays, so do I."

Ravenel grunted. "All right, bring the damn dog and let's go."

We marched to an unmarked Crown Victoria and I waved Olive into the backseat. The car roared to life and Ravenel drove too fast along a route I was getting to know by heart. We were heading back to Jamestown's police station.

"Look, if this is some shyster cruising for work or a public defender – " I said as we drove over the speed limit through East Ferry, the island's quaint hub.

"Don't jerk me around," Ravenel ordered. "This guy's your legal beagle, so stop denying it. I want you to get him and his wife out of the station. Hear me? They've been one hell of a distraction since they showed up two hours ago."

His wife? I tried unraveling the puzzle but came up blank as Ravenel screeched into the police parking lot. Olive made an excited leap out of the Ford and followed Ravenel and me into the small building. A few cops clogged the narrow front corridor and all had their eyes on a woman who had her back to me. One glimpse of the long, multitoned blonde hair was all I needed to see.

"Oh, my God," I gasped.

The woman turned, her fire-red chiffon baby doll dress barely covering her oversized breasts.

"Oh, no, no, no," I groaned.

"BULLET!" the woman yelled and charged past the uniformed line of lascivious grins and a lot of drool. "Oh, Bullet! Can you believe it! It's me!"

Certainly was. Twyla Tharp Rosenblatt. Ex-stripper, one-time hooker, aspiring dancer, and the niece of the last of the big-time mob bosses on the East Coast.

"Twyla!" I exclaimed. "What are you doing here?"

"Oh, Bullet!" Twyla squealed as she pushed into me, her boobs dangerously close to escaping their polyester harness. "We're here! Isn't this amazing! Did you ever dream this would happen?"

Truthfully, I had. Usually after eating green peppers, which is when most of my sweat-producing nightmares showed up. Twyla was one of my bad-dream regulars but she wasn't nearly as unsettling as the odd-looking man who stepped out of the small bathroom at the far end of the corridor.

"Bullet!" squawked Yigal Rosenblatt, Esquire. "Here we are! Yes, we are!"

Yigal zigzagged through the cop gauntlet. He braked to a stop in front of me and grabbed my hand. "Nothing to worry about. Not at all."

Olive circled around Twyla, wagging her tail vigorously. When she spotted Yigal, she stopped cold, sat on the tile floor and stared at the man in the black suit and yarmulke. Like most living creatures, the poodle was too mystified by Yigal to render an opinion. No wag. No bark.

"Bullet?" Ravenel's question cut through the mayhem.

"Blame my grandmother," I tossed out an explanation over the din. "Nicknamed at two years old and it won't go away."

"Oh, Bullet," Twyla purred. "It's so great to see you! Do you know how long it's been?"

To the day. When I last saw the woman a year and a half ago, she was on a premarital cusp. Yigal hadn't quite mustered the courage to propose marriage, but not long after I left the two of them in Orlando, he went to bended knee. After Twyla's conversion to Judaism, the two exchanged vows in a temple only a few miles from Disney World.

"Why didn't you come to the wedding?" Twyla hopped up and down on her four-and-a-half-inch stripper pumps. "We really wished you had come, Bullet."

"You should have been there," Yigal chimed in.

"Well, like I said at the time, I couldn't shake out of a shelter directors' regional meeting I had to go to," I lied.

Twyla turned to Ravenel and spoke to him as if he were her closest friend – or one-time client. "Isn't he something, Detective Ravenous? There's nobody who loves homelessness more than Bullet."

Wide-eyed and open-mouthed, Ravenel pulled me to one side. "Get these lunatics outta here, Bullock or Bullet – whatever the hell your name is."

It was understandable why the lieutenant wanted to separate the Rosen - blatts from the Jamestown station house. The town's police force clustered around Twyla was in a stupor mesmerized by every bounce of the woman's body. An audible gasp filled the corridor when Twyla made an excited leap that lifted the hem of her mid-thigh dress over her hips and exposed her satin and rhinestone thong.

"Yigal, let's go someplace where we can talk," I suggested.

"Oh, yes. That's what we should do. We have business to discuss."

Since I was without wheels, I asked Yigal if he had a car. He did. A new Mercedes S550 four-door coupe that Doug Kool, who knew all things expensive, once told me was a dream machine priced close to six figures. Olive and I climbed into the rear seat and Yigal switched on the thirty-two-valve engine.

"We're going to find a quiet place where you're going to hear a lot of loud questions," I warned the Rosenblatts.

A short drive later, I told Yigal to pull into the parking lot of an East Ferry restaurant called Trattoria Simpatico. Olive dragged me toward a large outdoor seating area and a waiter wearing a name tag, Rinaldo.

"*Olive!*" Rinaldo called out and shook the poodle's paw. The dog should run for mayor, I thought.

"Maybe you could seat us outside so we can be with the dog," I suggested to Rinaldo.

"Inside, outside. With Olive it don't matter," the waiter said. "Hey, but wait a minute – You must be the guy stayin' at the O'Connor's, right? You're the one whose picture was on TV this mornin'! So, you popped Harold Mason, right?"

"No, I didn't pop him or anyone else," I corrected, wondering which old photo the networks were using.

"Come over here and sit," Rinaldo instructed and guided us to a table under a massive beech tree. "You get a free dessert today. Whaddaya want? Tiramisu? Somethin' else? On the house for takin' out that rotten son o' bitch."

I ordered coffee and Twyla picked a slice of chocolate banana brownie cake and an espresso. Yigal explained that he couldn't eat or drink anything since Trattoria Simpatico wasn't kosher.

"I'm kosher at home but not when we're away," said Twyla. "Except if there's a rabbi or one of them Hasidic Jews around. Then I have to stop eating or pretend I'm not Yigee's wife or even his sister."

There were two other couples drinking wine at a patio table too far away to hear the madness.

"Yigal, what the hell are you doing here?" I asked Rosenblatt, who was wiggling out of his suit jacket. The early afternoon sun was battling the increasingly chilly air but it wasn't warm enough to keep goose bumps off Twyla's overexposed body. Yigal's coat covered as much of his wife's upper anatomy as was possible. Hard to believe that love was still in the air for the oddest of all couples – an ambulance-chasing lawyer who was Orthodox from his hand-crocheted yarmulke down to his scuffed black oxfords and a Gentile lap dancer whose maiden name had been changed to match her idol, the famed choreographer, Twyla Tharp.

"In Newport," Yigal said. "That's where we're staying."

"Can you believe it, Bullet?" Twyla cut in. "Our first anniversary!"

It was never easy to read Yigal's face because it was mostly hair. His black beard rode high on his cheeks and his thick eyebrows ran in a straight uninterrupted line over the top of his nose, coming close to his hairline that dropped low on his forehead. Look hard, though, and it was possible to see the glint in Yigal's eyes whenever his wife spoke.

"Congratulations," I said, trying to exhibit a semblance of enthusiasm.

"Our hotel is so close to Jamestown," Twyla continued, "which is why Uncle Manny called."

I jerked my chair back. "Manny? Manny Maglio? Twyla, you *hate* your uncle."

"I used to. I really did. But that was before he changed, Bullet. He's been so nice, hasn't he, Yigee? Even bought us our new car!" She waved at the restaurant parking lot.

"But Manny runs an organized-crime syndicate, Twyla. He's not a man you should be spending time with."

"I thought so too!" chirped Twyla. "Then Uncle Manny offered Yigee this wonderful job and all."

Yigal shrugged – at least, I thought he did. Figuring out Yigal's body mannerisms was tricky because the lawyer was in constant motion. His twitching and spasms were nonstop and extreme. A vibrator stuck on high speed.

"What job?" I asked Yigal.

"General counsel," Yigal replied a little too quickly. "But just for his legitimate businesses, is all."

"Jesus, Yigal."

"But it's so great, Bullet!" Twyla rejoined the discussion. "And you know why? Want to know why? Because this wonderful job gives us a lot more money for the three of us!"

"What?"

"Bullet, I'm PREGNANT!"

Twyla jumped from her chair, stood and did a slow, jiggling turn. The two couples at the back end of the patio watched the show and one woman applauded the announcement. Rinaldo also caught the bulletin as he hustled toward our table with a tray of desserts and coffee.

"This is such good news!" Rinaldo said as he helped Twyla back into her seat. "First Harold Mason and now a new bambino!" He turned to me and patted my back. "You know how to take care of business, hey, mister? You get rid of some scum and you make something worthwhile."

"Oh, no, no –" I tried making the correction.

"You know what?" the waiter asked rhetorically while passing his hand over the table. "This whole thing here is no charge. You two are going to be good parents." He gave Twyla and me a simultaneous tap on our backs.

I reached for Rinaldo's apron, but he stooped out of reach to give Olive a garlic breadstick. Then he whisked off. I looked at Yigal and was ready to apologize for the mix-up but Rosenblatt's head was bobbing up and down over clasped hands.

"Barechu et adonai hamevorach leloam vaed."

"Isn't he adorable?" Twyla asked, her eyes locked lovingly on her entranced husband. "Even if he doesn't have a speck of food himself, he still prays that whatever I eat won't get stuck in me or anything."

I poked Yigal and the Hebrew stopped. "Why do I think there's more to this visit than baby talk?"

"Very important you see Manny," the lawyer said deliberately looking off to the side when dropping his A-bomb.

"What?"

"He has to see you, Bullet. It's very important."

"Are you insane? The reason the cops think I might be a murderer is because I met Maglio once. Just once! If I'm caught chatting up a mob boss now, I might as well plea-bargain for life in prison."

"He says he has information about what happened to Harold Mason," Yigal whispered.

"Then he should check in with his nearest law enforcement office."

"He can't. That's why he has to see you. Yes, he does. Says it could clear your name."

It was either an overload of caffeine or Yigal Rosenblatt that triggered the first pang of a monumental headache.

"Manny wants to give you confidential information," Yigal went on. "Has to do with the Arab's island that's been in all the news. Dutch Island."

"And just how are we supposed to pull this off? Uncle Manny stops by for a quick business lunch?"

"Oh, no. He can't come here. Can't be seen around Jamestown. Not at all."

"Then where?"

"One of his clubs in Providence – Sinsations."

The already exuberant Twyla Rosenblatt got even more energized. "Sinsations? Oh, I danced there once, Yigee! It was so nice a place. I wanna go with you tomorrow. That'll be okay, won't it?"

Yigal nodded his approval. We talked a while longer until I gave in to a worsening headache and the image of one of Maglio's goons clipping off my pinkie finger. Since I was under strict orders not to wander off Conanicut Island, Yigal would need to pick me up on the sly. I told him to drive to one of the few undeveloped waterfront lots on Jamestown's east side. It was the same overgrown patch of land Harold Mason apparently used as his halfway mark when taking one of his low tide hikes.

Anticipating the front of the O'Connor house might be under surveillance courtesy of Lieutenant Ravenel, tomorrow morning Olive and I would exit the back screen porch entrance and scramble south to the empty lot where Yigal and spouse would be waiting. It was the kind of absurdity that comes from a lack of sleep and ten cups of java.

"This will be so much fun," Twyla promised. "I'll meet some of the girls I haven't seen in years. And you can talk to Uncle Manny about Douche Island."

"Dutch," I made the correction. "Dutch Island."

"What is that, Bullet? I never heard of Dutch Island."

Current affairs that fell into a nonsexual category never were Twyla's strong suit. Even so, I was surprised that anyone over the age of five didn't have at least some awareness of Dutch Island. I drew a deep breath and spilled out an abridged version of a story that continued to rankle America's masses.

It started with Harold Mason's development and construction company making a seemingly magnanimous offer. The Masons owned chunks of land on Jamestown and a stretch of oceanfront near Rhode Island's Point Judith. The company proposed a swap. Give the Masons title to Dutch Island, an eighty-two acre plug of uninhabited rock and weeds stuck in the middle of Narragansett Bay and the company would donate two parcels of land adding up to exactly the same acreage that the state could then develop into far more useable park property. Rhode Island's Department of Environmental Management was immediately suspicious because most everyone knew Harold Mason's favorite pastime was the kind of screwing that could make Twyla look like a nun.

"Where is this island?" Twyla wanted to know.

"Less than a mile off the Jamestown shoreline," I said. "To the west."

I continued the story.

It took a while, but a few bags of money and a truckload of Sony fifty-two-inch plasma televisions later, the deal was sealed Rhode Island style. At the same time the Masons were negotiating to become proud owners of Dutch Island, they worked out an agreement with the Army Corps of Engineers to build a tunnel from Jamestown to Dutch Island. The idea was so crazy and expensive that the army along with federal and state environmental agencies humored the Masons by signing off on the request. If it were ever built, the tunnel would stretch three thousand feet from the eight acres Mason owned near Jamestown's Fort Getty to the southern tip of Dutch Island.

Twyla was enthralled with the story. "Building a tunnel underwater would cost a lot, wouldn't it?"

"A whole lot," I replied. "Something like five hundred million for a small, two-lane passageway if I remember right. The water between Jamestown and the island is deep – fifty feet or more. Building a tunnel was so expensive that no one thought it would ever happen. People let their guard down, which turned out to be a big mistake."

"It was?"

"A very big mistake."

I went on with the story.

Less than a year after the Masons took title to Dutch Island, a reporter for the *Providence Journal Bulletin* discovered Mohammad al-Talal, the world's fourth richest Arab, was secretly involved in the land swap. *Forbes* estimated al-Talal's worth at around ten billion dollars most of which was invested in subsidiary companies based in Kuwait and Saudi Arabia. Of all the power brokers in the Middle East, al-Talal had long been among the most contemptuous of the United States. If he didn't have his hand on the oil valve that pumped life into America, the Arab would probably have run into a CIA drone a long time ago.

"Why would he want anything to do with Dutch's Island?" asked Twyla.

"To make a statement," I said and finished the tale.

Al-Talal and the Masons eventually came clean. Mason didn't sell property to the Arab, but negotiated a hundred-year lease that kept some of the financial details under the radar. The Mason company was in line to make millions as the lead contractor for the construction of the underwater tunnel *and* a forty thousand square-foot structure on Dutch Island that al-Talal planned to use as a residence and as a Muslim shrine.

"With a tall tower," Yigal joined the narration.

"Actually, a minaret," I confirmed. "A really tall minaret. When it's done, al-Talal will have one of the largest privately owned properties in the country sitting at the entrance to Narragansett Bay. The minaret will be the Arab's middle finger the U.S. Navy won't be able to miss each time it moves ships in or out of Newport."

"That's not good, Bullet." Twyla looked appalled. Better late than never.

"Nope, it's not," I agreed and checked my watch. "Gotta go. How about a ride back to my summer house?"

"Arabs have strange names," Twyla pondered as we walked to the parking lot. Weird Arabic monikers seemed to be Mrs. Rosenblatt's main take-away from my long story. "Speakin' of names, Bullet, guess what we're gonna call our baby?"

"Yigal Junior?" I gritted my teeth, hoping I was wrong.

"No," Twyla laughed. "There can never be another Yigee."

For sure.

"If it's a boy, we're going to call him Boaz. Boaz Rosenblatt."

I waited for the second shoe to hit me hard. It didn't take long.

"We don't think it will be a girl, but if it is, we'll call her Tzufit. That means hummingbird in Hebrew."

My headache rocketed into migraine territory. Olive and I parked ourselves in the backseat of Yigal's car and the Mercedes headed toward the O'Connor house. Drive time was five minutes but the trip seemed to take a lifetime.

– Chapter 5 –

I learned early in life about humanity's shortcomings. My father worked overtime as a public defender and my mother was a volunteer fixture at Camden's Fourth Street Mission, a feeding trough for the broken and luckless. My parents didn't allow for much downtime from their respective crusades. But on rare occasions, they would retreat to the living room of our three-bedroom tract house and give themselves over to an old RCA turntable that cranked out one Perry Como or Frank Sinatra tune after another. But *Catch a Falling Star* and *Strangers in the Night* were never quite enough to stomp out an awareness that misery prevailed, and it wouldn't be long before they scurried off to resume the never-ending fight against social injustice.

Were they still alive, even my parents might have had trouble warding off the spell of the O'Connor's mesmerizing back-window view of Narragansett Bay. Watching herring gulls and gannets circle Hull Cove or tracking the flock of J-class and Catalina keelboats as they cut through light chop on an easterly wind could sedate almost anyone. But I knew in the end, Jamestown's tranquility would have been overrun by unfairness and prejudice that hitched themselves to my father and mother like steel to a magnet.

According to my friend Doug Kool, the Bullock family's "save-the-world" DNA had been passed along to me big time. "Ridiculous!" I argued. Doug's predictable retort would follow: "Bullshit! If that were the case, you wouldn't be burying yourself for eighteen hours a day in a men's shelter!" All right, so I worked overtime at the Gateway Men's Shelter. I couldn't debate that point. But the reason why had nothing to do with an inherited obsession to save mankind. It was a diversion – my way of warding off a depression that had clouded my life since the death of my wife thirteen years ago.

"Hey, Angie," I said to the always-pleasant admin stationed outside Doug Kool's office on the fortieth floor of a Manhattan high-rise. It was four o'clock and I decided to activate my cell just long enough to make two calls before taking a quick nap.

"Is the man in?"

"He is, but you sure put him in a funk, honey," said Angie. "Been trying to call you like forever."

"Life in the slammer. The warden took my roll-over minutes."

The woman giggled. "Sure you want to talk to him? He's got a bug the size of a hamster up his keister."

"Ouch," I laughed.

"Tell him his proctologist is on the line."

Angie chuckled again and pressed the hold button.

"Damnit, Bullet!" Doug shouted a few seconds later. "What is it about you? Trouble sticks to you like shit on a diaper!"

Douglas Kool generally personified his name. He was, in most every way, cool. However, when life rattled his cage, the star performer for the largest fund-raising firm in the country who made a handsome living tapping wealth for good causes, quickly became unhinged.

"I tripped over a dead guy," I explained. "There's not much more to the story."

"You tripped over *Harold Mason!* Jesus H., Bullet! You remember whose house you're using for a free two-week vacation? A vacation I worked out for you? Ken O'Connor. *Ken O'Connor!* The guy who pumps in a half a mil a year to the United Way, not to mention what he gives to five other charities I hand pick!"

"Yeah, you've mentioned that a few thousand times," I said. "I'm just calling to let you know everything's fine."

"Fine? Your picture's in every paper in the country and worse, in whatever rag the O'Connors are reading while they're floating around the French Riviera."

"I discovered a body. Simple as that. End of story."

Doug moaned. "Nothing's simple with you. Oh, God – What about the dog! Tell me the dog's all right."

Olive was lying at my feet, her long black nose resting on my shoe. "She's doing great. Well, except for her left ear. Odds are it can be reattached."

One of my pleasures in life was to elevate Doug's blood pressure.

"You think this is funny? Your ass is hanging out there as a suspect in one of the most sensational murders of the decade. See how long you laugh when you're buck naked in a prison shower."

"Listen, when you talk to the O'Connors again tell them Olive's having a ball and the house is shipshape. Oh, and just in case they ask, the driveway gate still hasn't been fixed."

"What the hell are you talking about? What gate – is this another joke? What did you do? And why don't you keep your cell phone on? Bullet, can you hear me?"

"You're breaking up. But trust me, I'll keep you posted, Douglas."

The second call was to Alyana Genesee who told me we had a date with Lloyd Noka at eight p.m.

"Earlier would have been better," she said.

"How come?"

"You'll understand when we see Lloyd," she said. "I'll pick you up at quarter to eight."

I switched off my cell and stretched out on the king-sized bed that barely made a dent in the O'Connor's spacious guest room. Olive curled up on a nearby shag rug, and we were on the cusp of oblivion when the front doorbell rang. And rang again. And again. I stumbled through the house, Olive trotting alongside. The poodle began barking even before I opened the door.

Two men stood on the front porch, their feet apart, arms crossed. Both had facial features that hinted at their common genealogy. Graying brown hair, the kind of protruding jaw that's usually a billboard for arrogance and a body mass that put each of them at around two hundred pounds – maybe more. One wore mud-splotched jeans, a V-neck pullover, and work boots. The other was dapper. The press lines on his pants were razor sharp and his cotton poplin shirt oozed money.

Olive was working herself into hysteria. She crouched low to the floor and pulled her tail under her body. The piercing barks gave way to a loud menacing snarl.

"Sorry," I said, wiggling outside and closing the door. "She's usually not like that."

"You Bullock?" asked the man in jeans. It was a pointless question. In his hand was a copy of the *Newport Daily News* folded to an inside page with a two column by five-inch photo of the "Person of Interest" in last night's homicide.

"You here to fix the gate?" Hardly. I knew exactly who they were.

"No," the jeans man grunted. "But you best get that thing repaired. Anybody could get in here."

So it seems. I looked past the two men and saw a pair of vehicles parked in the driveway. An Escalade and a Bentley.

"Working on it," I said.

"We've got a couple of questions," the better-dressed man shouted over Olive's continued barking. "How about moving away from the noise."

"Hate dogs," jeans man muttered as we walked off the porch and along a paved sidewalk to the O'Connor's long oyster-shell driveway. Our footsteps took on a bone crunching sound.

"You know who we are?" the better-dressed man grabbed the conversation's lead.

"Church of the Latter Day Saints?"

"Probably not the time to play wiseass," the man advised. "My name is Caleb Mason." He paused and wagged his head at the second man. "My brother, J. D."

"Condolences. I didn't know your father. But before he died, he gave me a few fishing tips. I never got a chance to thank him."

"Doesn't sound like dear old Dad," said Caleb. "Harold wasn't the type to hand out tips. Of any kind."

J. D. said, "In other words, the old man was a prick."

Caleb raised his right hand. "You're going to hear, if you haven't already, that my brother and I didn't always see eye to eye with our father. But he was still our blood and we're not taking kindly to the fact that somebody killed him."

"I can understand that," I said.

"It's our intention to find out what happened and resolve the situation," Caleb spoke calmly as if this were just another Mason Development Company business transaction.

"The police are working the case," I reminded the two.

"Yeah, well, so are we," J. D. noted. "And our playbook comes with a different set of rules."

"I didn't kill your father."

"Maybe you didn't," J. D. shrugged. "Could be you were there just as backup. To make sure whoever took care of business did it right."

Our short parade ended when we reached the front of the Escalade. "I'm the guy who found your father's body. That's the extent of it."

J. D. gripped my forearm and gave me a quarter turn. "A Jersey boy who's thick with the Maglio syndicate shows up and the next thing you know my old man has his head pounded in. Somethin' says there's a lot more to the extent of it than you're lettin' on, my friend."

Caleb pried J. D.'s mitt from my arm.

"It won't take us long to figure out if you're innocent or guilty, Mr. Bullock," Caleb promised.

A chilly breeze worked its way off the bay and up the O'Connor's driveway. The cool air sent a shutter through my frazzled body.

"Nervous, Bullock?" J. D. asked with a smirk.

"Try cold," I said. "And tired. Are we done?"

Caleb replied, "Not quite."

I leaned against the Escalade's passenger-side door and waited for Caleb to continue.

"We think dear old dad was carrying something when he was killed – something that could be the reason he was murdered."

"And that *something* is what?"

"A document," said Caleb. "Probably rolled up inside a mailing tube."

"What kind of document?"

"Our guess is you know what we're talking about," Caleb went on.

"Nope. Don't have a clue."

J. D. stepped in front of me, his face no more than six inches from mine. "Let's pretend the bullshit you're feeding the cops is true. You say some asshole jumped out of the water, took an axe to the old man's head, and disappeared back into the bay. But there was no way the killer could haul ass a mailing tube in the water without ruining the thing. Right? Which meant it was still there when you showed up."

The press had pulled together enough information about Harold Mason's death to fill the airways and newsprint with gruesome details that were fodder for the public. But the media had yet to learn about the man in the neoprene wet suit who dove into the water after pulverizing Harold Mason's skull. The Mason boys had apparently bought themselves at least one mole inside Jamestown's police department.

"There wasn't anything on or near your father's body," I said. "No mailing tube. Not even a flashlight." I paused and stroked my chin with my right hand. "Here's a thought. Instead of worrying about what your father was carrying, why don't we ask ourselves why an old man was picking his way over rocks and seaweed in the middle of the night?"

"Dementia," Caleb said without emotion. "His senility has been a problem for quite some time."

"So you two good sons let your father tiptoe along the water's edge in total darkness even in his state of mind?" Maybe it was the drop in temperature or my fatigue. Whatever the reason, I was getting frisky.

"If you knew Harold Mason, you'd understand," Caleb contended. "He wasn't someone who took orders from anyone regardless of his mental condition."

"That's for goddamned sure," J. D. added. "And how we dealt with him isn't what we're here to talk about. You've got something we want. And we want it now!"

Homeless shelter management lesson one: don't get rattled. Lesson number two: don't fall victim to intimidation. It's an infection that if allowed to spread turns everything to pus.

"Listen, asshole," I said to J. D., keeping my voice steady and my eyes locked on his. "I was held at gunpoint two minutes after I found your old man on the shore. Then I was put in handcuffs and hauled to an interrogation room for five hours of fun and games. Any idiot should be able to figure out I couldn't steal anything from your daddy even if I wanted to."

J. D. Mason outweighed me by thirty pounds of what looked to be hard muscle. His biceps were the size of my thighs and his neck was a tree stump. I could tell his anger was volcanic, and if Brother Caleb hadn't been on the scene, the explosion could have easily landed me in the hospital – or morgue.

"Here's what we're going to do," Caleb said, his voice still under control. "My father's viewing is the day after tomorrow. By the time people show up to pretend like they really cared for the man, we want the document that was taken last night. Now, if you don't have it, then we expect you to help us find it."

"I'll bet you have a lot of employees on the Mason Development Company payroll," I said, knocking Caleb off balance.

"We do."

"Well, I'm not one of them. Don't expect a helping hand."

"That would be a mistake," Caleb warned. "Given your underworld connections, no one would be surprised if you suddenly disappeared. J. D. and I certainly wouldn't want that to happen."

J. D. missed the sarcasm running through his brother's last words. He glared at Caleb the same way he probably looked at his crazy father.

"If you're telling the truth and don't have what we want, Mr. Bullock," Caleb kept talking, "then I suspect you probably have a thought or two about where to find what we're looking for. So, come through for us and we'll be certain to keep you safe and sound."

Caleb turned and stepped toward his Bentley but J. D. was frozen in place, his eyes more threatening than any words his brother had thrown my way. Caleb did an about-face and pulled J. D. backward. A half minute later, the two vehicles raced ahead, their rear tires tearing shell shards from the driveway and firing them toward me like shrapnel.

The face-off with the Mason brothers drained what little energy I had left and the walk back to the house was slow. Ignoring the uncomfortable sea breeze, I tried to fathom how two sons could assign more importance to a piece of paper than the passing of their father. As revolting as Harold Mason may have been, death had a way of shaking out respect from the most disenfranchised relatives or friends. Unless – unless the old man's loathsomeness crossed all boundaries. Or unless he bred offspring who were equally as despicable. Or maybe both.

When I opened the O'Connor's front door, Olive dashed outside, nose to the ground. She tracked the Mason scent from the porch to the ruts left in the oyster-shell driveway. When the poodle was satisfied that the grounds were clear, she bounded back to my side and barked once. *Glad those bastards are gone,* was her message I guessed.

My sentiments exactly.

– Chapter 6 –

The sun's remnants colored the sky a muted purple-gray when Alyana Genesee drove her Odyssey minivan to the O'Connor's front entrance. Dusk had gotten a one-hour, daylight savings time reprieve and the lingering glow in the west backlit the woman who stepped out of the vehicle. Alyana had changed into a beige jersey top and casual slacks that were tailored perfectly to her trim body. She threw back her shoulder-length dark hair as she walked toward me. I don't remember ever meeting a woman with such an astonishing blend of class, sensuality, and beauty.

"Anyone ever tell you you're an oxymoron?" I asked.

Alyana stopped a couple of feet short of Olive and me. "Not until now."

"You live in an *Architectural Digest* house with a view to die for. But you drive a three-year-old Honda."

Alyana smiled. "Four years old. And the van is a professional necessity. Remember? I'm in the animal business. A Mazerati and a German shepherd aren't a good combination."

I bought some but not all of what she was saying. "And what would be in your driveway if you weren't a vet?"

"Probably a Prius," she laughed.

I believed her. Luxury and pretension were more of what she married than what she was. At least that's what I theorized based on a grand total of two encounters with the woman.

"Mind if Olive tags along tonight?" I asked. "I need to keep the dog safe or Maureen O'Connor will turn me into a eunuch."

"That's no exaggeration, Mr. Bullock – sorry, Rick. But for the record, after you left Maureen's dog in an unlocked porch last night, castration could still be in your future."

Alyana triggered the van's automatic tailgate.

I said to the dog, "Hey, Olive, tell the lady I treated you like platinum since the minute we met."

"You took a full-coat show poodle into Narragansett Bay."

"Yup," I admitted. "She had a blast."

"And ended up caked with salt and sand. Know how I spent two hours after you asked me to take over your dog sitting duties? I gave Olive a freshwater bath, blow dried her coat, and combed her out."

"Oh," I mumbled. "Dog grooming's not one of my strong suits."

"Really?" Alyana feigned surprise. "Because Maureen told me your friend Dr. Kool made a big deal about your poodle expertise."

"He tends to exaggerate. Fact is that aside from watching the Westminster Dog Show once, I don't have much of a puppy track record. I'm hoping Maureen doesn't figure that out."

"Look, Rick, this isn't about the O'Connors – it's about making sure nothing bad happens to this dog." Alyana stooped and ran a hand over Olive's back. "She's an extraordinary animal. I've been a vet for ten years and I've never come across a dog as intelligent as this one."

As if on cue, Olive jumped onto a narrow section of flooring at the rear of the Odyssey. The poodle grabbed a nine-inch tether hanging from the door of one of two metal crates that took up most of the van's back compartment. With a hard yank, the dog pulled open a sturdy slide latch and stepped inside. Alyana hand signaled Olive to use the tether to lock herself in the crate. When the job was finished, Olive barked once and threw me a see-what-we're-talking-about? stare.

"All right, I get it," I said to the dog. "You're a genius."

"Exactly. You're babysitting the Isaac Newton of dogdom," said Alyana while closing the minivan's tailgate. "Best not to forget that."

It was a short drive to Lloyd Noka's place, but long enough to ask Alyana about my two afternoon visitors.

"Know what caused the bad blood between the late Mr. Mason and his happy-go-lucky sons?"

Alyana steered the Honda north on Main Road, Jamestown's busiest street that ran the length of the island. "Harold wasn't exactly the dad-of-the-year type. From what I've been told, he was abusive to his sons when they were young. Nevertheless, when they were in their twenties, neither one wasted much time signing on to help run Harold's development company, which as you know, is worth millions."

"What about Harold's wife?"

"Died a long time ago. Don't know a whole lot about her."

"After they joined the company, the boys didn't warm up to Harold?"

"Definitely not," Alyana said. "And Harold wasn't thrilled with his kids either. J.D.'s paying alimony to three ex-wives and is well acquainted with every bar from here to the Massachusetts state line. He's been in more than his share of brawls."

"And Caleb?" I asked.

"Blows through money like a nor'easter. Has a minimansion in Newport and loves anything that goes fast on land, in water, or in a skirt."

I had a quick recall of Caleb's Bentley as it cut ruts into the O'Connor's driveway. "What about the deal with Mohammad al-Talal? Were father and sons on the same page?"

"Yes and no," Alyana answered. "From what I hear, all three would have sold Dutch Island to the devil if he came up with enough money. None of the Masons had or have a reputation for putting ethics or social responsibility over profit. But I've also heard the two boys wanted Harold to squeeze al-Talal for a whole lot more cash."

"A few hundred million wasn't enough?"

"Not for those two. There were even rumors Caleb and J. D. were considering a coup. If they could prove Harold's dementia was bad enough, he might be dethroned. But most people who knew Harold said he was still mentally competent enough to run the company."

The Honda turned right and twisted its way along a narrow road until Alyana reached a gravel drive that snaked through a stand of pine trees. She pulled to a stop in front of a small run-down cottage.

When the Honda's tailgate opened, Olive unlocked herself from the steel crate and hopped to the ground. The dog followed Alyana and me to a weathered door that was half open.

"Lloyd?" Alyana called out and waited for a response.

"Come in." The interior of the house was dim and overrun with clutter. The man with a deep, hoarse voice who had beckoned us inside sat in a tattered armchair. Olive raced ahead and did a full circle at the feet of a gaunt figure barely distinguishable from the ripped upholstery.

"Ah, my favorite *aním*," the thin man rasped. Olive rallied back with a bark and an excited tail wag.

Alyana walked to Noka and took his hand. "And what makes you think the dog speaks Narragansett, old man?"

"She understands the old language more than you and your kin who have little use for the past," Noka snorted.

"I'm Pequot and still know your Narragansett words, old man," said Alyana. "At least those you taught me."

Ah, yes, I did didn't I. If you have such a fine recall, prove it."

This was a game the two had played before, I guessed. Probably many times before.

"All right," Alyana complied. "*Mosq.* The man you still are."

The old man's laughter collapsed into a cough. "I wish that were true! Perhaps I once was a bear, but now – now nothing more than a *waûtuckques,* I'm afraid."

Alyana squeezed Noka's hand. "A rabbit? I don't think so. More like an old buck. An *attuck.*"

"Flattery will get you everywhere," Noka chuckled, his voice slightly slurred. He turned his head to me. "Who's the *neetop?*"

"My friend? His name is Richard Bullock."

"Ah," the old man leaned forward to catch a better look at my face. "You're the good soul who removed Harold Mason from our ranks."

"Well, not really," I corrected Noka. "Just showed up after the fact."

The old man grunted and for the first time gave me a good look at his face. His cheeks and forehead were a crisscross of deep furrows capped by an unkempt mop of long black hair. Wads of flesh hung below his dark eyes and the lobe of one ear was missing. An unlit cigarette drooped from the side of his broad mouth.

"Mr. Bullock needs to clear his name," Alyana explained, getting right to the point of our visit. "Which is why he wants to find out who really killed Mason last night."

"Should I confess now or later?" Noka asked with a grin. His cigarette magically attached to his lips even as he talked.

Alyana smiled back. "A few years ago, you'd be first on the list of suspects, old man."

Noka nodded and shrugged. He pointed at a bottle of Old Crow bourbon well within reach of his chair. "Would you mind, my dear?" he asked Alyana.

She said, "You know I don't like being an accomplice to your bad habit."

Noka lifted both hands that were noticeably shaking. "Think of it as a calmative – something to smooth over the reflections of a difficult life. It will help me tell the *neetop* what he needs to know."

Alyana walked to the table next to Noka's chair and half filled a water glass with bourbon. The old man took the tumbler and drained it with two swallows, his cigarette still stuck in his mouth as he drank. Olive, who had curled herself into a half-moon at Noka's feet, shot the man with a one-eye look that didn't go unnoticed. The Indian tried to dismiss the poodle with a wave of his quivering hand but the dog didn't blink.

"Do you sense their disapproval, Mr. Bullock?" Noka asked me as he lowered the empty glass to his lap. "Perhaps you share their displeasure. Or is that distain I see in your eyes?"

"Sorry?"

"Indians and liquor. The red man's curse. That's what you're thinking, isn't it?"

"No. Not really," I answered honestly.

"Then you are indeed an oddity." Noka's voice was thick. "Most Caucasians speak about Native Americans and alcoholism in the same breath. Of course, I have to admit that on occasion I prove them right!"

The old man chortled, his body rocking under the low light of a floor lamp that stood beside his chair.

Alyana broke in. "Let's move off this path, old man. I'm not here to watch you drown in sour mash whiskey."

Noka sighed and sank back into his chair. It was obvious the two were accustomed to wrestling over the old man's drinking. I had seen a few Lloyd Nokas before – Native Americans who were shoved into the Gateway Shelter, usually the result of their alcoholism. "Indians metabolize liquor differently," a physician once explained to me while signing a death certificate for a booze-ravaged Cree ironworker. Not everyone bought that theory, I learned later. But right or wrong, the explanation got legs each time the media did a data dip that had anything to do with Indians and liquor. Like the Centers for Disease Control and Prevention report that found Native Americans three times more likely to die from alcohol-related disease or accidents than the population at large. Another look at Lloyd Noka and I conjectured he'd soon be pumping up that statistic.

"How your name fits you, my love," Noka said to Alyana, a much too apparent ploy to soften the woman's sharp criticism of his drinking. "Do you know what her Indian name means, Mr. Bullock? Alyana – eternal bloom. She makes everything look like spring, doesn't she? Even an old man's addiction."

Alyana ignored Noka's increasingly tipsy comments and turned to me. "You've heard the word sachem, Rick?"

"I have," I answered and was grateful Alyana didn't ask why. As a preteen, I was a YMCA Indian Guide. My sachem or great chief was a fat Portuguese-American who was fond of kiddy porn and ended up in East Jersey State Prison. The sachem died in 2002 the same year the Y ditched the Indian Guide label, calling it insensitive to Native Americans.

"Lloyd is an advisor to tribal sachems throughout the country," Alyana said. "There's a reason why so many come to him for advice. Take a good look at this room."

Difficult to do given the bad lighting. But what I could make out told a story. Stacks of books stood four or five feet high against the walls. Copies of the *Congressional Record Daily Digest* were spread out next to a laptop computer sitting on a beat-up desk. Newspapers and periodicals were strewn around Noka's armchair.

"Lloyd is a sponge," Alyana continued. "He absorbs everything – "

"Including Old Crow," Noka broke in with a belly laugh.

"You'd best not get clever or cute about your drinking, old man," warned Alyana. Olive plugged in an exclamation point with a single, high-pitched bark.

Noka clutched his empty glass and pulled his chin into his neck the way a man might do when he's about to get smacked hard.

"There's very little Lloyd doesn't know about Native American affairs," Alyana said. "Tribal leaders come to him not just for information but also for counsel. He's the wisest man I know."

"Ah," the old man muttered either flattered or embarrassed by the woman's compliment.

Alyana shifted her attention back to Noka. "So, old man, this is why I am here with my *neetop*. To find out if there's a Narragansett who might have killed Harold Mason."

Noka grunted and looked at Alyana the way a father connects with a daughter. "All Narragansetts hated Harold," he said. "But I doubt there's a killer among us."

"What about someone from another tribe?"

The old man hesitated with his answer. I couldn't tell whether he was adverse to speculation or just didn't trust handing out this kind of information in front of a stranger. Finally he said softly: *Wushawunun.*"

"The Hawk?" Alyana asked.

"Yes."

"William Nonesuch?"

The old man bobbed his head.

"You heard this from the Niantics?"

"Today they call themselves Nehantics," Noka corrected. "What I hear is that Nonesuch has always been a hothead. After the smoke shop raid, he's been nothing but vicious."

"I'm lost," I confessed. "Smoke shop?"

Alyana gave me a brief tutorial. In 2003, the Narragansetts opened a smoke shop on tribal land in Charlestown, Rhode Island, a mainland community not far from Jamestown. Although ordered not to do so, the tribe started selling tax-free cigarettes. Two days later after the first pack of Marlboros went out the door, Rhode Island's governor ordered a squad of state police officers to shut the operation down. The raid didn't go smoothly and TV cameras were there to catch the action. The smoke shop was put out of business and several Indians were charged with assault, disorderly conduct, and resisting arrest. Five years of legal wrangling later, most of the Narragansetts were cleared and a few required to do community service. But for many, the bitterness that billowed out of the raid never went away.

"So, this man William Nonesuch," I said to Noka, "isn't connected to the Narragansett tribe?"

"He might not even be a Nehantic," the old man disclosed. "Nonesuch, or Hawk as he likes to be called, insists he has a bloodline connection to the tribe. However, the few Nehantics who are still left don't lay claim to the man."

"Hawk has a bad reputation," Alyana added more background. "He's been in and out of prison most of his life. Locked up for aggravated assault and harassment. Not exactly a stellar citizen."

"When Harold Mason desecrated the burial site on the island, Nonesuch and a few others said it was time for a payback," Noka said. "Could have been just talk. But maybe not."

The room went quiet for several seconds. This was all too obvious, I thought. When lining up suspects after a possible hate crime, a badass like William Nonesuch had to have made the top ten. "The cops must have this guy on their radar screens," I said to both Noka and Alyana. "Why haven't they worked him over?"

"Probably have," the old man replied. "Hawk knows how to cover his tracks. He'll have a solid alibi, you can be assured of that."

"Where can I find him?" I asked.

Noka didn't answer but instead looked at Alyana. "Hawk is what in Algonquian we call a *quenobpuuncke*. Did I ever teach you that word, my dear?"

"I don't think so."

Noka laughed. "Because it means *shit*. Nothing could better describe William Nonesuch, the Hawk."

"Where can I find him?" I repeated my question, drawing the old man's attention back to me.

"You don't want to do that," advised Noka.

"You're right – I don't want to. I just need to. Does he live around here?"

The old man shrugged and yawned. "Has a place near Lyme, Connecticut, which is where most of the Nehantics live. But if you go, bring a small army. You'll need it."

Noka's eyelids closed, a clear signal he was about to surrender to the bourbon. Before the old man drifted into an alcohol-induced oblivion, I wanted his take on another matter.

"Earlier today, Harold Mason's two sons paid me a visit," I said.

"Bad seeds, both of them," Noka grumbled, his eyes still shut. "Possibly worse than their father."

"They came looking for a document. Something they think Harold Mason might have had with him when he was killed last night."

The old man unexpectedly shook off his stupor and looked at me. "Was it a deed?"

"A deed?"

"Yes, a deed. Was that what they were looking for?"

"They didn't say," I replied. "A deed to what?"

"Dutch Island."

"I don't understand."

Noka tried pulling himself forward in his chair. Moving his body a couple of inches left the old man tired and he stopped to draw in a long breath before continuing our conversation.

"Some say the sale of Dutch Island may not have been legal."

"So, what does that mean? The deed between the state of Rhode Island and Mason isn't legitimate?" I asked.

"No. I'm sure that transaction is fine since Mason hired the best lawyers money can buy to put the deal together. But one of those attorneys is a friend. A Passamaquoddy."

"A tribe in Maine," Alyana clarified. "One of the largest in New England."

"He told me a title search firm uncovered a glitch that Mason's company has been working overtime to keep under wraps."

"What kind of glitch?"

"A glitch that says a part of Dutch Island may not have been Rhode Island's land to sell in the first place. There may be an enforceable deed out there that proves a section of the island belongs to someone else."

"The Narragansetts?"

"No," the old man huffed. "Rightfully the island probably does belong to our tribe. But centuries ago, Indians were easily weaseled out of their property. No, the deed in question goes back to the seventeen hundreds – between the King of England and a private landholder. Apparently that deed was never signed over to any other party by the owner or his or her heirs."

The picture was coming into focus. "Even if a deed like that exists, wouldn't a team of high-priced lawyers punch so many holes in the thing that it would be worthless?"

"My Passamaquoddy friend says that's exactly what would happen," replied Noka. "The state would have eminent domain on its side and a bagful of other slippery tactics to show it actually had ownership rights to the island before it cut a deal with Mason."

"Then why should Harold's sons be worried about finding the deed?" asked Alyana.

"Restraining order," Noka said. "Even if a claim against the state wouldn't stand a chance, it would need to be reviewed. So if the deed is located and the owner's heirs start making a stink, al-Talal's deal is put a hold. Everything grinds to a halt, including the tunnel construction."

Which would be good news for the Narragansetts. Whatever Indian bones the Masons hadn't already excavated would remain safely buried, possibly long enough to discourage Mohammad al-Talal from moving ahead with his much-criticized project. Native Americans had a lot to gain if the deed was found. So much of a benefit, in fact, that it stirred up a theory. Supposing William Nonesuch had been recruited to shake down Harold Mason. Nonesuch ambushes Harold, can't find the deed, things get out of control, and Mason ends up dead. A strong hypothesis except for one gaping hole: Noka's contention that Hawk was going to be flying around with an airtight alibi.

"How long would construction be delayed if a restraining order was issued?" I asked Noka.

"Normally, the whole problem might go away in just a few weeks," the old man said, probably repeating what he had been told by the Passamaquoddy lawyer. "But a judge or judges interested in slowing down the process could drag things out a long time. Months. Who knows? Even years."

"Public sentiment being what it is, any judge in New England wouldn't hesitate to drag his or her feet," Alyana predicted.

I said, "And I gather a long delay wouldn't sit well with Mohammad al-Talal."

Noka nodded. "The Arab isn't the patient type. Probably would figure out another way to use nearly a billion dollars to humiliate America."

The old man sank back into his chair and closed his eyes.

"Something I don't understand." I pumped up the volume, hoping to draw more information out of Noka before the bourbon took him away. "There are a lot of reasons why the Mason boys want the deed. Fine. I get that. But from what Caleb and J. D. Mason told me earlier today, they think their father had the deed with him last night. Why would the old man carry around something so important? That makes absolutely no sense to me."

"Precious cargo, *neetop*," Noka explained with a yawn. "A crazy man might not want something that valuable out of his possession even if he went wading in the bay. Of course, it's more likely Harold didn't have the deed on him. There's a good chance he didn't know where the deed was or even if such a document existed."

Alyana took Noka's hand. The old man smiled and forced his eyes open. "Why would Harold bother to pretend?" she asked.

"To torment his offspring. Could have wanted both his kids to have an anxiety attack wondering if the demented old fart – ah, excuse my language my dear," Noka apologized to Alyana.

"Go on," she urged.

"Harold might cough up the deed out of unadulterated spite. Wouldn't that be a great way to give a couple of miserable reprobates a multimillion slap on the ass?" Noka chuckled.

"But how can we be sure that Mason didn't have the deed hidden away somewhere?" I asked.

"My Passamaquoddy friend says it has yet to be found," the old man's voice faded to a whisper. "Yet to be found."

"He must have some idea of where it could be," Alyana conjectured but got no response. "Old man?"

Lloyd Noka's grizzled head angled to the left and he belted out a thunderous snore that brought Olive to her feet. Alyana released the old man's hand and patted him on his arm.

"That's all we'll get from him tonight," she said with the kind of certainty that comes from earlier experience. Alyana capped the Old Crow and moved the bottle to a table at the far side of the room. Then she switched off the floor lamp. With some difficulty, we worked our way through the dark room to the front door.

"There's no lock," I said to Alyana.

"Never has been," she responded. "At least not for the thirty years I've known Lloyd."

– Chapter 7 –

Hemlock and sycamore trees overhanging Noka's dilapidated house fractured the fall moonlight into pale yellow-white shafts that stabbed a low forest of weeds blanketing the old man's front yard. I took Alyana's hand and guided her off Noka's rundown porch. We walked slowly along a narrow alley of trodden-down sow thistle and crabgrass that ran from the house to the Odyssey. The poodle trotted ahead, her dark coat quickly lost in the night.

"Come on, Olive," Alyana called out as she unlocked the driver's side door and reached for the tailgate switch. When we first pulled into Noka's property, Alyana had maneuvered the vehicle so its nose pointed away from the front of the house. The minivan's back end gaped open and we waited for the dog.

"Olive?"

Alyana did a full circle, her concern immediately apparent.

"*Olive!*"

The poodle had a Velcro temperament and Alyana had mentioned earlier that Olive rarely separated herself from her pack. Whatever had drawn the dog away tonight was rustling the underbrush fifty yards from the van. Olive uncorked a furious round of barking and the distant unseen commotion turned into a frenzy. Then came one sickening grunt. After that, a gut-churning silence.

"Oh, God," Alyana cried out. She snapped on the Odyssey's headlights. Twin beams lit the unpaved driveway and in the distance, a tan pickup truck parked broadside across the entrance to Noka's property. Closer to us, Olive stumbled into view, took a half dozen unsteady steps and staggered behind a stand of white pine bordering the driveway.

"Jesus," I gasped and charged toward the injured dog. It was a short run.

A hulking figure stepped into the minivan's high beams. A glint of light flashed off a handgun the man pointed at my head.

"Back up, asshole!"

I stepped to my rear but not fast enough. The big man slammed me against the Odyssey and yanked Alyana to my side.

"Where is it?" the man growled, peering through two round openings cut out of a black ski mask pulled down to the collar of his jeans jacket. He pumped out a miasma of sweat and liquor so strong it was repulsive.

I could feel Alyana trembling, but her fear couldn't suppress her anger. "If you hurt that dog –" she began.

"Forget the goddamned dog!" the man screamed, his slurred words divulging the extent of his drunkenness. "Where is it?"

"Where is what?" I asked.

I guessed the man's height at over six feet and he had to weigh in at two hundred fifty pounds – maybe more. The pistol was a garden-variety twenty-two that I had seen far too often on the streets of New Brunswick. It wasn't the most lethal weapon around but with its barrel six inches from my nose, I knew it could drill out most of my brain.

"Whatever you took from Noka's house," he snarled, "gets put in my hand. Now!"

"What the hell are you talking about?" I bellowed. It was a homeless shelter tactic learned long ago. Intimidation sometimes falls apart when it barrels into loud-mouthed resistance. Of course, there are other times when it doesn't.

"Don't play with me," the drunk warned, staggering slightly as he spoke. "I know about the deed – the property deed. One way or another, you're gonna give it to me!"

"There is no deed, you dumb ass," I shot back. That dose of arrogance won me a fierce jab to my left kidney.

"Turn around!" the man ordered. Alyana did a slow half circle but I stayed put face-to-face with the drunk.

"Do what he says, Rick," Alyana said softly.

I turned trying to ignore the pain that tore at my left side.

"Take off your clothes," the man ordered.

"Are you crazy?" I yelled. The man answered with the steel toe of his work boot. He kicked the back of my calf nearly sending me to my knees.

"Your clothes! Everything comes off. Ladies first."

"Look, she has nothing to do with this," I insisted. And to some extent, I was telling the truth. Alyana Genesee was about to get naked because she had been dragged into a morass that should have been all mine.

The man held his pistol against my back and with his other hand, thumbed open a SwingBlade knife. He pressed the tip of the spring-loaded weapon under the hem of Alyana's tee top and ripped the fabric apart.

"Please don't do this," Alyana begged.

"Want this to end?" the man ignored Alyana and spoke to me. "Then give me what I'm here for." He slipped his switchblade under the thin cross strap of her bra, his hand noticeably quivering.

"Is this really what this is about?" I gave the drunk a sideways glance. He was breathing heavily, the liquor stench overwhelming. "Want your own private strip show?"

"What I want is the goddamned deed. Everything else is a bonus, shit head."

"I told you. We don't have the deed!"

The blade cut through the elasticized strap. Alyana caught the remnants of the torn shirt and bra and held the shredded clothing against her chest.

"What comes next is me having a good time with your lady," the man promised. "Then I start cutting flesh."

The movement was nearly imperceptible and went completely unnoticed by the drunk who was growling into my right ear. I moved my head back and blocked the man's view of the dark form working its way along the periphery of the van's headlights.

"OLIVE!" Alyana suddenly screamed. "*Fass! Fass!*"

The drunk never saw the dog charge. The usually affable Olive roared into the unsuspecting man, sinking her teeth into his right forearm. The force of the attack drove the drunk backward, the SwingBlade slipping out of his hand. I spun around and grabbed the man's left arm but not before he fired the twenty-two. Olive dodged to the side and the bullet drilled into the Odyssey's front fender. As the drunk tried desperately to shake off the dog, the pistol fell to the driveway.

I picked the twenty-two out of the dirt and leveled it at the man's head. "Table's turned, you son of a bitch."

Whether too stupid or too drunk, the man whirled around and ran toward his pickup truck, Olive still attached to his now bloodied right arm. I fired once over his head, but the panicked man didn't stop.

"Don't shoot, Rick!" Alyana shouted, obviously concerned about the dog. "*Aus*, Olive! *Aus!*"

The poodle instantly released her grip. She trotted back to us, a slight limp hindering her gait. Still holding the ripped remains of her blouse and bra to her breasts, Alyana opened the driver's side door of the van and reached behind the front seat. She retrieved a white lab coat and, using the vehicle's door for privacy, dropped her ruined clothing and turned the smock into a makeshift top.

When she walked back into the van's high beams, Alyana knelt beside Olive. Her hands shook as she examined the dog's torso and legs.

"My God!" I stammered. "What the hell just happened?"

"Schutzhund commands," Alyana explained. "The first German word I used means bite or attack. The second, release or let go."

"But this is a *poodle!*" I pointed at Olive. "You already figured out how little I know about animals. But if I remember right, those are commands for attack dogs. Since when does a poodle –?"

"Olive isn't officially Schutzhund trained. About a year ago, I invited Maureen O'Connor to a couple of sessions when a friend and I were working with a Rottweiler and Doberman. Olive tagged along. Everything you just saw was what she picked up from the sidelines."

I went to one knee on the other side of the dog. "Unbelievable."

"She's got a few sore ribs and a bruise on her left rear leg," Alyana said. "I'll need to give her a more thorough exam when we get back home, but I think she'll be fine."

Fine but banged-up. An even slightly wounded Olive could put me in the doghouse once the O'Connors caught wind of their poodle's close call.

"Should we let Lloyd know what happened?" I asked.

"No. He's too far gone to have heard anything. I'll fill him in tomorrow. Best to let him alone for now."

"Feel steady enough to drive to the police station?"

"Yeah," Alyana nodded and removed the minivan's keys from her purse. "Can you help Olive into her crate?"

I lifted the dog to the van's rear platform. She did the rest. Once Olive fastened the crate shut with the slide lock, Alyana closed the tailgate and we pulled away from Noka's decrepit house.

"What just happened – it's connected to Harold Mason's murder, isn't it?" Alyana asked as we turned out of Lloyd's driveway.

"I think so."

"The guy wasn't fooling around, Rick. Who is he? And how did he know we'd be at Lloyd's place?"

"I don't have answers, Alyana. At least not yet."

The van worked its way along the winding back road that connected to the island's main north-south highway. We rounded a sharp curve and Alyana braked hard narrowly missing the back end of a too-familiar tan pickup that had its front end wrapped around a massive white oak tree.

"Oh, no," Alyana gasped. She bolted from the van and raced to the pickup's driver who was buckled into a heap several feet from the tree. The side of the man's head was crushed, one eye and half his jaw pulverized. The ski mask was nowhere in sight, but the clothing and the smell of alcohol left no doubt who had just catapulted through the windshield of the '96 GMC Sonoma.

"Anything?" I asked as Alyana probed for a pulse. She was careful to avoid the blood and body fluids that soaked the man's jacket and jeans.

"No. He's dead."

I was no stranger to dead men. New Brunswick's Gateway was a magnet for tortured souls and the county coroner knew my address by heart. Even so, I was usually troubled when confronted by death. Tonight, though, was an exception. The deformed mass of broken bones and mutilated flesh left me cold.

Alyana walked back to the van, picked up her cell phone, and dialed 911.

"You okay?" I asked.

"Think so."

I knew close to nothing about veterinary medicine. But in Alyana's world, watching four-legged creatures die had to be a common part of the job. The look on Alyana's face made it apparent that a human fatality was different.

"Do you have any latex gloves in the van?" I called out. If Alyana had a lab coat in her vehicle, I guessed she also had a box of medical exam gloves on board. She did.

"He's got a wad of money in his pocket," I said after donning the powderless gloves. It would be several minutes before any police or emergency respondents would arrive on the scene. Plenty of time to do my own detective work without leaving any telltale fingerprints or other DNA evidence.

"Those are hundred dollar bills," Alyana said, her voice still unsteady. She pointed to the paper currency that I had carefully removed from the drunk's front pocket.

"About three thousand dollars," I guessed and pushed the money back into the man's jeans. Rolling the body to one side, I fished out the drunk's wallet. A Connecticut driver's license gave me the name of the deceased: Charles Kenyon.

I couldn't find anything else of importance on the body, so I moved on to the wrecked truck. The driver's-side door was badly bent and could only be opened a couple of feet, but room enough for me to squeeze into the cab and pop open the glove compartment. On top of a vehicle registration slip was a folded sheet of paper.

"Know anything about Corrigan-Radgowski Correctional Center?" I called out to Alyana.

"A prison, I think. Somewhere in Connecticut."

"According to this," I held up the paper, "it's in a town called Uncasville."

"That's not far from here, between New London and Norwich."

The city references didn't mean a lot to me since I was an infrequent traveler to New England. But I had no trouble figuring out that Charles Kenyon had recently been doing jail time.

"It's a paper listing standard conditions of parole," I explained, holding up the sheet. "From the Connecticut Department of Corrections."

"An ex-con?"

"Based on the date at the top of this thing, I'd say just barely an ex. Looks like he was released on parole only three weeks ago."

In the distance, a siren wailed as a Jamestown police cruiser raced toward the location Alyana had phoned in. I maneuvered out of the pickup, slipped off the latex gloves, and pocketed them. I walked to Alyana who was leaning against the Odyssey, her trembling diminished but still obvious.

"Hey," I said softly. "You doing all right?"

She didn't speak but instead put her arms around my waist and pressed her body into mine. I held her tightly; bewildered by how such a terrifying night could end with my feeling something that had been missing from my life for more than a decade.

– Chapter 8 -

"No, I don't know him."

Lieutenant Ravenel rubbed the back of his thick neck. Heavy eyes showed his fatigue.

"Aren't you getting tired of spending time in this place?" Ravenel asked, gesturing to the cramped interior of the small interrogation room. "Because I sure as hell am."

"The only reason I'm here is to report an accident."

"And an armed assault," Ravenel added. "Which is why I was dragged back to Jamestown. For the second damn night in a row."

I pointed to the wall-mounted video camera. "Do you always interrogate victims like they're serial killers?"

"When it comes to people who have friends in questionable places, that's exactly what we do." Ravenel leaned forward and repeated a question he had fired at me at least a dozen times earlier. "Did you know Charles Kenyon?"

"Never saw the man until tonight."

Ravenel checked the notes given to him by the Jamestown patrol officer first on the scene of the pickup truck accident. "We found a twenty-two slug in the front of Alyana Genesee's van. We'll run a match but you claim it comes from Kenyon's pistol."

I sucked in a deep breath. "Look, Lieutenant, you've got the story so why don't you and I go home and get some sleep?"

"We're not through yet."

"I think we are."

"Not until I say so."

"Maybe it's time for a lawyer," I threatened.

Ravenel smiled. "That lunatic shyster from Orlando?"

I grimaced at the thought of Yigal Rosenblatt protecting my legal rights. "Touché," I conceded and couldn't stop myself from matching Ravenel's grin with my own. "If we're going to continue waltzing until the wee hours, how about throwing me a couple of new questions."

The lieutenant shrugged. "All right. Try this one. Why were you at Lloyd Noka's house?"

"You told me to stay on the island. Noka was inside the boundary lines."

"Fine. You were a good boy and obeyed the rules. Now answer the question. Why did you go see Noka?"

Before Ravenel arrived, Alyana and I agreed we would disclose everything that went on during and after our visit to Noka with one exception. At least for another twenty-four hours, nothing would be said about the mysterious deed Charles Kenyon so desperately wanted. Before every Rhode Islander with a badge began sniffing for clues, I wanted time to do my own investigating.

"Alyana Genesee knows Noka," I explained. "She offered to make an introduction."

"And why did you want to see him?"

"From what I've heard, Noka knows most everything that goes on in Jamestown."

Ravenel wasn't surprised. "So you asked a few questions and Lloyd gave you answers."

"That's about it."

"What did he tell you?" Ravenel asked, his eyes fixed on mine.

"He gave me a name. Somebody he thought might have more than just a passing grudge against Harold Mason."

Ravenel spread his hands in a give-me-more gesture.

"Nonesuch."

"William Nonesuch?"

I nodded. Ravenel's expression didn't change, which told me Nonesuch was already on the state police Rolodex of suspects.

"What did Noka tell you about Nonesuch?"

"Apparently the man didn't care for people who desecrated Indian graves."

"Anything else?"

I shrugged. "Only that he did prison time."

What happened next caught me off guard. Ravenel momentarily stopped using the detective's playbook and served up information that a lead interrogator would normally never do.

"A lot of prison time," the lieutenant said. "Just got out of Corrigan-Radgowski."

Maybe it was just a slip that came from too little sleep. Or maybe Ravenel was throwing me a bone. The detective had learned enough about me to know I had to have thoroughly inspected Charles Kenyon and his truck before the police got involved and now would be connecting the prison dots between Nonesuch and Kenyon. But why put this on the table? Could be he was looking for help.

"What else did Noka tell you?" Ravenel wanted to know. I rubbed my forehead, glad that Alyana had escaped the relentless questioning. She and Olive had been sent home hours ago.

"Nothing you couldn't find out if you talked to Lloyd."

"Hard to do."

"Why"

"Lloyd Noka hung himself about the time you left his house."

Part II

– Chapter 9 –

Months before I buried my wife, death waited patiently for cancer to do its slow, agonizing work. But death came at Alyana Genesee in a much different way. It lunged at her. No warning. No preliminaries. Her husband died violently and unexpectedly. And tonight, death mounted another surprise assault, this time snatching a man who meant as much to Alyana as her father. Perhaps even more.

I overheard Michael Ravenel's phone call to Alyana while waiting for a squad car to haul me back to the O'Connor residence. The lieutenant's tone was surprisingly compassionate as he passed along the bad news about Lloyd Noka. Apparently, Lieutenant Ravenel had been given the word that Alyana and her sachem were close. Very close.

A few minutes later, I thanked a Jamestown cop for playing chauffer and then walked the now familiar path that ran between the O'Connor and Genesee lots.

"He didn't kill himself," Alyana said as I stepped into her imposing foyer. As she spoke, Olive greeted me with just a reserved wag or two of her tail. The dog's affection meter had been tamped down by an awareness of Alyana's sadness.

"I know."

"The man didn't have the strength to pull himself out of his chair, for godsakes!" Alyana snapped, her anger momentarily pushing aside her grief.

"Kenyon had one, maybe two others with him last night," I guessed. "While we were getting pushed around outside, Kenyon's friends were walking through Lloyd's back door." Which couldn't have been difficult to do, I thought, remembering Noka didn't believe in locks.

"Jesus, Rick," Alyana began to sob. "They hung him!"

They also tore apart Noka's cluttered quarters. Ravenel had leaked that bit of information during his brief conversation with Alyana – a detail the lieutenant seemed to want me to overhear.

"They're ruling it a suicide," Alyana continued.

"For now," I said. "It's about trying to keep a lid on things. Harold Mason's murder and an armed assault by an ex-felon is a lot to handle in less than forty-eight hours. Throw in another homicide and it could put Jamestown over the edge. Eventually, the facts will come out."

"I'm going to do whatever it takes to make sure that happens." There was no mistaking the determination in Alyana's voice.

"I watched both of you last night. Lloyd was more than just an acquaintance."

"Much more. Lloyd helped raise me after my father died."

"I wish I could say something that would make all of this a lost less painful than it is," I said. "I'm so sorry."

Alyana's composure broke apart and she wept uncontrollably. For the second time in only a few hours, I reached out to comfort a woman I hardly knew but who was fast becoming someone I wanted in my life.

We talked for an hour, a conversation mixed with rage and sorrow that gradually moved to remembrances of Noka the sachem – a man filled with intelligence, kindness and wisdom. Before Olive and I left, Alyana embraced me.

"Thank you," she said softly and kissed me lightly on my cheek.

The short walk back to the O'Connor house was buoyed by feelings that hadn't been part of me since a flatline ran over my emotions thirteen years ago.

# #

After four hours of sleep, I woke to a bright sun that brought unpredicted warmth to a September morning. On the road that bordered the front of the O'Connor and Genesee properties, a Jamestown patrol car stood guard. The Charles Kenyon incident and Lloyd Noka's death must have nudged Michael Ravenel into giving Alyana and me round-the-clock protection. Not that it meant much. Both properties were vulnerable from the back where they rolled down to the rocky shores of Narragansett Bay.

At nine thirty, Olive and I walked through the O'Connor's rear screen porch and made our way to the water's edge. Then we followed the same route as Harold Mason regularly traveled, carefully negotiating the jagged line of slippery stones and seaweed that separated land from the bay. The tide was nearly low, which made walking relatively easy. We picked up speed as we passed the Standish house, hoping to avoid another encounter with the man who only two nights ago had his rifle pointed at my head. Olive chirped out a low bark once we cleared the Standish property.

When we reached an undeveloped, wooded lot, I looked for Yigal Rosenblatt's expensive Mercedes. It wasn't hard to find. Olive and I scrambled through a barely passable path that zigzagged from the bay to the street.

"Oh, Bullet!" Twyla Tharp Rosenblatt leaped out of the passenger-side front seat. "You brought that adorable dog!"

Yigal stumbled from the Mercedes, his yarmulke askew. "Oh, I don't know. I don't know about the dog. Mr. Maglio doesn't like dogs. Not since that thing in Virginia Beach."

"What thing?" Five seconds with the Rosenblatts and I was already in the twilight zone.

"Oh, Yiggy," Twyla broke in. "That was different! What Candi did with that dog was just simple-ated."

"Simulated?" I wanted clarification, hoping maybe my mental image of Candi and her canine was just a revolting mistake.

"It was pretend," Twyla confirmed. "That's all it was."

"Could be, could be," Yigal agreed. "But it got the club shut down for a month and Manny had to pay that fine. A big fine."

"Uncle Manny won't mind about the dog," Twyla promised. "Besides, Bullet's puppy isn't a Great Dane like the one Candi used."

"Used" hung in the morning air as Olive and I boarded the backseat of the Rosenblatt's car which, I remembered clearly, was Yigal's thanks to Uncle Manny's largess. We motored north and then crossed the Jamestown-Verrazzano Bridge, which is exactly what Michael Ravenel had warned me not to do. Forty minutes later we rolled to a stop in front of a tan-colored, single-story building sprawled out under a towering neon sign that screamed: *Sinsations*.

"Oh, I'm so excited!" Twyla squeaked. "I haven't seen Destiny since she got infected by that recycled vaginal ring Manny sold her."

Yigal and Twyla got out of the Mercedes and headed toward the back entrance of the strip club with Olive and me in the rear.

"Destiny!" Twyla cried out as a woman with a chest the size of Massachusetts walked through the door.

"Ohmygod! Twyla! I ain't seen you since the weddin'."

Which scraped a sore spot on the relationship I had with the Rosenblatts. The fact that I wasn't in the temple when the couple exchanged vows had never been put aside. Even as Twyla and Destiny bumped boobs, Mrs. Rosenblatt tossed me a how-could-you stare.

"So, how come you're workin' Providence?" Twyla asked excitedly. "I thought you were doin' Boston?"

"I was until your asshole uncle told me I had to fill in here for a week," Destiny complained. "I'm blowing off five nights in Beantown all because Chastity got the clap."

Olive and I had yet to penetrate Sinsations, and we were already knee-deep in the backroom goings on of the triple-X business. Twyla and Destiny drifted off toward the parking lot chattering about why erotic dancers should be unionized. Yigal motioned me inside the building and past a "No Smoking" wall sign, which explained why Destiny was standing in a handicap parking space tapping out a cigarette from an ornate gold case. The irony made me blink. Performers and patrons could remove clothing and commit various consensual acts as long as they didn't inhale.

"Excuse me!" yelled a matronly lady as Olive and I moved through Sinsations' rear door. "*Excuse me!*"

There was no mistaking the voice. It was Mildred, Manny Maglio's personal assistant, who wheezed out her words like a tire going flat. I had met Mildred once before during a command appearance at Manny's corporate office, a dingy but well-protected building in Edison, New Jersey. The woman was in her late fifties, carried an extra forty pounds mostly on her hips, and wore her gray hair in a huge bun. "That dog can't come in here!"

"Special circumstance is what it is, Mildred," Yigal said and pulled the lady out of earshot. The two carried on a whispered conversation for about a minute, and then Mildred stomped back toward Olive and me.

"Rosenblatt says the dog doesn't got a thing? Is he tellin' the truth? Does it have a thing?"

"Excuse me?"

"A thing. You know – a ding-a-ling. A pecker."

I looked to Yigal for help but all I got was a shrug as the lawyer bounced from one foot to another behind Mildred.

"Well, no, the dog's a female," I said, hoping I had understood the question.

Mildred turned around and glared at Yigal. "If that dog's got a thing, it can't be within a hundred yards of this place. That's a court order, for godsakes! You want us shut down again?"

"Oh, no, Miss Mildred," Yigal stammered. "The dog doesn't have a thing. I'm sure of it."

"You better be damn sure. It's not always easy to see a thing until it's too late. Believe me, I know."

"I promise you," I broke in, "the poodle here doesn't have a thing. Never did."

"Jesus," Mildred grunted and gave Yigal another disapproving look. "Can't ever tell what the hell's gonna show up around here."

As if to prove the point, Twyla and Destiny paraded through Sinsations' back entrance.

Mildred led the way to a closet-sized office at the far end of a narrow corridor. She motioned me inside where once again I was face-to-face with the undisputed impresario of the skin trade. Manny Maglio was everything one wouldn't expect in a flesh purveyor and the reputed boss of an organized-crime network that ran from the top to bottom of the East Coast. His bald dome was rimmed with gray-black hair overdue for a trim. Manny had a pair of out-of-style bifocals perched on his bulbous nose reddened by the cheap hooch all thirty of his clubs sold to their over-testosteroned clients.

"What the hell!" Manny jumped from his fake leather office chair. "No dogs! Jesus H! We can't have no dogs here. Didn't nobody tell you?"

I gave Olive an apologetic look for exposing her to such madness. "Uh, the dog doesn't have a – She's a female."

Dots of sweat instantly speckled Manny's forehead. "That don't matter! One more count of bestiality and every D.A. from here to Florida will be pounding me like a Saturday night hooker."

"Look, Mr. Maglio, I have this deal with the dog's owner," I explained. "There's no way I can let her out of my sight. Long story but that's the way it's got to be."

"What the hell," Manny moaned and wiped his face. "Then we're gonna have to make this quick."

Fine with me.

Manny said, "You walked into some bad shit the other night."

"Harold Mason?"

"Here's the thing –" Manny started but was cut off by an exasperated Mildred barging into the office.

"Roanoke's on the line," said Mildred. "Fantasia's not going to shave it."

Manny sank back into his chair. "Oh, jeez, not again."

"Can't stand the itching and she says she's got a rash so bad there's pimples all over it."

Manny slipped off his glasses. "Mildred, you tell her she can't go on if she don't shave. That thing grows so fast that she'll look like ZZ Top in two days."

"You can't make her shave if it starts to crust up or weep. That's what's in the contract which, by the way, you shouldn't-a ever signed!"

"Yeah, but the thing is, who's gonna pay to see something that looks like a goddamned out-a-control Chia Pet? It's disgusting, for chrissakes!"

Mildred propped her chubby hands on her chubby hips. "So what do you want us to do?"

"All right! All right. If she wants to look like she's ridin' a box of Brillo pads, then the hell with her. But I'll tell you this – once the contract's done –"

"Yeah, yeah," Mildred sputtered and walked away.

Manny shook his head and looked to me for a little sympathy. "Nobody understands what I put up with. People think I'm gettin' laid every ten minutes, but you know what it's about? Yeast infections, urinary tract infections, and genital warts. That's what it's about."

I winced. Olive whined.

"Anyways, let's get back to what I was sayin'," Manny flipped off his glasses. "The thing of it is, I've got these investors who got a bug up their butts about Arabs takin' over this part of New England."

"You've got investors?" I considered myself reasonably street-smart. But it was news to me that an organized-crime syndicate had shareholders.

"That's what I got. And they're a royal pain in the ass. Listen to what this note says." Manny rustled through a stack of papers on a grimy desk that looked like it might have been used in one too many of Maglio's porno flicks.

"Mohammad al-Talal is a strict Issil mist or Izzle mast or somethin' like that," Manny read.

"Islamist?"

"I dunno–whatever," Manny shrugged and continued reading. "As such, al-Talal will hold every Arab to passage 5:90 of the Koran, which says, 'Intoxicants and gambling are impure of shaytan's handiwork: refrain from such abomination that ye may prosper.'"

"So, your investors think Mohammad will bring in a crowd that won't be playing the slots or shelling out for a two-drink minimum at any of your gentlemen's clubs?"

"Exactly! Even worse, they think al-Talal's gonna go on a crusade to convince every customer we got in Connecticut, Rhode Island, and Massachusetts that God don't like people who play blackjack or belt down a few beers."

Manny had a way of making his point. "Your investors want Mohammad to go away," I surmised.

"Big time. Which is why we got people on Jamestown Island trying to find that goddamned deed you probably already know about."

"Wait a minute!" I said. "Did your people have anything to do with Harold Mason's murder?"

68

"See, here's the thing. Nowadays this kinda work is outsourced. Didn't used to be that way but it's just how it goes today. We hire in talent for what needs doin'. Problem is, some of these contractors get a little carried away."

"Oh, my God," I groaned.

"Now I ain't sayin' the guys we recruited had anythin' to do with the Mason hit," Manny clarified. "I just can't be certain."

"Last night," I said, "an Indian named Lloyd Noka was killed."

"Yeah, yeah," Manny shook his head. "I heard. Terrible. But here's the thing –"

Mildred reappeared and Maglio's explanation fell to another business dilemma. "Atlanta is on line one. Nipple problem."

"Again?" Manny wailed. "Who is it? Linda Lust?"

"Yeah."

"Jeez, Mildred, can't this wait? I'm tryin' to hurry this meetin' along. Remember? We got a dog lyin' here, for godsakes."

"All they need to know is if she can go on this afternoon," said Mildred.

"What are we talkin' about? The same deal as last month?"

"Her left nipple's stuck inside."

Olive and I exchanged glances. I could tell even the dog thought this was surreal.

"Jeez," Manny sighed and turned to me as if I was owed an explanation. "Know what an inverted nipple is?"

"Me? No, can't say as I do."

"Linda Lust has nipples the size of the Statue of Liberty. Great draw for the club in Atlanta. But here's the thing, every once and a while one nipple disappears faster than a groundhog in winter. So now you got one nipple stickin' out like a telephone pole and another one that's playing hide-and-seek."

"So whaddya want to do?" Mildred asked impatiently.

"She can't go on unless both of 'em are out. Looks ridiculous. Nothin' erotic about a nipple takin' a goddamned siesta."

"And how in hell is she supposed to get the thing to pop out?" It was obvious from Mildred's tone that Linda's nipple had misbehaved a number of times in the past.

"What about the Electrolux?" Manny asked.

"I can tell you right now, that isn't gonna happen. Remember last time you told her to do that? God, Manny! Making the woman use a vacuum cleaner. It practically ripped her boob off."

Manny's exasperation ignited his rose-colored nose into a fiery beak. "All right, all right! Tell her to wear pasties."

"Pasties? Who wears pasties anymore?"

"She does! Until that thing looks like it's supposed to!"

Mildred grunted and stormed out of the office.

"See, this is what I gotta deal with all damn day long," Manny whined. "So where was I?"

"Harold Mason and Lloyd Noka."

"Yeah, like I was tryin' to say. I don't know for sure what happened. All I can tell you is we got people in Jamestown and we think the Arab does too."

"Mohammad al-Talal?"

Manny nodded.

"Know anything about a Native American named William Nonesuch?"

"Yeah, he's a crazy Indian who just got out of the joint. But he don't belong to us and as far as I know, he's not workin' for the Arab either."

"What are the odds he's in the hunt for the deed?" I asked.

"Pretty high," Manny answered. "Probably figures if he gets his redskin hands on the thing, he can sell it to the highest bidder."

Three insurgent forces had infiltrated Jamestown Island all trying for the same gold ring. That spelled big trouble. The body count could easily start going higher.

"So why did you want to see me, Mr. Maglio?"

"Here's the thing," Manny licked his puffy lips and flipped his glasses back onto his globular nose. "I gotta get that deed before anybody else. So if you find out where it is, we're gonna make it worth your while to give us a call. You catch my drift, right?"

"I'm catching it."

"What we got is a judge who's ready to use the deed to slap a stop-work injunction on those rat bastard Mason boys and their Arab pal. I don't exactly know why that deed is so important but it has somethin' to do with who really owns Dutch Island, or at least the important part of it."

"So I've been told."

"Yeah, well, my lawyers – and I'm not talkin' about my niece's idiot husband – tell me the deed can't hold up the project forever. But they think they can dig enough legal potholes to stall the deal for years. Not exactly what my investors want but, for the time being, it will keep me from gettin' my ass kicked."

"I don't know where the deed is," I said.

"Yeah, but you're good at findin' things," Manny threw me what I took as a compliment. Like most people with a TV or newspaper subscription, he remembered how a year ago I tracked down a missing book of the Bible. It was a search-and-find mission that turned a lot of people bloody. Still, my questionable detective work had given me fifteen minutes of fame that apparently hadn't gone unnoticed by the gangster community. "You're the kinda guy who's gonna end up findin' the deed. I got a way of seein' how these things work out."

"Doubt it. I wouldn't know where to start."

"See, that's why I wanted to have this talk. What you're good at is lookin' back instead of dealin' with what's right in front of you. You've got what's sort of a rearview mirror way of goin' at things."

Was I being stroked or maligned? Impossible to tell.

"So here's the thing," Manny continued. "If you find the deed, we want you to give it to us. Not the cops. Not anybody else. See what I'm talkin' about?"

"Yup." My vision was twenty-twenty when talking to a mobster who had a reputation for cracking kneecaps and shipping dismembered bodies to landfills.

"Thing of it is, we can use the deed to stop that Arab bastard faster than if the police get ahold of it. I mean, it would be goddamned un-American not to give it to us, right? And you're not un-American, right?"

"Right."

"See, this is good. It's all good."

I reached for Olive's fuzzy head and gave her a couple of strokes. The dog had become my sanity anchor. "Anything else?" I asked.

"Yeah, do me a favor, will ya?" Manny crunched forward, his large gut jammed against the edge of the desk. "You've got yourself in the news a lot these days. Be sure you don't mention nothin' about our knowin' each other."

"We know each other?"

"Enough to cause a problem. Here's the thing. It's not good for my reputation to be connected to any of the shit that's happenin' in Jamestown. That's all I'm sayin'."

I was getting dizzy. A mob boss who didn't want his reputation sullied. I might have passed out if Mildred hadn't made her third appearance of the morning.

"Cherry's manager is on the phone," Mildred said. "Wants you to pay for another month's worth of Lidocaine."

"Oh, jeez, Mildred!" Manny growled. "The broad is suckin' me dry!"

"She's got vulvodynia, Manny. Or did you forget?"

"With the medical bills I gotta pay for her? No I didn't forget, Mildred." Manny moved his eyes from Mildred to me. "Know what vulvodynia is?"

I didn't have a clue. "Motor oil?"

"No, that's Valvoline. This here is another one of those goddamned female crotch problems."

"Uh-huh," was all I could say. Olive reacted with a snort and then began licking herself.

"So what do you want me to do about Cherry?" Mildred demanded an answer.

"Jesus, when is this gonna end?" Manny wailed.

"It'll end when her vulva gets better. If you hadn't made her do that pole dance with a broom stick −"

"Yeah, yeah," Manny waved her off, stood up and looked at Olive and me. "Listen, I gotta tell you, I'm real uncomfortable with that dog bein' here."

"Right. Well I guess we should be heading back." I motioned Olive to her feet.

"The thing of it is," Manny said as he rounded the desk, "we really need that deed. If we don't get it and somebody else does, things could get uncomfortable, see what I'm sayin'?"

"I understand."

"That's good. And don't forget to forget my name if you talk to any cops or reporters."

"Manny!" Mildred cut in. "Are we buyin' the ointment or not?"

I flapped my hand at Maglio and headed out the office door with Olive leading the way. The poodle did a fast trot down the long corridor and bounded out Sinsations' back exit. She stopped and shook herself hard, probably trying to slough off the lunacy that clung to us both like a swarm of disease-infected cooties.

– Chapter 10 –

Yigal Rosenblatt's Mercedes bucked its way through midday traffic on Route 95 heading south toward exit 9, the connector that hooked the interstate to Jamestown Island. Manny Maglio's general counsel drove like he walked and talked. For a quarter of a mile, the car's V8 engine let loose and we rocketed ahead. Then without reason or warning, Yigal braked and the ninety-thousand dollar Mercedes slowed to a crawl. A line of cars blasted their complaints with a tirade of horn blowing. An irate truck driver pulled his eighteen-wheeler next to Yigal's Mercedes and punched the air with his middle finger.

Riding shotgun in the front seat, Twyla Rosenblatt jabbered incessantly, oblivious to her husband's erratic driving. Things were different in the back of the car. My gut was in an uproar and Olive wasn't faring much better. The poodle's rapid-fire panting steamed up the Mercedes' rear windows as we jerked our way past the exit to Rhode Island's busy Green Airport.

"Oh, Bullet!" Twyla babbled over her shoulder. "Guess what? The girls are going to throw me a baby shower! Can you believe it?"

"Terrific."

"And here's the best part. They're going to do it right in Jamestown!"

"Oh?" Apprehension wormed its way through the bile I felt creeping into my throat.

"It's going to be tomorrow night 'cause that's when they can get a room at the Jamestown library."

"Huh?"

"Destiny did a favor for some guy who donates a lot to the library. So, we can get to use some sorta museum at the library for two hours for free."

Destiny doing a favor gave me several seconds of a much needed distraction.

"You're not supposed to bring in liquor or nothin' like that," Twyla blathered. "But Destiny can slip things in like you couldn't believe."

I believed.

Twyla turned and fixed her eyes on mine. "Y'know, baby showers aren't just for ladies no more."

"Uh, no, I didn't know."

"That's why I want you and Yigal to come."

"Ex – excuse me?" I stammered.

"You'll be there Yigee, right?" Twyla asked the question without looking at her husband. Instead she kept her stare glued to my woozy-looking face. It was easy to read between her lines. *Yigal's going to say yes and you better too. You blew off our wedding so don't even think about skipping my baby shower.*

"I'll go," Yigal said as our thrill ride continued. "I can pick you up, Bullet."

I turned a darker shade of green. "No, no! I'll get there on my own."

Twyla pulled her high-glossed lips into a wide smile. "Did you hear that, Yigee? Bullet's definitely going to be at the party!"

"If I'm not dead or in jail –" I qualified.

Twyla faced forward, and I fumbled for my cell phone hoping a diversion might keep me from barfing on Yigal's climate-controlled leather seats. I ran through a string of messages. A couple of irrelevant calls from the stand-in manager at the Gateway Men's Shelter. Four from Douglas Kool. And one from Caleb Mason. I speed dialed Harris & Gilbarton in New York.

"Hey, Bullet." Doug's admin, Angie, answered. "Wow, you've really got him in orbit today."

"One of my few talents in life," I replied modestly. Not many people could frazzle the usually supercomposed Douglas Kool. For me, unhinging my friend was one of my few hobbies.

Angie put me on hold and a nanosecond later, Doug screams rattled my iPhone.

"WHAT THE HELL ARE YOU DOING? AND WHY AREN'T YOU ANSWERING YOUR DAMN PHONE?"

"Really bad cell reception on the island," I rallied back with a lie.

"Jesus, Bullet! I had a call from a state cop named Michael Ravenel. You know what he wanted? Anything I could tell him about you and an Indian named Lloyd Noka. An *Indian* for godsakes!"

"We New Englanders prefer the term Native American."

"You're not going to be such a smart-ass when I tell you the rest of the story," Doug warned. "After I finished with Ravenel, I called a Newport reporter I know. He sniffed around and caught the unmistakable whiff of Rick Bullock."

"Imagine that."

"Here's what my reporter friend told me. Lloyd Noka died last night – rumored to be a suicide. But the medical examiner hasn't officially ruled on the death, which means they're holding back letting the public know the damn Indian was actually executed!"

"Really?" I tried expressing some level of surprise, but my reaction was dulled by the knot in my stomach.

"My reporter pal gets more and more curious. So he calls a Jamestown cop he knows. Finds out you and a woman named Alyana Genesee were the last known visitors to Noka's house. And on top of that, you and this woman reported an accident near Noka's place – an accident which killed an ex-con named Charles Kenyon."

"It was a busy night."

"WHAT IN GOD'S NAME IS GOING ON, BULLET?"

"Nothing to worry about, Doug. Just a string of coincidences."

"Lloyd Noka was probably murdered! That bit of information is going to float across the Atlantic and right into Ken O'Connor's chartered yacht. If and when that happens, your ass is grass and so is mine!"

"Not to worry. The only thing we're responsible for is the O'Connor's house and their dog. The house is still standing and the dog –" I stopped to smile at Olive, "– is sort of okay."

Doug took the bait. "What are you talking about?"

"It happened at the dog park. O'Connor's poodle isn't even in heat but that damn Saint Bernard –" I stopped to smile at Olive. "Hey, do you know if there's such a thing as dog rape?"

"What?"

"Have another call coming in, Doug. Stay in touch."

I disconnected and swallowed my stomach as a string of sedans lined up behind the Mercedes. Minutes later, the parade of cars was forced to abandon the passing lane because Yigal refused to give way to faster-moving vehicles. Light blue, navy, and white car flags fluttered furiously as the caravan whizzed by on our right. I recognized the University of Rhode Island school colors and guessed the kids were on their way to a warm-up event for URI's Saturday football contest with archrival University of Connecticut.

"Hey *asshole!*" one student screamed out the side of a beat-up Honda. "Get off the road!"

Yigal nodded and tipped his yarmulke at the furious kid. The Mercedes bucked ahead for a quarter mile and then dropped to half speed.

"Oh, I love college boys!" Twyla clapped, unmoved by the verbal shots aimed at her husband. "They never have much money, but they can be so much fun!"

Yigal seemed at ease with Twyla's dreamy recollection of the sexual potency of an eighteen to twenty-one-year-old male. It was a peculiar pairing all right. Whether or not these two oddballs could make a marriage last for the long haul was still up in the air. But for the moment, the relationship was solid and that meant big points for me. Because I was the one responsible for introducing Manny Maglio's call girl niece to a struggling Orlando lawyer who wallowed chin deep in his Orthodox Judaism. As far as Manny was concerned, getting Twyla hitched to an attorney – any attorney – was akin to sending a man to Uranus. So when the engagement was announced and the wedding actually happened, Maglio thought I was golden. I wondered if his opinion had changed.

Yigal jockeyed his car into thickening traffic as we got closer to the Jamestown-Verrazzano Bridge. The Mercedes convulsed east, Yigal's foot tap dancing on the gas pedal and brake. Six or seven more miles, I estimated. The only way my nausea wouldn't give way to full-scale vomiting was with another distraction. So I punched in the callback number for Caleb Mason.

"My brother and I may have come on a little too strong yesterday," Caleb began after a few meaningless preliminaries. "I hope you understand we were upset – a death in the family and all."

Practically inconsolable, I thought. "What can I do for you?"

"Give J.D. and me a chance to show you why the project we're working on is so important," Caleb said. "Take a look at our plans for the al-Talal tunnel and buildings. When you see what we're doing, you'll understand why we can't let it get derailed."

Caleb Mason was the consummate sleazeball. Everything he said came with a veneer that coated the truth. Still, I was curious as to why the Mason boys wanted to play nice after yesterday's tough-guy act. "All right," I accepted the invitation. "When?"

"This afternoon if possible. Say about four at our work site near Fort Getty."

"Can't promise but I'll try to make it," I said.

"You won't regret carving out a little time, Mr. Bullock."

I ended the call as the Mercedes rolled onto the bridge and began a shuddering ascent to the span's highest point. At one hundred thirty five feet, Olive and I had a spectacular north-south view of Narragansett Bay. Calm winds and a sunny early afternoon turned the water's surface into a shimmering plane. Fall weather had chased most recreational boats back to their slips or dry docks. At Jamestown's northern end, a small fishing trawler rounded Conanicut Point. A ferry pushed away from its terminal at Quonset Point, once a major hub for the Navy's air-and-sea operations but converted to a National Guard air wing and commercial industrial park after the Vietnam War.

Looking south, I had my first decent view of Dutch Island, a pollywog-shaped splotch of brown and green not far from Jamestown's western shoreline. The small island was the only plug of rock and turf visible in what was called the West Passage. Farther to the south and east, I could make out a large clearing near Fort Getty, the abandoned garrison built to protect Narragansett Bay during World Wars I and II. Heavy equipment and several contractor trailers ran along the perimeter of the clearing. I couldn't be certain, but assumed this was where the Mason Brothers were digging the entrance to what would become al-Talal's tunnel to Dutch Island.

Yigal's Mercedes jerked down the backside of the bridge and shortly after, turned right on Main Road. Olive recognized the central artery that would bring us back to the O'Connor estate. The poodle let loose with one elated bark in anticipation of finishing the road trip without tossing her dog biscuits. I held off celebrating until the Mercedes closed in on the empty lot where Olive and I had been picked up hours earlier.

"Drop us off here," I instructed Yigal.

"But Bullet we can drive you to your place like we did yesterday," said Twyla. "It's easy to find because your house is the only one with a broken gate."

"Yeah, so I've been told," I said, climbing out of the backseat. "Thanks for the offer, but Olive needs exercise."

Fortunately, Twyla didn't argue. "Okay, then. Just don't forget the shower tomorrow night. At the library."

Yigal started to pull away but squeaked to a stop when his wife cracked open the passenger-side door. "And Bullet!" Twyla yelled back at me, all the usual giddiness gone from her voice. "Be sure you show up!"

I gave Mrs. Rosenblatt a halfhearted nod and continued my walk toward the O'Connor house. The ground never felt so good.

"Oh, jeez!" croaked a surprised uniformed cop as we neared his Jamestown P.D. cruiser. The young officer, who looked like he was barely old enough to shave, tumbled out of the Ford Interceptor and ran toward us. Olive gave the cop a mild tail wag of approval.

"How'd you – when did you –?" the cop stammered.

"Taking the dog for a walk. We went out the back door and hiked along the shoreline for a few blocks."

"Damn!" the cop looked panic stricken. "Lieutenant Ravenel's orders. I wasn't supposed to let you or Mrs. Genesee out of my sight."

"Hey, no harm done. And there's no reason Lieutenant Ravenel needs to know."

"I'd really appreciate your not telling him, Mr. Bullock."

"Not a problem." Olive and I were at the broken gate when the cop called out again.

"Say, do you mind if I ask what you'll be doing this afternoon? In case I get asked."

I put a hand on my chin as if having to think about a decision I had made more than an hour ago, midway through my conversation with Manny Maglio. "I'm going to call an old man and ask him to lend me a hand."

"A friend of yours?" the cop inquired.

"Sort of. As much as the most brilliant eccentric on the planet can be anybody's friend."

"Lieutenant Ravenel says you have a lot of interesting friends."

"That how he put it – interesting friends?"

"Actually," the cop looked at his shoes, "he said you're tied in with the weirdest assortment of idiots and misfits he's ever run across."

I laughed and trailed Olive toward the O'Connor house. "He's right," I called back over my shoulder. "In fact, he doesn't know how right he is."

– Chapter 11 –

Doc Waters lost his left testicle in a Port Richmond warehouse five miles from center city Philadelphia. The reverberating clamor of cranes and trucks offloading Delaware River container ships blotted out Doc's screams as two enforcers did their work. Slip joint pliers squeezed Doc's two-inch gonad tighter and tighter until it burst with a sickening *pop* and sent such an agonizing bolt of pain through the spermatic plexus that Doc went unconscious.

When they were through, the Scarfo syndicate dumped Doc Waters on the Jersey side of the Ben Franklin Bridge. Hours later, the one-time history professor was carted half dead into the emergency room at Camden's Cooper University Hospital. Miraculously, Doc survived and it was during the murkiness of his heavily medicated recovery that he uncorked a story that eventually made it to the cover of *Philadelphia Magazine.*

How an esteemed academic slid off his ivory tower and tumbled into a mob-infested gambling pit read like dime-novel fiction. "One-Nut" Walters had been a tenured professor at Rutgers University until his uncontrolled penchant for games of chance killed both his career and his marriage. A genius-level IQ wasn't enough to stomp out his addiction to laying down a bet on anything from a backroom round of Texas hold 'em to a no-limit craps shoot-out. When Doc's debt swamped his net worth, he turned to a Philly loan shark for a short-term loan that quickly became a long-term nightmare. At the time, Nicki Scarfo headed the Cosa Nostra family that ruled Philadelphia and South Jersey. Bumping up against Scarfo and his notoriously violent henchmen was almost always painful and commonly lethal. Doc's story which didn't take long to move from magazine to TV and radio underscored that reality with bloody, gut-clenching details.

Doc's deballing was Scarfo's third attempt to collect the professor's principal plus one hundred percent interest. Months earlier, the tip of

Doc's ring finger had been hacked off and tossed into Philly's Schuylkill River. Then came an early morning attack that left the professor with three broken ribs and a missing earlobe. Doc tried gambling his way out of debt, which only accelerated his spiraling descent into ruin. After he was partially castrated, the professor had little left to lose. So when the FBI showed up at his Camden hospital bedside, he unlocked his photographic memory and blurted out the kind of details that landed a half dozen Mafioso in federal prison.

One Nut's heroic stand against organized crime gave him about a month's worth of public acclaim – and a lifetime of fear. Doc's name was not only high on the underworld's hit list, it was marked with an asterisk. The professor was to be subjected to a special kind of retaliation at a time and place to be determined by Nicki Scarfo himself.

Doc showed up at New Brunswick's Gateway Men's Shelter six months after Philadelphia celebrated and then mostly forgot the man whose damaged scrotum had put the mob temporarily on its back. There was no safe haven for someone like Doc Waters but the nooks and crannies of Central Jersey gave him the best hope for survival. Until his fall from academic grace, Doc had spent years shuttling between Rutgers' campuses in New Brunswick and Piscataway so he knew the territory. But as familiar as he was with the state's midsection, he still came up short when looking for a place to stay. He landed at the Gateway by default, a marked man with no money, weighed down by the Scarfo family's promise of revenge.

"How's the textbook business?" I asked when Doc fielded my call.

"Dull as dirt. But fact checking footnotes pays the bills."

The professor had snagged a job at John Wiley & Sons, a Jersey-based publisher. Routine editing was far below Doc's competency level but with his background, he was high risk for any kind of employment. So he had wisely taken what he could get.

"It's been more than a year," I said thinking back to when Doc moved out of the Gateway and into a rented room in nearby Milltown.

"Yeah, miracles happen," Doc quipped. "Lot's wife turned into salt, Lazarus was raised from the dead, and I still have a job and a roof over my head."

Next to gambling, the professor's favorite hobby was plundering Biblical references and using them as conversational attention getters.

"I need your help, Doc."

"That you do. From what I've seen on TV the last couple of nights, you're one handcuff away from making license plates."

"Don't believe everything you see or hear."

"I don't. And for good reason. Do you know sixty percent of people lie at least once during any ten-minute conversation? *Journal of Basic and Applied Social Psychology*, June 2002."

Pure, unadulterated Doc Waters, I thought with a smile. Although he was now in his late sixties, the professor hadn't lost his quick wit or blasphemous irreverence.

"A couple of favors, Doc," I said. "First, I need you to help me find a land deed for Dutch Island."

"Dutch Island? Mohammad al-Talal's Dutch Island?"

"The same."

"You are up to your knickers in poop, aren't you?" Doc shot back.

"Been there before and so have you."

Doc got the message. He hadn't forgotten what life was like when he had been forced into the shadows. Nor had he forgotten how I was the one who bargained with Manny Maglio to convince the mob that Scarfo's bull's eye should be taken off Doc's back. Today, One-Nut Walters was a free man while, incredibly, the tables had turned on Nicki Scarfo. Tried and convicted of murder and racketeering charges, Scarfo was locked up for life in a federal prison. The ironic switch of fortunes made Doc's pardon all the more gratifying and his indebtedness to me all the more profound.

"What do you want me to do?" asked Doc.

"A deep dive. Get as much information as possible about the deed. And then track down who has the original document – assuming there is an original."

The professor paused to think. "Give me a place to start."

"I'm staying in Jamestown, which is as close to Dutch Island as you can get. Probably somebody here has information that could be useful."

"Does Jamestown have a town hall?"

"Yes," I said, remembering a building Yigal Rosenblatt passed on Narragansett Avenue when driving me to the O'Connor house after our lunch at Trattoria Simpatico.

"What about an historical society?"

"Don't know. But probably so. This is New England and history is like cannabis to a lot of these people."

"All right. Here's what needs to happen. I spend a few hours in the town clerk's office and then make nice with the right history buffs."

I had expected Doc's involvement to be long distance, but he was taking my call for help in a different direction. "You need to come here?"

"No other way. I'm at the front end of a week's vacation so I can be there tomorrow. Rhode Island is a four-or five-hour drive, right? So look for me around noon."

Bringing One-Nut Waters to Jamestown had its risks. The professor's presence wasn't likely to earn me points with Lieutenant Michael Ravenel. Nevertheless, when it came to following historical footprints, Doc was the best around. The possible benefits slightly outdistanced the definite downsides.

"Okay," I said. "You can spend a couple of days in one of Ken O'Connor's guest rooms."

"Enlighten me. Is that *the* Ken O'Connor who deep-fat fried his way onto *Fortune's* list of rich Americans?"

"The same. One other thing, Doc. I need a background check on an ex-con named William Nonesuch." I tacked on a few additional bits of information about the man, including his alias, the Hawk, and his Nehantic tribal affiliation.

"I can work on that tonight."

"Appreciate it," I said. After feeding Doc driving instructions, I disconnected.

At two p.m., I took Olive outside for a mid-afternoon bathroom break, and saw Alyana Genesee's minivan pull into her driveway. I switched on my cell and called next door. "Everything okay? Thought you were at work."

"I juggled things around so I could get home early," she explained. "I can't seem to shake what happen to Lloyd."

"Anything I can do?"

"Come over for a few minutes. I need someone to talk to – just for a while."

Olive and I cut across the O'Connor-Genesee property line. When the young cop still doing roadside guard duty spotted us, he tumbled out of his patrol car. I waved him off with a shout that all was well; just a neighborly next-door visit. The cop retreated back to his car, looking relieved.

"Thanks for coming," Alyana said after greeting me with a half smile. She poured us each a cup of coffee and led me from the kitchen to the great room where we sat on a three-seat sofa facing the home's rear windows. Outside a late September breeze chopped the bay frosting Narragansett's deep blue surface with peaks of white.

The conversation started out light. I told Alyana about Doc Waters and my plan to house him in one of the O'Connor's bedrooms for a couple of nights.

"Is this the Rutgers professor who went up against the Mafia in Philadelphia?" she asked.

"Amazing how people still remember him," I said, certain she also recalled, but purposely didn't mention, Doc's testicular misfortune.

Alyana looked worried. "Rick, if Maureen finds out –"

"How about putting this in the what-Mrs.-O'Connor-doesn't-know-won't-hurt-her category?"

"Not exactly the easiest secret to keep. Remember, it doesn't take much to get Maureen unhinged."

If Doug Kool's prediction was right, Mrs. O'Connor was already unhinged. Reading about how her house and dog-sitter was linked to Harold Mason's murder had to have Maureen doubling up her Prozac. With my name in the news again after last night's events at and around Lloyd Noka's house, Mrs. O'Connor's anxiety level was certain to be in the red zone.

"I had a call this morning," Alyana moved to a new topic. "From a woman I know who lives in Lyme, Connecticut. She's on the Nehantic Tribal Council."

I waited for Alyana to continue. Her long pause was a hint of what was to come, and it wasn't good news.

"William Nonesuch is accusing you of telling police that he's the one responsible for what happened to Harold Mason."

"Where did he come up with that gem?"

"He has a connection inside the Jamestown Police Department. Probably one of the clerks."

The Jamestown P.D. had more leaks than a chinois. "Could you get word back to the Tribal Council that Nonesuch has it wrong? I'm not pointing a finger at him or anyone else. At least not for now."

Alyana put her hand on my forearm. "Rick, anyone who knows Nonesuch will tell you it doesn't take much to turn him violent. If he thinks you're a threat, then you need to consider him very dangerous. Please be careful."

I placed my hand on hers. "I will," I promised. For a few seconds neither of us moved, our eyes locked and our fingers pressed together. Olive sensed the emotional charge heating up the room. The poodle gave us a soft bark and settled under a hand-carved coffee table adjacent to the sofa.

"I'm making the arrangements for Lloyd's funeral," Alyana broke what had become a long silence. She gently withdrew her hand. "He had no children and all his immediate family members are gone. I want to give him a Native American burial."

"How does that work?"

"The body isn't embalmed. It's kept cold and then buried in a simple shroud or wooden casket."

"Can I help?"

"I can handle the details. But having someone to talk to about him, that's the help I need right now."

And so I listened. Alyana talked the way a favorite daughter would speak about a father she adored. Noka was driven by his determination to restore the honor and stature of Native Americans, particularly those tribes in the Northeast that had been pushed into obscurity. But that passion never crowded out his concern and commitment for Alyana. She talked for almost a half hour, recounting times when the sachem would help her navigate around problems, sometimes with words and, on occasion, even with money.

"I can remember only one time when we went in different directions," she confided.

"When was that?"

"The day I told him I was going to marry Jeff Genesee. Lloyd was never a fan. 'Rich and reckless make for a bad combination,' he said. As things turned out, he was right. Jeff had the money to buy a toy that he used so carelessly it killed him."

I caught a spark of resentment in the comment. "But you had a good marriage, didn't you?"

"Better than good. Jeff was dedicated to me and generous to a fault. My student loans were paid off. He helped set up my practice. We had a beautiful home. More importantly, he was always faithful and attentive."

"Sounds like a perfect relationship."

"In most ways it was," Alyana agreed. "But Lloyd was right to warn me. It was a mistake to invest so much of myself in a man who lived such a risky life. When he died, I was shattered. His death left me completely empty. And angry."

I heard my own story in Alyana's words. I felt the same rage the night a young oncologist stuttered out his condolences. *I'm sorry. I wish we could have done more for your wife.*

"After Jeff died, I pulled back," Alyana confessed. "Retreated into a job that ate up the days and nights."

"Did you talk to Lloyd about how you felt?"

"All the time. There was no better counselor. He wasn't critical or judgmental about how I was dealing with Jeff's death. But in his own way, he let me know I had put myself in a cage and it wasn't a place I could stay forever. I've been trying to find a way out but –"

I reached across the sofa and took Alyana's hand. Her thumb ran over my fingers and an emotional bolt cut through my body. "You asked me here to listen," I said. "It would mean a lot if I could ask you to do the same. There are things I've bottled up for a long time. Maybe too long."

And so I spilled out thirteen years of bitterness and resentment. I had never admitted to anyone how I had given in to self-pity and misery after my wife died. Maybe Doug Kool was right. Maybe I took to hiding in a men's shelter because I didn't have the guts to go head-to-head with depression.

"Has there been anyone else?" Alyana began and stopped. The discomfort was obvious. "It's none of my business, but thirteen years is a long time. Along the way weren't there friends? Another woman?"

"Friends, yes. But nothing close to a serious relationship. Until –"

Alyana pulled close to me, lifted her hands to my face, and softly brushed her lips across mine. The kiss was subtle but there was no mistaking the voltage that passed between us. I reached around Alyana and drew her closer, the tenderness of our kisses growing more intense. I couldn't dissect the tangle of emotions that exploded inside me. The heated passion was boiling into a desire I thought had been buried long ago.

"Oh, God, Rick," Alyana whispered into my ear. "What's happening?"

We were both breathing heavily and the cool interior of the high-ceilinged great room felt overheated. Alyana inched back and closed her eyes.

"I didn't mean to come on so strong," I apologized.

Alyana stroked the side of my face. "Please don't be sorry. Not for making me feel the way I'm feeling now. But God, Rick, we've known each other for just a couple of days!"

"Feels like decades."

"It does. But I need more time to think about what's going on between us."

I drew in a long breath. "Okay. I'll slow this down. But it won't be easy."

She smiled and kissed me again. "I think Lloyd Noka would be very pleased with you, *neetop*."

"Why? Because I'm not rich and reckless?"

Alyana laughed. "No, you're not. And that would have suited Lloyd just fine."

"What I need is a distraction for at least the rest of the afternoon," I said. "Something to keep my mind from wandering in the wrong direction."

"Wander back in time for dinner tonight, okay?"

"Definitely!"

Alyana asked, "So got any thoughts about an afternoon's diversion?"

"Caleb Mason wants to give me a personal tour of the Jamestown side of his tunnel project. Thinks if I see the big picture, I'll join the al-Talal fan club."

"That's not how Caleb usually operates. He and his brother are the kind who run over anyone who happens to be in their way. Taking time to explain and build consensus isn't in their playbook."

"That's also my impression," I nodded and scratched Olive's chest. She had scrambled out from under the coffee table when hearing Caleb Mason's name. The poodle's tail was locked in her don't-like-the-bastard position. "So I think we should pay him a visit and see what he has up his sleeve."

"We?"

"Why not? Caleb didn't say I couldn't bring company."

"Rick, I've been a thorn in Caleb's side for a long time," Alyana said. "Next to Lloyd Noka, there's been no one who's done more to stop the Masons from doing a deal with al-Talal than me."

"All the more reason for you to tag along. If Caleb rolls out one side of the story, I have someone who can give me the other."

Alyana looked concerned. "I don't know –"

"Hey, I'm looking for a *really* big diversion," I joked.

"All right," she laughed. "But when Caleb asks why I'm with you, what's the answer?"

"You're my next-door neighbor. I happened to run into you while buying a present."

"A present?"

"Yeah, a gift."

"What kind of gift?"

"Something I need for tomorrow night. A baby shower."

– Chapter 12 –

Narragansett Avenue cuts across Conanicut Island in an east-to-west straight line, its tree-bordered sidewalks running alongside cedar-shingled houses and shops. Most of the weathered exteriors have a similar look, all aged to a dignified, gray-white palette. Blocks before its end, the avenue spears the town's village center, Jamestown's tiny and picturesque commercial hub.

"We'll find something here," Alyana said assuredly as she opened the door to a quaint gift shop and art gallery. "Tell me more about the mom-to-be."

"She's – she's unusual," I answered avoiding a detailed description of Twyla Tharp Rosenblatt. "Married to a very Orthodox Jewish lawyer."

"Do we know if she's having a boy or girl?"

"Nope. But either way, she has names picked out."

"Really? What are they?"

"Tzufit if it's a girl. Boaz if it's a boy."

"Yeah, right," Alyana grinned, her first smile since learning about Lloyd Noka's death.

"I'm serious."

"Uh-huh. Let's get serious about getting your friends a gift." Alyana pointed to a twenty-five dollar pewter baby photo album and a minute later, I was handing the clerk my credit card.

"A coed baby shower," Alyana mused as we left the store. "That's pretty uncommon."

"Just like the parents."

We walked to my decade-old Buick Century I had strategically parked to keep Olive in view while shower shopping. The poodle's tail was a Mixmaster as I unlocked the car.

"I'm still not comfortable bringing Olive with us," Alyana repeated an earlier concern. "And tell me again why we're using your car instead of my dog-friendly Odyssey."

"After seeing what Olive did to Charles Kenyon, I couldn't hire a better bodyguard. As for using the Buick instead of your minivan, think of it as a Trojan Horse."

A sharp left onto North Main Road sent Olive sliding across the car's vinyl rear seat. She let loose with a disapproving yap.

"So you use your Buick to sneak me into Caleb's world," Alyana said.

"Caleb comes across as a calculating kind of guy. There's a reason why he wants me to pay him a visit and it isn't just for tunnel talk. Bringing you and your Odyssey along could give him second thoughts."

The Buick crossed a narrow strip of land that linked the bulk of Conanicut Island to the smaller, less-developed area appropriately called Beavertail because of its resemblance to the semiaquatic rodent's back end. We passed Jamestown's deserted community beach, the cool autumn weather having shut down the bathing season weeks earlier. Looking westward across Sheffield Cove, I could make out the tip of Dutch Island, its thick shrubbery taking on a deep brown-green tone in the late afternoon sun. The yellow booms of two large excavators marked a small section of the island's vegetation that had been scraped away.

"Mason's equipment?" I nodded toward the heavy machinery.

"Yes. The company started work about two weeks ago, totally disregarding the complaint Lloyd filed last month."

"Complaint?"

"Violation of the Native American Graves Protection and Repatriation Act."

"I'm not familiar –"

"Most people aren't," Alyana interrupted, a trace of irritation rippling through her words. "The act was passed in 1990. Among other things, it protects locations where human remains are placed during a death rite or ceremony."

"So where does the complaint stand?"

"In limbo. Mason is using Mohammad al-Talal's money to buy lawyers who know how to send these kinds of problems into a perpetual state of indecision."

"And in the interim, Mason Development keeps on building."

"You've got it," Alyana said. "Of course that hasn't stopped some of us from raising public hell about what's going on."

"Some of us including Alyana Genesee?"

"At the front of the line."

I turned right on Fort Getty Road, an avenue that led to a defunct garrison used as an observation and defense facility during World Wars I and II. The area was now a town-owned public recreation site open to trailers and campers. Along the northern side of the road, twin ten-foot-high chain-link fences defined the boundary line for property purchased by Mason Development on behalf of Mohammad al-Talal. Coils of barbed wire topped the fence lines that stretched nearly the entire length of the access road to Fort Getty. My Buick coasted past several "No Trespassing" signs until reaching a gated entrance where two uniformed security guards had been posted.

"Rick Bullock to see Caleb Mason," I said to one of the gatekeepers. The man made a phone call, and then pointed us toward a pair of connected doublewide construction trailers. The on-site executive offices of the Mason Development Company.

I drove slowly along a makeshift gravel road passing stacks of building materials along with an impressive assortment of heavy-duty trucks, excavators, cranes, and land graders.

After parking the Buick, Alyana leashed Olive and we walked into a small but surprisingly nicely appointed reception area where a young woman greeted us with a forced smile.

"I don't have the lady on my visitor's list," the woman said looking at Alyana.

"An associate," I explained.

"And the poodle?"

"Companion dog," I whispered.

"Oh, does the lady have a handicap?" the woman whispered back.

"She keeps tripping over injustices," I said softly.

The befuddled woman didn't have a response. She picked up the phone and informed Caleb Mason that he had a visitor. Make that visitors.

We were escorted into a poorly lit room with a modest desk, small circular table with four chairs, and an architect table piled with dozens of rolled-up blueprints. Caleb choked back his dismay when Alyana made her entrance and Olive barged into the room with a growl.

"I don't believe I said anything about bringing a guest." Caleb's anger bled through his attempt to sound unruffled.

"Alyana's my next-door neighbor," I threw back a needless explanation. "I mentioned I was on my way to see you and asked if she wanted to tag along. Is there a problem?"

Caleb wore stylish tan pants and an expensive polo shirt with a D&G monogram I recognized instantly. Doug Kool's casual wardrobe was loaded with Dolce & Gabanna designs. More than once, my friend educated me about how the clothing line as hot as it was pricey.

"I'm afraid there is a problem," Caleb said. "Ms. Genesee is one of the plaintiffs in a class-action suit against our company." Caleb turned to Alyana. "Under other circumstances, it would be a pleasure having you here. But given our legal differences –"

"Are you asking me to leave, Caleb?" Alyana asked at the same time Olive snarled out her dislike for anything Mason.

"Let's not make this unpleasant, Alyana," Caleb urged. "I have a thought. Since you're here, I'd like you to see the Native American museum we're developing. Let me have Evelyn show you our plans while Mr. Bullock and I have a short conversation."

Without waiting for Alyana's response, Caleb hit the intercom button on his phone and the woman with the fake smile reappeared. Evelyn.

"Bring Mrs. Genesee to trailer C," Caleb instructed. "And the dog, too." Evelyn bared more teeth and motioned Alyana and Olive out the office door.

"Next time, call ahead to let me know if you're bringing company," Caleb scolded me. "That's just common courtesy."

"Sorry." I tried to make the apology sound sincere. Caleb wasn't fooled.

"As I told you on the phone, my brother and I were upset about what happened to our father when we stopped by the O'Connor's house," Caleb claimed. "If we insinuated you had anything to do with his death, I want to set the record straight. I hardly think you're a killer, Mr. Bullock."

"That's comforting."

"But I do think you could help us locate the missing document we mentioned . A property deed. It's something that could cause a needless delay with our Dutch Island project."

"I told you before. I don't know anything about a deed. When I found your father, he had nothing with him. No deed. Nothing."

"I believe you. I don't think my father had the deed when he was killed. In fact, I don't think my father ever had the deed. Why he claimed otherwise probably has to do with his dementia."

"So why are we having this conversation?"

Caleb circled his desk and pulled back a curtain from a small window overlooking the cleared work site that sloped down to the edge of Narragansett Bay. There were no trees and shrubs on the wide expanse of land, only rows of heavy equipment.

"You have a connection to the Maglio syndicate in New Jersey and Philadelphia," Caleb said.

"'Connection' is a loaded word. I know Manny Maglio if that's what you mean."

"Maglio wants this project to fail. So do people who value the past more so than the future. People like Alyana Genesee."

"Let's not forget the millions of Americans who apparently aren't ecstatic about a fanatical Islamic extremist building a nest in their tree."

"An unfounded fear, Mr. Bullock." Caleb backed away from the window, picked up a set of blueprints, and unfurled one of the large sheets. "Mohammad al-Talal's only interest is promoting a better understanding of Islam and, by doing so, finding a way to lessen Muslim tensions within the United States."

This didn't line up with al-Talal's oft-reported tirades against Western immorality and, in particular, certain American behaviors he considered contrary to the Koran. But before I could debate Caleb, he shifted gears. "Did you ever drive through the McHenry Tunnel in Baltimore?" he asked.

"A few times." Actually, quite a few times. I-95, one of the busiest interstate highways in the nation, ran under Baltimore Harbor through the eight-lane tunnel.

"More or less the same engineering we're using to build the al-Talal tunnel."

"Fascinating."

My sarcasm hit a nerve. "You don't get the significance of what we're doing here, do you?" asked Caleb.

"I'm not an engineer," I shrugged.

"You don't need to be to appreciate that this is one of the largest private construction projects in the nation. We'll be working three years on the tunnel alone."

"A lot of digging."

"Dredging," Caleb corrected. "Let me show you what it takes to build an underwater tunnel."

Caleb flipped open another architectural rendering of the passage that would eventually connect Jamestown to Dutch Island. With growing excitement, he gave me a tutorial on a procedure called sunken tube tunnel construction. First, he explained, Mason Development would scrape a 50-foot-wide trench across the bottom of Narragansett Bay. Over a million cubic yards of rock and muck would be transported by slurry pipeline to a disposal site near the Pettaquamscutt Cove National Wildlife Refuge on Rhode Island's mainland. Then several three-hundred-twenty-foot tunnel sections would be lowered into the trench and connected.

"By the time we're done, we will have used a half million cubic yards of concrete and fifty million pounds of structural steel," Caleb continued. "All this is going to have a huge economic impact not just here in Rhode Island but throughout much of southern New England."

"Also quite an impact on al-Talal's wallet," I quipped.

"You're right. This is a very expensive project made all the more so by two electric trams we'll be installing in the tunnel. Adding in the cost of the wall and ceiling tiles we're importing along with a state-of-the-art ventilation system, we could top half a billion dollars."

"A lot of money for a driveway."

"Hardly just a driveway," Caleb corrected. "Let me show you."

He opened the door to an anteroom and we maneuvered around a pair of four-foot-square, waist-high platforms – specially built pedestals for two spectacular architectural models. Caleb waved his hand over the model closest to the door as if he were blessing the replica.

"The American Islamic Educational and Cultural Center," Caleb proclaimed proudly. "It will be built here in Jamestown – not Dutch Island. In fact, a wing of the center will be right where we're standing. Much of the design is based on one section of a mosque in Medina, Saudi Arabia. The Prophet's Mosque."

Pointed arches and columns tipped with copper gave the exterior of the two-story structure a distinctively different appearance. Two minarets stood like sentinels on each end of the building. The interior looked overly ornate with glazed wall tiles and sculptured domed ceilings.

"Everything one could ever want to learn about Islam," said Caleb. "From the Prophet Muhammad's teachings to a look at what life is like for over a billion Muslims today. All open to the public and completely funded by al-Talal. Never an admission charge and –" Caleb paused to chuckle, "– free tea brewed in authentic Persian copper teapots. Nice touch, don't you think?"

I answered with a disingenuous grin and then wagged my head at the larger model in the room. "That's the Dutch Island building?"

"Ah, yes," Caleb practically purred, "Impressive, isn't it?"

"So the tunnel runs from the Islamic cultural center to al-Talal's island home?"

"What we're putting on Dutch Island is far more than a home. Did you ever hear of al-Masjid al-Haram?"

"No."

"It's the holiest mosque in the world. Millions make a pilgrimage to Mecca to worship at the mosque."

"A theological magnet."

Caleb smiled. "One way of putting it. We'll be building a replica of the Holy Mosque. Not the same size, of course. The mosque in Mecca can accommodate over eight hundred thousand worshipers."

"Maybe you should look for a larger island."

"Dutch Island is big enough. Not all its eighty-plus acres are suitable for building, but there's enough land to handle the footprint for the al-Talal Mosque."

"Interesting. Al-Talal gets his name on a scaled-down version of the holiest mosque on the planet," I said. "That should buy him a few virgins in paradise."

Caleb turned and faced me, his expression stern and his cheeks slightly red. "Cheap shots like that are the reason al-Talal wants a place in America to help beat back discrimination against Muslims."

The heated reaction was out of character for the Mason brother who was normally even keeled. Al-Talal had bought himself more than a developer. He had acquired a passionate front man. Or was Caleb just posturing? With him it was difficult to tell.

"I'm an equal-opportunity critic when it comes to any organized religion," I clarified. "To me, Muslims who have wet dreams about virgins in paradise are no more wacky than Christians who think they'll spend the hereafter sitting on clouds and playing their golden harps."

Realizing I was an all-faiths detractor took the air out of Caleb's annoyance. He turned away from me and his eyes swept over the intricately constructed model of the al-Talal mosque. "Extraordinary, isn't it?" he asked.

It was. The octagon-shaped building walled in a handsomely tiled courtyard. Four sections of roof had been removed from the model to expose the mosque's interior. Beautiful mosaics decorated marble columns and sculptured arches that linked one large room to another. But it was the exterior of the mosque that was most impressive. Arched windows each framed in brass were cut into gray marble walls. An enormous gate that framed the mosque's main entrance faced east, its stone voussoirs looking like compass needles all pointing across the Atlantic Ocean toward Mecca.

"Al-Masjid al-Haram has seven minarets," Caleb said. "But as you can see, our mosque has only three. To compensate, we modified the design to make the tower at the front of the building more dominant." He gestured to a multisided structure that spiked higher than the three minarets.

"Gold leaf?" I asked, looking at the jagged exterior of the tower.

"Some of the tower is gilded with twenty-four-karat gold. But you'll notice there are several glass and mirror plates also included in the design."

That feature was hard to miss. The tower had a patchwork appearance that fought with the smooth lines of the rest of the mosque.

"What you're looking at is an architectural interpretation of a design gemologists call a Mazarin or a double-cut brilliant," said Caleb. "Think of the tower as a diamond. It has seventeen facets, each of which catches light in a way that makes this mosque radiate."

"An Islamic beacon."

"More like a beacon of religious and cultural understanding," Caleb corrected. "One that gets lit around the clock. During the day regardless of weather, it's going to be a showstopper. And at night, truly amazing. You'll be able to see the glow miles offshore."

"Nice that I'll see the glow, but will I get to see the inside?" I asked.

"Excuse me?"

"The inside of the al-Talal mosque – can I ride the tram through your tunnel, buy a guided tour ticket and enjoy a few hours on Dutch Island?"

"Only if you're Muslim. This is to be a holy place just as is al-Masjid al-Haram in Mecca."

"So the Islamic center here on Jamestown Island is for everyone. Dutch Island is strictly for Muslims."

"Dutch Island will be a place of religious worship and study," Caleb's voice tightened.

I scanned the miniaturized ring of shrubbery that bordered the island. "What's behind the bushes – high voltage fencing?" I asked, already knowing the answer.

Caleb hesitated and then acknowledged the mosque would be protected with the most advanced security system available. "There will be no water access to the island. The only way in or out will be through the al-Talal tunnel."

"You do understand why some people are apprehensive about all this, don't you?" I asked, gesturing to the al-Talal mosque. "You're building a fortress inside America for a man who thinks people living here are a bunch of immoral imperialists."

"It's hardly a fortress. And al-Talal isn't a jihadist."

"Maybe not. But there's no arguing he's a billionaire with a chip on his shoulder when it comes to the U.S. of A. He's not exactly the neighbor most Americans want living next door or even across town."

"All this paranoia will evaporate a year or two after the project's completed," Caleb predicted. "In the meantime, I want you to consider the added benefits of what we're doing."

We moved back into the construction trailer's main office and Caleb punched a push-to-talk button on a cordless phone. "Can you break away from the meeting? We have a visitor."

Five minutes later after listening to more of Caleb's prattling about the importance of the new American Islamic Center, J. D. Mason bulled his way into the office. "What the hell is he doing here?" Caleb's brother yelled, clearly shocked to see me.

For a second time in only a couple of days, I was privy to a side-by-side comparison of the Mason brothers. While the pair had some common physical similarities, their differences trumped their likenesses. Caleb's facial features were refined, his high cheekbones and straight nose giving him a near regal look. In contrast, J. D.'s head was thick with an uninterrupted line of bushy brown hair running above his sunken eyes. While Caleb was meticulously dressed and groomed, J. D. was a mess. His mud-caked work boots were partially hidden by a pair of filthy jeans and his blue denim shirt was worn through at the sleeves.

"I think it would be helpful if Mr. Bullock had a better understanding of just how important our Dutch Island project is to New England," Caleb said to his still-stunned brother.

"Are you out of your goddamned mind?" J. D. clomped his way to the front of Caleb's desk. "What the hell's goin' on, Caleb?"

"I'd like Mr. Bullock to leave here today feeling the way we do – that our work shouldn't be delayed by a meaningless property claim. I have a feeling he doesn't quite get what the consequences will be if things get bogged down. And who better to get that point across than our friends in the meeting room next door."

J. D. looked baffled. "What?"

Caleb turned to me. "My brother is playing host to about a dozen union leaders this afternoon. You should meet them, Mr. Bullock. Let's say hello, shall we?"

"Jesus!" J. D. screeched.

Caleb disregarded his brother's protest and led us out of the Mason Development Company's main office trailer to an adjacent doublewide, vinyl-sided modular building. Once inside, I was maneuvered to the front of a long conference table surrounded by twelve megasized men all wearing mini stick-on name tags.

"Gentlemen, this is Rick Bullock," Caleb announced to the group. As if I needed an introduction. My mug shot had been in every paper and on every TV station in New England. Publicity came easy to the lone person of interest connected to Harold Mason's murder.

For a few seconds, the room went still. Then a burly man in his fifties wearing a badge that read "United Steelworkers of America" broke through the puzzlement that was temporarily mummifying the group. "Isn't this the asshole who put down your old man?"

"I don't think so," Caleb answered. "But he is someone who could help put most of your dues-paying members on an unemployment line."

A buzz ran through the room. "What's this about, Caleb?" the rep from the International Brotherhood of Electrical Workers shouted.

"You've all heard rumors about a Dutch Island property deed?" Heads bobbed and Caleb rolled on. "Let's assume the rumor's right. And let's assume the deed ends up in the wrong hands. The al-Talal project could get stalled for months maybe even longer. Worst case? We never get this thing off the ground."

"What are the odds that the deed even exists?" asked the only man in the room wearing a jacket and tie. Thin and balding, he was more an accountant look-alike than a union boss except for a gravely voice that gave away his inner toughness. "And if it does, what's Bullock got to do with any of this?"

Caleb looked at me and spoke through a thin smile. "When it comes to finding things, Mr. Bullock has a *very* impressive track record. Over the past couple of days, he's been on a hunt and my guess is he's picked up a scent. If there's a deed out there, our man here is likely to be the first to trip across it. And should that happen, Mr. Bullock, what will you do?"

I answered with a glare that could pierce steel. I had been suspicious of Caleb's invitation from the start, but being set up in front of a dozen Jimmy Hoffa clones went beyond any expectation.

"Hey, dickhead, did you hear the question?" J. D. grabbed my arm and turned me in a quarter circle. "What happens if you find the thing?" J. D. was standing on my left, his brother to my right. I was sandwiched in-between.

"Let's get something straight," I drew myself up trying to sound tough in a room so full of testosterone it was practically growing body hair. "I'm not on a search-and-find mission. This is supposed to be my vacation. The only thing I'm looking for is a decent steamed lobster – nothing else."

The poor attempt at humor didn't score so much as a grin. "Vacation or not, the question's still on the table," a man twice my size sporting an AFL-CIO badge said. "Let's say you do find the deed. Then what?"

"Not likely to happen."

"Cut the bullshit!" J. D. demanded. His square jaw was so close to my face that I felt his spit with each angry word he spoke. "What if you find the goddamned deed?"

"I don't play the what-if game."

"Meaning?" Caleb asked with a hint of a smile. He was enjoying the show.

"Meaning I don't answer what-if questions. It's a ticket to a rathole. So I don't go there."

"What the hell are you talking about?" J. D. jumped back in.

"What-ifs are dangerous," I replied. "Let me give you an example. Here's a what-if. What-if your brother found out you're actually gay, J. D.?"

The room broke into guarded laughter. J. D., however, wasn't amused. "You're one stupid son of a bitch." J. D. sputtered and shoved me hard. I stumbled backward into Caleb, who had braced himself, possibly expecting his brother's reaction.

"Hold it!" a man wearing a Carpenters Local badge at the far end of the table shouted as J. D. balled up his right fist. The man was older than most in the room and his gruff voice had an authoritative tone that commanded full attention. "Everybody relax," he ordered.

The room went quiet and even J. D. lowered his arms in deference to the man. Slowly inching his chair back, the carpenters' rep uncurled his six-foot-six frame into a mass so large that he blocked the back wall.

"Bullock, I don't expect you know Rhode Island is an unemployment shit hole," the man continued. "Fact is, we got more people out of work here than a lot of places around the country. Been like that for a long time. Which is why this project is too important to get screwed up. If this deal gets delayed or worse, we'll be lookin' for somebody to blame. Understand what I'm sayin'?"

J. D. grabbed me a second time and pulled himself to within an inch of my nose. "Let me make this so simple even an asshole like you will get it," he growled, the stink of his breath coating me like paint. "If you find the deed, bring it here. If you don't, I'll personally stuff your Jersey nuts down your goddamned throat."

I slapped J. D.'s hand off my shoulder and jabbed an index finger at his box-shaped chin. "Listen, pea brain, you or anyone else who threatens me is a phone call away from a lot of pain. Think I'm bullshitting you, J. D.? Ask your brother. He knows I have friends in all the wrong places. Keep pushing and you're going to end up in a body bag."

J. D. blinked not sure how to react to my bravado. If we'd been in a barroom, I'd be fending off uppercuts from a man who outweighed me by fifty pounds. But J. D. was in front of a different audience and his uncertainty gave me an opening and I headed for the exit.

"Oh, there's something else," I said to everyone else in the room. "The Dutch Island property deed means only one thing to me. Finding it might force whoever murdered Harold Mason to come out from under a rock. Once that happens, the Jamestown Police Department takes me off its hassle list. So if you want me to stop rummaging around for the deed, then figure out who left the Mason boys here without a daddy."

I barreled out the door expecting a dozen irate labor leaders to be on my tail. Instead I walked alone and untouched to my parked Buick where Evelyn, Caleb's toothy secretary, stood alongside Alyana and Olive. Seconds later, my car was crunching its way over the temporary gravel road that led to the construction site gate. The Buick stirred up a hazy cloud of dust and for a time, the Mason Development Company didn't exist.

If only.

– Chapter 13 –

"Caleb's warped idea of what it takes to be a respectable corporate citizen."

Alyana held up a rendering of a three-room exhibit area sketched above a caption that read: New England Museum of the American Indian.

"Big name, small space," I glanced at the color copy and shifted my eyes back to the road. We were midway between the future site of the American Islamic Educational and Cultural Center and Jamestown's high-priced neighborhood that was home to Alyana and the O'Connors.

"Caleb throws a few arrowheads and pottery shards into a converted out-of-the-way shack and he thinks the Narragansetts and every other tribe within a hundred miles will do cartwheels. That's not going to work."

Minutes later I pulled into the Genesee driveway, wondering what happened to the Jamestown cop who had been on guard during the day. There was no patrol car in sight.

"Maybe Caleb thought you'd stand down if he tossed you a bone," I said and pulled the Buick to a stop.

"Not a chance. He knew exactly how I'd react when I saw his idiotic excuse for a museum. He was also smart enough not to be in his back room when I exploded."

"Putting people in unpleasant situations seems to be his strong suit." Like pushing a homeless shelter director through a gauntlet of discontented union leaders.

"That's Caleb. He's a master at manipulation. He had no idea I'd be showing up at his place today and yet on the spot he still figured out a way to infuriate me. J. D. is a drunk and a thug but he's got nothing on his slime-ball brother."

I got out of the car and opened the rear door. Olive jumped from the backseat and bounded across the front yard.

As we walked toward the front porch, I took Alyana's hand. "Listen, I did a stupid thing. I shouldn't have dragged you along this afternoon. You had enough to handle trying to deal with Lloyd's death. If I'd known what Caleb –"

"No apology needed, Rick. I would have found out about Mason's asinine museum plan sooner or later. And besides, if I hadn't been there, Caleb might have fed you to the union wolves. Think of me as a kind of life insurance."

In so many ways, I told myself.

"Did Caleb ruin your appetite or are we still on for dinner?" I asked.

Alyana laughed. "You've got a lot to learn about me, mister. It will take more than a jerk like Mason to keep me from a decent meal."

"Great. But since Lieutenant Ravenel has me on a leash, we can't wander off this island. Any suggestion as to what qualifies as decent here in Jamestown?"

"Actually, I do have a place in mind," Alyana replied, her gentle personality returning. Olive picked up the change in demeanor and trotted back to us. "There's a small French restaurant that's about to close for the season. We shouldn't have a problem getting a table but we'll have to bring our own wine. Interested?"

"Sounds terrific. You make the reservations, and I'm good for the wine. How about I pick you up at six-thirty?"

Alyana turned and kissed me.

Olive boarded the Buick and we made a quick loop from the Genesee driveway to the sprawling house next door. After a brief pit stop at the O'Connor's, I loaded Olive back into the car and drove to a wine and spirits store I recalled seeing near the center of town. A clerk convinced me a cabernet would be a safe choice for a fine French dinner. The transaction took five minutes and thirty-five dollars. With some unexpected time to spare, I informed Olive we would be making a short side trip to the West Ferry section of town before returning to the O'Connor's for a shower and shave.

During my few fateful minutes with Lloyd Noka, I had seen a map of Conanicut Island spread out on a table near the old man's chair. A thick black circle had been drawn around an area on the western side of the island, near Narragansett and Watson Avenues. Scrawled on the bottom of the map were the words: The Shame of our Past.

I parked the car, leashed Olive and walked west on Narragansett Avenue. It took two conversations with passersby to find what I was looking for. An elderly man directed me to several acres of overgrown land that butted up to a paved school parking lot and tennis court. There might be an Indian burial site somewhere in the brush, he said.

"Indian cemeteries face west toward the setting sun," the man explained. "West Ferry's got its share of Indian bones, most in unmarked graves. The only marked burial site I know about is one hardly anybody else would remember."

After trampling through weeds and high grass, I found a small plot cordoned off by a shin-high, dilapidated fence. A thick blanket of brambles and vines covered the crumbled remains of a half dozen flat slabs of stone. The squared-off section of land looked as if might have been tended years, maybe decades ago. But now it was nothing more than an overgrown eyesore. If this was indeed a cemetery of sorts, Noka was right. It shamed the Narragansett's past.

Twenty minutes later, I drove back to the O'Connor residence and after a quick cleanup, called Alyana to check on restaurant arrangements. With the tourist season long gone, the fine dining business had slowed to a crawl. We would be the only patrons for the evening, which meant there would be no problem if we wanted Olive to join us.

The poodle and I drove up the Genesee driveway where Alyana was already out the front door and waiting. She wore a form-fitting black dress, simple but incredibly complimentary to her trim body. Her gold chain necklace and matching earrings caught the last glint of sun as it hovered over the western horizon.

"You look spectacular," I exclaimed while opening the passenger-side door. "Then there's me. I didn't even bring a tie."

Alyana did a quick scan of my dress slacks and sport coat. "Just right."

Acceptable, maybe, but not great. I had come to Conanicut Island to fish, read, and unwind. I hadn't packed to socialize, especially with a woman who was turning my world on its head.

Alyana directed me to a nondescript restaurant tucked into a small street that ran perpendicular to Jamestown's main drag. La Bergerie had little going for it except its culinary excellence. If you could find the place, it was because you were looking for the best food in the area. You didn't come for the water view. There wasn't any. And if you were in the mood for live entertainment, you needed to keep searching.

"*Bonsoir!*" a plump woman greeted us at the door. "And you, *beau chien*! How I've missed my favorite poodle!"

Olive's tail gyrated wildly.

"*Tellement bon de vous voir, Ayana!*"

"It's wonderful to see you too, Aurélie." Alyana embraced the woman with a warm hug.

"It's much too long since you were here. And my Olive. How I missed this *chien*."

Alyana laughed and took my hand. "This is my friend Rick Bullock. And this –" she nodded at the woman "– this is Aurélie Benoit. She and her husband, Yves, run the finest restaurant in New England."

"Don't forget Sarasota."

"*Quelle tragédie!*" Alyana shook her head. "Tonight the Benoits close La Bergerie for the winter season. Tomorrow Chef Benoit heads to Florida with Aurélie soon to follow."

"So perhaps you and Mr. Bullock come visit us where it's warm," Aurélie suggested and gave Alyana a quizzical glance. Le Bergerie's owner was probing the depth of the relationship.

"Maybe we will," Alyana smiled and shrugged.

"*Je suis tellement heureux pour vous, Alyana!*" the lady bubbled. I didn't speak French but needed no translation to understand the crux of the exchange.

Aurélie bustled away and disappeared through a double door I assumed led to the kitchen. "I take it you're a regular."

"Used to be," said Alyana. "But it's been a long time."

"Aurélie's glad you're back."

"So am I, Rick."

I asked about a menu and Alyana explained La Bergerie gave its best patrons the option of allowing Chef Yves to prepare whatever happened to inspire him. "I told Aurélie we were in their hands for the night. I hope you don't mind."

It was the right decision. The first course was a small, but an incredibly succulent, serving of dinner scallops Meiterranée with tomato.

"Ah, cabernet," Aurélie sighed with a hint of disapproval as she opened and poured my thirty-five dollar wine.

"White would have been better," I apologized.

"Oui, but how could you have known?" the woman hunched up her puffy shoulders. "*C'est une leçon.* Next time you bring one of each."

The main course was basil frog legs Provencal sautéed in butter and garlic. It arrived with a small dish of liver-colored meat that Aurélie placed on the floor next to Alyana's chair. Olive uncurled herself from beneath the table and slowly ate the treat with the kind of dignity that could only come from good breeding.

"Looks like foie gras," I nodded at the poodle's treat.

"Exactly."

"Foie gras? For a dog?"

"Sort of a tradition," Alyana said. "Aurélie is a little over the top when it comes to Olive."

"Isn't everyone?"

"Well, not everyone. Truthfully, Yves Benoit isn't crazy about dogs of any kind. Then, of course, there are Neanderthals like Caleb and J. D. Mason who would just as soon see Olive euthanized."

"Neanderthals don't count."

"If only that were true."

After crème brûlée and café au lait, we walked from the restaurant to my Buick parked on a street side about two blocks from La Bergerie. It was after nine and the narrow avenue was deserted. Olive trotted off leash at Alyana's side until we were a few yards from the car when the poodle suddenly charged forward.

"*Olive!*" Alyana shouted.

The dog braked to a stop and held her nose a fraction of an inch from a dark streak that blemished part of the Buick's grille and the lower half of the left headlight.

"What a shame dogs can't talk," a voice called out from behind us. Lieutenant Michael Ravenel's bulky frame emerged from the darkness. Two uniformed cops followed in his wake. As they moved a few steps closer, I recognized one of the pair – the young patrolman who had been guarding the O'Connor and Genesee households. "If the poodle could give us a deposition, I bet we could save Rhode Island taxpayers the cost of a DNA test."

"Or maybe she'd sue your ass for unlawful intimidation," I fired back unsuccessfully trying to cover up my shock at being ambushed. "Lurking in the shadows doesn't become you, Lieutenant."

Ravenel drew closer, his ebony face now fully visible. "The keys to your Buick, let me have them." One of the Jamestown policemen squawked into a shoulder-strapped mic as the lieutenant waited for my reaction. Seconds later a tow truck clattered toward us, its headlights giving me the first full view of the lieutenant and his backup team.

"What's this about?" I asked.

"It's about taking your car to the state police barracks in Scituate," Ravenel said matter-of-factly.

"For what?"

"Obvious, isn't it?" Ravenel jerked his head toward the smear across the front of the car.

"There's a law against driving a dirty car?"

"There's a law against running over somebody's head."

Alyana and I exchanged the same bewildered look. "Can you come to the point, Lieutenant?

"The point is your car is going to be picked apart for every shred of evidence –"

"Evidence?" I interrupted.

Ravenel ignored my intrusion. "While that's happening, you're going to get reacquainted with the Jamestown Police Department's interrogation room. Mrs. Genesee, one of the officers will be driving you and the O'Connor's dog to your home."

"Look, you owe us a better explanation, Lieutenant."

"Here's all the explanation you need, Bullock. You're a millimeter away from either a first- or second-degree murder charge."

"How many times are we going to walk down that trail? I didn't kill Harold Mason and had nothing to do with Lloyd Noka's death."

"That's yet to be determined," said Ravenel. "The picture's a lot less fuzzy when it comes to what you did this afternoon."

Alyana stepped toward Ravenel to get his full attention. "Lieutenant, enough! What's going on here?"

"Between five and six this afternoon, we believe Mr. Bullock beat a man to a pulp and used his car to finish the job."

"That's impossible!" Alyana said. "Rick was with me all afternoon."

Ravenel shook his head. "Not all afternoon. One of Jamestown's finest followed him to town after he left your house around four thirty. Didn't get back to the O'Connor house until shortly before six."

The tow truck driver, a scruffy, pot-bellied man in his fifties yelled at Ravenel. "Need to release the emergency brake on this hunk of shit. Get me them keys or I ain't responsible for damages."

Ravenel gave me a what's-it-going-to-be? look. I dug the keys out of my pocket and tossed them to the truck operator.

"This is insane, Lieutenant," Alyana continued defending me. "Rick went to buy wine –"

Ravenel signaled time out. "We know that. We also know he spent no more than ten minutes in the liquor store. After that, he was off the radar screen for about an hour."

"So you stopped spying after he bought a bottle of wine?" Alyana pressed.

"We had an officer assigned to both Bullock and you because we were concerned about your safety. That doesn't quite fit the definition of spying."

"Either way," Alyana continued, "why didn't anyone track Rick after he left the liquor store?"

"A car explosion and fire at a campground in Fort Getty Park late this afternoon made things interesting," the lieutenant volunteered more information than expected. It was difficult to hold back details from an attractive woman in a tight-fitting black dress.

Alyana said, "So we don't know where Rick went after he left the liquor store."

Ravenel pointed to the front end of the Buick being hoisted on to the tow truck's flat bed. "If the blood on Bullock's car matches what's left of the victim, I think we have a reasonably good idea."

"Is this about a hit and run?" I asked.

"No. This is about either a premeditated homicide or maybe second-degree murder if it turns out this was a messy end to an altercation that got out of hand."

"I haven't been on this island long enough to meet anybody I'd want to fight or kill," I claimed.

"Really?" Ravenel asked. "That's not what a dozen union boys tell me."

"What?"

"You threatened J. D. Mason earlier today."

"No threat. I just let him know there's a line he shouldn't cross."

"Which he apparently did cross after the two of you met for a private conversation at the end of a dirt road near Conanicut Point."

"Are you saying –"

"I'm saying you beat the hell out of J. D. Mason and then used your car to put him down permanently."

The news rocked me. First Harold Mason gets killed and now his younger son. What the hell was going on?

"This is ridiculous!" Alyana shouted. "Are you arresting him?"

"Maybe," Ravenel answered. "We'll see how I feel after Mr. Bullock and I spend another night together."

# #

It was a replay of my last visit to the Jamestown PD interrogation room. Two hours of taped questions and answers, a short break, and two more hours of grilling that might have gone longer if a uniformed cop hadn't intervened with a whispered message to Michael Ravenel.

"Your lawyer's here," the lieutenant announced.

"Oh no," I groaned.

On cue, Yigal Rosenblatt bounced into the room. "You shouldn't say anything. Nothing else should be said. Because if you say something it could be something you shouldn't say. I'm here because that's why I'm here. Which means I can handle all of this."

Handle it all the way to the gas chamber. "Yigal," I sighed, "you don't need to get involved with this. How'd you even hear that I –"

"We have connections, you know."

I knew. The only logical way Yigal could have learned about my being hauled back to Jamestown's lockup was because Manny Maglio had someone in the department on retainer. I already suspected William Nonesuch had bought himself a snitch inside the police force. Now add the mob to the list of outsiders getting regular updates from an informant.

"Everything's different now," Yigal said pointing his words toward Ravenel and the uniformed spectators whom we all knew were clustered behind the one-way glass panel that took up one wall of the interrogation room. "Because I'm here."

He certainly was. Yigal jittered from one side of the small room to the other, his frantic movements spinning his yarmulke off his head like a Frisbee. Lieutenant Ravenel watched the spectacle and then pressed his hands against his temple.

"We're done for now," the lieutenant said softly. Whether it was sheer exhaustion or Yigal's insanity, Ravenel was spent.

"What's the charge?" Yigal squawked. "Did you Miranda him? Because if you didn't, I can cause trouble. I'm good at trouble."

Ravenel raised his hand. "Counselor! Put it in neutral. It's after two in the morning and you're giving me a goddamned migraine. Your client hasn't been charged. He's still a person of interest and that means I want him close-by in case we decide to slap him with a warrant."

"I'll drive him home is what I'll do," Yigal announced as he spun out the interrogation room door. "To his vacation house is what I mean."

When the lawyer was out of earshot, Ravenel pulled me aside. "Two minutes in private," he said. We walked into the station's men's room.

"You keep bringing Manny Maglio's mouthpiece into my world and I'll make you pay," Ravenel warned.

"He's not Maglio's mouthpiece. He's his nephew-in-law. And only extraterrestrials know when, where, and how Yigal shows up."

"Yeah, that's hilarious," Ravenel said without a smile. "He's a pain in my ass and let me tell you something, he's not helping your situation."

"What exactly *is* my situation, Lieutenant?"

"You're being set up. I don't know why and I don't know who definitely doesn't love you. But it's as obvious as your lawyer's psychosis that somebody out there wants you to take the hit."

I leaned against the washroom's stained porcelain sink. "Is this just a hunch or do you have something else to back up your theory?"

"We got an anonymous call about six-thirty telling us where to find what was left of J. D. Mason. The same caller says an older American-made car the same color as yours was seen tearing away from the dirt road where Mason's head was flattened."

"Any lead on the caller?"

"No. A disposable prepaid cell phone and a garbled voice. Not sure if it was a male or female."

"The tip was for real and you found Mason's body," I conjectured.

"And since the car's description matched your Buick, we started searching the island. Not to be found until we got a second call from the same phone."

"While we were in La Bergerie, somebody plasters my car with J. D. Mason's blood."

"You Jersey boys aren't the brightest bulbs in the chandelier but you're not dumb enough to ride around with evidence dripping off your Buick's grille."

"You had no one on my tail tonight?"

"After the Fort Getty fire was put out, I sent a patrol car back to the O'Connor house. You were long gone."

"That fire –"

"Abandoned car somebody deliberately torched. Burned two acres of brush and scared the hell out of a half dozen campers in the area."

I turned on the corroded cold-water tap and splashed my face. Fatigue had me too far gone and the cool minishower did nothing to clear my head.

"If you're convinced I'm being setup, why work me over with four hours of pointless questioning?" I asked.

"To send a message that we think you're a prime suspect. If you're in the running as a candidate for a murder one charge, somebody's going to keep piling on reasons for putting you behind bars. The more that happens, the more likely mistakes will be made. And we like mistakes. They usually point in a direction that leads to a conviction."

"Well, the message is getting out, isn't it? Especially from Jamestown's law enforcement epicenter."

Ravenel pulled a paper towel from a wall dispenser and wiped his neck and face. "We know we have a leak."

"Leaks," I corrected.

"Yeah, maybe more than one. That's our problem and we're working on it. Your problem isn't inside the police department. It's strolling around Jamestown looking for ways to get you convicted of two or three counts of first-degree murder. Which is why I told you before and I'm telling you again, watch your ass."

I pushed my hand out and Ravenel responded with the kind of hard grip I expected. "You're giving me more than you need to. I don't know why, but I appreciate it."

"I read your file, Bullock. You're not the type who gets off cracking heads or stringing up an old Indian. But you *are* the type who just can't keep from tripping over piles of somebody else's shit."

No argument there. I moved toward the men's room door and braced myself for my ride back to the O'Connor house with Yigal Rosenblatt. "One more question," I said. "Tonight when I was at the restaurant. Who could have known where my car was parked?

Ravenel shrugged. "Only one person I can think of."

"Who?"

"Your new girlfriend. Alyana Genesee."

– Chapter 14 –

Yigal Rosenblatt dropped me off at the O'Connor house at three-thirty a.m. and within minutes I fell into a fitful sleep. The seeds of doubt Michael Ravenel had planted about Alyana Genesee turned into a nightmare. As exhausted as I was, it was a relief when the bedside alarm woke me at eight. A half hour later, I called my next-door neighbor.

"I was about to come over to see if you were okay," Alyana said.

"Yeah, sorry," I apologized. "I should have called earlier but Lieutenant Ravenel had me on the griddle until three o'clock."

"Listen, I have office hours most of the day today. Is there anything I can get for you before I leave?"

"Huh?" I tried shaking off the fatigue. Or was it my newly acquired doubts about Alyana? "Oh, no. Thanks. I'm fine."

"You sure? You don't sound fine."

"I think it's my sleep debt," I fibbed. "Is Olive okay?"

"She's great. If it will help, I can take her with me today."

"Oh," I mumbled, "that would be great."

"Go back to bed for a few hours. I'll come over around dinnertime."

"How about after dinner? I've got that baby shower –"

"Oh, right!" Alyana laughed. "But you don't have a car. How will you get to the wild side tonight? Need a ride?"

"No. I'm going to ask the mother-to-be to send her husband to pick me up."

There was coolness in my tone that came from something other than lack of sleep.

"Are you sure you're all right?" Alyana pressed.

"I am. See you after the shower."

I went back to wrestling with the prospect that a woman who might be able to tug me out of thirteen years of despondency was in reality nudging me toward a jail cell. On one hand, I thought Lieutenant Ravenel's implication was one-hundred percent ridiculous. On the other, it made absolutely no sense that a wealthy, beautiful woman would be attracted to a middle-aged, slightly balding Penn State graduate who ran a men's homeless shelter.

I ended the point, counterpoint mental fencing by checking the calls that had piled up in my phone's message vault. The three most recent were from my New York pal, Dr. Doug Kool.

"Hey, Angie," I said to Doug's amiable admin. "He there?"

"Oh, honey, you don't want to talk to him. He's at the far end of a megameltdown and all the credit goes to you."

"What else is new?"

"No, darling, this one's special. The man says you're a festering hemorrhoid that he's going to lance with a jackhammer."

My first chuckle since last night's dinner at La Bergerie. "Has he no mercy? Put me through, and be sure to say nice things at my funeral."

"I'll never forget you, Bullet," Angie said. Two seconds later, the phone roared.

"THEY"RE COMING HOME!"

"Hello to you, too, Doug. It's your buddy up here vacationing in the Ocean State."

"Do you understand what's going on, Bullet? *The O'Connors are coming back to Jamestown!*"

If Doug expected shock or panic, he got neither. "There's a bed and breakfast not far from here. I'll see if I can get them a room."

"You think this is funny? Ken O'Connor is cutting short a zillion-dollar cruise because you've managed to get yourself on the ten most wanted list in just two days!"

"Hard as this may be to believe, the only thing I've done that's close to illegal is catch a fish without a license."

"Bullet, your name's in the paper this morning – again! You're a suspect in another murder! Again! Christ, man! Can you guess why the O'Connors want you out of their house as fast as you can throw your stuff in that thing you call a car?"

"That's going to be a bit of a problem, Doug," I said, but wasn't given a chance to explain.

"No!" Doug snapped back. "No, it's not! The O'Connors are trying to track down Alyana Genesee, the veterinarian who lives next door. They want her to take over dog-sitting until they get back to the States in two or three days. Once you play pass the poodle, you're out of there."

"And when is all this supposed to happen?"

"Soon. Pack your bags."

"I'll stay until the dog leaves," I promised.

Doug hesitated, trying to detect the loophole in what I had just said. "Don't screw with me on this one, Bullet. I'm already on life support with Ken O'Connor. You may have lost me one of my biggest charity cash registers."

"And a chunk of your year-end bonus."

"That too."

I listened to two more minutes of Doug's ranting, disconnected, and phoned Alyana's office hoping I could preempt a call from the O'Connors. "Dr. Genesee is doing surgery this morning," a vet tech informed me. No phone contact until around lunchtime "but if it's really important, text her because Dr. Genesee reads those messages first thing when she's out of the operating room." I told the tech I would send a text, but it was urgent that Alyana check her messages before accepting any other phone calls. Then I clicked into the SMS texting world and typed –

Alyana – critical! Do NOT talk to O'Connors by phone before talking to me. Will explain later. Rick

I toasted two bagels and microwaved a cup of instant coffee before making several calls all dealing with backed-up Gateway problems. It was noon before I finished taking care of business. Shortly after, the O'Connor's two-tone door chime called me to the front entrance.

"Your driveway gate is broken," Doc Waters said skipping all customary salutations.

"So I've been told." I opened the door wide and my one-time Gateway resident and longer-time friend walked over the threshold. "Good to see you Doc."

Doc Waters scanned the eye-popping interior of the O'Connor home and blew out a whistle. "The house that fast food built."

I waved the ex-Rutgers history professor inside and once Doc cleared the doorway, I saw his car – a badly rusted, ugly brown four-door sedan. "You drove from Jersey in that?" I asked, pointing to the dilapidated vehicle.

"It's an eighty two Opel Commodore Berlina. Helluva a car, isn't it?"

Vintage Doc Waters. The man knew something about everything and a lot about most things. Including automobiles. A few years ago when I thought my Buick was a tow away to the junkyard, the professor did radical engine surgery. For the price of a few parts, the car got a second life thanks to an academic who looked no more like an auto mechanic than I did. Doc's hunched-over posture and untamed mop of white hair gave him the appearance of an aging intellectual. But his face told another story. The telltale effects of hard drinking and uncontrolled gambling creased his pasty complexion. As for his body, it wore the scars of a man who had done battle with the Philadelphia Mafia back in the 1980s. The tip of a finger on his right hand was missing and so was one of his testicles. Fortunately "One Nut Waters" as he was sensationalized by the media no longer wore a target on his back. Thanks to the pardon I had managed to negotiate with Manny Maglio, Doc's name had been scratched off the mob's hit list.

"Letting the world know you're on the scene isn't going to be good for you or me," I told Doc. "So how about you pull that piece of junk into the O'Connor's garage?"

"That piece of junk has a rebuilt six cylinder engine with a displacement that's off the charts. After I do a little bodywork, you'll see saliva pouring out of every Opel Club in the world."

Rarely did Doc say anything that didn't beg a broader explanation or a long list of follow-up questions. Like – there are Opel Clubs? What the hell *is* an Opel anyway? The trick was not to get sucked into the professor's verbal wake because it would lead you so far off course that you could never get back to your original bearings.

"Doc, just get the thing under cover," I ordered. "The garage door closest to the house."

Doc dropped his military-style duffel bag and worked his way back to the Opel. I headed for the interior door that opened to the three-bay garage and a minute later, the professor's car pulled into the only vacant parking space available.

"Mother of God!" Doc exclaimed as he climbed out of the Opel, "a new Bentley Mulsanne! You're talking three hundred k!"

I wasn't impressed, which seemed to stun the professor. So he quick stepped to the second O'Connor car parked in the garage and his knees literally went weak. "Jesus, Mary. Do you know what this is?"

"Popemobile?"

"Not funny, Bullet," Doc insisted. "This is a Bugatti Veyron. The most expensive car you can buy for regular street use. Goes from zero to sixty in two-point-six seconds. If I had to guess, we're probably looking at a million and half dollars."

I was so not a car person that the revelation didn't make a dent. "Half the East Coast got its arteries clogged from the junk food O'Connor sold to buy this buggy," I said, which only rankled my new guest even more.

"You know your problem?" Doc asked. "The Gateway's destroyed your taste for the finer things in life."

A clear, full-color image of Alyana Genesee shanghaied my brain. "Not entirely," I corrected without adding an explanation.

I led Doc through the garage entrance to the O'Connor house, retrieved his duffel bag, and walked to another guest bedroom only one door away from my own temporary quarters. I explained we needed to be ready to make a quick exit within the next day or two once we got word the O'Connors were closing in on Jamestown. Giving Doc time to settle in, I moved to the dining alcove with its wide-angle view of Narragansett Bay and checked my cell for text messages. Just one.

Rick – O'Connors called three times but haven't taken their calls. Will wait until we talk. What's going on? Alyana

I was about to key in a short text reply when the front door chime sounded for a second time in less than a half hour.

"Here to fix the gate," a muscular man about as tall and wide as Michael Ravenel said. Aside from their physical frames, the repairman and police lieutenant had nothing else in common. The man at the door was white and had a face as ugly as it was frightening. A jagged scar ran from his left ear to a huge nose that hung over a black mustache like an awning. The repairman's long hair was pulled back into a ponytail fully exposing two badly deformed ears.

"Thought you couldn't be here until later this week," I said. My brain's usually reliable warning signal began ringing.

"Got a cancellation," the man explained. "Where's the breaker box? I gotta shut off the juice to the gate."

I looked past the man and did a quick inspection of his unmarked panel truck. Then I scanned the black toolbox he was carrying along with his wrinkled tee shirt, stained jeans, and worn work boots. It was one of those fifty-fifty moments. Half of me screamed danger and the other half yelled that I was already in trouble up to my neck with the O'Connors. If the repairman was for real and if I told him to get lost, the gate might remain out of commission for weeks to come. I did a mental coin flip and the call went in favor of the repairman.

Mistake.

I led the way toward the laundry room where I remembered seeing a large circuit breaker panel. The repairman followed on my heels. After taking a few steps, the man grabbed the back of my shirt collar and tossed me hard to the right. I stumbled through the great room and into a mahogany wall table. Two antique vases worth more than my annual Gateway operating budget hit the floor and disintegrated.

Although I didn't end up on the floor, I was off balance. Before I found my equilibrium, my unwelcomed visitor had opened his tool box and pulled out a handgun.

"Here's what's gonna happen!" the man yelled, apparently all too familiar with rule one for cops and thugs: scream to intimidate. "Tell me where the deed is and we're done! Don't tell me and I use the shit in this box!"

I couldn't see all the "shit," but what was visible made me yearn for a pee break. A box cutter, a thin strand of steel wire, and a pair of needle-nose pliers were lined up on the upper shelf of the toolbox like an assortment of surgical instruments.

"I don't have the deed," I said forcing myself to stay calm.

"If you don't, you know where to find it!" the man said, waving the pistol at my chest. It was a Saturday night special, which was as common as a cockroach in New Jersey and I assumed also had to be an underworld favorite here in New England. If a crook couldn't find a Raven MP25 semiautomatic to steal, buying one on the streets was both easy and cheap.

I took three steps toward the man, using a technique perfected in far-too-many Gateway encounters. Like facing a grizzly bear, you don't run from a weapon. That can activate a triggerman's finger. Best to move toward a gunman but not so close as to pose a threat. Do the unexpected and confusion is the usual by-product. Right now, a little bewilderment was exactly what I needed to take my intruder off his game.

"Hey, asshole," the man warned, motioning a stop sign with his gun-free hand. Wrapped around his forearm was a tattoo of a large bird, its talons spread and its wing feathers pointed toward the man's thick shoulder. "There are six rounds in this pistol. Give me a reason and you're gonna eat every one of them."

"You're William Nonesuch," I said, my words nearly as loud as the man with the impressive image of a hawk inked into his arm that I read like a nametag. "I was hoping we could get together."

Nonesuch's eyes fluttered. "How'd you know who I –"

"Not important. Actually, you saved me a trip, Hawk. I was planning to visit you in Lyme. That's where you live, right? I would have made the drive to Connecticut, but getting around is a little difficult these days."

"Yeah, so I hear," Nonesuch said with a smirk letting me know that he had as much inside information about me as I did about him. "You can't go off the island. I heard all about that."

Which was bigger? Narragansett Bay or the leak in Jamestown's Police Department?

"Did you also get the word that I'm setting you up as a suspect in the Harold Mason and Lloyd Noka murders?" I continued amplifying my voice. "Because if that's why you're here, you need to get your facts right."

"I don't give a shit what you said or didn't say about me. There's not a cop around here who can tie me to what happened to those two assholes. What I want from you is the damn deed. That's all."

"Well maybe we can work something out. Maybe if you give me your take on who killed Mason and Noka —"

Nonesuch squinted. "You think I'm here to bargain? I'm not givin' you squat! This is a one-way road, pal. By the time I finish with you, I guarantee I'll be walkin' out the front door with all the information I want."

I hoped the exchange between Nonesuch and me was loud enough to blast into the guest room where Doc Waters was unpacking his secondhand duffel bag. It was. I watched the professor's shadow creep on to the foyer wall as Nonesuch continued rattling off his threats. Doc had perfected the art of blending into whatever surroundings he happened upon. This afternoon, Doc's drab brown pants and equally as plain tan pullover were nearly indistinguishable from the O'Connor's beige interior wall paint. Not that it mattered since Nonesuch had his back to the hallway connecting the great room to the guest quarters. Doc took a few shoeless steps until he was only two feet from Hawk's rear.

At nearly seventy years old, Doc was no match for an armed ex-con. I braced myself for a bad ending but as he had managed to do so often in the past, Doc turned things around this time with a simple touch to the Hawk's spine.

William Nonesuch lifted up on his toes, his body trembling violently. The Raven semiautomatic rattled from his hand and clattered to the Italian travertine floor. Doc stepped back a pace and gave Hawk room to stagger backward and sideways. When Nonesuch's Jello-legs began to steady, Doc walked calmly behind the man and once again pressed something against the base of his spine. Two doses of Doc's medicine were too much for Hawk. He crumpled to the floor, his legs and arms convulsing.

"Doc, what the hell?" I croaked. The way Nonesuch's eyes were rolled back I assumed only a breath or two separated him from his happy hunting ground.

"It's the mini," Doc said proudly, holding up a device about the size of a cell phone. "Strongest stun gun in the world and the damn thing operates off three lithium batteries."

"Is he —?"

"Dead? Nah. Although two shots of a 975,000-volt charge will make you wish you were somewhere else."

Nonesuch continued squirming on the tile. The dark iris of each eye rolled back in place and suddenly Hawk began to wail like a baby.

"Shut up!" Doc shouted and shook the stun gun at the man lying at his feet. Nonesuch pulled himself into a ball and muffled his bawling.

"God, Doc, a stun gun? They're illegal in Jersey and probably Rhode Island too."

Doc Waters and the law enforcement world bumped into each other on a fairly regular basis. Although the professor had only done spurts of time, largely for minor offenses, he was banned from carrying a weapon.

"I camouflaged the exterior of the thing so it looks like an automatic garage door opener," Doc grinned. He pointed to a Sears Craftsman label on the small device.

"You don't have a garage."

"I do if the cops tell me to empty my pockets."

"Help me Hannah," I muttered. "Is he going to be all right?"

"Depends," Doc answered and knelt down beside Hawk. "It's rare that a stun gun kills somebody. But you have to understand how this thing works."

"Doc –"

"An electric charge scrambles communications between the brain and the muscles. Like when an electrical signal screws up the picture on your TV."

Nonesuch slowly straightened his body out.

"Stress causes the muscles to convert their source of energy – that's blood sugar – into lactic acid. When a muscle can't get energized, it instantly gets disabled."

"Interesting," I said, "But this isn't the time for a science lesson."

"Mr. Nonesuch might disagree. Because it's important to understand that while it only takes five or ten minutes to recover from a short high-voltage shock, a charge that's continuously applied especially against the spine – well, the results can be more long lasting. Like forever."

I collected the handgun from the floor, closed the metal toolbox, and bent over Hawk whose cries had subsided into deep raspy breaths. "You came here to get a property deed," I said to Hawk. "I told you the truth. I don't have the deed and I don't have a clue where to find the thing. Now it's your turn to open up. Who killed Harold and J. D. Mason? Who murdered Lloyd Noka?"

"Kiss my ass," Nonesuch mumbled.

"Hmmm," Doc shook his head and tapped Hawk on the leg with his mini garage door opener. Nonesuch screamed but his reaction was far less severe than when the professor electrocuted his lower lumbar region.

"May I have a word?" Doc asked, and tugged me away from Nonesuch.

"Doc, go easy with that thing," I begged.

"Not to worry. I know what it takes to keep a naughty boy in line. Problem is, the mini isn't very effective as a kind of truth serum. It has a way of turning a brain to peat moss. So if you want Nonesuch to be a bit more forthcoming –"

"What do you have in mind?"

"Ah, so glad you asked." Doc ran a hand through his thick white mop and cracked a smile that reminded me of Mr. Cronin, my old high school biology teacher. Mr. Cronin, who was one of the strangest, scariest animals on two legs, had a special affinity for frogs. I still have vivid memories of the day the teacher pinned an amphibian to a slab of balsa wood and ran an Exacto knife up its belly and chest. Mr. Cronin took a little too much pleasure in ripping apart the frog's rib cage to show off a miniature heart pitter-pattering away the last vestiges of life. The frog's eyes were as big as nickels and it died with the tiniest of grunts. The barely discernable sound rippled through the class like an A-bomb. Mr. Cronin stared at the green corpse splayed out on a lab table, his smile still there along with a hint of drool about to spill out one corner of his mouth. He seemed to be somewhere else, completely unaware how distress had taken command of the class or that Mary Pettrocino was barfing her macaroni and cheese school lunch over my new Woolworth's book bag.

"Don't take this too far," I urged Doc as we hauled the still disoriented Nonesuch toward the O'Connor master bathroom.

"Not to worry," the professor said through a Mr. Cronin-like grin that gave me the willies.

"I *am* worried. Jamestown already thinks I'm a serial killer. I don't need a fourth homicide hanging around my neck."

"We don't have to murder Mr. Nonesuch," Doc tried unsuccessfully to reassure me as we pulled Hawk onto a tiled seat built into an enormous walk-in shower chamber. "We simply have to make him uncomfortable enough to come clean – so to speak."

The professor yanked off Nonesuch's shoes and filthy socks. Hawk was surprisingly compliant when Doc removed the stained pullover shirt but less acquiescent when his belt was unbuckled. Another shot of the mini to Hawk's thigh and the chino pants and dirty Hanes briefs were easily taken off.

"Always amazes me," Doc chuckled and nodded at Hawk's shriveled penis. "The bigger the blowhard, the smaller the weapon."

"What – what the hell are you –?" Nonesuch groaned. His muscles were still malfunctioning but his diminutive brain was apparently still working.

"It's called interrogation, Mr. Nonesuch," Doc answered. "Unorthodox, but I can tell you from personal experience, *very* effective." With that, the professor marched out of the bathroom and headed toward the garage. He reappeared a couple of minutes later carrying a large roll of duct tape and a heavy-duty fishing rod equipped with a reel twice the size of the one I had used to haul in my memorable bluefish.

"Saw these when I pulled into the garage," Doc explained. "Jogged a memory or two I would have just as soon kept in the vault."

"Oh, no," I muttered, anticipating Doc's plan.

"This shower couldn't be better for this kind of work," said Doc. He peeled off a long strip of tape and attached one of Nonesuch's nonworking wrists to a stainless steel handrail installed on one side of the shower bench. Panic twisted Hawk's face into a knot as Doc wrapped Nonesuch's other wrist to the same handrail.

"Please don't tell me you're going to do something to his –" I gestured to Hawk's manhood that had all but gone into hibernation.

"Depends on how things go."

The hawk tattoo on Nonesuch's arm began to quiver. Seeing the muscle tone was making a comeback, the professor moved quickly to fashion one end of the monofilament fishing line into a slipknot and then placed it over the middle toe of Nonesuch's left foot. Doc clicked the release lever on the fishing reel and walked backward toward the bathroom door.

"Let me explain what's going on here," Doc said to Nonesuch and me as he ran the line under the bottom of the door. "I'm putting the reel outside the bathroom door and setting the drag tight. The door will keep the reel from moving when I turn its handle. The line gets taut and it starts cutting into your toe. Once the line gets *really* taut, four or five more cranks and most of the toe comes off."

"You sick son of a bitch!" Nonesuch yelled.

"Blood, tissue, and maybe a little bone ends up on the shower floor. A turn of the faucet and the whole thing's nothing but a memory. Well for us it is, Mr. Nonesuch. For you, it's a few months of shuffling around and cancelling your tap dancing lessons."

"You do this and I'll hunt you down," Nonesuch warned. "Take one of my toes and I'll hack off two of yours. That's a promise!"

"Not a good plan," Doc replied and pulled off his right shoe and sock. He waved a disfigured foot at Hawk. "There's not a lot to work with. Look –" Doc pointed to the remnants of two toes. "Unfortunately, the little piggy that's supposed to eat roast beef and his little next-door neighbor were snapped off in a Philadelphia warehouse a long time ago."

Nonesuch swallowed hard.

"I had a lot of things done to me back in the day," Doc continued. "But I can tell you the most painful torture of all was having a toe amputated. Can't explain why, except maybe it's because no matter how bad the pain is, you don't pass out."

I thought I knew all the gruesome details about Doc's run-in with the mob. His amputated ring fingertip. The way a pair of pliers had popped his left testicle into oblivion. But for all the years I had known the professor, he had not once talked about how his foot had been maimed.

"You crazy bastard!" Hawk shouted.

"There is another way, of course," Doc calmly explained. "We could tie the line to Mr. Johnson and pull him out of his hiding place."

We all peered at Nonesuch's crotch trying to spot Mister Happy that was still playing turtle.

"But I'm not big on handling those things. I'm not even crazy about my own. So, let's stick to the toes."

Doc half closed the bathroom door and I heard but couldn't see the turn of the reel's handle. Three clicks and the thin line lassoed around Nonesuch's toe stretched tight.

"Oh, Jesus!" Hawk screamed. *"Please! Please don't do this!"*

The professor stepped back into the bathroom. "Okay, I won't. As long as you answer a few questions."

"All right! All right!"

"Truthfully."

"Yeah, yeah."

"Mr. Bullock will be taking the lead," Doc said. "But before he begins, let me ask you a warm-up question. You're a full-blooded Nehantic Indian, is that right?"

"Yeah."

Doc wheeled around, walked behind the bathroom door and turned the fishing reel handle one click. The line jerked Nonesuch's foot forward, the monofilament digging deep into his toe.

"AAARGHH!"

Doc marched back into the room and wagged his forefinger at Nonesuch. "When I say truthfully that means no lying."

Nonesuch whimpered words I couldn't understand.

"I spent a lot of time studying you last night," said Doc. "Of course you didn't know I was picking apart your past. But I was."

"I was only–"

"You're not a full-blooded Nehantic, Mr. Nonesuch. In fact, your Indian blood is fairly watered down, isn't it? Your grandfather on your daddy's side was a Nehantic married to a white woman. A French Canadian lady originally from Quebec, I believe. In fact, you still have relatives on the other side of the border, don't you? Your father gave you his name but that's about it. He disappeared when you were two and left you with a mother who's as Caucasian as they come."

"I'm still a Nehantic," Nonesuch whimpered a defense.

"You play the Native American card because it buys you a few federally approved privileges, and makes your ex-con friends think you're a big man. You didn't get the name Hawk at some Nehantic ceremony. You gave it to yourself."

Nonesuch didn't refute Doc. Instead he sat silently looking at his toe that had lost all circulation and was turning red-brown. The professor looked at me and nodded. William Nonesuch was now all mine.

"Did you kill Harold Mason?" I asked

"No." The response was fast and sure. I believed the man.

"Did you kill J. D. Mason?"

"No."

"Did you kill Lloyd Noka?"

A slight hesitation and then, "No."

I walked to within two feet of Nonesuch and peered down at him. Hawk's bulky torso was covered with dark hair, giving him a simian look that suited his personality. Minutes ago, Nonesuch was as menacing as any man I had met. But now, naked and hog-tied, he was pure putty.

"Be careful how you answer the next question," I cautioned. "Do you know who killed Noka?"

The pause was long and I could almost see the war going on inside Nonesuch's ugly head. Another glance at his toe and Hawk made the right decision to come clean.

"Tommy Caddefeld."

"Keep talking."

"Did time at Corrigan-Radgowski. He's a nut job who was supposed to work Noka over to find out if he had the Dutch Island deed. Ended up hanging the old asshole."

"He was there with Charles Kenyon?"

Nonesuch nodded. "And another guy named Frank Purvis. Kenyon was the driver and outside man. Caddefeld and Purvis worked the inside. The whole goddamned deal was a joke."

"What happened?"

"You and the Genesee woman spooked Kenyon, who took off and left Caddefeld and Purvis without wheels. Once that happened, Purvis was done – he wanted to get as far away from Noka's place as he could. Caddefeld told him to hang around until you and the woman drove off. Then they both went inside for another look around. Which is when the drunken old fool woke up."

"And?"

"Caddefeld's half Nehantic so Noka knew who he was. Caddefeld is also up to his ass with the law and a breaking-and-entering charge would mean a big-time parole violation. So the old man had to go."

"They hung him to make it look like a suicide?"

"Caddefeld's idea. Purvis only helped. At least that's what Purvis told me. Afterward, they walked to Cranston Cove, where Purvis had parked his car."

Earlier, Alyana had pointed out Cranston Cove – nothing more than a wrinkle on Jamestown's eastern shoreline.

"Where are Caddefeld and Purvis now?"

"I dunno," Nonesuch answered. "Since Caddefeld broke parole, he's probably up north. Has relatives in Maine. Purvis is scared shitless and's holed up somewhere around Lyme."

"And you?" I caught Nonesuch's eyes to make sure he grasped the importance of the next question. "Kenyon, Caddefeld, and Purvis. They all worked for you, didn't they?"

It was toe or truth time. Nonesuch chose the truth. "I paid 'em to look for the damn deed. Not to kill nobody. Caddefeld is a maniac."

Nonesuch's toe was taking on a purple hue, a ripening concord grape capped with an ugly patch of thin black hair. "Paid them?" I asked. "If you're shelling out money then there has to be somebody else working the cash register. Who's putting up the wampum?"

"I dunno," Nonesuch croaked.

Doc took three giant steps toward the bathroom door.

"No!" Nonesuch screeched. "What I mean is I work through a middleman. The guy I deal with doesn't have the bankroll. He's just a go-between. I never found out who's puttin' up the cash."

"What would this go-between give you if you happened to find the deed?"

"A hundred grand."

The toe started to balloon.

"You don't know where the money's coming from, but you know who the man in the middle is."

"Yeah."

"Give me a name."

"The Frenchman."

"Frenchman?"

"Yeah, the cook. From the French restaurant in the village."

"La Bergerie?"

"That's the one."

"Yves Benoit?"

"I don't know his real name. On the street he's the 'Frenchman.'"

– Chapter 15 –

"Don't I know you?" Michael Ravenel studied Doc Waters, suspicion knotting his forehead. The two were a study in contrast. The police lieutenant had a tree-trunk body and a rugged black face capped with partially gray close-cropped hair. A foot shorter and slightly slouched, the professor appeared ghostlike, his crinkly mug punctuated with two hoary eyebrows as big as any caterpillars I had ever seen.

"You don't remember?" Doc feigned disappointment. "Our long weekend at that gay resort. The drinking. The passion." The professor wasn't big on cops, plainclothes or otherwise.

Ravenel was a half second away from a verbal counterpunch when I intervened.

"Doc Waters," I broke in with an introduction. "He happened to be in the neighborhood and since you've commandeered my car, he's going to chauffer me around for a couple of days."

Ravenel pulled back a faded curtain and looked out a dusty window at the Jamestown PD's pint-sized parking lot. "In *that?*" he jerked his head toward the professor's relic.

"Opel," Doc replied proudly. "Aged to perfection."

Ravenel turned to me and snarled. "I don't give a rat's ass who does the driving, Bullock. Or Bullet. Whatever you're called, you're not leaving this island until I say so."

"Why would I want to do that? I'm on vacation. Rest. Relaxation, Not a worry in the world except maybe doing a life sentence for a crime I didn't commit,"

"Cry me a river." Ravenel sat behind a table covered with manila folders and stacks of police reports. The paper pile was much higher than when I left the lieutenant last night. "You said you have information about Lloyd Noka. What is it?"

"An ex-con named Tommy Caddefeld killed Noka."

123

Ravenel was the type who had trained himself not to show a reaction. He was a hardened cop who could poke at a corpse, pick up a body part, or listen to the last gasps of a murder victim without so much as a blink of the eye. But when my headline came flying his way, he flinched. "And you know this how?" he asked.

"William Nonesuch. He did time with Caddefeld at Corrigan-Radgowski."

"Out of the blue, Nonesuch decides to do his civic duty and turn on his old cellmate? That's not how these things go down."

"Let's just say Nonesuch developed a leaky conscience and it just so happens Doc and I were standing around with a catch basin."

"Yeah, right," Ravenel instantly turned skeptical. "I don't believe a word of this and won't until Nonesuch whispers in my ear."

"Could be a problem," I explained. "Nonesuch has decided he doesn't want to be found. Not by you or his old prison pals."

Doc and I agreed to spare the police a detailed explanation of our interrogation tactics, and how we had allowed Hawk to make a hasty posttraumatic getaway.

"What about Caddefeld?" asked Ravenel.

"He's playing catch-me-if-you-can somewhere in Maine."

"So this is all a lot of nothing."

"It would be if it weren't for another upstanding citizen named Frank Purvis. Nonesuch says Purvis is holed up somewhere around Lyme, Connecticut. Dig him out and with a little away-from-the-video-camera encouragement he'll lead you to Caddefeld."

"If Caddefeld hung Noka, then he also did old man Mason and his kid, J. D. Is that what Nonsense claims?"

"It's Nonesuch," I corrected. "And no, he didn't say Caddefeld killed either of the Masons."

Lieutenant Ravenel measured us both with his steely cop eyes. "If Caddefeld didn't then we've got *two* killers roaming an island that hasn't seen a homicide since Eisenhower was president."

"Yeah, looks like it," I said. Doc Waters shook his head in agreement.

"Who else did Nonesuch finger?"

"No one," I lied. The professor and I agreed Yves Benoit shouldn't be thrown to the men in blue until we were certain Hawk was telling the truth about the Frenchman.

Ravenel leaned toward Doc and me. "This doesn't smell right. Until I figure out what the hell is going on, I don't want either one of you any more than a five-minute drive from here. Understand?"

"Whatever you say, Officer Krupke," Doc ran a bad *West Side Story* imitation into his words.

Ravenel's memory vault suddenly opened up. The lieutenant pointed a finger at the professor's chest. "Now I remember who you are, you wiseass. You're One Nut Waters."

Nothing good was going to come from hanging around any longer. "We'll be staying on the island, Lieutenant," I pledged.

"Make sure you do. Ditto for your friend if he knows what's good for the one gonad he has left."

Doc was ready with a retort but I pulled him away before he could do more damage. We boarded the Opel and headed back to the O'Connor house. I did a quick mental review of the afternoon's drama while pretending to listen to the professor ramble on about the similarities between the Khmer Rouge and the Rhode Island State Police.

Against Doc's advice, I was responsible for giving Nonesuch a free pass. I reasoned if we had dragged the ex-con back to jail, it would have meant hours, maybe even days, of legal entanglement not to mention having to deal with an ACLU complaint about toe mangling. The odds of my figuring out who was trying to cast me as a killer would sink even lower if I got bogged down with a pack of prosecutors who caught the scent of a conviction.

Of course, letting Nonesuch off the hook also opened the possibility he would soon be making a retaliatory comeback. But I didn't think that was likely, mostly because Doc had an iPhone recording of Hawk squealing on his associates. If either Doc or I were to experience so much as a bump on the elbow, all the incriminating evidence would be sent to Lieutenant Michael Ravenel via some unspecified but failsafe arrangement. At least that's what we told William Nonesuch.

"You think Hawk was stupid enough to buy a story about our secret system of notifying the cops?" I blurted out as we were driving.

"Yeah, he's stupid enough," said Doc. "Never got past junior high school, according to what I found doing research on your behalf until the wee hours last night, thank you very much."

"He's smart enough not to get his toe ripped off."

"It wouldn't have come to that. A couple of men I know, well, make that ladies I know who work in the admin office at Corrigan-Radgowski told me Nonesuch can't take the sight of blood. The boy's got a low threshold for gore – especially his own."

"But Jesus, Doc, why not just punch him in the nose? I mean you were going to rip off his toe! You of all people know what that's like."

"How would I know?"

"How? Because the Philly mob yanked off two of your tootsies."

"No they didn't."

"But – "

"A genetic thing. I was born with only eight toes. Five on one foot, three on the other. Made me very self-conscious when I was a kid. Everybody thought I had this paranoia about gang showers in high school because my weenie looked like a toothpick. Wrong. It was because I have a right foot two toes short of being normal."

"Unbelievable!" I said. "Christ, Doc, I'm never sure whether you're for real or running a scam."

"I prefer finesse over scam." The professor was a bridge player as competitive as they come.

"Whatever. The point is I can't tell if you're telling the truth or pulling off some kind of charade. I mean, for all I know you really don't have a recording of Nonesuch on your iPhone."

"Yeah, about that – "

"Oh, good God, no," I groaned.

"Let me explain. It's this whole new technology business, Bullet. I'm not a gadget guy, which is why I should have never bought that damn phone in the first place."

There were times when the professor's ability to blur reality into a thick fog was a tremendous asset. But there were other occasions when it was maddening.

Doc pulled his Opel into the O'Connor garage and we disembarked for a ten-minute pit stop. Then we followed the well-worn path to the Genesee front door where Olive gave me a more enthusiastic greeting than did Alyana.

"So you're the legendary Professor Waters," Alyana said.

"Hardly legendary," Doc chuckled. "Odysseus, Vlad the Impaler, and Robin Hood – now you're talking legends. Me? I'm nothing but a worn-out history teacher with a penchant for games of chance."

Alyana smiled. "More than that. There aren't many people who are courageous enough to go head-to-head with organized crime."

"And stupid enough to think they wouldn't lose body parts for doing so."

The two laughed like they had known each other for years.

"Doc, could you give Alyana and me a minute?" I broke in.

The professor hoisted his huge eyebrows and gave me a knowing look. Then he offered to take Olive for a backyard stroll.

"I owe you an apology," I said when Alyana and I were alone.

"First, you owe me an explanation. What's going on with you, Rick?"

I prattled through a recap of what Doug Kool had told me – that the O'Connors were on their way back to the States, that I was about to be put out on the street, and that Alyana was being recruited to take over all dog-sitting duties.

"What else?"

I could have tried dodging the question but Alyana's lie detector was on full blast. Falling into a deeper hole wasn't a good option.

"Last night, Lieutenant Ravenel led me to believe you had something to do with J. D. Mason's murder."

"*What?*"

"Ravenel thinks I'm being set up to take the fall for what happened to J. D. The only person who knew where my car was parked last night was you, according to Ravenel. His theory was that you got somebody to plaster the front grille of my Buick with what little brain matter J. D. happened to have."

"And you bought what he told you?"

"No – well, not exactly," I stumbled ahead. "I mean, what Ravenel did was to pull the cover off something that's been hanging out there since I met you. It makes no sense that a beautiful, rich woman would want anything to do with a homeless shelter director. Unless –"

"Unless what? Unless there happens be some underlying reason? Like framing you for murdering J. D. Mason?"

"Not that."

"Jesus, Rick!"

I swallowed hard and kept going. "There's more. Earlier today, Doc and I had a chat with William Nonesuch –"

"*What?*"

"Long story. But Hawk explained what happened last night. You didn't set me up. Yves Benoit did."

"*What?*"

The third revelation was too much for Alyana. She dropped into a Louis XVI chair and cupped her mouth with her right hand.

"From what Nonesuch told us, Benoit is a go-between. He manages lowlifes like Hawk, but gets his marching orders from a party yet to be determined."

Alyana shook off her dismay, and said, "I've known Aurélie and Yves Benoit for years. What you're saying is impossible."

"I don't know if Mrs. Benoit is involved. Nonesuch only mentioned Yves."

"This just can't be," Alyana said.

"Nonesuch isn't exactly the most credible character I've run across," I continued. "So Doc and I agreed to keep the cops out of this until we can check his story."

"And how will you do that? Yves is on his way to Sarasota."

"But Aurélie is still here."

"And you propose what? To put her on the rack and rip the truth out of her?"

Just a toe or two, I thought, hoping Alyana would never learn what happened in the O'Connor bathroom. "You know the woman, Alyana. Maybe you could talk to Aurélie –"

"Oh, no!" Alyana shot to her feet and paced to the double-storied windows that framed the white-capped waters of Narragansett Bay. "I'm not about to ruin a friendship by accusing Yves of anything."

"I understand."

"No, Rick. You *don't* understand. You also don't understand how deeply you hurt me by even listening to Ravenel's idiocy."

I walked to the window. Olive was scouting the bayside shoreline with the professor following in his tracks. Doc zipped up a light jacket as a late afternoon wind blew in a chill from the northeast.

"Alyana, I'm a man who's spent thirteen years thinking there's not a woman on the planet I would want in my life." I reached for Alyana's hands. She didn't pull away. "Then I meet someone so out of my league it's mind boggling. Instead of spinning around in ecstasy, I start looking for hidden flaws. Try to understand how unexpected this all is and how long it's been since I've felt this way about another person."

Alyana nodded. "*That* I do understand because you know I've been in a very similar place. Nowhere near as long as you but long enough."

"Then give me a chance to make this right."

Both of us knew we were at a critical intersection. Alyana weighed her response carefully and then spoke in an uncharacteristically uncertain voice. "Damn you, Rick. You can't be blind to what I'm feeling. I don't know you anymore than you know me. But I'm not looking for reasons to end what could be an important relationship."

"I'm not either, Alyana."

"Don't mistrust me again, Rick," Alyana warned.

Anything else I could say would be meaningless. I drew Alyana close and kissed her gently. The nearly out-of-control passion that heated both of us a day earlier wasn't there, replaced instead with a hint of an even more powerful connection.

"So you finally found a woman," Doc laughed. He and Olive had made their way back to the house and entered through a side French door.

I pulled back from Alyana but felt no sense of embarrassment. "I think maybe I have," I answered.

"About the hell time," Doc kept chuckling

Alyana drew a long breath. "Okay, let's deal with another matter, shall we? Looks to me like you boys have a housing problem."

Doc and I nodded.

"I have room for you here but somehow I think that could prove to be – complicated."

"Oh, don't mind me," the professor said with the kind of grin more suited for a peep show. "You won't even know Olive and I are around."

"It's not that kind of complication, Doc," Alyana clarified. "When the O'Connors show up – which knowing them could be as early as tonight – it will take a lot of explaining if you're my roommates. Then there's Lieutenant Ravenel. He apparently thinks I have blood on my hands."

I cleared my throat and kept my eyes pointed at a large silk Persian rug that covered two-thirds of the great room floor.

"I have a client who lives in a three-bedroom ranch a block away from the village," said Alyana. "He's not the most pleasant character around, but I know he's looking for off-season guests. I might be able to talk him into putting you up for a few days. Maybe longer if need be. If I can work things out, you should really think about making the move tonight."

"He's your client, which means he owns a dog, I suspect," Doc conjectured. To my knowledge, the professor had no history with canines but his introduction to Olive seemed to be turning him into a dog fan.

"No. Actually he doesn't. He has a pet ferret."

"A ferret?"

"Quite unusual in Rhode Island," Alyana explained. "You need a permit to own one in this state. And Saul's ferret is an absolutely beautiful female."

"Saul?" I asked.

"Saul Lipschitz. He's in his eighties but you'd never know it. Since his wife died a couple of years ago, Ellie has been his constant companion."

Doc twitched his bushy eye awnings. "The ferret's called Ellie?"

"Ellie Weasel. Saul named her after the Nobel Laureate Elie Wiesel. Very clever, don't you think?"

Doc and I shrugged. We were about to be shipped off to an octogenarian named Lipschitz who lived with a ferret. Frankly, we were both speechless.

"I'll call Saul while you're both –" Alyana stopped to laugh. "Oh, I guess I should ask. Is Doc going with you tonight, Rick?"

The professor looked understandably puzzled. I had yet to discuss what we would be doing for the next couple of hours.

"Yeah, he's coming with me."

"I am?" Doc asked.

"Well then, I'll try to get your residential needs squared away while you boys enjoy –" Alyana stopped and laughed again. "The baby shower."

– Chapter 16 –

The Sydney L. Wright Museum and Jamestown Philomenian Library share a long rectangular building atop a small rise on North Road. Six arched multipaned windows give the combination single-story structure a distinctive appearance, albeit not as impressive as many of the other much older properties that dot Conanicut Island.

"Opened in 1971," Doc said somewhat disapprovingly after glancing at a brass building marker. Anything younger than a century left the one-time history professor unimpressed. We entered the corbel course interior of the building with Olive walking a few paces in front of us on what seemingly would be our last outing together. Two days ago, Twyla Rosenblatt had invited Olive to her shower, probably expecting I would respectfully decline on the dog's behalf. But when Alyana decided to visit and not phone Saul Lipschitz, I thought it best to accept Twyla's invitation and not leave Olive on her own at the Genesee house. "I can't take her with me," Alyana explained. "Poodles have a strong prey drive and if Olive eats Ellie Weasel, you'll be looking for other quarters." A quick brushing and a couple of dabs of Alyana's Karl Lagerfeld perfume later, the poodle was shower ready.

"Hold it right there!" shouted a trim, gray-haired woman who could have been a Norman Rockwell model for the archetype American librarian. "No dogs allowed!"

I mumbled a few words that seemed to bounce off the steely exterior of the woman as she charged toward us.

"What do you think this is? A kennel? What's wrong with you?" The woman braked to a stop. "Oh, it's you, Olive. Well, come on in. Someone should have told me the O'Connor dog was part of this absurdity tonight. God knows I wasn't made aware of the other goings-on. I've never seen anything like this."

"Excuse me," said Doc as he closed in on the lady. The slouch seemed to disappear from the professor's body as he addressed her. "Are you – you couldn't be. Oh my word, it *is* you!"

"I beg your pardon."

"You're Miriam Constable."

"Miriam Reis. But my maiden name's Constable. How'd you know that?"

"Miriam, don't you recognize me?"

The woman's eyes and mouth opened simultaneously. "Are you – Doc? Doc Waters?"

"My God, how long's it been?" The professor was beaming.

"American Historical Association convention!" The woman peeled off her iron shell and gave Doc a warm smile. "Faneuil Hall."

"How many years ago was that?" Doc asked. "You were still a grad student."

Miriam gave her shoulder a coquettish tilt. "And you a faculty neophyte at Boston College."

Doc took Miriam's hands. "I can't believe it! I've thought about you so many times – about that night."

I looked at Olive hoping for some telepathic explanation. The dog took a few steps backward.

"Maybe we should leave you two to catch up," I suggested.

"Doc, you're not part of what's going on in there, are you?" Miriam totally ignored me and waved her neatly coiffed hair at the entrance to what I knew had to be the Wright Museum.

"Oh, no," the professor laughed. "I offered to give my friend here a ride, is all. I told him I'd stop in and say hello to the mother-to-be. After that, maybe you and I could spend a few minutes? So much to talk about."

"I'd love that," Miriam cooed and then turned sour. "I need to get my mind off this despicable insult to what little culture we have left here in Jamestown."

Doc turned to me and faked a look of repulsion. "And you told me this was a baby shower."

"You know what it is," I said.

"I doubt you do!" Miriam's no-nonsense librarian's voice rode over a wave of music that suddenly flooded the building's interior. "It's a gaggle of harlots violating every rule and regulation in the book!"

Doc tried looking appalled. I shook my head, gave Olive a pat on the rump, and headed toward the boom box pounding out "Be My Baby" by the Ronettes.

"And by the way," Miriam stopped me with a tug on my sleeve. "I know all about you. You're all over the papers and TV. Just to be clear, I'm letting you in only because you're on the guest list."

"Okay."

"If it were up to me, you wouldn't get through my library front door. Don't get me wrong – I didn't have any use for Harold Mason or his obnoxious son, J. D."

"Uh-huh."

"But I had a high regard for Lloyd Noka."

"I can understand that."

"What I'm saying is I don't condone killing people, Mr. Bullock. Not even Harold or J. D. Mason."

Doc intervened with a chuckle. "Believe me, Miriam, I know this man. He doesn't kill people. But it's a strange thing – a lot of folks who bump up against him do end up dead."

Miriam ran the tip of her pink tongue over her nearly nonexistent lips. "I see," she said, the irritation in her voice dissipated by uncertainty. I read her mind: *best not to screw with the angel of death, especially if he lives in New Jersey.* "All right then. Perhaps you should just move along."

Olive and I continued toward the Wright Museum entrance. After a few more words to Miriam, Doc followed in our wake and caught up just as we stepped through the doorway and into an altered state.

"Oh, Bullet!" Twyla Rosenblatt cried out. "It's you and Olive! And – oh my God! It's Doc! Doc Waters!"

Twyla charged toward us, an oversized tiara perilously attached to her mound of bleached hair, pulled up and held tight by an assortment of oversized pink-and-blue diaper pins and a fishnet snood. Sequin letters spelled out *How I Became a Mommy,* the words arched over an X-rated illustration of two copulating storks.

"Oh, Bullet," Twyla purred and looked at Doc. "This is the best present ever. Bringing Doc to my party."

"Well, he's not my –" I fumbled for words still trying to absorb what I was seeing. Olive nudged my right hand and I lifted the gift-wrapped picture frame that Alyana had helped select. "From Doc and me," I said and handed the present to Twyla. The poodle barked. "And from Olive," I added.

"Oh, you shouldn't have," Twyla gushed the way people do when they mean it's a damn good thing you brought something.

The overhead room lights had been turned off and the interior glowed with more votive candles than I had ever seen outside a cathedral. In a far corner near the ghetto blaster over-amplifying Buddy Holly's "Little Baby."

a multicolored strobe light made the room look more like a Manny Maglio gentleman's club than a museum.

"Hello, Doc," Yigal Rosenblatt said as he emerged from the darkness. Twyla's husband was dressed in his usual black suit and yarmulke but also sported a long white satin sash that matched another draped over Twyla's right shoulder. Yigal's banner had bright-blue lettering that screamed *I DID IT* and his wife's hot pink message read *I LET HIM*.

I squinted past Yigal, trying to sort out what else was happening in the room. Helium-filled colored balloons shaped like condoms were everywhere, some tied to museum display cases and others set free to dot the ceiling. Women in skintight or skimpy outfits giggled through confetti and streamers that littered the floor.

"Are you the only male here?" I asked Yigal.

"Until now," the lawyer answered, obviously relieved that a couple of other Y chromosomes had showed up.

"Well congratulations to you both," Doc shouted over the music to Mr. and Mrs. Rosenblatt. "Unfortunately I do have to run off for a bit."

"Oh, Doc, you can't," wailed Twyla. "You'll miss the games."

"I'll be back," Doc promised and without even attempting an explanation, backed out of the museum.

"Oh, I wish he could have stayed," Twyla pouted for two seconds before doing a one-eighty. "But at least we have *you*, Bullet!"

"Yes," Yigal bobbed up and down. "We have you."

The music abruptly stopped and a woman wearing a body-hugging spandex dress cut low on top and high on the bottom stepped to the center of the room. It was Destiny, the stripper Twyla had met at Sinsations.

"Now, before we begin, I wanna thank my friend who's on the board of this here museum," Destiny said and held up a sheet of paper. "After some special kind of negotiatin', my friend figured out a way to get us some exceptions to what's called the meetin' and event policy."

Destiny pulled on a pair of mini-reading glasses and moved to within viewing distance of a cluster of candles.

"First off, there's not supposed to be no open flames anywhere in the room," she read.

Laughter cut in from all sides. My eyes were slowly adjusting to the dim surroundings and I was able to make out fifteen to twenty women most of whom were remarkably similar in body and dress.

"Second of all," Destiny continued reading, "there's to be no alcohol or illegal drugs to be consumed or brought onto the property."

The woman roared. "To Destiny's friend!" one of the ladies shouted and lifted her plastic glass high. The crowd eagerly toasted the unnamed trustee.

"Vodka punch," Yigal explained and handed me a container. "Orange and pineapple juice. And the maraschino cherries are kosher. I'm sure of it."

Ready for any kind of mood enhancement, I emptied a quarter of the cup. "What the hell, Yigal!" I coughed. "This is almost all vodka!"

"Somebody changed the recipe. Doubled the alcohol."

Which explained Destiny's slight stagger and the general tipsy tenor of the room.

"It's present time!" Destiny yelled and the women tittered with excitement. Everyone moved toward a long linen-covered table weighed down with an assortment of wrapped gifts and a three-tier cake decorated with grosgrain ribbon and candy facsimiles of old-fashioned diaper pins.

Destiny plucked a box with a huge purple bow from the pile. "From Blaze!" she announced and handed the box to Twyla who was now seated next to the table. With appropriate fanfare, Twyla ripped open the gift and held up a blouse.

"Are those –" I asked Yigal.

"I think they are. At least they look like they are."

"Nipples?"

Yigal moved in to take a closer look and then danced back to me with a nod. The polyester shirt had been digitally printed with more anatomically correct nipples than I could count.

"Oh, Blaze," one woman cried out. "That is so cool!"

"Isn't it?" replied a woman in a ruched tan dress with an exposed front zipper. "What's so amazing are the Velcro pops."

Blaze yanked the blouse away from Twyla and pulled two strategically placed tabs. "You just stick your things through these holes and the kid can suck in public. Nobody'll know what the hell is goin' on 'cause you can't tell the difference between the real and fake ones."

"Oh my God!" chirped Twyla. "That is so clever!"

"All right, let's keep movin'," Destiny instructed. "We got a crap load of stuff to unwrap here."

I drained my punch and asked Yigal if he could get me a refill. Before he returned, Twyla was handed the smallest box on the table.

"From Fantasia," Twyla read the tag taped to the gift and unwrapped a strange looking device shaped like a cork. The women clustered around the item, studying it like the alien object it was. "What is it?" Twyla finally asked.

A platinum blonde wearing a blouson top dress with a revealing V-neck sashayed to Twyla's side. "It's a water siren," she explained with a haughtiness that only comes if you show up with the most incredible baby shower gift on earth.

"What's that?" Twyla asked.

"Before you go to bed, you stick it up you know where and when your water breaks, a siren goes off," said Fantasia.

"No way!"

"If you don't like the siren, you can exchange it for one that plays a few notes from that Diana Ross song 'I'm Coming Out.'"

I emptied my second glass of vodka punch.

The women passed around the water siren like it was the Hope Diamond. Someone named Velvet asked the obvious question. "What happens when you pee?"

"No siren – it just whistles a little," Fantasia assured the group.

I gripped Yigal's shoulder and told him I needed to sit down. We found a dark corner and spent most of the next hour wishing we were somewhere else. Things continued to go downhill when Yigal won stinky doo. It was a scratch-and-sniff game where everyone got a card with a picture of a diapered infant's butt prominently displayed. Only one guest had a card that smelled like poop and as fate would have it, Yigal unleashed an odor that nearly made both of us pass out.

"You lucky sucker!" a woman who called herself Cherrypop said to Yigal. She unwrapped his prize – a large pacifier laced with rum that she slowly and seductively slipped into his mouth. Olive let out a sympathetic moan even though she looked almost as pathetic as Yigal. One of the guests had dressed the dog in silk panties with a warning sign embroidered at the crotch: *OCCUPIED – DO NOT ENTER.*

It was after nine when a guest named Sapphire suggested a change of venue. Why not move the party to Newport's *Private Parts*, one of Manny Maglio's adult clubs that was only a twenty-minute drive away? Apparently this was an inspired idea because fifteen minutes later, the group was heading out the Wright Museum door.

"Come with us, Bullet!" Twyla pleaded.

"Can't," I said. "Not supposed to leave the island."

"But you went off the island to see Uncle Manny."

"True. But we're supposed to pretend that never happened, remember?" I reminded Twyla.

Yigal tugged me aside while Twyla trudged off to the long white table to stack her gifts. "I don't want to go, Bullet. These women give me hives."

"You're the daddy so you don't have much choice."

"I know," Yigal groaned. "But if you came with me, it would make –"

"Wish I could," I cut in.

"Do this and we'll invite you to the bris. I promise. You can stand right next to the mohel."

Something to look forward to, watching the Rosenblatt's kid get his foreskin chopped off. "That would only work if you have a son. According to Twyla, you have no idea what will show up after her water siren goes off. It could be a Boaz. Or it could be a Tzufit."

Yigal shuttered with such intensity that his *I DID IT* sash jiggled to the floor ending up in messy heap. "There must be something –" he grasped for another straw that wasn't there.

"Sorry. Fact is, Doc and I are late for another appointment. We have to check in with our new landlord." At least, I hoped we had a new landlord. A quick call to Alyana would decide whether the professor and I would be spending the night with Saul Lipschitz or bedding down in Doc's Opel.

"Come on, Yiggy!" Twyla called out. "Bullet, we love you! Call us tomorrow and let's you, Doc, and us get together."

The Rosenblatts marched off, Twyla in the lead and her forlorn, laden-down caboose, carrying a high tower of mostly off-color presents.

I removed Olive's underwear that Twyla wisely left behind and tossed the panties on the floor. Normally I don't litter but there was so much wreckage left behind in the Sydney L. Wright Museum that adding to the trash didn't seem to matter.

The poodle and I walked back to the library's front hall where Miriam Constable Reis had confronted us. There was no sign of Miriam or Doc Waters.

"Strange," I muttered to Olive. The dog woofed and tipped her muzzle to the floor. A minute later, we came to a halt outside the closed door of what appeared to be a small meeting room. At that instant, I heard the scream.

"Oh, my Jesus!" a woman's shriek pierced the door.

Three cups of double-strength vodka punch had thoroughly drowned my ability to think clearly. A logical reaction would have been to call 911 and stay on the sidelines until Lieutenant Ravenel and his posse arrived to handle matters. But waiting could mean still another homicide on Conanicut Island and semi-intoxicated or not, I wasn't about to let that happen.

I inhaled a deep breath and drove my shoulder into the door. It was unlocked but barricaded by three boxes of hardcover books. The door cracked open just wide enough for Olive and me to squeeze in.

"Good God in Heaven!" I yelled.

"What the hell?" Doc Waters screeched as he pulled back from Miriam Reis who was spread out on an oak table like one of Mr. Cronin's frogs.

"Doc, what are you doing?" I shouted.

"What does it *look* like I'm doing!" the professor roared back while desperately looking for whatever discarded clothing he could find to cover his manhood.

Miriam propped herself up, her naked torso shivering in shock. "Oh, noooo –" she wailed softly. Olive returned a sympathetic whine then began panting.

"Bullet, please!" Doc implored. "Give us some privacy. We need to dress."

"What?" The whole scene turned me catatonic. I couldn't move. It wasn't just the appalling sight of two old nudes, but the story their clothing told. Doc's pants, shirt, and underwear were thrown about the room in abandon. Miriam's gray suit was folded neatly on a chair with her bra and granny panties placed carefully to the side. The air reeked of Estée Lauder and sweat.

"Bullet!" Doc bellowed and I snapped out of my stupor. Olive and I backed out of the room and shut the door.

Ten minutes later, Miriam Reis made an appearance. Fully dressed, she marched past the poodle and me without saying a word. However, our eyes did meet long enough for me to catch a look of embarrassment and humiliation mixed with – no question about it – a lingering semblance of euphoria.

Doc Waters stumbled through the door a minute later, his hunched posture back in place, his face reddened, and his white hair damp and disheveled.

"Well, what are waiting for?" the professor asked as if nothing out of the ordinary had occurred. "Let's go meet Saul Lipschitz."

– Chapter 17 –

"She's married!" I screeched as the Opel headed toward Saul Lipschitz's house on Melrose Avenue. We were definitely booked for a week at the Lipschitz residence but with conditions. Saul wanted us in our rooms before ten thirty p.m., which was his bedtime. That gave us thirty minutes.

"Sort of," Doc countered.

"What do you mean sort of? She is or she isn't."

"Miriam's husband has Alzheimer's. Been zonked out for four years."

"But Doc, even so. I mean you just met the lady."

"Oh, no," the professor corrected. "I knew her back when. We were quite attracted to one another but never consummated our relationship."

"It's a half century later! And out of the blue the two of you decide to do the dirty deed in some dusty alcove of the Philharmonic Library?"

"Philomenian Library," Doc said. "Philomenian is a kind of debating and cultural society. Been around since the mid-eighteen hundreds. And so what if it took Miriam and I a few decades to do what we've long wanted to do. You remember the famous Einstein quote, don't you?"

I looked out the Opel passenger-side window and said nothing. It was my way of waving a white flag.

"'The only reason for time is so that everything doesn't happen at once,' is what Einstein said. The wait was long but well worth it. Well worth it indeed."

We drove too fast through a maze of narrow streets until we found a modest clapboard ranch house that matched Saul Lipschitz's address.

At ten twenty five, Doc parked and we unfolded ourselves from the cramped car.

"I just never thought of you as someone who was into women just for the sex." The buck-naked image of Miriam Constable Reis was stuck in my head, which probably accounted for why I couldn't stop talking about the lady.

"Oh, I could never enjoy sex if a woman wasn't cerebral," Doc said as we trekked toward the front door of the Lipschitz residence. A forty-watt light cast a dull yellow cone over the entryway. It reminded me of the middle bulb of a traffic light. The one that warns: caution.

"Cerebral?"

"Yes."

"So Miriam is cerebral."

"Very."

"In what way?"

"She's a first-class researcher and her deductive reasoning is incredible. In fact, after I told her what you were looking for, it took her less than a half hour to come up with an answer."

I dropped my suitcase. "Excuse me?"

"The deed to Dutch Island. She told me where it is."

Part III

– Chapter 18 –

The ten-by-twelve guest room was tight with mismatched furniture. Two scratched and chipped bedside tables looked older than they probably were, standing next to a modern twin-size bed. A large mahogany bureau blocked a quarter of the room's only window that faced west toward Dutch Harbor. Dominating what little space remained was a worn suede rocker recliner now occupied by Doc Waters.

"What the hell?" I sputtered trying to shake myself out of what had been seven hours of deep sleep.

The professor yawned and pulled the recliner to a ninety-degree angle. "Sorry, Bullet. Didn't mean to startle you."

"What – what are you doing here?" I complained and reached for my watch. Seven thirty a.m. "Why aren't you in your own room?"

Saul Lipschitz had assigned us each an equal-sized guest room separated by a jack-and-jill bathroom. The last memory I had before going unconscious was Doc dragging his duffel bag into his designated sleeping area.

"Had to get out of there," the professor explained. "I was attacked."

"Attacked? What are you talking about, Doc?"

"The weasel. Two or three in the morning, the thing came through a hole in the door, crawled over my feet and headed north. Scared the shit out of me."

"You couldn't have just thrown it out?"

"You know anything about ferrets, Bullet?"

"Not really," I admitted.

"Neither do I. But I went to bed with one, which makes me more of an expert than you. And this much I do know. It's got teeth. You don't go throwing around anything with teeth."

I rubbed my eyes wondering if this was reality or the tail end of a bad dream when Saul Lipschitz pounded on my door.

"What's goin' on in there?" Saul shouted.

"Uh, just getting ready to start the day." I sounded like a Cheerio commercial.

"Alyana Genesee," Saul said after a pause. "She didn't tell me you was happy boys."

"We are?" I asked as Doc disappeared into the bathroom connecting our two guest rooms.

"Don't favor what happy boys do," continued Saul.

"Oh, you mean gay."

"I mean this here arrangement's not gonna work out. I don't favor happy boys."

I pulled myself out of bed and cracked open the door. "We're not happy boys, Mr. Lipschitz," I said. "Not that we care if other boys are happy, but –" I peered into the hallway ready to continue rebutting Saul's sexual orientation assumption. Our landlord had disappeared.

A half hour later, the professor and I wandered into the kitchen. Saul was seated at a bistro kitchen table with Ellie Weasel at his feet. Both were working on generous servings of over-cooked scrambled eggs.

"Mr. Lipschitz, we need to talk," I began.

"No need," Saul responded without looking at either the professor or me. "You boys pack up and leave me be."

I pulled a beat-up maple chair to the table and sat. Ellie Weasel seemed oblivious to me but interrupted her eating long enough to make eye contact with Doc.

"Here's what happened last night," I said to Saul. "Somehow, your ferret got into Doc Waters' room and nearly gave him a heart attack. Doc didn't know what else to do other than protect himself by coming into my room."

Saul scratched a three-day-old beard and glanced at his pet. Ellie made a clucking noise and jammed her dark-masked face back into the plate of eggs.

"What are you sayin'? You're not happy boys?"

I shook my head. "I'm not happy, Mr. Lipschitz."

"And him?" Saul motioned to Doc.

"Definitely not a happy boy."

Saul's crinkled body loosened up and he looked at me for the first time since I strolled into the kitchen. "Shoulda told me what happened right off."

"How about you shoulda told *me* there's a hole my bedroom door," Doc joined the conversation with a growl. "And that your muskrat was a damned pervert."

Saul uncoiled his skinny body and stood. He was short, no more than five foot six, I guessed. Bristles of gray hair ran in a horseshoe pattern from one huge ear to another. His brown corduroy pants were spotted with stains as was his cotton long-sleeved shirt. "Ain't no muskrat!" Saul pointed to Ellie.

"Doesn't matter what it is," Doc volleyed back. "That thing was all over my legs and was on a beeline for my love muscle."

Saul pushed his thick-rimmed glasses up his hooked nose and took two steps toward the professor. I jumped between the two before they started whacking each other with their Medicare cards.

"Look," I said. "This is all a misunderstanding. Maybe you could stop up the hole in the door to Doc's room, Mr. Lipschitz."

"Ellie's favorite room," Saul said, looking affectionately at the ferret. "Will be hard keeping her on the outside."

"It'll be just for a few days," I reminded the old man. "Alyana said you could use the week's rent."

Saul considered the proposition and shrugged his approval. "Stay away from my ferret," Saul said to Doc.

"Don't worry about that," the professor answered. "You tell your weasel to keep its distance, especially from my noodle."

"And don't go feedin' Ellie no raisins," Saul ordered.

Doc's face scrunched into a hairy white ball. "What?"

"You don't know shit about ferrets. They ain't supposed to eat raisins."

"I haven't been near a raisin in forty years, you old fart."

Saul looked genuinely surprised. "You don't like raisins?"

"No," Doc answered.

"So you didn't have none on you last night?"

"No."

"Huh," Saul scratched his chin and gave the ferret an inquisitive look. "Thought Ellie had a thing for you because of raisins. Must be somethin' else."

Ellie Weasel pulled her slender snout away from her plate of eggs, looked up at Doc, and clucked.

"Oh, God," Doc whispered.

The tension stayed locked in the kitchen until I asked Saul if we might inconvenience him for a cup of coffee. Surprisingly, the old man turned hospitable and grabbed a pair of grimy mugs that he filled with brew from an ancient metal coffeepot. A half hour later, emotions leveled off and we were all on a first name basis. Except for Doc Waters and Ellie Weasel.

"You had two calls this morning," Saul said to me.

"Here? Somebody called your number asking for me?" I asked.

"Alyana was one. The other was from a fella in New York named Kook or Koop or Kool. Whatever. Got his number written down. Told me he didn't like that you keep your cell phone turned off."

I excused myself and returned to my room and phoned Doug Kool's office, expecting to get dumped into voice mail. It wasn't quite nine o'clock and Doug wasn't the type to punch in early. I was surprised when Doug's admin Angie picked up.

"What do you want first – the good news or the bad?" Angie asked.

"It's early. Start with the good."

"Mrs. O'Connor got her foot caught in a people mover at the Charles de Gaulle Airport. She's in a Paris hospital getting screws put in her ankle."

"That can't be fun. So that means she's not on her way back to Rhode Island?"

"Definitely not," Angie confirmed. "Neither is her fast-food hubby. Probably will be stuck in France for several more days."

"Too bad I didn't know about this yesterday. I could have stayed put at the O'Connor house."

"It's called premature evacuation."

I had to laugh. "You're hilarious, Angie."

"Yeah, well you won't be chuckling at the bad news."

"Which is?"

"My boss decided to take a road trip. To Rhode Island. He's going to take your place at the O'Connor's residence."

"Oh, no!"

"Oh yes. And the way he drives, it will be a short trip. The O'Connors made it crystal clear that he's to mind the store until they get back. And the standing order is to keep you away from their house and their dog."

"Doug's supposed to take care of the poodle? The only dog he likes is one that comes with mustard and a bun."

"No. Dr. Alyana Genesee, the next-door neighbor, gets the pooch. Doug called her earlier this morning. She agreed to keep the dog for the duration."

I thanked Angie and quickly dialed Alyana. I caught her as she was walking into her office.

"I just talked to Doug Kool's assistant and she told me –"

Alyana stopped me cold. "Rick, did you watch the news this morning?"

"What? No." I didn't take time to explain I was too busy playing referee to a pair of grizzled old men and a ferret.

"Yves Benoit is dead."

"*What?*"

"He was killed in a car accident somewhere near Tampa. I called Aurélie a few minutes ago. She's devastated."

I was too stunned to react.

146

"It was absolutely horrific, Rick. The car caught on fire and exploded. Yves was burned beyond recognition."

"Good God."

"Something else Aurélie told me," Alyana went on. "Michael Ravenel called her late last night. He said he wanted to talk to Yves, but wouldn't get into specifics. Then the Florida State Police called and told her Yves was dead."

We talked a few minutes more. I skipped over the ferret foray as well as the much bigger revelation – that Doc Waters seduced the town's librarian and may have discovered the whereabouts of the Dutch Island deed. Alyana suggested we touch base around dinnertime, after she got acquainted with her new neighbor Douglas Kool.

I returned to the kitchen where Doc and Saul were engaged in a friendly conversation. Apparently the professor knew something about Rudolph Lipschitz, a famous mathematician known for a confusing concept called a continuous function. That bit of trivia instantly converted Saul from adversary to admirer. Ellie Weasel seemed even more in tune with Doc Waters studying him with a milky look that reminded me just a tad of the glint in Miriam Reis's eyes last night.

"Doc, I need a ride to the Jamestown police station."

We excused ourselves and boarded the Opel for a quick cross-island trip to visit Lieutenant Ravenel.

"How did this happen?" I asked as we drove. "People have been digging around for the Dutch Island deed for a long time. A half hour of sweet talk and Miriam Reis suddenly knows where to hit the jackpot?"

"It was all a matter of guiding her in the right direction," said Doc.

I bet.

The professor continued. "Miriam has access to a ton of historical files that are being sorted through."

"Sorted through?"

"Brown University is doing a study of southern New England from the sixteen hundreds through the nineteenth century. A bunch of postgrad students have been picking apart old Conanicut Island records for the past six months."

"So a Brown researcher could reach the same conclusion as Miriam," I speculated.

"Absolutely."

"Which means others could get their hands on the same information we have now."

"And are likely to do so very soon," Doc agreed. "Tiny Templeton's already been sniffing around the Wright Museum and the Jamestown Historical Society according to Miriam."

"Tiny Templeton?"

"Three hundred pounds of don't stop until you find what you're looking for. Used to be big in the electronic surveillance world, but now spends most of his time doing records research. I hate his fat ass but have to admit he's good at what he does."

The Opel turned into the now all-too-familiar Jamestown Police Department parking lot. "Why would Tiny be interested in the deed?"

"Because somebody's paying him," said Doc. "He'll whore for just about anyone."

"Who's cutting him a check?"

Doc shrugged. "Don't know. Manny Maglio. Indians. Caleb Mason. Mohammad al-Talal. A dozen others. Take your pick."

It was all hunch that Lieutenant Ravenel would be on duty this morning. Jamestown's body count had become a headline-grabbing bonanza for the papers, television, and radio outlets throughout New England. So it was predictable Ravenel would be logging as many hours as he could to show the horde of news people the state police were on top of the case. I found the lieutenant slumped in an office chair, his eyes heavy, and exhaustion pulling his mouth into a frown.

"If you can spare a few minutes, I'd like to take a walk," I said.

"A walk?"

Yes. Anywhere outside this building."

A couple of uniformed cops overheard the exchange and looked surprised when Ravenel immediately stood and followed me toward the station door. On the way, Doc Waters intercepted us and asked the lieutenant if there was an Internet-connected computer he could use. The professor got permission to Google while Ravenel and I took our morning stroll.

"You called Yves Benoit's wife last night," I said leading us across the street to the grassy perimeter of Jamestown's only golf course.

"Word gets around."

"You wanted to question Yves. Why?"

Ravenel hesitated with a response. Then he said, "We got a call from DEA yesterday afternoon. Seems our local French chef was cooking more than escargot and confits."

"Drugs?" I guessed.

"Methamphetamine, mostly."

"Was he a serious player?"

"Very," Ravenel answered. "He was carrying phenylacetone and methylamine when his van hit a tree somewhere around Tampa. The chemicals caught fire and released a phosphine gas. Then *boom*. The Florida cops picked up pieces of Benoit fifty yards from where the van exploded. A couple of false teeth and a wedding ring are about the only things that didn't get incinerated."

To the right of the nine-hole golf course clubhouse, an elderly man hacked a ball off the first tee and sent it no more than ten yards down the fairway. He was too far away for me to decipher the profanity.

"How'd you know about my call to Aurélie Benoit?" Ravenel asked.

"Alyana Genesee. She phoned Aurélie after Yves made the morning news."

"I see," the lieutenant nodded quickly and smiled. Connecting the romantic dots between Alyana and me wasn't difficult. "We're trying to figure out how involved Aurélie might have been with her husband's side job. It's possible she knew little or nothing. On the other hand, she had to know Yves was spending a lot more money than the restaurant was pulling in."

"Drug trafficking filled the gap?"

"Some of it. Apparently our boy leaves behind a few IOUs past due for payment. Expenses go up when you're into high-stakes poker, not to mention more than a couple pricey hookers."

"So I should thank the DEA for getting you to dump the idiotic idea that Alyana had somebody plaster J. D. Mason's remains on the grille of my Buick."

Ravenel shrugged. "In my world, everyone's guilty until proven innocent."

"Yeah, well, in this case the DEA is the jury and it's in with a verdict. Alyana Genesee innocent – Yves Benoit guilty."

"I suspect you're right. According to the feds, Yves was getting a pile of cash each month over and above what he collected from his drug business. We think he was on retainer to handle certain odd jobs. Probably one of which was washing your car with Mason's cranial fluid."

"So Yves squished J. D.'s head and then – "

"No, he was strictly a post-mortem player. Yves was elbow deep in quiche Lorraine when Mason was murdered."

"Then whoever did the killing mops up J. D.'s brain matter, brings it to Yves and tells him on his next cigarette break, take a couple of minutes to splatter the front of my car."

"That's the theory. We think the killer didn't want to risk being seen anywhere near that piece of crap you drive. Could be he or she is a local and would be too easily recognized. Or maybe the perp is an out-of-towner who is so *not* Jamestown that he would have murder suspect written all over him."

"Like an Arab," I said.

"Or one of Manny Maglio's greaseballs."

I pulled to a halt and faced Ravenel. "What?

"Think about it. Drugs. A monthly bag of bucks for services rendered – like supervising William Nonesuch, Tommy Caddefeld, and Charles Kenyon. Has all the earmarks of organized crime."

"You've got it wrong. Manny's into adult entertainment with a smattering of prostitution and loan sharking."

Ravenel smiled again. "I think you underestimate the scope of Maglio's business."

I wanted to argue but knew Ravenel's supposition might be right. I remembered Manny's comment about hiring contractors and how some of those free agents went over the line. I knew Maglio wanted the Dutch Island deed. Without it, his business could take a major hit. But signing death warrants for Harold and J. D. Mason and maybe even for Lloyd Noka? No, I doubted Maglio would go that far.

"Something else makes all this smell like the mob," Ravenel kept talking.

"Yves Benoit's so-called accident?"

"Exactly. Which I'm guessing is why you wanted a private chat this morning."

"You're right," I said, not at all surprised the lieutenant was aware of my motive. "If we were having this conversation inside the Jamestown Police Station, we might as well be on CNN. The place is an open mic."

"I told you before. I know we have a leak in the department."

"More like a gusher."

"We're working on getting it plugged. In the meantime, I'm walking around a golf course waiting to hear what you have to say."

"Yves's death is too much of a coincidence."

Ravenel locked his huge hands behind his back and continued walking. "We're on the same page. Whoever was bankrolling Benoit may have gotten word the DEA was closing in. If Yves had been nailed with a major drug charge, he might have become a little too talkative."

"Problem solved when his car disintegrates."

"If Yves was murdered, two other people could be next in line." We did an about-face and began retracing our steps back to the police headquarters. "Two others?"

"Caleb Mason is top on the list. For whatever reason, there seems to be an open season on the Mason family. Since he's the only one left, Caleb's probably in the crosshairs. Plus he's not exactly the lovable kind. There wouldn't be a lot of weeping if he went down."

"So you're using Rhode Islander tax dollars to give Caleb round-the-clock protection?"

"No. He doesn't want it and doesn't need it. He beefed up his own security team, and I can't say I blame him given the porous condition of Jamestown's cop corps."

"Who's number two on your list?"

"Obvious isn't it? You, Bullet."

I anticipated the answer, but having Ravenel slap a target on my back gave me a chill. "No, it's not obvious. I'm just a vacationer trying to mind his own business."

We crossed Conanicus Road at the same time a foursome closed in on the ninth hole just behind us. I couldn't block out a tinge of annoyance that there were people on this island recreating while I was spending my vacation tripping over dead people, proclaiming my innocence, and staying one step ahead of a killer.

"You've got a knack for being in places where people looking for the Dutch Island deed don't want you. Like, for instance, having your professor friend rifle through records at the town library last night."

Oh, God. What else did Ravenel know about last night? Half of Jamestown probably heard Miriam Reis's orgasmic screaming. The more pertinent question: did Ravenel or anyone else know Doc Waters had uncovered the whereabouts of the missing deed?

"Just take me off your persons-of-interest list and I'll fade into obscurity," I promised.

"Not going to happen," said Ravenel. "You're still the best piece of fresh bait I have. You're going to continue to float around and help me draw the shark to the surface. Just do what you do naturally, Bullet. You're as good as chum on the water, my friend. Chum on the water."

– Chapter 19 –

"You know what ferrets and skunks have in common?" Doc asked as we drove away from the Jamestown Police Station. "Scent glands next to their poop chutes."

"Jesus, Doc, is that what you were doing?" I asked. "Using Ravenel's computer to Google animal anuses?"

"Listen, there's something about Ellie Weasel that gives me the heebie-jeebies. It's the way the thing looks at me. So big deal. I used a half hour of the state of Rhode Island's Internet time to do a quick study on *Mustela putorius furo* – otherwise known as your sometimes overly friendly ferret."

The professor ran a hand through his thick white mane and navigated the Opel toward the West side of the island. Traffic was light almost as if Jamestown was on hold, bracing for another punch to its serenity.

"Relax, Doc. Saul said he'd patch the hole in your door. Nothing's going to be touching your unit tonight." With the possible exception of Miriam Reis, I muttered to myself.

The professor braked his car in front of the ranch house. "I'm not just talking about how Ellie thinks of me as a boy toy. The ferret's also got a bad case of feminine odor. And don't tell me you haven't noticed, Bullet. Ellie stinks. Could be the anal situation or could be that she craps in every corner of the house."

I bit my lip. "Doc – enough about the ferret. Can we move on? Let's do a replay of how you and Miriam figured out where the Dutch Island deed is parked."

"Again?"

"Yeah, again." I wanted to be certain Doc's coital escapade hadn't rattled his brain.

"The island was originally called Quentenis. The Dutch West India Company set up a trading post on the island in the early sixteen hundreds. Hence the name change."

"So it was Dutch territory back in the day."

"A short day. The Dutch didn't find much use for the place and it reverted back to the Indians after about twenty years."

"Then what?"

"In 1657, a tribal leader named Cashanaquont was paid one hundred pounds sterling and wampum for both Conanicut and Dutch Islands. Over a hundred colonists invested in the deal but there were two men at the front of the line. William Coddington and Benedict Arnold."

"Benedict Arnold the traitor?"

"Nope. The traitor's grandfather who happened to have the same name."

"Okay. So now we have a bunch of colonists who are the owners."

Doc shut off the Opel's ignition. "Oh, look at that." The professor's eyes glazed and he pointed to a black BMW parked in front of Saul's house.

"Stay focused, Doc."

"Hard to do when I'm staring at the second most expensive car BMW makes. The Alpina B7. Has a sticker price north of a hundred K."

I scanned the car thinking it looked familiar. But luxury vehicles rarely got stuck in my memory bank so I didn't waste energy trying to recall where I had seen the BMW. Frankly, the only car of interest to me was my Buick that was undergoing invasive exploratory surgery at a state police chop shop.

"Let's get back to Dutch Island."

"Huh?" the professor blinked away from the Alpina's aerodynamically correct rear spoiler. "You're so not a car person."

"It's a curse. More about the island please."

"Jamestown and Dutch Islands were eventually carved into parcels and handed over to investors. Acreage changed hands over the years. But the last deed of record shows a transaction that gave ownership of the island, or at least an important part of the island, to a man named Daniel Weeden."

"And this is the deed everyone wants?"

"Seems to be. It's dated 1743 and from everything we can find, it was never legally superseded by anything that's happened on that island since."

I pictured the triangular-shaped bump of land sticking out of Narragansett Bay a mile to the west of Jamestown's shoreline. It was difficult to envision the island as anything more than a poison ivy-covered impediment to the

Narragansett's ever-shifting tidal waters. "Just exactly what did happen on that island since 1743?"

"Quite a bit actually," said Doc. "A lighthouse was built on the southern tip. Somebody set up a fish oil business that went bust. Off and on, the land was used for sheep grazing. But nothing tops what happened when the government showed up on the island in 1863."

"Enlighten me."

"It was turned into a training camp for the 14th Rhode Island Heavy Artillery, which just so happened to be a regiment of black soldiers."

"You're sure about that?"

"Positive. Blacks were brought to the island from all over the north. Once they were battle ready, at least three batteries of the 14th Regiment were sent south to fight the Confederacy."

Doc's historical fragments constantly amazed me. "Keep going."

"After Lee surrendered at Appomattox, the feds decided to stay on to the island. In 1898, the Spanish-American War broke out and the government updated the old Civil War fortification. Named it Fort Greble."

"A fort on an island that small?"

"Look hard enough and you'll find remnants. But more obvious would be the leftovers from the First World War when a few Rhode Island National Guard companies were stationed on the island to defend the entrance of the Bay."

"After that?"

"Once the U.S. built battleships that had more firepower than the island's guns, the place lost its strategic usefulness."

"So the military left?"

"Yup. In 1958, Dutch Island went on a government surplus list and was handed over to the state of Rhode Island."

"Then along came Harold Mason and his sons who talked the state into a land switch."

"With the help of Mohammad al-Talal," Doc added.

"All these transactions are documented?"

"Everything but the disposition of Daniel Weeden's property. Like I said, there's no record of a property sale or any order of eminent domain. What Miriam did find, though, was an odd notation. Seems all rights of ownership are restricted to Daniel Weeden or his heirs and that ownership can only be validated by the original deed."

"So the deed isn't worth squat unless the original and one of Daniel's descendents can be found."

"That's about it."

"Even if somebody could prove they're related to Daniel, showing up with the deed probably wouldn't mean much. I've been told such a claim wouldn't stand up to a legal challenge."

Doc shrugged. "Probably a moot point. My guess is the whole deal won't ever get argued legally."

"Why?"

"Money. Whoever has the deed marches up to al-Talal and says his problem will go away if he parts with a couple of million. That's loose change for the Arab."

"Could happen, I suppose. Or maybe the deed's owner is more interested in keeping a mosque off Dutch Island than adding a few zeros to his bank balance."

"Yeah, and maybe Rhode Islanders will stop eating clam chowda."

"Not everyone thinks money is the high card," I said. Doc gave me his you-should-know look. "Has Miriam uncovered any Weedens who could be candidates?"

"Possibly. She wants to dig deeper before feeding me a name. I might hear from her later today."

We paused outside Saul's house. Even with the front door shut, the distinctive odor of Ellie Weasel was already obvious.

"William Nonesuch and his band of banditos must have figured out al-Talal would be good for a ton of money if they got their hands on the deed," I guessed.

"If not Nonesuch and company then their manager, Yves Benoit. Of course, the dearly departed French chef is now out of the running."

Saul Lipschitz opened the front door. Ellie Weasel was at his side, the ferret propped up on her hind legs with her front paws partially crossed. She looked like an irritated housewife, her body language matching Saul's very cranky welcome.

"Where the hell you been?" Saul asked.

Doc and I traded confused looks.

"This dandy here has been waitin' for you for more than a half hour." Saul jerked his head toward the small living room. From where I was standing, I could only see a pair of Prada men's shoes worth more than my Buick. No doubt about it – Dr. Douglas Kool was on the scene.

"What a surprise!" I said strolling into the house. My fake greeting did nothing to soften Doug's aggravated expression.

"You're new friend, Alyana Genesee, told me you'd be here," Doug began. "You and I need to – what the *hell*, Bullet!" My Manhattan friend caught his first glimpse of the professor and gasped. "*One Nut Waters*? Good God, are you crazy? You've got *him* involved in this mess?"

Doug wasn't one of Doc Waters' fans nor, for that matter, of any of the Gateway's residents past or present. For someone in Doug's position, getting too close to riffraff was not just unseemly, it was also a career hazard. My longtime friend made his living by grazing with the elite and he worked tirelessly to keep his image untainted. That meant keeping the underclass at arm's length.

"You drive the BMW?" Doc asked totally ignoring the fact that Dr. Kool had not even offered him a hello.

"Yeah," Doug admitted, clearly not pleased about being forced into a conversation with Doc.

"Alpina B760Li, right? Got the 6-liter with the V-12?"

Doug's metamorphosis was staggering. "You know the car?"

"I dream about that car. Best yaw rate and engine torque going."

Doug's expression went from hostile to affable in a fraction of a second. "Five hundred thirty-five horses."

Doc smacked his lips. "I know. I know. Twin turbo with four overhead camshafts. Worth every penny of the hundred twenty-five grand sticker price."

"Hundred forty with accessories."

I couldn't help jumping in. "*Hundred forty?* What the hell, Doug! You're a *fund-raiser*. Of all those donations you hustle, how much are you stuffing in your pocket?"

"It's an art, and I get paid well because I'm good at what I do," Doug said defensively.

Doc could care less about how much Doug scraped off the top of each charitable gift he solicited. What mattered was the BMW parked outside. "Zero to sixty – how fast? Under five seconds?"

"Four point five."

"Oh, my God!" Doc exclaimed and Doug grinned. Probably his first smile in days, I thought.

"Love to listen to more car talk," I said. "But, Doc, you and I have business to tend to."

Doug grimaced and yanked me into Saul's kitchen for a private chat. "You're not going to tend to anything until you tell me what the hell is happening!" he snarled.

"I'll tell you what's happening. I got bumped out of my bayside vacation home by a New York fund-raiser who drives a car that costs more than the Gateway Men's Shelter."

"Damnit, Bullet! Ken O'Connor's going to deep-fat fry my manjigglies because of what you've done."

Why? I've vacated his property, and I'm not dog-sitting his poodle. So what's his problem?"

"His *problem* is that he's getting calls from every newspaper and TV station in New England about why he let a murder suspect hole up in his goddamned estate!"

I was ready with a comeback about how Doug was a fair-weather pal more interested in scoring points with the high and mighty than standing up for a friend – a friend he *knew* was guilty of nothing more than being a magnet for bad karma. My tirade never made it off the launch pad.

HKKREEK

The shriek was shrill, alienlike. Doug and I charged back into the living room and found Doc Waters kneeling over Saul Lipschitz who lay crumpled on a worn braided rug. Ellie Weasel was on her haunches, her four canines spiking out of her open mouth.

HKKREEK

Saul clawed at his chest. "*Mein zeit*," he muttered. "*Mein zeit.*"

"What's he saying?" I asked Doc. If anyone could do the translation, it was the professor.

"Yiddish, I think," Doc said. "Something about time. *My time*, I think."

"And no *rozshinke*," Saul wheezed. "No *rozchinke!*"

Doc leaned forward. "I – I don't know that much Yiddish. I don't understand what you're saying."

"*Rozchinke!*" Saul rasped. "No *raisins*, you shmuck! Don't feed her raisins!"

Ellie cried out again. Her screech gave way to a mournful wail.

"Damn!" Doug cursed. "He's not dying, is he? Tell me he's not dying!"

Saul hoisted his right hand, grasped Doc's shirt, and pulled the professor's face close to his. "Ellie – take her. You hear me? You take Ellie!"

"What?" Doc's eyes widened. He tried pulling away but Saul had the professor in a death grip

"No one else," Saul whispered. "Got no one left. Ellie's got some kinda connection to you. No raisins. Just take care of her and you'll have the best *blik*, good *masl*."

"Oh no, no, no. I'm not into ferrets."

"Treat her bad and I'll *schiltn* you from the grave."

Doc's face reddened. He yanked hard at Saul's fingers but they were locked tight on the professor's secondhand Jersey polo.

Ellie lowered herself to all fours as her master sucked in his last breath. The ferret slowly crawled onto Saul's body and curled herself on his chest.

Doug sank into a tattered armchair and stared at the motionless body. "Oh, Mother of God. Is he – is he dead? *Is he dead?*"

Doc nodded and finally pulled himself free from Saul's grasp. The professor probed Saul's carotid for a pulse. Nothing.

"I've never seen anybody die before," Doug wheezed and lowered his head between his knees. "I think I'm going to faint."

"Myocardial infarction," Doc pronounced as he put a hand on the dead man's chest to double-check for any cardiac activity. Ellie Weasel moaned and gently put a paw over Doc's fingers.

"Oh, God," Doug moaned.

"Yeah, he's gone," Doc said calmly. Death was nothing new to the professor. "Definitely a heart attack."

Doug stood, staggered to the Lipshitz bathroom, and threw up.

"This is unbelievable," I said to Doc. "If Ravenel finds me within a half mile of another corpse –"

Doc shrugged. "Natural cause. Nobody can hang this one on you."

"Don't bet on it." I could see the future and it looked like another marathon session with Lieutenant Ravenel and company.

"Then let's not be here," Doc said.

"What?"

"Let Kool handle this one. He calls 911 and waits around for the EMT team. While he's taking care of business here, you and I will be somewhere else. Like the Jamestown library, for instance." The prospect of another rendezvous with Miriam Constable Reis pulled Doc's mouth into a smile.

"Doug," I said to my New York friend when he stumbled back into the living room, "you're going to have to handle this."

Doug Kool gagged again and stared at me. His man-tanned face had turned almost as white as Saul Lipschitz's lifeless mug. "What?"

"Call the police. Tell them you and Saul were having a chat when he dropped dead."

"Are you *crazy?*" Doug stammered.

"Here's the situation," I explained. "If I'm in this house when the cops show up, Saul's death is ruled suspicious. You, Doc, me and even the ferret get hauled in for questioning. That's when your name gets tarred with the same brush that's being used to work me over. You want that?"

"But I –"

"Tell the cops you came here looking for me," I went on. "While you and Saul were talking, he keeled over. You did a few minutes of CPR but couldn't bring him back."

"I can't –"

"Yeah, you can. You're an upstanding citizen who did his best to save an old man."

The room went quiet for a few seconds. Ellie uncurled her twenty inches of body and tail and nuzzled Doc's leg. Doug used the arm of his Brunello-Cucinelli cashmere Henley sweater to swab his brow.

"Jesus, Bullet!" Doug wailed.

"Just call 911," I ordered and motioned Doc to head for the front door. The professor took a step and Ellie clamped on to his pant leg.

"Ah, shit!" Doc whined. The ferret wrapped its stubby legs around the professor's limb and clucked.

"Pick her up and let's go," I ordered.

"I'm not touching that thing!"

I gently tugged Ellie free from the professor's pant leg and placed the ferret in Doc's arm. Ellie cuddled against the chest of her newly appointed guardian. I opened the front door and pushed Doc Waters and friend toward the Opel.

We were half way to the Jamestown library when Doc's cell rang. The professor stopped the car and carefully maneuvered Ellie's tail away from the phone's holster.

"That was Miriam," Doc said after finishing the brief call.

"And?"

"She's ninety nine percent sure who has the original Dutch Island deed."

I blinked. Mohammad al-Talal and Manny Maglio were lifting every rock in Jamestown trying to find the deed. And in less than twenty-four hours, a librarian strikes gold? It seemed implausible. "Who?"

"A married couple on the other side of the bay. Live in a town called Portsmouth."

"Does Miriam have an address? Phone number?"

"Yes and then some. She knows the people."

"She *knows* them?"

"As do a lot of others around here," Doc said. "From what Miriam says, they're a pretty incredible pair. Oh, and by the way, guess who else knows them?"

"Who?"

"Your new inamorato." Doc said. "Alyana Genesee."

– Chapter 20 –

A row of fetterbush evergreens bordered a small clearing directly across the road from Alyana Genesee's front yard. Doc Waters stood dead center in the small open patch of land, a faint afternoon breeze rustling his disheveled white hair. Ellie Weasel had wrapped herself around Doc's left leg and was now staring defiantly at the champion poodle Olive parked twenty feet away in a sit-stay.

"You sure about this?" Doc called out.

Alyana smiled and tugged gently on Olive's leather leash. The dog rose to all fours and began a slow walk toward the ferret. "The trick is to let them get to know each other on neutral ground," Alyana said assuredly. "Once that happens, things will work out fine."

Doc kneeled and stroked Ellie as she shivered in anticipation. Alyana had explained that Olive's strong prey drive would be easier to control if the dog were introduced to the ferret someplace other than on territory the poodle considered her own. The professor wasn't totally sold. He maneuvered himself between the two animals.

"For a ferret bigot, you've come a long way, Doc," I chuckled.

"Don't mistake what's going on here," Doc said defensively. "I'm no weasel lover. I just don't want to end up in court on animal cruelty charge."

"Whatever you say," I laughed louder as the professor continued petting Ellie's long, slender body.

Alayana guided Olive to the ferret's side. The usual animal-to-animal naso-genital greeting played out for nearly a minute. Then Ellie relaxed, the quiver in her small mouth no longer evident. Olive settled into a sitting position only a few inches from her new acquaintance.

"The start of a new friendship," Alyana predicted and unclipped the leash from Olive's collar.

Doc pulled Ellie closer and gave Olive a nervous glance. "Maybe you shouldn't cut that puppy loose until we're sure where things stand."

"That would be a smart move if we were dealing with a different dog," Alyana said. "With Olive, it's a lesson learned. She's not going to bother your pet."

"She's not my pet!" Doc argued.

Alyana laughed and shrugged. "Could have fooled me."

Doc scooped Ellie into his arms and crossed the street to the manicured front lawn of the Genesee estate.

"Thanks for ducking out of work," I said. Alayana had rearranged her afternoon appointments after my call to her office only an hour earlier.

"When you told me Saul was dead, I had to get back here. Later this afternoon, I'm going to head over to his place to see if there's anything I can do."

"Bring smelling salts. The guy passed out on Saul's living room floor will be Dr. Douglas Kool."

Alyana didn't smile.

"About the couple Miriam Reis thinks has the Dutch Island deed," I pushed the conversation in a different direction. "According to Miriam, you're their vet."

"Was," Alyana corrected. "Was their vet. Their Welsh Corgi died a year or two ago. I haven't seen them since we put the dog down. But they're not people you tend to forget."

"Because –?"

"Because they set the high bar when it comes to being married."

"In what way?"

"You'll understand when you meet them. Which is what I am guessing you're planning to do, right?"

"That's the plan."

"Easier said than done," Alyana noted what was already obvious to me. "They're nice people but I'm not sure they'll be putting out a welcome mat for a murder suspect."

I nodded. "Which is why I need a door opener."

"Let me guess. That would be me?"

"Bingo. It's either you or Miriam the librarian. And if I go with Miriam, Doc's erotic powers might get her so sidetracked we'd never make it out of Jamestown."

The line cracked through Alyana's sadness. "Okay," she smiled. "I'm in. Speaking of leaving Jamestown, how do you plan to get through Michael Ravenel's blocade? In case you forgot, it's jail time if you're caught off the island."

That wasn't something easily forgotten. I had slipped off the island once without being detected. Rolling the dice a second time was high risk. But if the Dutch Island deed was actually in Portsmouth, then that's where I needed to go.

"Flying under Ravenel's radar won't be easy," I admitted.

"True," Alyana said, "Of course for me it's a different story. Stopping by a former client's house in Portsmouth shouldn't be all that suspicious. Maybe there's a way I could smuggle you –"

"Not a chance."

"What about Doc? Or Doug Kool?"

"My guess is both are being watched."

Doc arrived first at Alyana's front door. He gently placed Ellie on the brick landing and looked on with trepidation as Olive nuzzled the ferret. Ellie responded with a soft murmur and Doc grunted his approval.

"Then how *do* you make the great escape?" Alyana asked.

"Yigal Rosenblatt," I answered. "I don't think Ravenel and company have him under surveillance. And even if the cops do spot him, they'll probably avoid him like the plague. That's the effect Yigal has on most people."

Alyana opened the door and Ellie followed Olive across the threshold. "So somehow Rosenblatt gets you to Portsmouth. Then what?"

"That's when you make a house call – about a half hour before I show up for my grand entrance."

"And mine," Doc broke in.

I turned to the professor. "What?"

"You're taking me with you."

"I am?"

"Yes, you are. And I'll tell you why. If these people actually do have a deed, are you savvy enough to know if it's for real?"

Good point. "You're telling me you could authenticate the deed?"

"You know anybody else with a Ph.D. in history who could do the job?"

Doc was right as usual. Which meant I would be taking a ride with old One Ball Waters joining me in the backseat of Yigal Rosenblatt's fancy Mercedes.

"You're not bringing the ferret," I insisted.

Doc thought for a moment. "Listen, Bullet, I've got this eerie feeling Saul is circling over me with a wrecking ball. If anything happens to Ellie Weasel –"

"You two can hash out whether Ellie goes or stays," Alyana cut in. "How soon should we do this?"

"As soon as we can," I replied. "Maybe tomorrow morning if you can work it out."

Alyana thought for a few seconds. "I'll use Olive as an excuse to visit the couple. They're considering getting another dog and Olive will be on display as a possible choice of breed. At least that's what I'll tell Ravenel if need be."

The pieces of the plan fell into place. Alyana phoned the Portsmouth residence and had no trouble scheduling a visit for ten o'clock tomorrow morning. Next, I called Yigal Rosenblatt and arranged for him to meet Doc and me at the undeveloped plot of land we used to rendezvous before driving to Manny Maglio's strip club. Yigal would time the trip to Portsmouth so as to arrive about a half hour after Alyana and Olive paved the way for our arrival.

"What about tonight?" asked Alyana. "Staying at Saul's place is not a good idea."

Doc quickly agreed. For as long as I had known him, the professor had an aversion to getting too close to the spirit world. When Saul's lights went out, I knew Doc would want to put as much distance as possible between him and the Lipschitz house.

"We'll bunk in with Doug Kool," I said.

"What about my place?" Alyana offered.

"Tempting," I said. "But Ravenel already has you in his crosshairs. Moving in with you will only make him more suspicious."

Alyana hiked her shoulders. "But if you stay at the O'Connors and they find out –"

"One night," I interrupted. "Maybe two. As long as Ken and Maureen are stuck in Europe, we should be okay."

Alyana asked, "What about Dr. Kool?"

"Given what happened at Saul's house, Doug's in a compromising position. He'll be Mister Hospitality."

Doc, Ellie Weasel, and I left Alyana's home and made a quick return trip to Saul's ranch house. Afternoon shadows ran over the clapboard exterior of the place giving its off-white color a tombstone hue. Doc scooped up the ferret from the Opel's backseat and we walked to the Lipschitz front entrance. I used the key Saul had given me to open the door.

The house was vacant. No Doug Kool. No EMT. No cops. No coroner. The living room where Saul sucked in his last breath was eerily still. Doc lowered Ellie to the faded braided rug in the center of the room and the ferret nosed out a scent that belonged to the dead. Doc scurried to retrieve his duffel bag from the hole-in-the-door room at the rear of the house. In the adjacent bedroom, I repacked the few belongings I had taken out of my suitcase and headed back to the front entrance. Ellie gave a mournful wail as Doc lifted her into his arms. Although I had never given much credence to the professor's spirit theory, I felt a need to get out of the Lipschitz house as fast as possible.

We climbed into the Opel and drove toward Beavertail and Kenneth O'Connor's estate as a late afternoon fog blew in from Narragansett Bay's West Passage.

# #

"A low pressure trough has moved much closer to land than anticipated. Get ready. It's looking more and more like a classic nor'easter –"

The sexy blonde weatherwoman swished her hand at a satellite picture of a slow-spinning gray mass sliding east toward the New England coast.

"Next twenty-four hours should be interesting," I gestured at the kitchen television with my coffee cup.

Doug Kool gave me the same fiery-eye glare that he had shot at Doc and me when we unexpectedly appeared at the O'Connor's front door last evening.

"I don't give a shit about the weather, Bullet," Doug snarled. "You're outta here tonight."

"What a cruel man you are, Douglas," I smiled just as Doc walked into the room with Ellie Weasel draped over his right shoulder.

Doug's shoulders sagged. "Jesus help me. If the O'Connors ever find out you brought that thing into their house –"

"It's a *mustela putorius furo,*" said Doc and cruised to the Bunn Pour-o-Matic coffee brewer. "She's a ferret, Dr. Kool."

"It's a flea-infested rodent crawling around one of the most expensive houses in Rhode Island!" Doug roared. "And I swear to God, it better not be here after today!"

The bargain struck with Doug late yesterday afternoon was to let Doc and me back into the O'Connor residence for one night. In exchange, we agreed not to punch holes in the false account Doug had given to a pair of Jamestown cops who were first to respond to Dr. Kool's 911 call. Doug had claimed he was alone with Saul Lipschitz when the old man collapsed and died.

"You *told* me to feed that line to the cops!" Doug resurfaced a complaint we had heard several times.

"Doesn't matter. You were the one who lied to the police. If the media finds out, your Park Avenue friends and associates are going to think twice about their charitable giving."

"Damn you, Bullet!"

Doug continued brooding as Doc and I finished our coffee.

"How about a walk, Doc?" I asked.

"Ellie could use the exercise," Doc answered and clipped a leash onto a nylon harness that hugged the ferret's small frame. Doc had found the harness hanging on a hook in Saul's kitchen.

I turned away from Doug and glowered at Doc. We were still at odds about whether the ferret should be part of the morning's trip to Portsmouth. Now that Ellie was hooked to the professor with an eight-foot leash, the issue was resolved. The ferret was coming with us.

We walked out the O'Connor's rear door and through the spacious screened-in porch. Ellie romped toward the bay's shoreline, the tiny locator bell and ID tag on her harness jangling as she trotted down the grassy incline to the water's edge. Once we stepped onto the narrow, shell-covered beach, Doc gently hoisted the ferret into his arms and followed me as I marched quickly toward the vacant lot where I hoped to find Yigal Rosenblatt and his Mercedes S550 courtesy of Manny Maglio.

"Oh, my God!" squealed Twyla Tharp when she spotted Doc and me. Miraculously, Yigal was on time and parked at our agreed-upon location. "It's one of them Italian pigs!" Twyla pointed at Ellie.

"No, no," Doc corrected as we climbed into the Mercedes' rear seat. "Not a guinea pig. It's a ferret."

"Whatever!" Twyla chirped. "I *love* it! After it dies, can I have its skin? One of my Uncle Manny's cousins is a taxi attorney. Sometimes he makes muffs outta animals. Oh, wouldn't it be a beautiful muff, Yigee?"

Yigal put the Mercedes in drive and jerked forward. "Does it bite?" Rosenblatt asked. "Don't like anything that bites. I can take a nibble but not a bite."

The Mercedes lurched across the Claiborne Pell Bridge that linked Jamestown to Newport and then headed north to Portsmouth, a small town bordered on one side by Narragansett Bay and on the other by the Sakonnet River. Doc, Ellie Weasel, and I were hunkered down out of sight in the rear of the car as we jerked our way onto a quiet road called Water Street.

"Is that the house?" Yigal asked as he approached a small but neatly maintained one-level home on the left. Doc and I lifted our heads for quick peek.

"That's it," I said. As planned, Alyana had used her Honda as a marker, having parked on the street in front of the place.

"Oh, Yigee!" Twyla cried out. "Look, a motor house! We should buy one of them. We *really* should."

Doc and I pulled ourselves up for another quick inspection. A thirty-foot Winnebago RV took up most of the blacktopped driveway that stretched from Water Street to the door of a single-car garage.

I shrunk back into my incognito position and expected Doc to do the same. Instead he turned his head one eighty and stared out the Mercedes' rear window.

"Couldn't be –" Doc whispered.

"Couldn't be what?" I asked.

Doc squinted, trying for a clearer long-distance view. "A car parked a few blocks back. It looks like –"

"Like *what?*" This guessing game was getting annoying.

Doc shook his head and slid down in the seat until he was once again out of view. Ellie Weasel climbed onto his lap and curled into a half circle. "It's nothing," Doc said.

Later we would learn that this was one of those rare times when the professor was totally wrong.

– Chapter 21 –

"Come in, Mr. Bullock."

Betty Weeden's voice was warm and upbeat.

"My husband, Rick," Betty said, motioning to a man in his sixties seated in a recliner. Rick Weeden looked to be about six feet, thin but not wiry. He wore glasses and sported a close-cropped white beard. He didn't get up when introduced and I knew why.

"Hi," Rick said softly and offered me a wave. Alyana had told me about the man's advanced Parkinson's disease. The Weedens had been married for nearly forty-five years and for all but fifteen, Rick had battled a debilitating sickness that tore at his central nervous system.

"Two Ricks!" Twyla squealed, her head swiveling first toward me and then toward Rick Weeden. "I've never been with two Ricks before!"

Somehow, I doubted that.

"Know what everyone should do?" Twyla pointed to me as she continued blathering. "Call this Rick by his other name – Bullet. That way none of us will get our Ricks mixed."

Rick gave Twyla the same involuntary wide-eyed look most people couldn't hide when first meeting the blonde.

"Actually, that's not a bad idea," Doc Waters added a second to Twyla's suggestion and turned to the two Weedens. "Allow me to introduce myself –"

"You must be Professor Waters," Betty interjected, a strong New England accent coating her words. "Alyana told me about you." Betty turned and faced Yigal and Twyla with a smile. "And about you, Mr. and Mrs. Rosenblatt."

There was an exchange of handshakes.

"And who is this little guy?" Betty asked, nodding at Doc's ferret.

"Actually, it's a she," said Doc. "Meet Ellie Weasel."

Doc lowered Ellie to the floor and unclipped the leash from her harness. The ferret quickly trotted across the room to join Olive who was obediently holding to a sit-stay.

"They certainly seem to get along," Betty observed.

"Don't they though?" Alyana smiled and gave Doc an I-told-you-so look.

Betty waved us to a corner room with a large bay window that presented a spectacular view of the Sakonnet River. The two Rosenblatts parked themselves on a divan and the rest of us found chairs facing Rick Weeden's recliner. "Alyana tells us we have quite a precious item hanging on our wall," Betty said.

"On your wall?" I asked.

Betty excused herself and walked to an adjacent room. Seconds later, she returned with a framed document about a foot wide and eighteen inches long.

"A few of Rick's family items have been passed down over the years," she explained and handed me what looked like an old property deed. "We've had this on our spare bedroom wall for I don't know how long. Rick and I figured it might have some historical value, but Alyana says it's much more important than we thought."

"Might be," I said and passed the document to Doc. The professor stood and walked to the bay window. The morning sunlight was dulled by the first bank of storm clouds pushed in by the fast-moving storm that was moving up the Eastern seaboard. Doc closed one eye and scrutinized the deed's handwritten text made distinctive by its elaborate penmanship.

"I need to study this more closely," Doc said. "But first impression? It's what we've been looking for."

"What is it, Doc?" Twyla asked. Until now, the Rosenblatts had deliberately been kept in the dark about the missing deed.

"An old document," said Doc. He glanced up at Twyla and realized she needed more of an explanation. "It's a deed that turns over a portion of Dutch Island to a man named Daniel Weeden. Signed in 1741."

"Does it say what part of Dutch Island Daniel Weeden owned?" I asked.

"Well, there are lot numbers listed on the deed," Doc answered. "So if I can get my hands on the right old plat maps, I should be able to figure out exactly where those lots are. Miriam could probably dig those up. But I think we can assume the property is where Mohamad al-Talal and friends don't want them to be."

"The deed is signed by an agent of King George the Second," Alyana said after scanning the document. "Wouldn't any legal transaction made before the United States was born be invalid?"

Doc shrugged. "That's the multimillion-dollar question. The deed says Daniel Weeden's heirs, executors, or administrators have rights to the land. But is a British deed worth the paper it was written on when it was signed before 1787 when the United States officially got its start? Who knows? It's the kind of cud lawyers love to chew on."

"Alayana told us there are folks who'd do just about anything to get this deed." Betty took the document from Doc and looked at me, a slight hint of apprehension showing on her face. "Is that true, Mr. Bull... Is that true, Bullet?"

I could have tried sugarcoating a reply but recalling what Alyana had told me about Betty, she wanted her answers straight up.

I said, "Yes."

"Should we be worried?" Betty asked, her anxiety mounting. Rick's face briefly showed the same apprehension and then his eyelids clamped shut. Doc would later explain that an involuntary closure of the eyes was called blepharospasm and it was just one of the miserable maladies brought on by Parkinson's disease.

"There's a possibility you and Rick could be in danger."

Betty took a breath. "So what should we do?"

"You have options. You could sell the deed –"

"To al-Talal?"

"Yes."

"Or to the company al-Talal hired to build his Islamic Center?" she asked.

"Yes, the Mason Development Company," I said.

"Anyone else?"

I answered with a nod. "Just about anyone who's lined up against al-Talal. The deed could muck up his plans – at least that's what some people think."

"I see." Betty extended the deed to arm's length and ran her eyes over the document. Then she scanned the room, making sure she made eye contact with each one of us. "So what would you do if you were in Rick's and my shoes?"

There was an awkward silence none of us was willing to fill.

Betty's smile returned. She placed the deed on a teak coffee table. "I didn't mean to put everyone on the spot. Let me ask the question differently. What if money weren't a consideration? What would you do with this deed?"

"But money *is* a consideration," Doc said.

"You're right, Professor Waters," Betty agreed. "However, it's clear that there's more on the line here than a payoff to Rick and me. If the deed goes in one direction, al-Talal gets to build his mosque and thousands of Rhode Islanders get great paying jobs. If it's handed over to the other side, there's a good chance the Islamic Center goes away, which more than a few national security experts think would be a good thing."

"Whatever you do, make money," Yigal broke in. "You should sell, is what you should do."

Betty's smile grew. "Having a fatter bank account wouldn't be a bad thing for Rick and me, Mr. Rosenblatt. But thankfully it's not a necessity. We're fortunate enough to have a nice home that's paid for. Insurance covers most of Rick's medical expenses. Mine too. Our needs are pretty much met. More so, in fact. We even have an RV."

"Oh, Yigee, the RV!" Twyla yelped and grabbed her husband's arm. "We *have* to get one of them. After I pop out Tzufit or Boaz, you can drive us all over, Yigee. Can't you just see that?"

I could. Yigal Rosenblatt behind the wheel of a monster rig would be the National Safety Council's worst nightmare.

"I'm not sure any of us is in a position to decide what's best to do," I tried answering Betty's question. "If it were me, I'd give it to someone who knows what's going on but doesn't have a dog in the hunt."

"Meaning?" Doc asked.

"Let somebody who's more informed about where things stand with al-Talal and who can be trusted to make the call," I explained. "There are going to be upsides and downsides no matter what's decided."

Betty ran a hand over the back of her steel-gray hair that was styled in a short pixie cut. "You have someone in mind, Bullet?"

"I do," I replied. "A state cop named Ravenel. Lieutenant Michael Ravenel."

"Ravenel?" Alyana asked, obviously surprised by my suggestion. "The man thinks you're a murderer, Rick!"

"He knows I didn't kill Harold or J. D. Mason – or anyone else for that matter. He's using me as a decoy to draw the real killer out of the woods."

"I'm not sure about this, Bullet," Doc muttered. "You think a cop can be trusted?"

"Yes." And I meant what I said. Ravenel and I had spent more time with one another than either of us wanted. The lieutenant had a less-than-enviable bedside manner but I was positive he wasn't in anyone's pocket. Al-Talal, Caleb Mason, or the Maglio crime syndicate didn't own the man. Nor did anyone else. At least that's how I read Ravenel and reading people was one of my more keenly developed aptitudes.

Betty leaned over her husband and gave him a gentle nudge. Rick strained to open his eyes and then looked up. The two never spoke but it was apparent they were connecting in a way that went far beyond an exchange of words.

I recalled what Alyana had said about the couple – that they had knitted themselves together in the closest relationship she had ever seen.

Rick's eyes fell shut again and Betty turned to me. "Okay."

"Okay?" I asked, surprised by the quick response.

"Rick's in agreement. Bring the deed to Lieutenant Ravenel. It's our best option."

"All right," I said. "I'll call Ravenel and we'll work out a time and place for the handover."

I reached for my cell but before I could punch in Ravenel's number, the Weeden's front door was kicked off its hinges. A huge man holding a 9 mm pistol bulled past the splintered doorjamb and charged into the entryway of the corner den where we were seated.

"My God!" Doc yelled. "Tiny Templeton!"

I recalled the name. He was the overweight historical records researcher Doc had spotted digging through Jamestown's archives looking for the Dutch Island deed.

"Nobody needs to get hurt!" Tiny shouted waving a Springfield XD9 handgun from one side of the room to the other. Salty rivulets ran down his neck and were soaked up by the collar of a faded turtleneck.

"What the hell is this, Tiny?" Doc was the first to shake off the shock and find his voice.

"Just stay where you are," Tiny warned. "I got people comin' who'll handle this. All I'm supposed to do is make sure you're here when they show."

Olive barked furiously at the intruder. Ellie chattered and disappeared behind the divan.

"The goddamned dog needs to shut up!" Tiny growled.

Alyana leaned toward the poodle and put an open hand in front of the dog's muzzle. Olive immediately went silent.

Doc's eyes turned to slits. "I thought I saw your car, you fat pig!"

Tiny licked his plump lips. "You want to lose another nut, Doc? Is that what you want? Just keep pushing me. Go ahead, keep pushing me."

"You're back in the eavesdropping business, I see," Doc snapped back. "What's a sleazebag like you using these days? A laser listener?"

"When I'm dealin' with assholes like you, I don't need a directional," Tiny said and held up a small black box with a pair of earplugs dangling from one end.

"Well, look at that," Doc said, totally unfazed by Tiny's pistol. "A cheap acoustic listening mike. My God, Tiny, is that all you can afford these days?"

"Like I said. Why bother with the good stuff when it's not necessary."

"When Tiny here didn't weigh six hundred pounds," Doc explained, "he was a pretty decent private dick who made a living spying on naughty people. After he turned into a walrus, it was hard to stay in the shadows."

"Up yours, Doc!" Tiny's flabby face turned burgundy red. So completely focused on the professor, Tiny didn't spot a narrow band of fur slinking along the floor molding and heading toward Templeton's pant leg.

"Tiny's as behind the times as he is fat," Doc continued the insults. "See that thing in his paw? It's an old-school amplifying box that's about as unsophisticated as you can get. Mostly used by voyeurs who slap it on a wall or glass pane to catch a little bedroom action."

Tiny billowed out his chunky cheeks and snorted at Doc. "Hey, you piece of crap! Let me tell you about *old school*. You had no idea I was outside the back window for the last ten minutes. Nobody did! I taped everything I needed to know about the goddamned deed. The same deed that's gonna make me –"

Two things happened at once. First, Rick Weeden's right leg jerked straight out and struck a small table. It was a spastic, involuntary movement called dyskinesia common to many Parkinson's patients. But to Tiny, it was a threat. He swung his handgun toward Rick just as Ellie Weasel clamored up the loose fitting right leg of the big man's extra-large cotton pants.

"AUGGHOWEE!" Tiny screamed.

Ellie chomped hard into the man's fatty tissue and Tiny screamed again.

"Oh, Christ! It's on my leg! It's on my –"

Tiny pulled his arm down and aimed the 9 mm at the back of his right calf. Off balance and panicked, he fired once. His shot went high, the bullet ripping into his thigh. A small dot of blood instantly smeared Tiny's pants and quickly grew larger. Ellie Weasel unlatched herself and scampered out from under Tiny's pant leg. The ferret dashed for cover back behind the divan where Yigal and Twyla sat mummified.

Alyana pressed her hands to her face. "Oh, God! He hit his femoral!"

"What was it? What was it?" Tiny yelled, more concerned about whatever had chewed his leg than the blood welling from his severed artery.

"Listen to me!" Alyana implored. "We have to stop the bleeding. You're going to be in serious trouble if –"

"Shut up!" Tiny shrieked. Blood gushed from the bullet wound and puffed out Tiny's pant leg. Glassy-eyed, Tiny fell to a sitting position, a widening dark red pool surrounding his corpulent bottom.

"You've cut your femoral artery!" Alyana tried another time to break through to the injured man. "You could bleed to death if we don't do something–"

"Don't!" Tiny said, his speech slightly slurred. "Don't jerk me around. I got people comin' who'll handle this."

"Who are you working for, Tiny?" I asked after a two-minute silent standoff. Twice before I had watched men die after their femorals had been sliced open. In my world, you learn a lot about injury and death – much more than any sane person would want to know. The fat man was losing consciousness faster than I expected. "Who's coming, Tiny? Who are you working for?"

Tiny muttered a few garbled words. Then unexpectedly, he found enough strength to lift his 9 mm and squeeze off a final round. Before it shattered the river-facing bay window, the slug zipped within a foot of Yigal Rosenblatt's thick black beard. Tiny's eyes fluttered and the fat man fell flat, his body sloshing in his own blood.

Alyana rushed toward Tiny. "Get his pants off!" she yelled at Doc and me. "Give me his belt and we'll tourniquet his thigh."

Disrobing Tiny proved to be a messy business. His extra-large cotton trousers were the perfect sponge for the fountain of blood that kept jetting from Tiny's leg. Doc and I worked for a long minute before we exposed the lower half of his body.

"He's not going to make it," Alyana said while holding her fingers to Templeton's neck. His carotid pulse was barely detectable.

"Oh, Yigee!" Twyla Rosenblatt screeched and pointed at the ferret. "The little weasel ate that man and saved our lives! Can you believe it? A weasel saved our lives, Yigee!"

As if on cue, Ellie reappeared and scampered back to Olive's side.

I wiped as much of Tiny's blood from my hands as possible. "We need to get out of here. Now!"

Alyana looped the fake-leather belt around Tiny's thigh and pulled hard. The blood flow subsided. "We can't leave him like this," she said.

"Yeah, we can," I argued.

I knew Alyana wouldn't have moved had it not been for Tiny. His body shuddered once and went limp. Alyana probed for a pulse but the man was dead.

"A heart attack, I think," she guessed.

I said, "Whatever. Let's do our mourning somewhere other than here."

Betty grabbed a derby walking cane and handed it to her husband. Doc and I helped Rick to his feet and jockey him past Tiny's lifeless body. Then we navigated our way to and around the splintered remains of the Weeden's front door. Doc jogged toward the street and made a sudden U-turn.

"We've got a problem," Doc said.

One of the day's more monumental understatements, I thought. "What?"

"Tiny cut the tires on the Mercedes. Ditto for Alyana's Honda."

"Damn it," I cursed. "Where's Templeton's car?"

Doc pointed to a nondescript two-door Chevy Colbalt.

"He could fit into that?" I blinked at the small yellow compact parked three doors away from the Weeden's lot.

Doc shrugged. "In his business, you don't want to stand out. Somehow, the fat slob shoehorned himself into the thing."

"If it's got a motor and air in its tires, we can use it," I said. "Go inside and fish through Tiny's pockets and get the keys."

Doc wasn't happy with the assignment, but didn't protest.

"Even if we can into his car, it's not big enough for all of us," Betty put into words what I had already been thinking. "We should use the RV. I don't know why, but Templeton didn't cut the tires."

I checked the Winnebago and wondered aloud why Tiny had ignored the RV. For sure, he wasn't about to give us an explanation. "You can drive this thing?" I asked Betty.

"Like a pro," she answered confidently.

We helped Rick into the Winnebago. Olive jumped on board and I followed carrying Ellie Weasel in one arm and the Dutch Island deed in the other. Alyana and the Rosenblatts boarded next, just as Doc stormed out of the house holding a blood-soaked key fob. He dashed to Tiny's Colbalt, opened the car door, and tried to turn the engine. Nothing.

Doc abandoned the Chevy and sprinted to the RV. "The fat bastard installed a backup ignition kill switch that I couldn't find. Antitheft protection in a *Colbalt*? Jesus! That's how crazy Tiny is – or was."

"Not a problem, Doc, we don't need the car," I said as Betty revved up the Winnebago's engine and put the vehicle in reverse. "Shake anything else out of Tiny's pockets other than car keys?"

Doc looked back at Ellie Weasel curled up on the RV's couch next to Olive. "Yeah, something that explains why our ferret here turned hero."

"What did you find, Doc?" Twyla joined the conversation.

The Winnebago banked right and headed for Portsmouth's main drag. A pair of black Escalades passed us going the opposite direction. They were traveling too fast toward Water Street.

Doc shook a finger at his ferret. "Ellie wasn't after Tiny Templeton."

"It was," Twyla protested. "It knew the fat man was going to shoot us, Doc!"

"No. The only thing Ellie wanted was what Tiny had in his pocket." Doc held up a small cardboard container, its front panel made illegible by Templeton's blood.

"What is that, Doc?" Twyla asked.

The ferret hoisted its tiny head and cackled.

"A box of Sun-Maid raisins."

– Chapter 22 –

The nor'easter's opening salvo drove quarter-sized raindrops against the Winnebago's tinted side windows. A fierce wind rocked the Weeden's motor home but a forty-foot Gulf Stream parked between us and the entrance to the Melville Campground was taking the worst of the storm.

"Good enough?" Betty wanted to know. I had asked her to find a place where Tiny Templeton's backup squad would least likely locate us. The hundred-fifty acre campsite owned and managed by the Town of Portsmouth was an easy choice. It was only a few miles from the Weeden's Water Street address and was populated with enough recreational rigs to give us the camouflage we needed.

"Perfect for now," I said nodding at the Gulf Stream keeping us hidden from anyone entering or leaving the campsite. "But once we pull out of here, different story. Whoever's been bankrolling Tiny probably has your plate number."

Alyana knew I was right. "In this weather, there won't be many RVs on the road," she said. "We'll be easy to spot."

"Storm might help," Rick spoke unexpectedly. His voice was low and we all strained to catch his words. "Visibility's bad. Could be nobody's going to expect us to leave. Not for a while."

On the drive to the campground, Betty had explained that like many Parkinson's patients, Rick had trouble speaking. "Getting the words out is hardly the worst of it," she had said and explained how tremors, stiff muscles, and drooling made Rick's life a living hell. "But it's the hallucinations, depression, and anxiety that turn everything into a nightmare."

"I can't imagine what that must be like," I had reacted. "With everything he's dealing with, Rick still manages a smile. He's pretty amazing." As is his wife, I thought.

"What's really amazing is how Rick's brain continues to function even though the disease has chewed up his body," Betty had noted. "When his meds kick in, he's got incredible recall. A walking encyclopedia. Ask him about weather, sailing, or anything about Narragansett Bay. He'll have an answer."

I wasn't sure if Betty was exaggerating but it was an opportune time to find out. "The bridge that runs from Newport to Jamestown," I said to Rick, "will it be closed for vans and RVs if the wind gets any stronger?"

"The Claiborne Pell Bridge," Rick said without a pause. He had folded himself into an awkward position on the RV's pull-out couch. "Part of it stands a couple hundred feet above the waterline. If winds hit fifty knots, some trucks, small cars and buses won't be allowed to cross. Big RVs like ours –"

Rick finished the sentence but only Betty could discern the words.

"Bottom line is the police will probably keep us off the bridge if the winds top fifty knots," she said.

I looked back at Rick. "Best guess. What's the wind speed right now?"

Rick struggled to keep his eyes opened. "Gale force. Somewhere around thirty-five to forty knots."

Doc was monitoring a radio weather channel as Rick spoke. "Based on the latest forecast, we have about three hours before winds reach fifty knots."

Olive sensed the growing tension and whined. Alyana ran her hand through the poodle's thick coat and the dog settled.

"Whoever's after us will be watching traffic heading over the bridge from Newport to Jamestown," I said.

"Which is why we should use the back door," Alyana said.

We waited for more.

"There are two bridges that connect to Jamestown," Alyana reminded us. "Since we're only a few miles from Newport, common sense says we'll be using the Pell Bridge. But suppose we drive north to Providence and then circle back on the other side of the bay to the second bridge – the Jamestown-Verrazzano Bridge."

"How long would that take?" I asked.

Betty had the answer. "It's about a fifty-mile drive. Normally it would take less than an hour. But in an RV and with the wind the way it is, it could be twice as long."

"Worth a shot," Doc said.

We circled a vinyl ottoman and hatched our next moves. As a starter, we agreed I should call Lieutenant Ravenel. After a couple of mea culpas for ignoring his order to stay put on Jamestown Island, I would work out a time and place for handing over the Dutch Island deed. In case Ravenel's phone was compromised, I would lie – we were heading back to Jamestown via the Claiborne Pell Bridge. And if the lieutenant hadn't already heard about the Tiny Templeton development, I would fill him in.

Doc Waters turned to Yigal. "Earlier this afternoon, you told me Manny Maglio would be in Newport today. Did I hear you right?"

"Oh, yes – that's true," Yigal replied. "Here for a meeting. Probably on the *Aroused*."

"He is, Doc," chirped Twyla. "The *Aroused* is the best bachelor boat ever. If there's a really big nighttime party, Uncle Manny always shows up in the afternoon to check on the arrangements."

"So that means the boat's going to be busy tonight," Doc guessed.

"Oh, it will!" Twyla squealed. "A lot of the Sinsations girls are working so I know the *Aroused* is going to be really bouncing up and down."

I censored a few mental images, and asked Doc why the interest in Maglio and his party plans.

"It's the best defense is a great offense theory," Doc stated.

"What's your point?"

"Confrontation. Get in Manny's face and find out if he was pulling Tiny's strings."

"Have you lost your marbles?" I glanced at the professor's crotch regretting my poor choice of words.

"Hear me out," Doc urged. "If it's Maglio who's looking for us, where would we least likely show up?"

"On board the *Aroused*," I played along.

Doc nodded.

"Sounds as risky as it is dumb, Doc."

"It would be if Manny's niece and counselor Rosenblatt weren't part of the plan."

"Meaning what?"

Doc leaned forward. "Maglio isn't going to mess with a blood relative or anyone his niece happens to have in tow. We ask him straight up – was Tiny in his pocket? If he was, we tell Maglio that Tiny's dead and the deed's been handed over to the state cops. Game over. Manny lets us go and we're back in Jamestown in time for dinner."

"And if Tiny wasn't on Maglio's payroll?"

Doc shrugged. "Consider it a process of elimination. If you believe what Manny says, it probably means Tiny was working for Mohammad al-Talal."

Twyla flipped back her streaked blonde hair and stared open-mouthed while Doc and I went over the pros and cons of a nose-to-nose confrontation with the East Coast's reigning strip club king. Yigal looked equally as perplexed and a lot more anxious. Until now, it hadn't registered with either Mr. or Mrs. Rosenblatt that Maglio was high up on the list of suspects.

"Uncle Manny?" Twyla yelped. "Oh, Bullet, that can't be. He's changed. He really has."

Yigal bounced in his seat and shook his head in agreement. "Changed man is what he is. Only two indictments this year and he's paid all his fines."

"Doc, Doc," Twyla grabbed the professor's arm with both hands. "Uncle Manny's not a bad man. Not anymore at least. And besides, he's gonna pay for a huge bar mixer party when Tzufit or Boaz gets old enough."

I bit my lip hard, thinking this all might be a bizarre dream. No such luck.

"Listen," I said to Twyla, "Maybe Doc's plan isn't all that crazy. If Manny comes up clean, we'll make sure the police get off his back. We'll be doing him a big favor and maybe he'll do the same for us if we need his help down the line."

Twyla and Yigal chewed on the convoluted logic for a few seconds. Then they both shrugged in unison and mumbled, "Okay."

"Do you know where we can find the *Aroused*?" I asked Twyla.

"Definitely!" she answered a little too quickly. "It's still where it was when I did my shows on it. At the Newport Shipyard."

There was a story or two tucked into her words. Maybe someday when Yigal wasn't in earshot.

Betty explained the Shipyard was a popular docking location near Newport's Goat Island Causeway. "Just a few miles from here."

The Winnebago's interior turned sound chamber as the rain pounded the roof. We all sat quiet for a time considering Doc's proposal that we walk into a lion's den.

"All right, let's go see Manny," I broke the silence. "After that, we'll take the long way around and use the Jamestown-Verrazzano Bridge to get back on the island."

A worried look crossed Alyana's face. She stood and put her hand on my shoulder. "Could I speak to you? Alone."

We squeezed into the Winnebago's sleeping quarters and Alayana closed the bedroom door.

"Rick, you of all people know Manny Maglio's a very dangerous man. Confronting him makes absolutely no sense. Please don't do this."

"I wouldn't give it a second thought if it weren't for Twyla," I said. "Before Maglio's brother was killed, he got Manny to promise to look after his niece. Maglio's family ties run deep. There's no way Twyla's going to get hurt and neither will I if I hang on to her coattails."

Alyana wasn't convinced. "You remember how my husband died?"

"Yes, I do." Jeff Genesee's violent powerboat accident was not something easily forgotten.

"And you remember Lloyd Noka's warning? That marrying Jeff was risky?"

"Because rich and reckless are a bad combination," I recalled.

"It wasn't Jeff's money that killed him, it was his recklessness. I don't want to go down that road again, Rick. Do you understand?"

I brought Alyana close and kissed her softly. The tension in her body eased but it was obvious she still had concerns.

"Even if Manny's responsible for what happened to Harold and J. D. Mason, he's not going to hurt me," I said. "Twyla's protective shield is very wide."

There was still a hint of skepticism in Alyana's eyes. "Wide enough to protect me?"

"What?"

"If you think meeting Maglio is risk free, then take me along."

"No."

Alyana pulled back. "That's what I thought. You're not being honest, Rick."

"Maglio knows me, Alyana. My showing up with Twyla may come as a surprise, but he'll understand the connection. If you're with us, he's going to be a lot more suspicious."

"He's poked around Jamestown enough to know who I am," Alyana said. "Tell him you've brought me along to corroborate that we really did find the Dutch Island deed."

Given more time, I would have continued the debate, although I realized the outcome wasn't going to change. Alyana would be part of the delegation visiting Manny Maglio. End of discussion.

We returned to the RV's mid-coach living area, and I placed the call to Michael Ravenel's cell. Four rings later, I was forwarded to Jamestown's police dispatcher, a grizzled old man whom I remembered seeing during one of my visits to the station.

"I'm trying to reach Lieutenant Ravenel," I said.

"Storm's screwed up our cell phones," the man told me. "Ravenel's in the field. If it's important, we can get a message to him on his two-way."

I was torn between hanging up and asking for a callback. I made the wrong decision. "Tell him I have what he wants and I can get it to him around five this afternoon. We need him to pick a place to meet."

"I'll get back to you," the old man snorted and disconnected.

Betty fired up the Winnebago and was maneuvering out of the parking area when I got the return call.

"He's working a crime scene at Beavertail State Park," the dispatcher said "Meet him there at five sharp. Near the lighthouse."

The RV's windshield wipers flapped wildly as we pulled out of Melville Campground. Betty kept the speed low but even at a crawl, it was difficult to see the road marker that read: *NEWPORT 5 MILES*.

# #

"You wanna go now?" The man doing the asking had a nasty voice and a face that matched.

I answered, "Yes."

"It's a goddamn hurricane out there!"

"We need a ride." The *Aroused* was moored at the farthest dock from the Newport Shipyard's main office. Yacht owners who paid by the foot to tie up at any of the marina piers got free ground transportation for themselves and their guests. Regardless of weather conditions.

The man cursed and pulled on a black poly-nylon slicker. "How many I gotta take?"

"Four of us. And a dog."

"We're not supposed to do no animals," the man snarled as we scrambled aboard a six-seat golf cart customized with a canvas roof and side panels. Alyana ignored the complaint and gave a hand command to Olive. The drenched poodle hopped on the seat next to the driver. The man shot Olive a disgusted look and the dog volleyed back with a single sharp bark.

"Is that the *Aroused?*" I asked, pointing to the misty outline of a megayacht tied to a T dock that the storm made nearly invisible.

"Yeah," the driver grunted and switched on the cart's battery-operated motor. We pulled away from the ship's store and adjacent lot where the Weeden's Winnnebago had been parked. I caught a glimpse of Betty and Rick at one of the RV's oversized windows. And in another, Doc and Ellie Weasel. The professor had argued heatedly that he should be part of the boarding party, especially since the unannounced visit to the yacht had been his idea. However, it wasn't that long ago when I convinced Maglio to take Doc off the mob's hit list. In exchange for my chaperoning his niece, Manny granted me a favor. He leaned on his gangster pals to forgive and forget the professor had cooperated with *Philadelphia Magazine* in publicly yanking the rug from under more than a few East Coast wise guys. Maglio's one stipulation for doing the deal: Don't ever let me lay eyes on that shaggy-headed piece of shit again. To renege on my promise would be the wrong way to get Maglio's attention.

The fierce wind and rain made the drive to the *Aroused* wet and uncomfortable. When we jerked to a stop just short of the yacht's boarding ramp, the driver was seething with annoyance. We rushed from the cart to the deck of the *Aroused* as the driver did a quick U-turn and headed back to the shipyard's office.

"*Mildred!*" Twyla squealed at an overweight woman blocking the entryway to the yacht's main salon.

Manny Maglio's stressed-out personal assistant stopped short. "Miss *Twyla?*" Mildred's eyes fluttered and her lower lip dropped into her double chin.

"Isn't this something?" Twyla chirped. "Can you believe it? I'm back on the *Aroused*! I just *loved* doing things on this boat."

Considering the yacht's five staterooms, that added up to a lot of "things." I looked at Yigal, who didn't seem at all curious about his wife's shipboard escapades. He was definitely in another zone, hopping from one foot to the other the way a man might be expected to act minutes before an unannounced visit with his employer who also happened to be one of the nation's last mob bosses.

"Your uncle didn't say he was expecting you," Mildred managed to cough through her shock.

"I know!" Twyla said gleefully. "This will be a really big surprise, won't it?"

"Yes, but – " Mildred's words fell away when she spotted Olive. "Oh, no, no. That's the dog that showed up at Sinsations."

"I know!" said Twyla. "When she's not all wet, she's got really nice fur, doesn't she?"

Mildred took a breath. "Miss Twyla, your uncle isn't supposed to be around animals. There's a court order –"

"Yes there is," Yigal broke in. "Because it has to do with a Great Dane that never did anything to Candi Kane. At least not on stage. It was an illusion, is what it was."

"Unfortunately, that's not how the undercover cop in Virginia Beach saw it," she reminded Yigal. "Mr. Maglio has to keep his distance from dogs."

"Oh, he won't mind this once," Twyla bubbled and wiggled her way into the yacht's interior. The rest of us followed in her wake. "Where is Uncle Manny, Mildred?"

"Miss Twyla," Mildred's said sternly, her shock wearing off. "Your uncle can't be interrupted. He's in a meeting."

"With Tommy Turnip?" Twyla asked.

"Turnort," Mildred corrected. "Yes. He and Mr. Maglio are making final arrangements for tonight. We booked a large party – "

"I know!" Twyla exclaimed. "The girls told me all about it. I knew Tommy had to be here because nobody does bachelor parties like him. He's so awesome."

Mildred pushed a clump of stray gray hairs into an oversized bun that resembled a large ball of steel twine. "This really isn't a good time."

"They're on the bridge deck, right?" Twyla guessed and turned to give me an explanation, "Upstairs is the most beautiful bar, Bullet. Tommy loves bars and this one's his favorite."

Twyla beckoned us toward a circular teak stairway that wound its way to the yacht's top deck and a stunned Manny Maglio.

"Twyla?"

"Uncle Manny! And look at you, Tommy Turnip!"

Manny Maglio sat frozen on a leather barstool, his mouth agape. Seated to his side, a wiry man with stringy black hair and a long nose that hooked slightly to the left.

"What are you doin' here?" Manny managed to sputter. Before his niece could answer, Maglio spotted the odd lineup behind Twyla. He yanked his plump butt off the stool and wagged a chubby finger at the rest of us as we corkscrewed up the yacht's stairs.

"What the hell!"

"I know I shoulda called, Uncle Manny," Twyla apologized. "But we were passing by and everybody wanted to clear up something."

"Is that you, Twyla Tharp?" Tommy said after thoroughly eyeballing the woman's torso. "I ain't seen you in years."

"I know!" Twyla jogged to Tommy's seat and kissed him on the cheek. "It's like the olden days!"

"You lookin' for work?" Tommy asked. "You still do that thing with the avocado?"

"I can't no more," Twyla said sorrowfully. "I'm married now. To Uncle Manny's lawyer, Yigal Rosenblatt. Oh, and guess what? I'm knocked up! Isn't that wonderful?"

Tommy shrugged. Twyla's marital and maternal status seemed to instantly snuff out his interest.

"What?" Manny gagged and took two steps to his rear. "It's that dog! Jesus, it's back! How'd that thing get on this ship?"

Olive had been at the rear of our odd parade and was just now padding into view.

"It's okay," Twyla assured her uncle. "It's not like that Great Danish dog that got you in so much trouble. This here's a female puddle, which means she doesn't have a weenie. No weenie means no problem. Right?"

Manny blubbered something none of us could understand and then screamed, *"Mildred!"*

Maglio's assistant schlepped up the stairs.

"This is supposed to be a business meeting, Mildred!" Manny shouted. "No interruptions!" The insinuation was obvious. Mildred's job was to be omniscient. Impromptu intrusions were her fault, not his.

"She's *your* niece!" Mildred shot back. "You should have told me she was going to show up!"

"The thing of it is, Mildred, I didn't know she was comin'. You're the one who's supposed to be on top of crap like this. That's your job! To take care of things!"

"Really?" Mildred glared at Manny. Her bun had unraveled into a crown of gray thorns. "You mean like taking care of *things* like Lynda Lypps's snake?"

"That's got nothin' to do with this," Maglio protested.

Mildred drew her hands to her wide hips. "It did this morning when you told me to take care of things! The point is, Manny, when I do take care of things you get pissed. And when I don't take care of things it's no different."

Maglio pulled his tongue across his thick lips. "Mildred, I didn't tell you to *kill* Lynda's snake, for chrissakes! That's not takin' the right care of things!"

"Oh, really! The snake ate the woman's vulva!"

"Bit!" Manny corrected. "Bit it. Which, by the way, wasn't the end of the world since her vulva looks like a couple of mud flaps."

"Lynda *Lypps!* Remember, Manny? It's her schtick. That oversized labia majora has made you plenty of money."

Maglio's puffy face reddened. "Nobody comes to see her Labrador major, Mildred. It was the goddamned python that brought them in. And you *killed* the snake!"

I looked around. We had fanned out into a half circle watching this theatre of the absurd. Even Tommy Turnort was captivated by the exchange playing out on the yacht's high-gloss teak floor.

Mildred pointed her nose at Manny's flabby chin. "Yes, I killed the snake! I took care of things! Just like last week when I took care of the Chinese G-strings?"

"Not the way I wanted you to!"

"I shipped them back. Because half the girls got vulvodynia!"

"A little itchin', for godsakes, Mildred. I had to pay that rat bastard supplier in Jersey City three times as much for replacements. *Three times!*

And besides, this is got nothin' to do with keepin' people from breakin' into a meeting that's supposed to be private!"

Mildred's mouth curled into a snarl. "I'll tell you what it has to do with. It has to do with me quitting, you ungrateful bastard!"

Mildred arched her shoulders, did a quick about face and then coiled down the yacht's spiral stairs. Not a word was spoken until the last of Mildred's gray quills disappeared from view.

Manny broke the silence with a moan. "See, this is what I gotta deal with. There's always goddamned something!"

Twyla moved to Maglio's side and held his arm. "Oh, Uncle Manny. I'm so sorry! It's all my fault. I shoulda called."

Manny gave a wave with his free hand. "Nah, it's nothin'. The thing of it is, Mildred does this a lot. She'll get over it in an hour or two."

Tommy Turnort stood and pushed his skinny frame between Twyla and her uncle. "Can we finish this?" he asked Manny.

"Yeah, yeah," Manny answered and looked at Twyla. "Listen, what's this about? Tommy and I got business. Then there's the dog thing."

Twyla motioned me forward. Manny and I needed no reintroduction.

"Tiny Templeton." I got right to the point. "You know him?"

"Yeah. A lot of us know him, right, Tommy?"

Tommy responded with an indifferent shrug.

"Did Tiny call you earlier today?" I asked.

"Me?"

"Yes."

"Why would he call me?"

"Does he work for you?" I continued.

"You mean now?"

"Yes, now."

Manny pulled on his chin. "I don't think so."

"Does that mean he does work for you sometimes?"

"Off and on," said Manny. "He hires out to whoever. Why? What's goin' on with Tiny?"

"Templeton shot himself sort of by accident," I went on purposely omitting details about a raisin-obsessed ferret. "He's dead. But before he checked out, Tiny said he had been hired to find the Dutch Island deed. Somebody told him we had the thing."

"The deed?" Manny blinked. "That fat bastard was after the deed? Did he find it? Who's payin' him? Who?"

Manny was definitely not an actor. He didn't need to be. His actions and reactions were all real, even if often despicable. What you saw or heard was genuine Maglio. His words and perplexed expression told us everything we needed to know. Tiny Templeton was not on Manny's payroll.

"He didn't get the deed," I said.

"No? Well, that's good. So who told him you had the thing?"

The bridge of the *Aroused* had become a crossroad. I could take us in one direction and leave Manny mystified about why we had crashed his bachelor party's warm-up meeting. Or I could come clean – sort of.

"Actually, we have the deed. Or at least we did,"

Manny took two steps to his rear and crumpled onto one of the bar stools. "You had the deed?"

"Turned it over to the state police," I lied.

"Ah, shit," Manny moaned and stroked his bald head.

"We had no choice, Manny," I said. "Things were getting out of hand. A lot of people were in danger. Including your niece."

Manny glanced at Twyla, who looked as baffled by my story as Maglio.

"You shoulda told me you found the goddamned thing," Manny whined.

I manufactured a chagrinned look. "Maybe. But we were boxed in and there wasn't much choice at the time."

"But, Jesus, the cops – " moaned Manny.

"I know. I know. But better than the Arabs, right? Which is why we're here, Manny."

The man looked up, his face drawn by disappointment.

"What?"

"Mohammad al-Talal," I continued. "His people still think we have the deed. Just before he died, Tiny Templeton made a call. All of us – Twyla, Yigal, me and a bunch of other people – we're all targets."

Maglio shook his head. "So what you want?"

"Maybe a little protection if it comes to that," I answered. "For Twyla's sake."

The upper deck went quiet except for the sound of the wind and rain pounding the yacht's white exterior.

"The thing of it is, when you got the deed, you shoulda called," Manny finally said.

"Again, I'm sorry about that." Was I repentant enough? I wasn't sure.

"All right, I'll give you a couple of guys. Where should I send 'em?"

"Beavertail Lighthouse on Jamestown Island. Have them meet us there at five this afternoon."

– Chapter 23 –

The Winnebago snaked through Newport's warren of side streets, deliberately avoiding the city's main arteries. Once well north of the Claiborne Pell Bridge, Betty pulled the thirty-foot RV onto West Main Road and headed toward Fall River.

"From road to roof, we stand twelve feet high," Betty said, and turned left at an exit marked *PROVIDENCE*. We were the only large vehicle traveling in either direction on the rain-soaked highway. "If anybody's looking for us, we won't be hard to find."

Betty's apprehension grew as we skirted Rhode Island's capital city and connected with southbound Route 95. Several miles later, we pulled onto a secondary road that ran to the west end of the Jamestown-Verrazzano Bridge. Betty's uneasiness began to fade.

"Nobody behind us," Doc yelled from the sleeping quarters at the back of the RV. For the past hour, he had monitored our wake from the vehicle's rear window.

Betty kept a steady speed and the Winnebago rolled onto the bridge. Then, without trees or buildings to buffet the wind, we caught the full brunt of the storm. The RV rocked sideways dumping maps, magazines, and Yigal Rosenblatt to the carpeted floor.

We inched toward a line of tollbooths and a bridge worker in a yellow slicker, who flagged us to a stop. Betty slid open her driver's side window.

"Wind's too strong!" the man screamed over the howling gusts. "No trucks, trailers or RVs!"

Before Betty could respond, the professor nudged her aside. "I'm Doctor Waters! They want me in Jamestown! And they want me there now!"

"Who wants you?" the man shouted.

"State police! Call Lieutenant Michael Ravenel!"

The toll taker glanced at the phone inside the booth. A burst of rain blasted his face, and any thought of taking time to run a check on Doc's fabricated story never had a chance. "Yeah, well, just know I ain't responsible if you don't make it!"

Betty nodded, closed the RV window, and drove forward. The professor took a few unsteady steps back to his seat.

"For an old coot, you're still quick on the draw," I said with a smile.

Rick handed the professor a towel and Doc wiped his shaggy white hair. "It's in the genes."

No arguing that point. Doc's brilliance showed itself often and fast. His swift thinking and impromptu moves had yanked me out of trouble more than a few times. Unfortunately, his brains and wit also brought him plenty of grief along with a half-empty testicular sac.

The Winnebago wobbled over the bridge at no more than twenty miles an hour. The constantly changing wind rocked the RV violently. Olive crawled between the stationary metal legs of the Winnebago's dining table and Ellie Weasel followed tucking herself hard against the dog. The rest of us kept a white-knuckled grip on whatever was handy.

"Terra firma," Betty called over her shoulder when we finally reached Jamestown Island. The ride smoothed and we made a slow turn right toward Beavertail – the rodent-shaped scrap of land that hung off the island's southern tip.

"Third oldest beacon in the country," Doc muttered more to himself than the rest of us.

"What?"

"Where we're going – the lighthouse at Beavertail State Park," Doc explained. "Dates back to before the Revolutionary War. The original light is gone but the one there now was put up in 1856."

"Fascinating," I said unconvincingly. "But how about we focus on finding Michael Ravenel? Save the lighthouse lecture for another time."

The Winnebago's windshield wipers muffled Doc's obscenity. Nothing irked the professor more than a cheap shot aimed at anything historical, especially icons of the past that apparently included old lighthouses.

"Look for Ravenel's car," I said. "An unmarked white Crown Victoria."

We crept along a road that bordered Beavertail's craggy perimeter and headed toward the lighthouse that was all but invisible except for the sweep of its rotating beacon.

"There's a truck up ahead," Betty squinted through the blurry windshield.

As the RV drew closer, we caught a better view of a large bulky vehicle parked on the grass adjacent to the narrow road that traced the edge of Beavertail's shoreline.

Doc cleared the condensation from one of the Winnebago's windows. He snapped out of his funk and said, "That's a class-eight side loader and a decent one at that."

"What's a side loader, Doc?" asked Twyla.

"Trash truck."

Doc's astonishing storehouse of information still amazed me.

"And not just any trash truck," Doc continued. "A dual-axle Freightliner Condor. That's sixty thousand pounds of heavy-duty power sitting there."

"Two men in the cab," Betty called back to me. "The one on the passenger side is getting out."

"Ravenel maybe?" Alyana asked me.

"Doubt it," I answered. Michael Ravenel and a trash truck were not a logical pairing.

The man who had stepped into the storm wore a black neoprene slicker with a hood pulled tight over his head. He waved the Winnebago forward until we came to a stop in front of the parked truck.

Pushing his way through the wind and rain, the man approached the RV and knocked on the door. Betty slipped out from behind the steering wheel, opened up and motioned him on board.

With this left hand, the man pulled back his hood.

"Oh, my God!" Alyana shouted and grabbed my arm.

"*Bonjour*, Alyana."

"You know him?" I asked

"It's Aurélie's husband – Yves Benoit!" she gasped.

I don't believe in apparitions. Not even the Holy Ghost. La Bergerie's chef had been incinerated in a car accident near Tampa. His carload of phenylacetone and methylamine had turned the Frenchman into a cinder. Comebacks don't happen, especially after you've been charbroiled.

"*Un tel miracle, no?*" the man asked through a half smile. He had a raspy voice that fit perfectly with his pockmarked face and greasy hair. "*Revenir du mort, je signifie.*"

"What's he saying?" cried Twyla. "And why is he talking Jewish, Yigee?"

Yigal swallowed and whispered the subtle differences between French and Yiddish.

"Ah, *pardoner me manqué*," Benoit said to Twyla and drew a small 9 mm Walther handgun from his slicker pocket. "In English, yes?" He paused to study Twyla's chest. "You see, *ma beauté*, there is such surprise because I have come back from the dead."

"Yves, how could you be – ?" Alyana struggled with her words.

"Alive, my dear?"

"The accident," Alyana went on. "You were burned –"

Benoit laughed and prodded Betty with his pistol. She was pushed to the rear of the RV's main cabin. Now all of us were packed together with Benoit in full command of the Winnebago.

"It's about getting police to see what you want them to see, *n'est pas si vrai*?" Benoit chuckled. "I have a dental plate," he explained. "Well, two actually – the one in my mouth," he pointed the business end of his handgun to his cheek, "and the other a spare. Or was a spare until it was cooked like a fine *canard rôti*."

"Let me guess," Doc jumped in. "You find some miserable homeless slob about your size. Bust a few bones and toast him to a crisp. Nothing's left to identify the body except your false teeth that miraculously weren't fried in a one-car accident with a fatality."

"*Voilà!*" Benoit laughed with a wink. "Uhmm. You sound like a man who knows a little too much about how to do this. *Suis je redresse?*"

Doc hooked his left shoulder slightly. "*Faire j'admets une telle chose?*" the professor answered in near-perfect French.

"Ah, *bien sûr!*" Benoit snorted. "Of course! You are the professor, no? The Doctor Waters I've heard about. Such a brilliant man."

"Yves!" Alyana shouted. "Please stop this! Tell us what's going on!"

"Just finishing a job, my dear," Yves answered, his voice hollow, emotionless.

"Job?" Alyana pressed. "What job?"

"A job that got Harold Mason murdered," I said. "And it was you who recruited three thugs to work over Lloyd Noka. Then you put in a little overtime when you ducked out of the kitchen to crush J. D. Mason's head."

Alyana still had her hand on my arm. I felt the tremor shaking her body.

"*Félicitations*," Benoit said at the same moment we heard the diesel behind us roar to life. The truck's headlights snapped on and the Freightliner inched ahead until its front grille tapped the back of the RV. "I have not formally met you, Monsieur Bullock. But I have heard you are a *magnifique* detective."

"Did I hit the bull's eye, Benoit?"

"Not dead center but you're close."

"Yves, what's happened to you?" Alyana asked. "What about Aurélie?"

"Ah yes, my dear fat Aurélie," Benoit smiled. "You know, I could have divorced. But this is so much better. She lives well with the life insurance, no?"

Alyana's disbelief wouldn't go away. "This doesn't make sense, Yves. You and Aurélie had everything. A good life here and winters down south –"

"So a good life is sweating twelve hours a day over a stove?" Benoit got suddenly serious. "Living with a *gros cochon*? Ah, no, no. A good life is the freedom to pick and choose what ripens best." He glanced at Twyla and grinned.

"That's the kind of good life that can cost a man a lot of money," I said, recollecting Benoit's penchant for prostitutes and dice.

"*Très vrai*," Benoit agreed. "Which, of course, is why I am here."

"To collect the Dutch Island deed."

"Exactly."

"Satisfy my curiosity, Benoit. How much are you getting paid to play go fetch?"

"Let us say it is a sizeable sum. But what does it matter? You know where the money comes from. For the Arab paying the bill, it is mere pocket change."

"But to you, a small fortune."

"*Tellement vrai*. Enough for a long and happy life."

"But only if you deliver the deed."

"Quite correct," Benoit agreed.

"It's not here," I lied forcing myself not to look at Rick, who had pushed the deed behind his seat cushion.

Benoit laughed and reached into his slicker's left pocket. He removed an eight-inch-long silver canister and placed it on the end of the RV's sofa. "I doubt it could be anywhere else. My friend Monsieur Templeton told us you have the deed. And since it wasn't found at the Portsmouth house after you made your *départ hâtif*, then *par consequent*, it has to be here. On board this bus."

"Maybe the search-and-find crew didn't look in all the right places when they ransacked the Weeden's house." My hunch about the two Escalades speeding toward the Weeden residence had been right.

"Good try," Benoit laughed. "They are very competent professionals."

"Don't you wish everyone on your team was so capable?"

"I'm happy with my team."

"Really? Like the dispatcher at the Jamestown Police Station. The one who works the phone lines any way you want him to?"

"Ah, so harsh. He's just an old man who's been underpaid all his life," Benoit explained, confirming my suspicions about who was responsible for the department's leaks. "He earns extra for telling us what we need to know and sending people who could be a problem on a *poursuite de l'impossible*.

"A wild-goose chase," I said. "People like Michael Ravenel."

"*Exactement!* Our good lieutenant has been sent to talk to Caleb Mason about a development that means nothing. But such a helpful diversion, no?"

"Too bad Tiny Templeton wasn't as good at his job."

"Ah, *oui*. But sometimes we have to make the best hand from the cards we are dealt."

Benoit took out another canister – a clone of the first. He gently placed it on the couch.

"There's another card in your deck, isn't there. A wild card named William Nonesuch."

Benoit squeezed his eyes. Was he angry or impressed? Hard to tell. Maybe both. "You really *are* quite the detective, Mr. Bullock. But yes, you are right about Mr. Nonesuch – or Hawk as calls himself. Not always dependable. Today though, he is very focused. Very determined. He has what we say in French a *score de régler.*"

"Score to settle," Doc translated.

"Yes, yes," Benoit chuckled. "To settle with you, Doctor Waters. Oh, and with Mr. Bullock here as well. Apparently you both humiliated him. He wouldn't give me details. Ah, but the rage! *Oh mon Dieu!* Which is why I relented and allowed him to join me tonight." Benoit wagged his head toward the truck that had its front bumper pressed firmly against the back of the RV.

Jesus. A pissed-off faux-Indian behind the wheel of a truck big enough to push the Winnebago six ways to Sunday. I was putting together all the pieces of Benoit's sick plan and I didn't like the looks of the jigsaw.

"Very clever," Doc Waters chimed in and pointed to the two cylinders. "That's gas, right? You pop those canisters, take off with the deed, and buy an island somewhere near Borneo."

"Something like that."

"What are you using?" Doc asked. "Carbon dioxide? Nitrous oxide?"

"Hardly," Benoit replied. "Even in this closed space, that would require much too much product. Fentanyl works better."

"Ah," Doc sighed. "Methylfentanyl. What the Russians used in 2002 after the Chechens took over the Dubrovka Theater in Moscow."

"You are a smart one."

"Maybe you forgot," Doc said. "Methylfentanyl killed over a hundred hostages in that theater."

"*Si terrible.*" Benoit's left hand fished out a gas mask from beneath his rain gear.

"Oh, oh," Doc shook his head at the mask. "That's Russian, right? I know a guy who bought one on the Internet. Not worth crap."

Benoit wasn't phased. "It's been thoroughly tested, I can assure you."

Twyla suddenly grasped the gravity of the situation. "Oh, Yigee!" she screamed at her husband. "This man has *gas!*"

Yigal clasped his hands and begged Benoit with his eyes. "This won't be good for Boaz or Tzufit!"

Benoit ignored the Rosenblatt's craziness and turned to Betty and Rick. "I've been told you two own the Dutch Island deed, *oui?* And you own this bus, too, right?"

"It's not a bus," said Betty.

"So as owners, I am asking you to hand over the deed. If you do that, it will make things much less uncomfortable for you and your friends."

"What deed?" Betty asked.

Benoit sighed and lifted one of the canisters. "Being uncooperative has consequences. So it's off to sleep you all go."

"More like into the bay, right, Benoit?" I asked. "Before you dump us over a cliff, think about this. You're about to lose a fortune."

"Now, now, Mr. Bullock. Let's not *remuer le pot.*"

"It's not about stirring the pot," I said, hoping my guess at the translation was right. "You want something you'll never find without our help."

Benoit looked at the canister and then at me. "I'll give you a minute to explain, Mr. Bullock."

"If you gas us into oblivion, I guarantee you'll never find the deed."

"You're wrong."

"What if I'm not? What if you don't locate the thing? Then what?"

"I'll find the deed," Benoit insisted.

"You won't. And that screws up the rest of your plan big time."

"What *is* the rest of your plan, Mr. Ben-Nut?" Tywla squealed.

Benoit disregarded the question but I didn't. "He's going to put the RV in neutral and bail out after giving Nonesuch the high sign to push us into the water," I answered.

"Oh, my God," Alyana murmured. Beavertail State Park sat on a plain that at ebb tide was high above Narragansett Bay. If the fall didn't kill us, the water turbulence would do the job. We were parked near a partially flattened guardrail that stood as nothing more than a speed bump between us and certain death.

I asked, "How much is the deed worth if it ends up in Narragansett Bay?"

"It won't," Benoit said, sounding less certain than a minute earlier.

"You're not a man who leaves loose ends," I said making the statement sound like a compliment. "So you manufacture an accident that kills six people –"

"Not to mention a dog and a rodent," Benoit added with a sadistic grin. He looked at Alyana, the professor, and finally the two animals still huddled under the table.

Olive subdued a growl turning it more into a moan than an angry rebuttal. The ferret pushed harder into the poodle's midsection.

"The RV nosedives into the bay and gets pulverized by the waves," I kept talking.

"Une telle trégedie."

"You're not going to use that pistol unless absolutely necessary. It would raise too many questions if 9 mm holes are found in whatever bone fragments are recovered after the accident."

Benoit shook his head and chuckled. "You misjudge me, *mon ami*. I am not worried about bone fragments. I prefer not to use a gun when I can –" He lifted one of the canisters. "– make all this as painless as possible. With the gas, you'll feel nothing. So you see, I'm not a cruel man, Mr. Bullock."

I wondered if Harold Mason felt the same way before his throat was slit.

"There's one reason why your plan is –" "Dumb" would have been the preferred word but insulting a man who has a finger on the trigger of a pistol would be – well, dumb. "– going to keep you from becoming a very rich man."

"You're stalling, Mr. Bullock."

How true. "You're right about the deed. It's on board the RV."

"Old news."

"What's new news is that it's in a place that you can't get to without help."

"I don't believe you."

"Then go ahead and try it on your own. You'll come up empty."

"So what are you proposing, Mr. Bullock?"

"A trade-off of sorts. You give us something and I'll give you the deed."

This was the kind of fabrication Doc Waters usually concocted. The professor wiggled his bushy eyebrows that I took as an expression of admiration. Neither of us looked at Rick, who pressed his back harder against his seat cushion and the hidden deed.

"What are you doing?" Doc pretended to complain. "Even if he drags us outside, he's not going to find –"

"Ah, outside," Benoit took the bait. "Hidden somewhere outside the vehicle. How clever."

"Jesus, Doc!" I shouted.

"What difference does it make?" Doc shot back. "So he knows it's outside. Without our help, there's no way he's going to find the thing."

The Frenchman broke in, "Let's hear what kind of bargain you're proposing, Mr. Bullock."

"There's a house next to the lighthouse tower." I could make out the shape of a structure that looked to be about a hundred yards away.

"What about it?"

"Park everyone inside," I continued. "There's duct tape in the cabinet behind me. Nobody's going to get out of that place until help shows up tomorrow."

Benoit hoisted one of the canisters. "Then you tell me where the deed is?"

"Yes. But not until Mr. Nonesuch joins you and me for a little RV excursion."

"Is that what we're doing to do?"

"It is. We drive for a few hours – long enough so there's not enough time for you to circle back to Beavertail before help arrives in the morning."

Benoit asked, "And how do we even begin our little *trébucher* when the bridges on both sides of this island are closed to traffic?"

The professor turned to me. "The only way that'll happen is if I'm the guy who takes the joyride. I can get the RV off the island."

"Because?" Benoit asked.

"Because I'm a doctor of sorts," the professor shrugged back a response. "I can go just about anywhere."

"I see," said Benoit. "And after many hours of driving, we stop, you tell us where the deed is hidden, and then you help us get it."

"If I'm certain everyone else is okay, you'll get the deed."

"Then I dispose of you."

Doc shrugged again. "Probably."

"Why would you give your life up so easily? *La vie est tellement bon marché?*"

Doc pushed his hand through his white mop. "No I don't think life is cheap. But I'm an old man. *De sacrifice est de vivre.*"

"Ah," Benoit sighed. "I have to say I am impressed with you, Mr. Bullock, and Professor Waters. But *je suis désolé*. I'm afraid I cannot go along with your plan."

"Why not, Mr. Ben-Nut?" Twyla asked. "It sounds like such a good plan except you shouldn't kill Doc Waters because he's got what they call karma."

Benoit blinked.

"If you hurt people with karma, especially if they come from New Jersey, you'll end up with a lot of bad luck," Twyla said. "It happened to my cousin Tony who got pimples after he shot a guy in Trenton and –"

"*Stop!*" Benoit screamed. "Enough, mademoiselle! I've heard all the *absurdité* I can handle. There's a much easier way to get you to tell me where to find the deed."

We waited for what all of us knew was going to be very bad news.

"Mr. Nonesuch is going to send you over the cliff one by one until I have the deed in my hand. After that – well, for those of you who are still alive, perhaps we can reach some kind of *réglement négocié*. So let us start with the dog and the muskrat, shall we?"

"It's a *ferret*, you miserable *scélérat!*" Doc snapped.

"Ah, my apologies. I was misinformed. *Pardonnez-moi.*" Benoit stepped back from the RV's side door. "Madame Genesee, please bring your dog outside. And Professor Waters, I've been told the rodent is yours, no? It also needs to go outside."

Whether he walked away with the deed or not, I knew Benoit couldn't afford to leave any of us alive. He wasn't about to let the world know how he faked his death. Everyone was in line to die and that included, I suspected, William Nonesuch.

Alyana reached under the table and grasped Olive's collar. The dog got to her feet and I watched Alyana give the poodle a nearly undetectable hand signal. Olive reacted with a soft bark. Alyana turned to me and her anguished expression gave away her plan. She was about to give the poodle the same Schutzhund command used to send the dog's teeth first into Charles Kenyon's right forearm. Olive had won the battle with Kenyon, who was as drunk as he was stupid. Yves Benoit was no Kenyon. He was on alert, sober, and ready to kill. A sudden charge by the dog might give me an opening to get to Benoit – but a more likely outcome would be a dead poodle and a *really* incensed Frenchman.

I reached for Alyana's arm and held her firmly. I mouthed a silent "No" and followed with: "Let's do what he wants." Alyana's confusion was obvious. But I pressed her forearm twice letting her know that things weren't quite as bleak as she thought. At least, that's what I hoped. My optimism was hooked to a dark blur I had seen outside the RV's left window. Was it a man or just some windswept debris? I couldn't be sure.

Benoit stepped from the Winnebago into the storm and waved at Nonesuch to exit the trash truck's cab. Hawk walked to Benoit's side and watched as we spilled out of the Winnebago. A cruel smile turned his thin lips into a happy face when he spotted Doc and me. He glared at both of us and then looked down at his left foot. Promise kept. He had hunted us down and now it was payback time.

Benoit wagged his pistol at Ellie Weasel, an unspoken command for Nonesuch to grab the animal. The ferret was to be casualty number one. Hawk took two steps forward but abruptly stopped. He grunted and crumpled to the wet pavement.

"Ce que l'enfer est mal avec vouc?" Benoit roared at the man.

Nonesuch clutched his right lower leg and wailed. A bullet had cracked bone, leaving Hawk with a shattered tibia and a lot of pain.

The wind muffled the sound of two more shots. One creased Benoit's black slicker and a second pinged off the Freightliner Condor.

"Down!" I shouted and motioned everyone to the ground.

Benoit returned fire but the heavy rain made it impossible to make out a target. He pulled Nonesuch to his one functioning foot and the two staggered toward the trash truck.

More shots, and from the sound, I guessed the weapons to be in a different league than Benoit's Walther. The Frenchman apparently came to the same conclusion. He dropped Nonesuch and ran toward the Freightliner.

Benoit couldn't outrun a bullet that caught him in the right shoulder and spun him in a half circle. He was still on his feet when a second shot hit him square in the chest. The roar of the storm did nothing to mask the splintering sound of Benoit's sternum.

William The Hawk Nonesuch watched in horror as the Frenchman's lifeless body fell to the ground. His shock was short lived. A .38 slug blew out Hawk's left eye and macerated his brain.

"Tommy?" Twyla screeched at one of two men who drew close enough to be recognized. "Tommy Turnip?"

"How's it goin'?" Tommy Turnort flipped us a casual wave.

"Tommy, you saved us!" Twyla yelped and gave the skinny and totally soaked Turnort an open-mouthed kiss. "But how come you're here?"

"Manny asked me if I wanted a side job," Tommy explained, checking out Yigal's reaction to his wife's exuberant greeting. Not a jealous husband, Tommy correctly concluded, and said, "Damn bachelor party business has been slow as crap. So me and Guido here figured it would be an easy two bills each just to keep an eye on you's."

Tommy's sidekick was a hundred pounds overweight and definitely not a talker. Without a word, he hauled William Nonesuch into the Freightliner's cab. Next, Yves Benoit. Both bodies were pushed to the passenger side leaving enough room for Guido to squeeze into the driver's seat.

"Yo, Guido, you got this or you want help?" Tommy shouted over the wind.

Guido answered by putting the truck in gear and slowly maneuvering the Freightliner through a narrow band of low-lying shrubs that marked the outer rim of Beavertail's flat plateau. The truck flattened the bushes and stopped when its nose was perched over the steep, rocky drop-off. Keeping one foot firmly on the brake, Guido pulled Benoit's body forward until it was behind the steering column. He jockeyed the Frenchman's foot against the accelerator pedal. With a surprisingly agile move, Guido eased his bulky frame out of the cab while still continuing to press the brake with his foot. Then he jumped free and the truck rolled ahead.

"Jesus!" Doc whispered.

Tommy shook his head. "Yeah, it's a bitch of an accident, right? Two hard workin' garbage guys die. What a freakin' disaster. Right?"

Doc mulled over the question, and said, "Shit happens."

The Freightliner moved ahead, its front end now suspended in air over the rocks and ferocious sea. The truck's rear tires kept rotating and suddenly, the huge vehicle pitched forward and catapulted into Narragansett Bay.

Tommy shook his head. "Know what's a shame? All that garbage in the bay. It's what Manny wanted done. But if it was my deal, we'd do this without the garbage. No garbage in the water."

"You always was a conversationalist," Twyla sighed, still holding Tommy's hand. Yigal was bouncing in high speed seemingly unperturbed by the infatuated look on his wife's very wet face.

"Conservationist," Turnort corrected. "Yeah, I can't stand doin' anythin' that hurts Mother Nature."

Murdering human beings apparently fell in a different category, I thought. Not that I was complaining.

Alyana motioned Olive back into the RV. "We're done with all this, right Rick?" she asked as we followed the poodle inside.

I didn't answer.

"We have the deed. Benoit and Nonesuch are dead. So it has to be finished."

Betty and Rick boarded the Winnebago with Doc, Ellie and Yigal close behind. Outside Twyla continued jabbering with Tommy Turnort. The wind and rain distorted what was being said. Something about an avocado.

"Rick," Alyana put her hand on my cheek and we locked eyes. "Please. Tell me it's over."

"It's not."

– Chapter 24 –

"*Nous sommes heurtés à un problem!*"

Doc's French wasn't one hundred percent perfect but cell phone static and a roaring wind covered his flaws.

"Speak English, goddamnit!" a voice crackled back.

Doc yelled into the push-to-talk phone that Guido had shaken out of Yves Benoit's pocket just before the Frenchman had been rolled into the bay. "There was a problem!"

"Too much background noise! Doesn't even sound like you, for chrissakes! Say again!"

"A problem!" Doc repeated. "The deed's somewhere on the RV. But we can't find it."

"Can't find it?" the voice roared. "Can't find it! Why the hell not?"

"*L'un des panneaux muraux!*" Doc explained.

"English!"

"We think it's behind one of the wall panels."

"You *think?*"

"From what they told us, that's what we think."

"Then rip the thing apart, for chissakes!"

Doc said, "Not that easy. For a rig this size, it could take *éternellement* – forever."

"You got people there, right? So beat the shit of them until somebody starts talking."

Doc looked at me and I nodded. Time for the next big lie. "*Il n'y a pas de gens* –"

"Jesus Christ! Will you speak English?"

"We don't have people."

The phone hissed and the voice screeched, "What the hell are you talking about?"

203

"We moved them outside the RV. Some of the men rushed –"

"No! No! No! Don't tell me you killed them! Before they talked, you killed them?"

"Nothing we could do. If Nonesuch didn't have his Uzi –"

The voice was edging toward hysteria. "Uzi! That goddamned Indian! I told you to leave him out of this!"

"I know, but –"

"Did he shoot them? Wasn't I clear? No bullets in any of the remains. Isn't that what I told you? Did he shoot them?"

"*Ne pourrait être aide.* Couldn't be helped. But the bodies are getting *motif de bits* by the waves. There'll be nothing left to find."

The Nextel phone went quiet for several seconds. "What tools do you need?" the voice asked. It was more controlled, but the words boiled with anger.

"Hammers, crowbars, anything we can use to peel the skin off this RV," Doc answered. "If you could drive the tools over here, we could –"

"Drive over? Maybe you and the Indian should pull your heads out of your asses. I'm not driving anywhere."

Doc put the phone on mute and gave me a what-now? look.

"Try again," I said.

Doc pushed the talk button. "Just thinking this would go faster if there was three of us doing the work."

"Don't think!" the voice ordered. "I'm not going anywhere near that RV."

"*C'est ainsi.* We still need tools."

"Listen, I can't help you until I get back to the mainland."

Doc blinked. "Mainland? Where are you?"

"Dutch Island."

"Dutch Island?"

"That's right, Benoit. I'm sticking to the plan. I risked my damn neck coming over here because I wanted our overly curious detective friend to cash out in a way that wouldn't raise suspicion. Accidental death! Remember? The way the people on the RV were supposed to die!"

Doc muted the phone and looked to me for direction. We were dumbfounded. There was only one detective whose curiosity was so unquenchable that it was life threatening. Michael Ravenel. What the hell could he be doing on Dutch Island in the midst of a mini-typhoon with a man who wanted him dead?

Before I could figure out Doc's next move, the professor took off on his own. "We can drive the RV to your place. We're *à proximité*, no?"

The voice wasn't buying. "Are you out of your mind? Seven people disappear from a Winnebago and it ends up on my property?"

I motioned to Doc, and he hit the mute again. I snapped Tommy Turnort and Guido to attention. They were draining a pair of Yuenglings and showed absolutely zero aftereffects of having just disposed of two human beings.

"You drove here, right?" I asked.

Tommy replied, "Yeah. Guido and me each got a car. We parked by the lighthouse. Why?"

"What kind?"

"Huh?"

"What are you driving?" I asked.

"Guido's got a Camry and I got a Chevy cargo van."

Doc knew exactly where I was heading. He clicked on the phone.

"*Nous reviendrons à vous.* I'll drive to your place and pick up whatever tools we need. Should only take a few minutes since we're close."

"Not in that piece of shit trash truck you won't!" the voice said.

"No, no. Nonesuch drove the truck to the park. I followed in my van. I'll drive it to your place. *Ne sera pas un problem.*"

The voice was not quick with a response. Finally, an answer. "All right. I'll call security. When you're inside go to my office. Evelyn's still there. She'll tell you where to get the tools."

"*Va faire.*"

"Just find the deed and dump the damn RV in the bay. Then you, Nonesuch, and that trash truck get the hell out of there."

# #

"For the record, I'm totally against this," I said.

"You've been out voted, Bullet," Doc reminded me. He was seated to my right, riding shotgun in Tommy Turnort's van. The professor had the hood of his rain slicker pulled over his head. Good thing. He was supposed to be the much younger, taller, and heavier Yves Benoit. Which was almost as ridiculous as my passing myself off for William Nonesuch.

"What's the worst that can happen?" Doc asked. "Security blows our cover and won't let us in."

"Getting in is not what I'm worried about," I said. "It's what's in the back of the van that's got me rattled."

"Not a problem, Bullet," Yigal called out from behind me. "I got a gun."

Yigal Rosenblatt with a weapon. That made me feel *so* much more secure.

"Sticking together is a better option than splitting up," Alyana said. She was seated on the floor of the cargo van next to Betty and Rick Weeden. Olive was curled at her side. Twyla and Yigal squeezed themselves against the back of the van with Ellie Weasel shoehorned in amongst the tangle of bodies.

"We're getting close," I said.

I checked the rearview mirror and slowed to a crawl until the crew in the seatless section of the van disappeared under a grimy canvas tarp. When there was no movement, I drove to the entrance of the Mason Development Company's staging area for the big dig between Jamestown and Dutch Island.

The storm was still raging, and a tired looking guard whipped a beam of light into the interior of the van.

"You Benoit?" the guard asked.

I shook my head and pointed to Doc Waters.

"*Je suis* Benoit," Doc said and then waved at me. "He's Nonesuch."

The guard aimed his light at a foggy window. "What's in the back?"

"Hand truck, dollies, moving equipment is all," answered Doc.

"All right, go ahead," the guard ordered and triggered the one-arm security gate to an open position. I cruised forward following the crushed stone road toward the doublewides where I had last seen the two Mason boys.

"Oh, Bullet!" Twyla popped up from the back. "Isn't this exciting? It's like in the movies where they penetrate the enemy's lines. I love penetration."

That came as absolutely no surprise.

"Listen, I know you're not crazy about all of us rolling into Mason's backyard," Doc said to me. "But Alyana's right. We need to stay together. Any one of us could be a target."

I couldn't argue Doc's theory. Benoit might not have been the only one with orders to find the Dutch Island deed and to take no prisoners in the process.

"I should have parked all of you in some out-of-the-way place," I said. "Going head-to-head with Caleb Mason shouldn't be a group exercise."

Doc snorted. "First off, there's no guarantee we'd be safe no matter where you parked us. Second, the only reason you're taking on Mason is to save Michael Ravenel's ass, which to me is as worthless as seaweed."

"Maybe we should turn around and wait for the cops outside the gate is what we should do," said Yigal.

"Look, we've already been over this," I said. "We don't know how long it will take Turnort and Guido to get back here with help."

"It might be soon," said Yigal.

"Or it might not," I argued. Turnort and Guido claimed to have connections to a couple of Jamestown's finest. Since the dispatcher-on-the-take would block any other move we made to call the police, it would be up to Manny Maglio's boys to round up a posse. It had been a half hour since the two had driven in Guido's car toward Jamestown's East Ferry, and, so far, not a word from either of them.

Five minutes later, my cell rang.

"We're at Potter Cove near Newport Bridge," Turnort screamed over the wind. "A dozen boats are upside down and at least three people are missing."

"Christ!" I swore. "So what does that mean?" I remembered Potter Cove was on the other side of Jamestown Island.

"Means it could be a helluva a long time before our guys can make it to Mason's."

"Wonderful," I moaned and disconnected.

"What now?" asked Doc.

I eased the van to a stop in front of Mason's main construction office. "Let's see what I can find out from Caleb's assistant. What we do next depends on wherever Mason and Ravenel happen to be."

Rick asked, "Didn't Caleb tell Doc they're on Dutch Island?"

"That was a while ago. Could be they made it back to Jamestown."

"You might need this is what you might need." Yigal handed me the Smith & Wesson .38 Special Tommy Turnort had let us borrow.

I am not usually a gun fan, but in this case I made an exception. I took the pistol and stepped into the storm's fury. Alyana followed.

"What are you doing?" I asked.

"Going with you. If you want to get anything out of Caleb's admin, you're going need help. Remember, I know the woman. Evelyn and I spent a lot of uncomfortable time looking at Mason's poor excuse for a Native American museum while you were butting heads with organized labor."

Maybe she had a point. We hurried through the torrential rain to the door that led to Caleb's waiting room and office. Locked. After a few loud knocks, it opened. Evelyn was waiting – with a smile, of course.

"Mr. Benoi –" Evelyn's Cheshire grin turned upside down in a flash. "*You!* What are you doing here?"

I shoved my way into the office forcing Evelyn to backpedal. Alyana followed and shut the door.

"Mr. Benoit's indisposed," I said. "We need to talk to your boss."

"He's not here."

"Then where can we find him."

"I don't know."

I run a men's shelter, which means I haven't had a lot of experience interrogating women. With females, I tend to go slow and soft – a technique better reserved for the bedroom than when mining for information.

"Here's the deal, Evelyn," Alyana took a tougher tack. "Caleb Mason is a few minutes away from being arrested for murder. First-degree murder!"

Evelyn covered her mouth and gasped.

Alyana continued, "The police will be here shortly. Before they show up, I want you to listen carefully. Continue to play dumb, and you're going to be charged as an accessory. Do you know what that means? It means a lot of years in jail, Evelyn."

"But I –"

"Tell us where Caleb is," Alyana interrupted, "and we'll tell the police you did what you could to stop Mason from killing another man."

"Another man?" Evelyn whimpered. "Michael Ravenel," I said.

Evelyn slumped into a waiting room chair. "Oh, Lord Jesus. I didn't know. I didn't know. Please believe me."

Alyana squeezed harder. "That won't cut it. Denying you knew nothing isn't going to keep you out of prison, Evelyn. What you say now is what's critical. So, tell us where Caleb is!"

"He's on – last I heard, he's still on Dutch Island."

"With Ravenel?" I asked.

"Yes."

"You said last you heard." I continued. "What does that mean?"

"For the last half hour, I haven't been able to reach him on his walkie-talkie or cell. Both are out."

Alyana leaned forward, her face inches from Evelyn's. "Are you telling us the truth? Why would Mason take a boat ride in the middle of a storm?"

"The two of them left just before the wind got really bad. Something about the deed."

"What about the deed?" I asked.

"I heard Caleb tell the lieutenant the Dutch Island deed had been hidden on the island. Someplace where a flood could ruin it."

It was possible but improbable that Mason could have talked Ravenel into making the risky trip to Dutch Island to recover a piece of paper. I continued going after Evelyn.

"Lieutenant Ravenel is too smart a cop to take that kind of risk. For any reason. Which means you're lying."

"No! I'm not! Ravenel was on the crew boat Caleb took to Dutch Island. I'm sure of it because Caleb called me a few minutes after they left to tell me the lieutenant got injured."

Alyana pointed a worried look at me and then refocused on Evelyn. "Injured?" she asked.

"The lieutenant slipped and hit his head. Caleb said Ravenel would be okay."

"Damnit," I muttered. Ravenel hadn't slipped. He had either been immobilized or killed.

"Is there any way we can get to the island?" I asked Evelyn.

Alyana glared at me like I was insane.

"There's another crew boat," Evelyn said. "Exactly the same as the one Caleb used. It's at our dock at the landing."

I told Evelyn to find and hand over the keys to the boat. She rifled through the top drawer of a metal cabinet and gave me what I wanted. Then I took Alyana's arm and headed to the trailer door. "Wait here until the police show up, Evelyn. Then tell them everything you told us."

"I didn't know!" Evelyn cried.

"More like you didn't want to know," Alyana corrected.

We both ran from the trailer to Tommy Turnort's van.

– Chapter 25 –

Mason Development Company's stretch of Jamestown shoreline caught the worst of the winds screaming across Narragansett Bay's West Passage. Gusts blasted construction equipment and trailers scattered about the site.

"Stay away from that storage building," Doc pointed to our left as I jockeyed Tornort's van closer to the waterfront. "The roof's starting to ripple."

The professor finished his warning just as the storm peeled off a sheet of corrugated stainless steel and sent it flying to our rear.

"My God," Alyana whispered, "this is really getting bad."

Ellie Weasel scrambled into Doc's lap and Olive whined.

Doc nodded to a barely visible silhouette fifty yards in the distance. "That's the boat."

I pulled ahead and stopped at the foot of the pier. The van's high beams lit up the back end of a forty-five-foot crew boat.

Doc said, "Better keep the van off the pier. It doesn't look that stable."

A mountain of water shook the metal pilings and the pier shuddered. Point made. I turned the van's engine off.

"I've never seen the bay like this," Alyana said worriedly. "This isn't a good idea."

The *good idea* was all mine. We were less than a mile from the western edge of Dutch Island. How difficult could it be to sail from here to there if we had the right boat and an experienced crew, I had asked only a few minutes ago? Scanning the turbulent bay, I answered my own question. *Very difficult.* It would be a risky trip but in my landlubber opinion, it was still worth taking a chance. The Mason crew boat looked seaworthy. I guessed the beam to be fifteen feet and its hull rode high even in rough water. Just as important, I had a captain and mate who had years of experience navigating Narragansett Bay

"Sure you can handle this?" I asked Betty.

"With the right boat, it can be done," she answered confidently. The Weedens had sold their thirty-foot sloop-rigged keelboat years ago after Rick's Parkinson's worsened. But time hadn't diminished their memory of this part of the bay. At least that's what Betty had told me.

"Looks like she has radar and probably GPS," Betty peered through the van's cloudy window at the crew boat. "My guess is she's got twin diesels, which we've worked before. But for the record, engines can be temperamental especially in this kind of weather."

"Not to worry," Doc assured the Weedens. "If you keep the tub afloat, I'll keep the diesels running."

Alyana touched my shoulder. "Rick, you can't do this. The conditions are much worse than I thought. It isn't worth risking four lives to save one man who might already be dead."

She was right, of course. My plan had never been overloaded with logic. With help from Rick and his navigation skills, Betty would captain the boat while Doc worked the engine room. I was to be the only other passenger on board. The task was to cross the bay, land on Dutch Island, and hopefully arrive in time to prevent Caleb Mason from eliminating Michael Ravenel.

I turned to Alyana and took her hand. "If I could do this on my own, I would. I don't want anyone taking unnecessary chances. Problem is, I can't row a boat, never mind operate something one notch short of a ferry."

"Nobody should be out on that water, Rick. Nobody."

Her reaction was sharp and I knew why. The sea had taken her husband and was ready to claim another few souls.

I said, "If it weren't for Rick and Betty, I'd back off, Alyana. But the Weedens are experienced sailors. If they say we can make the crossing —"

"But why?" Alyana cried. "Ravenel's probably dead. And even if he's still alive, why should you put your life on the line to save him?"

Good question. One I heard before but put slightly differently by Doug Kool: aren't you tired of going out of your way to help every sorry ass you trip across?

"I have to try, Alyana," I said.

"Jesus, Rick!" Alyana snapped and pulled her hand away.

"I promise this will work out."

"I've heard that before," she said, tears inching down her cheeks. "Damnit! I've heard that before."

The others in the van were stone silent and obviously uncomfortable. I turned to Rick and Betty.

"Alyana's right. I can't put the two of you and Doc in jeopardy."

Betty looked at Rick and then at me. "We're not afraid of dying, Bullet. Death's paid us a call more than once and so far we're still here. Trust me, we can handle the crossing."

"I believe her," Doc said.

"But getting to Dutch Island may not be the issue here," Betty went on. "What happens after we land is what I'm worried about."

Yigal joined in. "You have the pistol Turnort let us borrow." He paused and pointed at the Smith & Wesson revolver jammed in my belt. "Will you use it is what I want to know?"

Yigal knew me well enough to know I favored guns about as much as I enjoyed liverwurst. But it was Doc who knew just how deep my repugnance for anything that discharged bullets really went.

"Yigal's asking the right question, Bullet," the professor said. "I've got my garage door opener stun gun but you've got the heavy artillery. If we run into Caleb, you can't diddle around. Shoot the bastard."

It wouldn't be easy pulling the trigger. For years, the Gateway had given me a front-row look at the damage firearms can do. Now I was packing a pistol with five .38 rounds that at close range could put Caleb Mason down permanently. Would I point and shoot? Frankly I wasn't sure, but decided against going public with my uncertainty.

"I'll take him out if it comes down to that," I said, sounding too much like John Wayne.

"Pop him in his eye," Twyla advised. "That's what Carmen Vittulo did to my cousin Angelo Hinkey. Angelo didn't die but his brain is pretty much dead. Oh, and they had to stitch up Angelo's bad eye, which is why everybody calls him Winky Hinky."

For a few seconds, no one knew what to say.

"Please don't do this," Alyana broke the silence with a whisper.

Betty put her hand on Alyana's arm. "You're right to feel the way you do. But there's a man's life at stake. For us to do nothing, Alyana, that's something that can eat at your conscience."

"How do can you be sure you'll make it to the island?"

"We'll make it," Betty insisted. "Rick and I know this bay and although it's been a while, we can handle a boat."

"There has to be another way."

"I can't think of one," Betty replied. "We'll be very careful, Alyana. You had your heart broken once and I won't be party to having it broken again. I promise you that."

I cranked my body around and pulled Alyana to me. Separated by the van's front seat, it was an awkward embrace that Alyana didn't resist.

"Damn you if you die or get hurt, Rick Bullock," she said softly.

"Won't happen," I said fully aware that it was a hollow assurance. Caleb Mason would kill me in a nanosecond if given a chance.

I kissed Alyana and stepped out of the van. Rick and Betty quickly followed. As planned Yigal climbed into the driver's seat, Benoit's 9 mm Walther handgun at his side. He would drive Twyla, Alyana, Olive, and Ellie Weasel back to Mason's doublewide where they would keep an eye on Evelyn until the police arrived. Yigal put the van in reverse, backed up a few feet, and abruptly stopped. Twyla opened the rear door and the ferret leaped out.

"Oh, jeez!" Twyla shouted over the wind at Doc. "Your weasel just had a panic attack! It was spinnin' around like a whirling derby. Take it, Doc! You gotta take it!"

Ellie zipped through the rain and attached herself to the professor's pant leg. Doc lifted the ferret to his left shoulder. I couldn't make out the expression on the professor's face but imagined it was a mix of aggravation and pure affection

"Saul Lipschitz sent a message from the other side," I said. "He thinks you're the greatest."

"Shove it," Doc growled. Ellie had a tight hold on the professor's shoulder, her head buried in Doc's overgrown white hair. The hissing had given way to stream of contented clucks.

I turned to Rick. "Can you make it?" The boarding ramp to the crew boat was at least seventy yards away and the wind was fierce. Rick's Parkinson's made it difficult for him to keep his balance even in the best of conditions. I knew he usually used a two-wheeled aluminum walker but it had been left behind when we made a hasty exit from the Weeden's Portsmouth home.

"Yeah, I can do it." Rick shifted most of his weight to a birch walking cane Betty handed to him. He kicked his left foot forward and marched toward the boat. He was a few feet from the gangplank when the toe of the cane jammed into a narrow gap between sections of the pier's polypropylene panels. The cane snapped and sent Rick sprawling to the wet surface.

Doc and I rushed to help but Betty was already at Rick's side. She waved us back. "It's okay," she said calmly. "If you have Parkinson's, you learn how to fall. It's part of the deal."

She hoisted Rick to his feet and retrieved the broken cane. It had splintered about a foot from the base and what remained of the shaft now looked more like a sharp spear than a walking stick.

"Damn thing's not much of a cane but it'll be great for Shish kabobs," Rick chuckled and ran a finger over the needlelike end of the stick. Betty laughed and grabbed her husband's right arm. The two walked in tandem to the gangplank and made their way on board. They were still giggling when Betty parked Rick in a chair adjacent to the captain's seat.

"Jesus, what an amazing pair," Doc said to me as we climbed into the boat and shoved the boarding platform aside. "If I kept getting curveballs thrown at me like those two, I'd be one pissy old man."

"You already are," I said.

"Of course there's one thing the Weedens may not be."

"Which is what?"

"Two people who can keep a boat from flipping over in the middle of a damn hurricane."

Doc stifled whatever doubts he had about the Weedens when Betty made it clear that not only did she know what she was doing, she was in full command. Doc was instructed to inspect the engine compartment and I was ordered to get ready to release the bow and stern lines. Doc yelled to Captain Weeden that the boat had two Hyundai diesel engines and a Cummins generator, all practically new.

"That's what I wanted to hear," Betty called back and turned the ignition key. The diesels instantly responded.

"Everyone come here," Betty shouted. Doc, Ellie Weasel, and I scrambled to the bridge. "Before we sail, I want you to understand what's going to happen. We'll be riding parallel to Dutch Island to start. For a time, we'll be pointing bow first into the wind and waves."

"This thing's just short of fifty feet and not that wide in the beam," noted Doc. "Can we handle the swells?"

Betty nodded confidently. "Yes. But we'll be fighting some very rough seas. So, Doc, make sure the bilge pump is working."

The professor saluted.

"The tricky part of the trip is making the turn toward Dutch Island. The boat will be broadside to both the wind and current for a short time. Once we come about, we should have no trouble heading to the dock Mason built on the island."

Ellie Weasel cackled her angst and I swallowed back what tasted too much like saltwater.

"Rick will work the GPS, depth finder, and radar," Betty continued. "Plus he knows this part of the bay like the back of his hand. He'll tell me how to clear a row of pilings just offshore and then it's up to him to keep us on the right side of a shoal buoy."

"Shoal buoy?" I asked.

Betty said, "There's some very shallow water out there. We definitely don't want to run aground. Not in this weather."

Doc looked skeptical. "Is this doable, Rick?"

"With a little luck."

"Which we're going to need," Betty added, "since we'll be sailing without lights. We're taking a chance we won't run into something."

"No lights?" Doc asked.

"Even in this bad weather, Caleb would see us coming if we're lit up."

"How long's this trip going take?" I wanted to know, hoping the answer would be in the five-minute range.

"If we don't sink, not long," Betty quipped. "Last word. If things go sour — if we take on too much water — if one of the engines quits — whatever — we abort. I'll turn if I can and then run with the wind back to Jamestown. Are we all on the same page?"

Everyone nodded yes and the preliminaries were finished. Betty sent me to untie the forward and aft lines. I unfastened the heavy, wet ropes from the dock cleats and the crew boat was free,

"Doc, get in the engine well and keep those diesels alive," Betty said.

"What can I do?" I asked.

"Find a seat in the cabin, hold on, and make sure your pistol stays dry. If we get to that island in one piece and your gun's not working, nobody's going to be your friend including the ferret."

The crew boat had chairs for twenty-four passengers so there was no shortage of seating options. I picked a spot near a window on the starboard side. Bad decision. A minute later, the boat hiked up and over the first monster wave then hurled down the backside with such speed and force that I was thrown out of my seat. The boat's bow plunged deep into the bay. The window where I had been sitting was partially underwater.

"Jesus!" I screamed to no one in particular. The boat had been pitched at such an angle that its stern was completely out of the bay, its twin props spinning wildly. Suddenly another huge wave pulled the bow upward and the boat righted itself.

"Sorry!" Betty yelled from the wheelhouse. "When we hit deeper water, the ride shouldn't be as rough. Do me a favor and check on Doc. Make sure he's okay."

I stumbled to the engine compartment. Doc was on his knees nursing a knot on his right temple. Ellie was at his side looking as displeased as she was dazed.

"Damn women drivers!" the professor shouted and pulled himself to his feet. He unzipped the top of his slicker and stuffed Ellie into a makeshift pouch.

"Probably not the best time to start with the sexist remarks," I said.

"She needs to back down on the speed."

"I think she already figured that out. Says things will improve when we hit deeper water."

"Yeah, well, she's right. More depth means the swells flatten out. Sometimes."

I didn't like Doc's caveat and I wanted an explanation. But another large wave ended our conversation. I was knocked back on my rump but Doc managed to stay upright by grabbing a handrail.

"Tell Betty we've got water," Doc yelled. "Not a lot, but we're taking in more than the bilge pump can spit out."

I staggered back to the wheelhouse and passed along the bad news. Betty was working the boat's dual throttles and Rick was hunched over the instrument panel calling out instructions to his wife. Moving the boat a degree to the port or starboard was no easy task given the weather. But it was critical to set a course that kept us away from the pilings near Fort Getty and the hazardous shallows along Jamestown's western shore. The two were fixated on their work, sweat beading down their faces.

The ride became a little less terrifying once we passed a buoy that I assumed marked the Beaverhead Point shoal. That meant we were in the deeper part of Dutch Harbor, the waterway separating Jamestown's West Ferry from Dutch Island. A few more minutes, and we'd be turning left, which would mean sailing broadside to the waves. I knew Betty was apprehensive about the maneuver, and for good reason. One good hit and capsizing was more than just a long shot.

"Tell Doc I'm going full throttle at the turn," Betty shouted back at me. "I don't want those engines to quit. When I find a smooth patch, we'll be doing an about face. So get ready."

I shuttled back to the engine compartment and told the professor to stand by. A minute later, the crew boat made a sharp turn tilting us dangerously to one side. A mountainous wall of water struck the vessel's hull. For a few seconds that morphed into an eternity, we teetered at a right angle to Dutch Harbor's muddy bottom. I was no sailor but knew the boat was at a tipping point. One more nudge and we would capsize.

Suddenly Betty cut the speed on the port engine and used the power of the starboard diesel to pull us out of trouble. The bow swung south and we began moving in the same direction as the wind and waves.

I lurched back to the wheelhouse.

"How I love you, Mr. Weeden!" Betty cried out with a laugh and high-fived her husband.

"Great work," I congratulated the pair, and asked the logical next question: when the hell was this rock-and-roll ride going to end?

Rick checked the radar screen. "A couple of minutes more to go."

Betty turned to me. "We're just northeast of Mason's pier on the western side of the island. Finding the dock won't be a problem – but we'll be going in fast."

"How fast?"

"Fast enough to get banged up. The storm's pushing us hard and I don't know if I can get enough reverse thrust out of our two engines to make this a soft landing."

What the hell! I thought. We had just cheated death on the high seas and now this?

"Doc should get out of the engine well just in case," said Betty. "The main cabin will be safer."

I helped Doc out of the engine room. He was smudged with grease and his shirt bulged at the stomach. Ellie Weasel was in hiding and not about to make an appearance. Smart ferret.

When the crew boat neared Mason's Dutch Island dock, Betty reversed both engines. The diesels shrieked and the boat slowed slightly but not enough to keep it from riding over a shard of steel that stuck up and out of the water like a shark fin. The piece of metal was thin and sharp. It slit through our boat's aluminum hull with ease nearly cutting it in half. Water gushed into the engine compartment and main cabin.

"Damnit!" Betty cursed and then bellowed at Doc and me. "We're close enough to the dock where we can get off. But there's not much time. So move!"

The current and wind pushed the fast-sinking boat against Mason Development Company's recently built pier. I yanked Doc to the aft deck and pushed him up and onto the pier's concrete surface. Rick was already out of the wheelhouse and Betty not far behind him.

"Your cane!" Doc called out to Rick who was struggling to get off the boat. "Give me one end and you hold the other!"

Rick poked the sharp end of the cane toward the professor, who grabbed the shaft and pulled. Betty and I were still on board the crew boat and boosted Rick to safety. Then we hoisted ourselves onto the pier.

"What the hell happened?" I asked Betty. Before getting an answer, the crew boat groaned and disappeared.

Betty caught her breath. "I don't know. There's something under water next to the pier. Whatever it is, we ran into it and the damn thing nearly killed us."

"What nearly killed you is your own stupidity."

There was no mistaking the voice. I pulled the Smith & Wesson from my belt and spun around.

"Not a good idea!" Caleb Mason yelled and pointed the nose of a Heckler and Koch MP5 submachine in my direction. He sprayed a half dozen 9 mm rounds over my head, and I dropped the pistol.

"What are you doing, you asshole!" Doc screamed at Caleb. "We came here to help you!"

"I don't think so." Mason drew closer. The usually impeccable Caleb was a mess. Rain had flattened his hair and the wind blew back his unzipped L.L. Bean jacket.

"Listen, you dumb bastard," Doc screeched, "we risked our asses –"

Caleb cut the professor off with a hard thwack to his right leg. Doc crumpled to the ground.

"You're not here to help me," Caleb said calmly. "You came here to help him." He motioned to his rear. Barely visible because of darkness and the relentless rain was a body lying motionless on the pier. We didn't need a closer look to know who it was.

"Damnit, you killed him!" I shouted, cursing myself more than Caleb. This ridiculous, treacherous rescue mission was everything Alyana said it was. An act of total stupidity that never had a chance from the get-go.

"Correction. He's still alive," Caleb said. "But not for long."

Michael Ravenel still had a pulse? That didn't make sense. Caleb had obviously found a way to knock the lieutenant unconscious. And since finishing him off was the goal, why the delay?

"I'm curious, Caleb –"

Mason cut me off. "Shut up! I want everyone on their knees with hands behind your backs except you." Caleb pointed at Rick.

I dropped to a prayer position. "Tell me if I have it right," I kept pressing Mason. "You didn't put a bullet in Ravenel because if his body gets found, the cause of death has to be accidental, right?"

Caleb ignored me, and pulled several nylon cord hand restraints from his pocket. He threw them at Rick. "That fat bastard Templeton was right," Caleb said. "He told me the owner of the Dutch Island deed has Parkinson's."

Rick stood at an angle, balancing himself on his shortened cane. He grabbed the braided ropes with his left hand but not without difficulty. The catch upset his equilibrium and for a second, it looked like he would land face first on the pier.

"You and your goddamned wife caused me a lot of grief," Caleb muttered. "All you had to do was hand over the deed and none of this would have been necessary."

I could see Rick fighting to stay alert. He was coming off what Betty called his "on" period that had lasted a couple of hours. Next would come a longer stretch of sleep or semiconsciousness.

"We didn't know you were looking for the deed," Rick managed to say in a raspy voice.

Caleb said, "Probably because you and your wife are as mindless as you are useless."

Rick's body shook more violently than I had seen since I had met the man. The tremor had nothing to do with his Parkinson's or the wind. It was pure, unadulterated rage.

"Know what I think?" Caleb kept talking at Rick. "I think a cripple like you can be of some use. Put those hand restraints on everyone's wrists and do it right or I'll pound the hell out of your wife's worthless head."

The restraints were Tuff-Ties, as common in New Jersey as traffic jams. Put on properly, they were as effective as handcuffs thanks to a double-locking polycarbonate block that made it nearly impossible to get the cord off.

I kept after Caleb hoping to buy time and a miracle. "I'm right, aren't I? Ravenel's still alive because you want him to die your way. Stick his head in the bay, let his lungs fill up, and then it's death by drowning. Any coroner in the country would rule it an accident."

"Quite the smart-ass, aren't you?" Caleb bent over me.

"Not smart enough. I should have figured long ago it was you who ordered the hit on your own father."

"A mercy killing," Caleb said without a hint of remorse. "The old man was a miserable prick. When he turned into a crazy miserable prick, getting rid of him was an act of kindness."

"What about getting rid of your brother? Killing J. D was another act of kindness?"

"Success means knowing how to get past impediments – or removing them."

"J. D. was an impediment?" I asked.

Instead of answering, Caleb kicked Tommy Tornort's Smith & Wesson into the water. "Any other weapons?"

"You must know you're chin deep in trouble, Caleb," I said. "There's no going back."

Rick had already cuffed Doc's and Betty's hands and began working on me. He was keeping the Tuff-Ties loose, but I knew Caleb would follow up and tighten the braided nylon cords. Once that happened, it was game over.

"Move out of the way," Caleb told Rick once he finished. Rick picked up his cane and stepped to the side.

As predicted, Caleb circled behind us and pulled the restraints taut. When he reached me, he leaned forward and spoke into my right ear.

"Going back is not a problem for me, Bullock," Caleb snarled. "That's because I think ahead. Unlike you who put yourself and your friends here in a very bad situation."

Score one for Caleb Mason.

"Nearly as bad a situation as you'll be in once Benoit and Nonesuch start talking," I lied assuming Caleb hadn't heard about the shootout at Beavertail Park.

"Using the two of them was a calculated risk," said Caleb. "Which is why there's always been a plan B."

"Which is?"

Caleb didn't say a word but gave me the answer with a smug expression and a look at the agitated surface of Narragansett Bay.

"So you've got a backdoor exit," I guessed. "What's the plan? A boat shows up in the middle of a cyclone to save your butt? How much is that costing you?"

"Boat doesn't do justice to a very sophisticated and very expensive submersible," Caleb disclosed.

"You're going to leave behind a deal that could be worth a lot of money, Caleb. Doesn't sound like you."

"I'm leaving behind the deal but not the money."

"Really? Because I don't see any bags of cash."

Caleb laughed. "Welcome to the electronic world, fool. The money's in a set-aside fund I have access to courtesy of Mohammad al-Talal."

I had to hand it to him – Caleb had indeed planned ahead. "Al-Talal's not going to let you tap that account."

"Already tapped."

"Then the sound you hear next will be the footsteps of a billion Muslims paid to hunt you down," I warned.

"That might happen if al-Talal thought I was alive. But why hunt for a dead man?"

I got the picture. "Ravenel and you died while crossing the bay."

"Exactly. The boat Ravenel and I took to the island sunk. It's what you ran into when docking a few minutes ago."

I finished the story. "Ravenel drowns and his body gets washed ashore but you're missing at sea."

"It's a bad storm," Caleb said and moved behind Betty to check her hands. "When they find my lifejacket floating in the bay, my name gets added to the list of victims who drowned."

"I don't think so," I argued. "When four more bodies are found with their hands tied behind their backs, it won't take a genius to figure out who's responsible."

Caleb stooped and picked up the end of a rope that looked to be at least twenty feet long. Tied to the other end was a heavy metal anchor. "There'll be nothing suspicious about your corpse, Bullock. I'm going to tie a weight and rope to your chest. Oh, you'll fight to stay afloat but not for long. After a few minutes underwater, I'll haul you to the surface. Clip. Clip. Your hand restraints are gone and so are you."

"You're one sick bastard," Doc muttered.

Caleb reached into his pocket for the last of the Tuff-Ties, and walked toward Rick. "As I said before, if you had handed over the Dutch Island deed, we wouldn't be here."

"Never too late," Rick said, his words labored.

Caleb said, "Meaning what?"

"Don't you know?" Rick paused and looked at Betty, Doc, and me. "Maybe he doesn't. Should I tell him?"

We didn't have a clue where Rick was heading. But it was apparent that wherever it was, this was likely to be our last shot at staying alive.

"What the hell are you talking about?" Caleb asked, his face no more than two inches from Rick's.

"You want the Dutch Island deed, right? Well, we have it."

"Horseshit," snarled Caleb.

Instantly, Doc Waters caught on. "Jesus, Rick. Don't go there! Not yet!"

Rick used his cane to steady himself. He was at war with his body trying to stay upright and awake. "Why not, Doc? That's why we brought it. Right? In case we needed a bargaining chip?"

"We had an agreement, damnit!" Doc swore. "I'm the one who starts the bargaining. Not you!"

Rick stumbled slightly and drew in a breath. "Then what are you waiting for?" he asked, his voice nearly lost in the wind and rain.

"All right, all right!" said Doc and looked up at Mason. "There's a buyer who wants the deed."

Caleb's suspicion was obvious. "Not after al-Talal pulls out. Dutch Island will be worthless and so will the deed."

"You and al-Talal have turned that island into the most-publicized chunk of land in the country," said Doc. "As soon as you and the Muslims move out of the way, the buyer has other plans for Dutch Island."

"What plans?"

"A casino on Dutch Island. Plus an upscale hotel on your Jamestown Island construction site. And a bunch of fancy water taxis in between."

"Ah, I see," Caleb smiled. "Manny Maglio has a dream."

"More than a dream," Rick said. "We've seen the plans. But the project won't happen unless al-Talal is out and the original deed is in Maglio's hands. Make those two things happen and a lot of money shows up."

"How much?" Caleb asked.

"A few million," I joined in.

"What does a 'few' mean?"

"It's negotiable," I said, hoping I was on the same track as Rick and Doc. "We know Manny's got backing for over a hundred fifty million for the full project. The deed's probably worth five million. Maybe more."

Greed was the only impediment between us and Narragansett Bay. And for the moment, it was standing tall.

"I see where this is going," said Caleb. "We all sail back to Jamestown, you hand over the deed, and I let you live. For five million, it's not worth the risk. Sorry."

Caleb moved toward Betty, his first victim.

"Hold it!" Rick shouted. "You don't need to go to Jamestown."

"What the hell are you talking about?"

"The deed's here," Rick said.

Caleb stepped back from Betty. "Here?"

"Jesus, Rick!" Doc shouted

"It's time, Doc," Rick insisted.

"If we give up the deed, we're dead!" Doc wailed.

"He doesn't believe we have it," Rick replied. "Let's hand it over."

Doc winced. "Then he kills us!"

"No, he won't," Rick said in a whisper

"Ah, but I will," Caleb corrected. "Frankly, I could care less whether you have the deed or not. You've all turned the goddamned thing into a worthless piece of paper."

Rick turned to Caleb. "Worthless? We can come up with five million reasons why you're wrong."

"Let me replay what I told you earlier. I have a very fat offshore account. What makes you think another five million would do anything for me?"

"Because you know al-Talal isn't an idiot," Rick answered. "He's not going to buy the lost-at-sea story. Take the deed and work out a long-distance sale with Maglio. You'll need another five million if you expect to outrun one of the richest Arabs in the world."

Caleb hiked his eyebrows. Maybe Rick's fabrication had Mason worried.

"Your professor here," Caleb nodded to Doc, "has a point. Once I have the deed, what's to keep me from killing all of you?"

"A phone call," Rick rasped back an answer.

"Phone call?"

"To Manny Maglio. He knows we have the deed. Unless we tell him we worked a deal to give it to you, Maglio won't believe you have the real thing."

Caleb leveled the MP5 at Rick's midsection and stroked the weapon's trigger. "All right. I'm curious enough to go the next step. Let me have the deed, and then we'll talk."

"Don't!" Doc shouted.

Rick pushed the gun's barrel to one side and steadied himself on his cane. "It's rolled up in a waterproof plastic shipping tube," he said. "Unzip Doc's jacket and you'll find what you're looking for."

"Damnit!" Doc screamed.

Caleb shifted the MP5 to his left hand and stepped toward Doc Waters. Rick took three unsteady steps and positioned himself behind Mason. Feet spread apart to hold his balance, Rick lifted his cane and pointed its tip toward Caleb's lower back. As if he knew the playbook by heart, Doc gave Rick a slight nod.

"Let's see if this is for real, old man," Caleb said and tugged on Doc's coat zipper with his right hand.

Suddenly exposed, Ellie Weasel shot out of her cocoon with an earsplitting shriek. Caleb jerked upright at the same instant Rick drove the needle point of his cane beneath Mason's jacket and into the man's flesh. With as much thrust as he could muster, Rick punched the wooden spear past Caleb's vertebral column and deep into his abdomen. The force of Rick's attack, Caleb's own backward momentum proved catastrophic. The cane ripped open Caleb's liver and right kidney.

Mason sank to his knees at the same time Doc shifted to a sitting position. Using both legs, the professor drove his feet into Caleb's stomach forcing the tip of Rick's cane deeper into the wounded man's gut.

Betty rolled to her right and kicked the MP5 from Caleb's hand. The weapon skittered over the slippery pier and into Narragansett Bay. I jockeyed myself close to Rick so he could use what little energy he had left to loosen my nylon handcuffs.

Exhausted, Rick fell backward and listened as the ferret's screams turned to an eerie moan and Caleb's labored gasps were caught up in the bawling wind.

– Chapter 26 –

Twyla Rosenblatt adjusted the sheer mesh shoulder straps on her body-hugging wrap dress. The leopard-print spandex wasn't something most mothers-to-be would even think about wearing. But Twyla was about as far from a typical pregnant woman as her husband was from a typical lawyer.

"Look at you!" Rinaldo the waiter squealed. "You're back!"

Indeed we were. Back at Jamestown's Trattoria Simpatico seated at the same outside table where Twyla and Yigal first told me they were expecting a Boaz or a Tzufit.

"And Olive!" Rinaldo got to one knee and stroked the poodle's fuzzy topknot all the while keeping his eyes glued to Twyla's supersized boobs. "You know what you are? All of you's? Celebrities, is what you are!"

"We are?" Twyla chirped with a smile.

Rinaldo said, "Yeah, of course! You're in the papers. You're famous!"

If fame comes from a one paragraph mention in an Associated Press wire release tagged *RHODE ISLAND BLOODBATH*, then the Rinaldo was right. The Rosenblatts were media sensations.

Rinaldo turned to me and winked. "What a story you and your wife are gonna tell your kid."

"Oh, no," I said. "She's not my – I mean, the baby's not –"

"Listen, this is what I'm gonna do," Rinaldo cut me off. "I remember what you like. Chocolate banana brownie cake and an espresso for everybody. Olive, you get ground sirloin. And you know what? There's no charge for anythin'."

Rinaldo unlatched his eyes from Twyla's chest, did an about face, and headed for the restaurant's interior. I checked Yigal, thinking he might want to straighten Rinaldo out about whose sperm was responsible for his wife' condition. But the lawyer was dealing with a more pressing issue. He had his cell pressed against his ear listening to Manny Maglio scream that a stripper named Daizee Chane was suing for wrongful termination.

Twyla settled into her chair and gave me a life-is-great smile. And why not? It was a beautiful early fall afternoon. Jamestown's East Ferry neighborhood had lost most of its tourists and was humming along at an easy pace. In the distance, we watched a few sailboats catch a light breeze that swept over Narragansett Bay.

"Everything worked out so great for everybody, Bullet!" said Twyla.

Well not for everybody.

Yves Benoit and William Nonesuch were dead. Caleb Mason was in guarded condition at Newport Hospital, Rick Weeden's cane having done a lot of damage to Mason's internal organs. Because of the violent storm that battered much of New England, it had taken the Coast Guard two hours to reach Dutch Island and then another hour to transport Mason to the hospital emergency room. By then, internal bleeding and other complications had taken their toll. It had been a week since Mason underwent his first surgery, and doctors were still on the fence as to whether he would make it.

Mohammad al-Talal didn't come out a winner either. The storm of negative publicity was too much for the Lebanese Arab who scrapped plans to build a replica of the al-Masjid al-Haram mosque on Dutch Island. Al-Talal made a brief public statement about disassociating himself and his money from what was left of the Mason Development Company – and from a nation of morally depraved degenerates.

There were other losers too. Hundreds maybe thousands of southern New Englanders whose employment hopes had been riding on Dutch Island turning into a multiyear construction boon.

Even Maureen O'Connor hadn't fared well. What was supposed to be a few days in the hospital to treat a broken foot had turned into an indefinite stay. I don't know what was worse for Mrs. O'Connor – fighting off a nosocomial infection or having to apologize to me. Maureen's fast-food maven hubby even begrudgingly threw me a mea culpa and insisted I return to the O'Connor's waterside mansion to spend the last couple of days of my so-called vacation.

"Oh, and how about Uncle Manny!" said Twyla. "Isn't he something? He's gonna buy Dutch Island if it goes up for sale, Bullet, and then donate the land back to Rhode Island. Didn't I tell you he was special?"

I don't know about special but for sure Manny was ecstatic. With al-Talal out and the Muslim tide having receded, Maglio's gambling and strip club investors were bullish. Sin was back in, and Manny couldn't be happier.

"The island will be for sale, is what I'm sure about," Yigal joined the conversation after scribbling a note on a yellow legal pad: $20,000 cash to

Daizee Chane. "A lot of creditors in line but Mason Development has assets. They'll all get sold off, is what I think."

I asked, "What happens to the property Mason owns here on Jamestown Island?"

"It'll be zoned residential," Yigal predicted. "It's on the water. Very valuable is what it is."

Rinaldo returned with a small bowl of uncooked beef and placed it in front of Olive's nose. The poodle waited until I gave her the command to eat and then she slowly and delicately consumed the meat.

"What manners she has!" Rinaldo said to me without unlocking his eyes from Twyla's chest. "Ah, such a lucky man! You have two beautiful ladies. Miss Olive here. And a gorgeous wife who's gonna give you a bambino."

"About that, I think you've got it wrong," I tried explaining again. Too late. Rinaldo was ten feet from our table and disappearing fast.

"Sooo –" Twyla grinned and took my hand. "What about you and Alyana?"

"I don't know," I said honestly. "We're taking it slow and we'll see how things work out."

"Are you going back to Jersey, Bullet?"

I said, "Day after tomorrow. Vacation's done. It's back to running the Gateway Shelter."

"Long distance isn't good for people in love," Twyla warned.

I wasn't sure but I think I blushed. "The drive time between Jamestown and central Jersey is less than five hours. I'm scheduling a few extra-long weekends between now and the end of the year."

"And?" Twyla cooed.

"And what?"

"And if the two of you decide to – you know – get married?"

"Oh, hold on. You've got that boat moving a little too fast."

"Yeah, but just suppose. Let's say you do get married. You know what?"

"What?"

Twyla's grin flattened into a stern look. "Yigee and I won't stand you up. We'll be at your wedding no matter when or where it is."

Touché. I had made more than a few bad decisions over the years. Blowing off the Rosenblatt's Florida wedding was one of the worst.

"We're going to Doc Water's wedding, too," Yigal intervened with what was a perfect diversion. As crazy as he might be, Yigal Rosenblatt had become a good friend who knew his wife had just gored my conscience. He was throwing me a lifeline.

"Doc's getting married?" I gasped.

"Miriam Constable Reis."

Wait a minute. Was this Yigal's way of sidetracking his wife or was this for real? "Miriam – the Jamestown librarian?" I asked.

Yigal fixed his yarmulke and nodded.

I said, "But Miriam's still got a husband."

"Doc says not for long."

Mother of God, I thought. What the hell kind of mess was the professor stumbling into now?

"Even if Miriam's real husband isn't dead, he sort of is because he's deminted," Twyla said. "So Doc shouldn't wait. You'd go to his weddin', right Bullet?"

"That's bigamy."

Twyla's face turned deadly serious. "Yes, it would be big of you. Too bad you didn't think that way when you got our wedding invitation!"

Two things happened at once that pulled me out of the surreal vortex that seemed to always swirl around the Rosenblatts. First, Rinaldo showed up with free cake. Twyla attacked her chocolate banana brownie with a vengeance while Yigal tried explaining why eating the dessert would be a violation of Jewish halakhic law and a surefire ticket to hell.

The second development showed up on wheels. Two cars braked to a stop in front of Trattoria Simpatico and Michel Ravenel unfolded his six two frame from the Crown Vic that was in the lead. Right behind was my old Buick driven by the young Jamestown police officer who had been assigned to keep watch over Alyana's property and the O'Connor estate.

"Thought I'd arrange for a door-to-door delivery," Michael Ravenel wagged his head at the Buick.

"I was wondering if I'd ever see it again."

Ravenel smiled, said hello to the Rosenblatts, and asked if he could talk to me in private. I guessed he was looking for separation not because he had anything confidential to say but because he wasn't fond of lunacy. We strolled to the sidewalk, Olive at my side.

"Listen, about the car," said Ravenel. "When the boys go pecking around for evidence, they take things apart. When it comes to putting all the pieces back together again sometimes there are parts left over."

"Sort of a Humpty Dumpty deal."

"Exactly. So if it doesn't run right, call me."

This was a different Lieutenant Ravenel. "All right."

"So I just wanted to –" Ravenal paused and ran a hand over the bandage covering the thirty stitches on the left side of his head. "Well, I know I jerked you around a lot –"

"That you did."

"Then you end up saving my ass."

"Not just me," I corrected.

"Yeah, I know. Betty and Rick Weeden. A pretty incredible couple."

"In a lot of ways."

"I probably wouldn't be here if it weren't for them."

"You got that right."

The lieutenant turned his head and looked toward the shoreline on the far side of the bay. "I'm heading over to Portsmouth to thank them."

"They'd appreciate that. While you're there, ask them to show you the copy of the Dutch Island deed they have hanging on their bedroom wall."

Ravenel looked surprised. "A copy? Where's the original?"

"The Sydney L. Wright Museum. Somebody I know whispered in Mariam Reis's ear about how the original has historical importance. Should be a big-time tourist attraction."

"Miriam Reis the librarian?"

"And museum curator," I said and then silently hoped she wouldn't earn another moniker: felon serving life for the murder of an Alzheimer's patient who also happened to be her husband.

"Anyway, I wanted to drop off the car and say thanks."

"Your welcome."

"By the way, Caleb's assistant has turned into a prosecutor's dream."

"Evelyn?"

"That's the one. She told us where to find Mason's private papers and a ledger that explains why Caleb wanted his daddy and brother out of the picture."

"Let me guess. Money."

"Bingo. Caleb has been skimming the company for years and losing just about everything he stole. One bad investment and one expensive woman after another."

"I don't get it. He said he embezzled millions from al-Talal – money he was going to collect after he faked his own death."

"Caleb convinced al-Talal to set up an offshore account for bribing whatever politician, union boss, or bureaucrat needed to be bought. Roughly thirty million, which Caleb had access to. Not a huge sum compared to what Mason might have sucked out of the tunnel project, but enough to live comfortably if he had to cut and run."

Ravenel was bringing a hazy picture into focus. I said, "So getting his hands on the Dutch Island deed –"

"It was part of what drove Caleb to do what he did," Ravenel interjected. "But he had other motives. As far as we know, his father's death had nothing to do with the deed. Harold Mason was murdered because he found out his son had his hand in the company cookie jar."

Flashback to Harold Mason's mangled skull and the ax-wielding man who slipped into Narragansett Bay. "Caleb hired Yves Benoit to do the dirty work."

"Yeah."

"And Caleb's brother?"

"J. D. was dumb as an earthworm. But somehow he got wind of what was going on. He forced a showdown and since there was no love lost between the two Mason brothers, Caleb had no qualms about killing the horse's ass."

I needed clarification. "Benoit didn't murder J.D.?"

"We don't think so. Seems it was strictly a brotherly act. Caleb took care of business and bagged a little cranial memento. Then he called Benoit who used his cigarette break to make a fast drive to meet Caleb someplace away from where you were eating dinner. Seems Mr. Mason didn't want to risk being seen anywhere near your vintage car. After Yves drove back to the restaurant, he slapped J.D.'s brains on your front bumper and grille."

"What about the rest of the body count?" I asked.

"Murder for hire," answered Ravenel. "Benoit and Nonesuch handled most of the work. We don't know if al-Talal's money was involved or if the Arab even knew anything about what was going on. But there are a lot of people in Washington pick axing their way through Mohammad's transactions with the Mason Development Company."

I nodded and ran a hand over Olive's shoulders and back. "What about you?" I asked and gestured to the bandage that covered much of his left temple.

Ravenel shrugged. "Headaches every now and then. But I'm doing better."

"I'm glad." And I meant what I said.

Ravenel shook my hand, gave me the keys to my Buick, and walked to his Crown Vic. The uniformed cop who had been behind the wheel of my car was now aboard Ravenel's Ford.

The lieutenant stopped and turned. "I hear you might be making a few more trips up this way."

"Might be."

"Probably will regret saying this since trouble sticks to you like a barnacle, but maybe one of those times we could get together."

"Interrogation room?"

Ravenel laughed. "There's a bar in Newport. Steamed clams and two-for-one beers on weeknights."

"First round's on me."

Ravenel smiled and coiled himself into his Ford. The car turned north on Conanicus Avenue heading toward the Newport Bridge.

After a few more minutes with the Rosenblatts, Olive and I slipped into my Buick and drove south toward Beavertail. The poodle was usually restricted to the rear of the car but not today. She sat in the front passenger seat where you'd want a good friend to be.

END

– Author's Epilogue –

To the publishing trade, *Dutch Island* is a comedic mystery. But this novel has deeper roots. Woven through the fiction are historical facts, unsettling medical truths, and a real-life tale of profound love and courage.

Dutch Island is not an imagined place. It is quite real. The eighty-two-acre dot of land sits about a mile west of Jamestown (also known as Conanicut) Island. Uninhabited and overgrown with catbriers, bittersweet and poison ivy, its current state belies an extraordinary past.

In 1636, the Dutch West India Company picked the little triangular-shaped island to trade cloth and liquor for furs and fish from the Narragansett Indians – hence the name Dutch Island. A dozen years later, a group of religious dissidents from the Massachusetts Bay Colony brokered a land deal that eventually turned the island into common pasture for grazing sheep. Then in 1657, Cashanaquont, the head sachem of the Narragansetts, sold Jamestown and Dutch Island to a group of 100 English settlers. The most prominent and wealthiest of the new landowners was Benedict Arnold (whose namesake great-grandson would become the notorious Revolutionary War traitor). Among the others, a Quaker named William Weeden whose father had fled England's intolerance in 1638 and landed in Boston aboard the three-masted ship *Martin.*

William produced nine children. Most of the present-day Weedens – at least those with East Coast roots – can trace their lineage to this prolific man. William's fourth son, John, inherited much of his father's land holdings, including property on Dutch Island. But John's good fortune was short lived. He drowned in Narragansett Bay in 1710 and in his will left "house and lands given to me by my father – also cattle, lands, tools, and shore at Dutch Island" to his son Daniel and bequeathed other Dutch Island property rights to another son, also named John.

In 1741, son John sold his Dutch Island holdings to brother Daniel for twenty-five pounds sterling (worth about $5,000 in today's currency). The original deed authorizing the transaction was signed in the name of Great Britain's King George the Second and is now framed and on display in the home of Richard Weeden, who twenty generations later lives in Portsmouth, Rhode Island, only a few miles from Dutch Island.

In the nineteenth century, Dutch Island and the fertile, bountiful lands bordering Narragansett Bay became known as the "Garden of New England." The island contributed to the growth of a livestock industry which met market demands from Boston to Barbados. Then in 1827, a thirty-foot stone beacon was erected on the southern tip of the island, changing the look and ultimately the purpose of "Little Dutch."

Like the fictitious Mohammad al-Talal, the U.S. government recognized the island's logistical importance. The "light station" built on six acres acquired by the government became an important navigational aid to the growing number of ships navigating Narragansett Bay's West Passage. Three decades later, the station was upgraded with a forty-two-foot light tower complete with fog bell. Construction was completed just before the onset of the Civil War and was a precursor to the transition of Dutch Island into a military encampment.

Although never attacked by the Confederates, Dutch Island still found its way into the wartime's history books – albeit as a footnote. An African-American regiment – the 14th Heavy Artillery – was assigned to the island and charged with defending the bay's strategically critical West Passage. The regiment's eight artillery pieces were never used in battle and once the war shifted in the Union's favor, the 14th (1,800 men strong) was sent to Texas and later New Orleans.

Dutch Island's military importance was even more significant just before and during the Spanish American War. Throughout the 1880s and 1890s, most of the island was transformed into a fortress. Antiquated gun batteries were replaced with mortars and heavy-duty weapons. Fort Greble, named after a West Point lieutenant killed during the Civil War, took over part of the island complete with tunnel-connected gun emplacements. But the island's fortifications were never tested. The 1898 Treaty of Paris ended all military engagements with the Spanish and the island was converted into a training venue for militia and naval units.

During the First and Second World Wars, Dutch Island met another need – a holding pen for German prisoners of war. After the armistices, the federal government's General Service Administration assumed control of the property until 1956 when it was officially handed over to the state of Rhode Island.

Today, Dutch Island stands uninhabited with the ruins of Fort Greble and the old, recently restored lighthouse the only visible mementoes of decades and centuries past. From Jamestown's West Ferry, the island's overgrown shore is clearly visible. Easily seen are the parcels of land once owned by Daniel Weeden, and by virtue of the 1741 deed, possibly (albeit improbably) still real estate that belongs to his multitude of descendents.

Had Daniel Weeden been in a position to name the modern-day protector of his Dutch Island land deed, Rick Weeden would have been his hands-down pick. Rick and his wife, Betty Weeden, are – like Dutch Island – far from illusory. Yes, the couple's encounters at the close of the novel are fabricated. But the everyday challenges met and overcome by these two remarkable people are no less heroic. Theirs is a true story about how misfortune can be trumped by determination and devotion.

Rick graduated from Worcester Polytechnic Institute with a mechanical engineering degree in 1968. Shortly after college, he accepted a job with the Raytheon Corporation, married a nurse named Betty Sargent, and settled in Portsmouth, Rhode Island, a near postcard-perfect New England community. The two had a daughter, a comfortable home, and an all-American life. That is until Rick turned thirty-three and was diagnosed with Parkinson's disease (PD).

An estimated one million Americans have PD, just one in twenty is under the age of forty. As a disease that mainly impacts older men and women, Rick's diagnosis made him a medical outlier of sorts. It also turned him into a valuable research subject. For decades, Rick became a central figure in PD experimentation, not only in the search for the cause of the disease but also in the pursuit of more effective treatments.

PD is idiopathic, meaning no clear explanation can be determined as to why some individuals contract the disease and others do not. In Rick's case, there is no known family history of PD, which led researchers to theorize the disease might not be genetic but possibly linked to an incident that took place while Rick was in college. During his junior year, Rick got caught in a campus brawl while trying to keep a young coed from getting injured. His chivalry cost him a serious head injury. The possibility that this could be a "Mohammad Ali" effect where a severe concussion was the precursor to PD has been folded into a database that researchers continue to refine in hopes of finding clues as to what causes the disease.

While Rick's background may help pinpoint *why* PD happens, it is *how* his disease has been treated that has added the most to the body of knowledge about Parkinson's. For ten years after his diagnosis, Rick's symptoms were

Betty and Rick Weeden

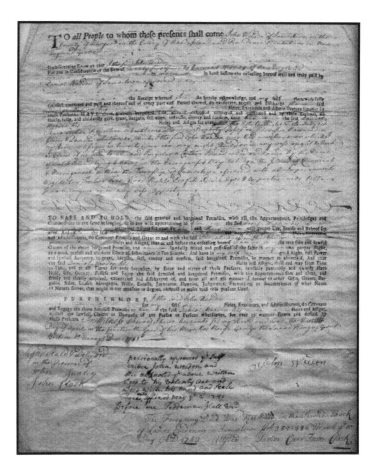

The original Dutch Island Deed signed in 1741 and registered two years later by Jamestown's town clerk on behalf of England's King George the Second.

Photo by Kraig Anderson

Dutch Island Lighthouse. The beacon was re-illuminated in 2007 after being dark for twenty-eight years. The Dutch Island Lighthouse Society is working to maintain the lighthouse and the solar-powered lantern that blinks a welcome to ships sailing into Narragansett Bay's West Passage.

Photo by Kraig Anderson

Beavertail Lighthouse. This rocky point at the southern tip of Jamestown Island is the scene of a life or death showndown for the novel's Rick Bullock and company.

238

controlled by medication. Trembling hands, rigid muscles, and general mobility problems were kept in check by different drugs. Then in 1989, Rick's body rebelled. He developed dyskinesias – a drug side effect all too familiar to many PD patients. His movements became uncontrollable. At rest, his legs constantly writhed. When walking, his feet would jerk up and to the side making a normal gait nearly impossible.

Rick was caught between two horrible options. Use the prescribed drugs, knowing his body would fight back with unmanageable consequences. Don't use the drugs and either freeze in place or deal with balance problems so severe that crawling was the only way to move from place to place.

With standard PD treatment alternatives exhausted, Rick sought the help of a Finnish neurosurgeon who had resurrected and refined a medical procedure called a pallidotomy. Surgeons made a small hole in Rick's skull and inserted a probe that carried an electrical current into the brain. An electrode was used to stimulate or inactivate cells that secrete dopamine, a neurotransmitter that carries signals between brain cells.

Rick underwent three pallidotomy procedures, one in Sweden and two others at the prestigious Massachusetts General Hospital. For a few years after the operations, Rick's quality of life improved. But a pallidotomy is not a PD cure. It buys time. The disease is degenerative and eventually Rick was back to battling the loss of functioning mobility along with many other debilitating problems associated with PD.

Today, Rick's fight with PD continues. And the combat isn't restricted to countering muscle rigidity or motion problems that are the more apparent PD symptoms. He also has to fend off emotional and psychological assaults that can make the disease especially devastating.

Anti-PD medications are known to cause hallucinations and delusions in some patients – Rick included. The disease can also trigger mood fluctuations that happen when the brain stops producing a steady flow of dopamine. A patient can transition from a deep sense of sadness to euphoria in just minutes. Some physicians equate these extreme swings to a kind of bipolar disorder that plays itself out over and over again each day. The fictional account of Rick's novel-ending resolve to keep from slipping into a mental as well as physical "down" period dramatizes what it is like for PD patients who must consistently cope with these "in" and "out" time brackets.

As with many other Parkinson's patients, Rick's medical problems can't be disguised. The challenges he faces are very obvious. What's not so evident is how the disease affects family and friends particularly his principal caretaker – his wife, Betty.

With a blend of toughness, intelligence, humor, and compassion, Betty has been Rick's PD navigator for nearly thirty-five years. Trained as an operating room nurse, Betty is able to give Rick around-the-clock, hands-on medical attention. Equally as valuable are Betty's administrative skills that she honed as director of surgical services at Rhode Island's Newport Hospital. Her knowledge, experience, and tenacity have made her the ideal patient advocate. She has left no stone unturned in the search for the best possible course of treatment for her husband; no avenue unexplored in the hunt for ways to make Rick's life as comfortable as possible.

What Betty *hasn't* done is to allow Parkinson's to get in the way of life. Determined that she and Rick should travel, Betty bought a used thirty-two-foot Class A motor home. For years, she has single-handedly driven Rick and family dog, Brandie, up and down the East Coast. A woman in her sixties operating a five-ton vehicle with a disabled husband on board might be inconceivable to some. But to those who know Betty, it's totally understandable. She's never had a shortage of fortitude and there's always been an oversupply of friendliness. So at campgrounds from Florida to New Hampshire, people have come to know and admire the Portsmouth Weedens. As well they should.

Betty and Rick are an extraordinary couple made all the more so by their extraordinary marriage. Few people are so bound together as these two. Betty has a devotion to her husband that is limitless and Rick's connection runs much deeper than what some might wrongly judge as dependency. Long before Rick's PD diagnosis, their relationship was out of the ordinary. These are people who truly care about each other; whose lives are totally interlocked.

For all the pain that Parkinson's inflicts on its victims and families, ironically it can also magnify what's good and right. It takes but a few minutes with Betty and Rick to discover this cruel disease gives definition to self-sacrifice, incredible resilience, and unconditional love.

# #

Over 270 years ago, a Dutch Island land transaction between John and Daniel Weeden was recorded as a deed of record and authorized with a signature and seal by a representative of His Majesty George II of Great Britain. Generations have passed and along the way, the Weeden family has savored the country's freedom and prosperity – and sometimes endured its challenges from the Revolutionary War days when the British invaded the Weeden's Jamestown homestead to the trying times of the Great Depression.

But nothing in the family's history matches the courage and inspiration exhibited every day by the couple now entrusted with the deed to Dutch Island.

Betty and Rick Weeden - *Ils sont les meilleurs d'entre nous.* They are indeed the best of us.

# # #

– Acknowledgments –

Shortly before his death, my father entrusted me with a small handwritten journal that traces the history of the Weeden family from the mid-1600s to the 20th century. He asked that I make the journal's information known to my children and grandchildren and to pass along the Weeden story to others connected to the family bloodline. My father was a voracious reader and loved mysteries. So I think he would approve of my using fiction as a way to draw attention to the Weeden saga that has been a part of America for over three and a half centuries.

Book writing is an exercise that steals time and diverts attention. Without the understanding and patience of my wife, children and grandchildren, I could not possibly have written *Dutch Island*. So very special thanks and much love to all of you.

My grandson Jordan Pugh did the original artwork for the Jametown-Dutch Island map that appears at the front of the book. He got a very helpful and talented hand from graphic artist Mat Brady.

The aerial photo of Jamestown and Dutch Islands is courtesy of the Town of Jamestown as well as the Rhode Island Geographic Information System – with special kudos to Justin Jobin, GIS coordinator. The beautiful pictures of the Beavertail and Dutch Island lighthouses are included with the permission of Kraig Anderson, a San Diego photographer who has somehow managed to capture on film every lighthouse in the U.S. (as well as some in Canada).

Photos posted on the website www.dutchislandnovel.com are courtesy of my son, Ryan, who (when not running the construction company Four Square Design/Build) is as talented with a camera as he is raising a family.

The help and hospitality of the Jamestown Town Clerk's office and Jamestown Historical Society is greatly appreciated (Deputy Town Clerk Karen Montoya held the door wide open). Sue Madden is a former nurse and current author, historian, and expert on all things Jamestown. Her insights were especially helpful.

When agreeing to give me access to Jamestown's Police Department, Sgt. Angela Deneault was the department's public information officer. In 2011, she was named Jamestown's police chief – and Rhode Island's first ever female chief of police. Good things happen when authors show up.

John Urban, an executive at Northeastern University and author of *A Single Deadly Truth* and other works, guided me through the ebook world. Another author, James R. Clifford *(Ten Days to Madness, Double Daggers)*, once again offered encouragement and guidance. My colleagues Donna Kraemer and Dana Frazeur offered consistent and much appreciated help. Friends and advisors – including Bob Fell – were generous with their time, comments and support. My wife Marti proved once again that she is a master editor.

No one has been more important to this book than Betty and Rick Weeden. They inspired this novel just as they inspire anyone who meets them.

Want More of Bullet, Doc, Twyla and Yigal?
Order *Book of Nathan* Today

"... A Wild Ride..."
- *Publishers Weekly*

"... An Edge-Of-Your Seat Read..."
- *ForeWord*

"...Hysterical, Touching And Interesting..."
- *FreshFiction*

"... Like slicing a knife through warm butter, readers will easily slip inside the pages..."
- *Examiner.com*

"... Fun story that builds to an explosive ending..."
- *Book Fetish*

Visit: **www.bookofnathan.net**

Available on Amazon.com and wherever books are sold.

Curt Weeden is a former Johnson & Johnson vice president and founder of the Association of Corporate Contributions Professionals. In addition to his novel, *Book of Nathan,* his nonfiction books include *Smart Giving Is Good Business, How Women Can Beat Terrorism,* and *Corporate Social Investing.*

Visit his website at www.curtweeden.com